STAFF NUD

After an unhappy love affair, Senior Staff Nurse Claire Graine channels all her energies into her work on the Eye Ward at The Royal. The last thing she wants now is to fall in love . . . But why does she continue to be so aware of consultant surgeon Gareth Bannerman?

# STAFF NURSE
# ON GLANELLY WARD

BY

JANET FERGUSON

**MILLS & BOON LIMITED**
London · Sydney · Toronto

First published in Great Britain 1983
by Robert Hale Limited, Clerkenwell House,
Clerkenwell Green, London EC1R 0HT

© Janet Ferguson 1983

Australian copyright 1984
Philippine copyright 1984

This edition published 1984
by Mills & Boon Limited, 15–16 Brook's Mews,
London W1A 1DR

ISBN 0 263 74649 6

Set in 11 on 12½ pt Linotron Times
03–0484–46,000

Photoset by Rowland Phototypesetting Ltd
Bury St Edmunds, Suffolk
Made and printed in Great Britain by
Richard Clay (The Chaucer Press) Ltd
Bungay, Suffolk

# CHAPTER ONE

PEOPLE often assumed I had specialised in ophthalmic nursing because my father, Richard Graine, was blind: 'But that simply isn't the case,' I would tell them, 'I'm interested in eyes; it has nothing to do with my father at all.'

I had trained at Seftonbridge General, I nursed there for a time, then came to The Royal Hospital, Cletford, to be nearer to my home. I had been at The Royal just over three months when Sir Hugh Wellesley emigrated, and the Registrar, Gareth Bannerman, got his job. But it was more than just a job, it was a top-of-the-tree post—that of Consultant Ophthalmic Surgeon, and G.B. wasn't old; he was in his mid-thirties, which is nothing for a man.

He was appointed at the end of May, when Sister was on leave, and when I, as Senior Staff Nurse, was left in charge of the ward. I was in the office sorting reports when Steve came along to tell me. Steve was our Houseman, he was very excited indeed: 'He's in the ante-room, outside the board room, having coffee,' he said, 'everyone's shaking him by the hand, he's taking it all in his stride.'

'He's a stridey man.' I shuffled my papers, 'Were there many applicants?'

'*Candidates*,' Steve corrected, 'there was a short-list of six. Three of the unsuccessfuls are just about to go in to be interviewed for the post of Registrar.'

'So, it's all happening,' I said slowly, watching him reach for my biscuits. There were times when Dr Stephen Bell seemed younger than twenty-five—he was exactly two years older than me.

'My money was on G.B., you know,' (Gareth Bannerman's name was pared down to initials behind his back). 'He's been doing most of the complicated surgery, anyway, just lately. He had Specialist qualifications when he came to us, you know—three years ago—after the death of his wife.'

'Is he likely to pay us a visit today?' I saw Steve shake his head as I glanced through the window into the ward. Nurse Islet was with Mr Shone, whilst Nurse Bayer and the Learner were at the Nurses' Station (the Central Desk). My thoughts still eddied round Gareth Bannerman. He'd be feeling pleased with himself. He was a tall, dark, strong-shouldered man, a little burly perhaps; he was dramatic-looking, he reminded me of Keith. Father knew him, said he liked him, said he had a good voice: 'He's a tenor, Claire, with a powerful range, I've heard him at Melton House.' Melton House was the Training Centre for the Blind on Armitage Hill. Father belonged to their Sports and Social Club.

'I think,' I said, as I saw Mrs Denton fiddling with her shade, 'that I'd better get on the ward and do my round.'

'I dare say it's not all beer and skittles being

Acting Sister!' Steve grinned, but he got up and took himself out of the room.

Glanelly Ward was twenty-four bedded, and had a T-shaped layout. The stem of the T was the ward corridor, with ancillary rooms leading off. The cross-top was the ward proper—females on the right, males on the left, a screen dividing the two. Nearly always, though, the screen was pushed back to allow for easy surveillance, for the entrance and exit of trolleys and stretcher-beds.

I persuaded Mrs Denton, who had had a lens extraction, to bear with her shade for just a few more days: 'I know you feel you want it off, but it won't be very long now. You're doing so well. Mr Bannerman is pleased.'

'I hear he's been made the boss now,' she said. 'I can't say I'm surprised. He's got a kind of important look—a presence, I suppose you'd call it.' Mrs Denton had excellent sight in her uncovered eye.

'But Mrs Denton—how did you know?' For how could she have found out?'

'The man who came to fix the shade told me about it, dear. He says it's all over the hospital.'

I laughed and moved away. I was quite sure it was, for no news—good or bad, or even just mild in content—ever stand still in a closed community.

Mr Mark Steadman, in the lefthand section, wasn't feeling very happy. He had glaucoma and was due to go to the theatre next day for an operation which would help to reduce the discomfort in his eye. At first he had been against surgery, holding the mistaken view than an operation would lessen what sight he had. It was G.B. seeing him in Outpatients' Clinic, who had finally persuaded him to undergo surgery, and rid himself of the pain.

'My work's getting all behind whilst I'm lying here, Nurse,' he said. He was a farmer, with a very small staff, and it must have been worrying for him. A deep frown made him look distraught. I tried my best to say the right things, and I hoped I reassured him, I went to the head of his bed and closed the blind.

We seldom made the ward dim, but harsh light was excluded. All the beds were so arranged that no patient looked straight at a window; there were numerous points for examination lamps. This, the Ophthalmic Unit, which included Outpatients downstairs, was the newest department in the whole of the hospital. The Royal, as it was affectionately called, was over a hundred years old. It had been modernised in the thirties, and during the Second World War half of it had been utilised as a military hospital, for Cletford, in those days, had been a garrison town. I knew all this from Father, who talked of those days often—the good days for him, when Mother had been alive.

Joyce Gale, the Learner Nurse, was still at the Nurses' Station. I asked her to take some specimens down to the Labs: 'And whilst you're down there, ask if they've got the result of Mrs Lloyd's culture—the conjunctival swab you helped me take yesterday.'

'Yes, Staff.' She was only eighteen, a fairylike doll of a girl. There were five of us on duty, for pre-op days were hectic. At one o'clock Kay Dellar, the Staff Nurse junior to me, would come on duty, releasing me for lunch.

I turned to glance at the clock, but my eye didn't quite reach it, for there by the doors, just coming in, standing sandwiched between their edges, was G.B. He was looking round for me: 'Sister off-duty?' He was always brief, never using more words then he need. He looked down at me, chin tucked into his chest.

'She's on leave, sir,' I remembered the 'sir'. It was due to him now, of course. And as for him, *he* had remembered to leave off his white coat. His dark suit fitted him like a glove.

'I don't remember her telling me.' Dismay was sharp in his voice.

'Well, I'm sure . . .'

'Yes, yes, I'm sure she did. I've had a lot on my mind. The simple explanation is that I clean forgot about it. Still, never mind, you're here, aren't you? Perhaps we could have a word—in the office, I think.' He leaned back and opened the doors.

I brushed past him, avoiding his feet, the doors snuffed to behind us. We crossed the passage and entered Sister's den. Once in there I felt her mantle of authority drape my shoulders—effecting a prompt, putting words into my mouth: 'I'm sure Sister would wish me,' I began, 'to say how glad we all are to hear of your appointment, and to offer congratulations.' I very nearly said, 'Well done', but bit that back in time. I put out my hand and felt him clasp it—a quick, warm grip—my face went red—I caught a glimpse of his smile. He was dark-complexioned—not swarthy, but dark—there's a subtle difference somehow—his teeth were white and a good shape, and his mouth had a sweeping curve; his eyes were slate, the glittery sort; they didn't miss very much: 'What did you want to see me about?' I asked.

'Tomorrow's theatre list, Staff. Have you sent it down to them yet?'

'To Theatre block—yes, I have, sir, but I've got a copy here.' I pulled a foolscap sheet of paper from under a pile of books. He sat down and read it, leaning forward to the desk. He looked very much the Consultant, he couldn't be anything else. There wasn't a single wrinkle in the straight back of his suit, his hair was jet—thick, and short, and neat.

'Mm . . .' he straightened, and looked up at me, 'I'm going to alter these times. Got a pencil?' I held one out, he attacked the list viciously, scoring deeply, going right through to the desk. 'I intend to start at nine a.m. and take the child first,' he said.

'Nine o'clock!' I gasped a little. Sister Theatre wouldn't be pleased.

'Yes, yes, I know,' he said (perhaps he could read my thoughts) 'but until I get a Registrar, which I hope will be next month, I'm going to be very hard put to it to keep up with patient demand. The last thing I want is to have to postpone, or cancel, any admissions. There's nothing worse than having to put people off.'

I nodded, he made me feel breathless.

'So, I've altered all these times. I'm operating at

Seftonbridge tomorrow afternoon.' (Seftonbridge General was in our hospital group). 'Still, I'll square things with Sister, you just follow this,' he gave me the list and drew up to his full height.

I wondered if he wanted anything else, for he made no move to go, and he was looking at me, wearing an expression I'd seen on his face before— one of faint curiosity, mixed with doubtfulness. It was the doubtfulness that made me rear up, set me on my mettle, made me determined to prove I could do my job:

'How old are you, Nurse?' The question was accompanied by the faintest of closed smiles.

'Twenty-three—well, close on.'

'And where did you nurse before?'

'At Seftonbridge, and if you're worried, I *am* ophthalmically trained, I obtained my OND as a post-graduate qualification. I took the course after my SRN.'

'Good, well, in that case, we've no problems,' he said. But he said it rather snappily. Perhaps he thought I was rude. He went on to ask me, all in one breath, about our small boy patient: 'How did he settle, Nurse, after his mother went home?'

'He was quiet at first, very subdued, right on the edge of tears, but Night Staff said he slept well. He doesn't seem to be fretting.'

'I'll go in and see him now, I think. I'd like you to come with me.' So once more I passed under the high arch of his arm, as he held the door for me, leaning forward from the jamb.

Paul was in Glanelly because the children's ward

was full. He was eight years old, and he had a squint—a right-sided strabismus. I knew that G.B. intended to effect a shortening of one of the tendons, thus pulling the eye (which turned inwards) round to straight.

'Hello, Paul, you remember me, don't you?' He sat down on the bed. The child stared back, and almost at once we could see the converging eye— the right one, turning inwards to his nose.

'I saw you in Outpatients, didn't I?' He was a very bright little boy. His eyes were big, and blue, and reproachful, his hair was fair and straight, and very clean, lying flat and close to his head. G.B.'s hand stroked it down, and the harsh lines of his face softened a little, as his smile appeared again.

'This time tomorrow,' he said, 'this eye of yours will be mended. I'm going to fix it so that it looks and behaves just like the other one. It'll be like magic. You'll be very pleased indeed.'

'Will it be like all the other boys' eyes?' He meant the boys at school. His mother had told me how they'd plagued him, calling him 'old boss eye'. Nothing, and no-one can be more cruel than a gang of little children, teasing and taunting the one who is different from them.

'*Exactly* like all the other boys' eyes,' G.B. promised him. Paul's face puckered into a smile.

'Poor little beast,' G.B. said, once we were out of earshot. 'When we're children we all want to be the same, when we're adult we strive to be different— to be individual, to stand out on our own.'

I gave a token nod of agreement, but I didn't

really agree—not, that is, with the second part; I had reservations on that. *He* might want to stand out in solitary, glorious splendour. I didn't, I liked to be in the fold.

'I think that's all, thank you, Staff,' he said when we reached the corridor. 'Unless you, or Dr Bell, are worried, you won't see me until Wednesday.' Then he took himself off, went striding off, towards the landing and lifts. He was a perfect example of walking tall, he carried his height so easily, as though he enjoyed it—head up, shoulders squared. And today, of course, he was feeling good, for success is a heady thing. I wished him well, I felt he deserved it, I even felt pleased for him—but I wished he'd reached his zenith somewhere else.

Just before noon the nurses began to prepare for the luncheon trolleys, which came down from the kitchens on the fifth floor. Some of the patients—those whose eyes were well on the way to healing—could feed themselves from tables swung over their beds. Others, even more advanced, and almost ready for home, were able to eat in the Day Room round a central family table. One of the latter was the cataract, Mr Shone. I went to help him put on his slippers, warning him not to stoop. He was wearing dark glasses, but no shade, he was dignified and stately, nearly eighty years old, with a little white wisp of moustache: 'Don't try to hurry,' I cautioned him, as he set off at a brisk trot. 'Remember that you won't see very clearly until you get your new glasses, the ones with the special lens built in.'

'My dear, I'm more pleased than I can say,' he whispered against my cheek, as I lowered him into one of the hardbacked chairs.

As I came out of the Day Room, Nurse Dane and Nurse Islet were bringing the luncheon trolleys into the ward. The lids were slipped back, I smelled mince and greens—strong fare for a hot June day, but there were salads as well, for those who preferred them, there was milk pudding or jelly, or both together; some patients liked them mixed. The food was served out carefully, there was little flutter or fuss, the trolleys were eased along with the greatest care. Noise in any hospital ward had to be kept to a minimum, but here on the Ophthalmic Unit, such care was especially important. Even ordinary sounds like the rattle of cutlery, could be a major hazard. The nurses knew this, and worked quietly, keeping their voices low. Even the blinds at the long sash windows seemed to shift cautiously in the soft warm breeze that fanned the sills.

The Royal stands at the top of the town in Charles II Street. Three of its sides overlook the heath. The heath is a feature of the town, a kind of crowning glory. Take the heath away and Cletford would be as bald and deprived as a seaside town without its beach. It has an ancient history too, for it was here that the Iceni, famed for their expert horsemanship and great scythed chariots, rode and dwelled in the time of Boadicea. Some people say that the ghost of Queen Boadicea haunts the heath, others have heard the rattle of chariots. These tall tales amused Father, he chuckled when he heard them. He heard many a tale and a great deal of gossip down on his Department. He was Chief Physiotherapist at The Royal, had four men under him. Over the years he built up a name for himself.

Kay Dellar came on duty, and free for lunch at last, I bought sandwiches from the hospital shop, and took them outside to eat. A short-cut through the laid-out gardens brought me to one of the exits, which led out to the road beside the heath. I crossed the road and began to walk over the grass to the trees, to a copse of silver birches a short way off. I walked slowly, lazily, enjoying the heat of the sun which rayed down through the shoulders of my dress. It was a lilac dress, a Staff Nurse dress, made of thick, crisp cotton, it was mid-calf length, had leg-of-mutton sleeves. I liked it, for as uniforms went it was flattering and attractive. It was well cut and the colour was fine with my hair. I have fair hair, kind friends call it golden, it's long and wavy and thick, but when in uniform it had to be fastened round my head, in a French pleat, to satisfy hospital rules. I have brown eyes and a large mouth, and my nose turns up. I'm tall for a girl—nearly five feet eight.

Keith used to say my looks would last, which made me feel good value, but that was nearly two years ago, when I'd been engaged to him—just about (although I didn't know it at the time) to be disengaged, for he'd found another girl. Keith had been a House Physician at Seftonbridge General Hospital, which was where we'd met in my very last training year. Our engagement lasted exactly six months, till Keith left the hospital service; when he gave in his notice he also gave me mine . . . 'I'm sorry, Clarry, but I've met someone else. It's just one of those things that happen. Fay's a doctor, we're getting married, setting up in practice together.' And that had been that. He had left at the end of the month.

If it hadn't been for Father, I too would have left the district, left it far behind, got a job abroad, perhaps. But I did have a father, widower father, a father who was blind, and however independent he was, however well-organised, it didn't seem fair to take such a drastic step. So I carried on at Sefton-bridge, I braved the sympathy, I braved the humiliation too, for there's always some of that when it's known that a man has turned his back on a girl. I took my Ophthalmic Nursing Course, which absorbed me completely. I worked and played hard. I whittled down the hurt.

After eighteen months I told myself I had got over Keith, and I felt this even more strongly when I got my job at The Royal, starting working on Glanelly Ward. There were times, it was true, when my pulses would leap at the sight of the back of a head—a jet-haired back of the head, that belonged to Gareth Bannerman, but which could, just *could* have belonged to Keith. Gareth Bannerman had the power, I knew, to destroy my new-found calm. Not that he'd try—why should he try—I was nothing at all to him. I was perfectly safe—just a Staff Nurse on the ward.

Four months ago I met David Cope, who worked

at Melton House. He wanted to marry me, had proposed to me last week. It had been a shock, a delicious shock, I hadn't known what to say, yet the sound of his words had touched me like a wand: 'Claire, I love you—we're right together—Claire will you marry me?' Dear David, darling David, so very different from Keith—so utterly, blessedly different from Keith, but I hadn't known what to say. He had been understanding, said he would ask me again.

I reached the copse of trees and sat down, I unwrapped my sandwiches, I began to eat, staring out over the heath. David was the Mobility Officer up at Melton House. I had met him there at the end of January, when there'd been a cocktail party to welcome the new Superintendent, Dr Shaw. Father had introduced us, had introduced me to David: 'Claire, you've not met David, have you, he's just been transferred from Cromer. David, this is my daughter, who's a trained ophthalmic nurse. She and Mrs Shoulder keep me in order back at The Larches. I can't get up to much with them around.'

'Who's Mrs Shoulder?' David had asked, as we made our way to the buffet.

'Our housekeeper, a daily one, she came when my mother died.' We had talked a lot that evening, had spent most of it together. He asked me if I would see him again, and that had been the start— the start of an era, a period of time which was proving very happy. I admired David, I trusted him, I admired the work he did—teaching the newly-blind how to move about with confidence, both at Melton House and out in the busy town. He was tall and shanky, athletically built, his fine textured hair was brown, light brown, it sloped down at one side. His face was long and thin like his body, he *could* look lugubrious, but his smile was sweet, and it always reached his eyes. He was what I needed, he was always there. Perhaps I was using him. I hoped not, he was far too decent and kind. I knew I liked being with him, I knew I enjoyed his company. He never set me on fire like Keith, there was no blinding magic, there was no cascade of love so strong that I thought I would die of it. But I didn't want that again—never, not ever again— never again, for I knew it didn't last.

I was thinking of David, eyes closed, when I heard someone approaching—heard a heavy-footed rustling in the grass. I looked up and saw Gareth Bannerman, jacket over his shoulder, coming towards me, he was looking down at the ground. He hadn't seen me, I leapt up. Shrieking out his name. Had I not acted quickly he'd have fallen over my legs.

'Great Scot!' he blinked rapidly, looking a little stunned. He must have been as deep in thought as me. He very soon recovered, though; he was that kind of snap-to man. He stood in the grass before me, legs apart. 'Enjoying a rest from the madding crowd?' He glanced back at the hospital, he straightened his tie—a blue one with a stripe.

'I come here sometimes when I want to escape,' I said. I debated on whether to sit down again. Surely he was going. He hadn't wanted to stumble on me, like this. But he seemed to be in no special hurry, he slid his jacket back on, stepped into the shade and leaned against a tree. I did the same, I felt I should, and once again, in his presence, I felt my heart turning over in slow hot bumps.

'It's very warm.' His face turned to me.

'Yes, I . . . yes, it is.'

We exchanged polite, social smiles across the grass space between us. The light fell on his face in pools, moving and shifting when he did. His ears were neat. I looked away over the heath.

'I came up here literally for air,' he said, breathing it in. Yes, and to be alone, I thought, for that had been my idea too. We neither of us wanted the other's company, or any company at all. Well, so be it—I picked up my shoulder bag. 'You're off, are you?' his voice came sharply, I saw his feet advance.

'I'd better get back.' The strap of my bag was biting into my shoulder. I moved it round. He was standing by my side.

'I think I'll come too. I really should. I've an Outpatients Clinic at two.' We walked down the slope together, and I tried to conceal my astonishment, for in no way was G.B. a matey type. All the nurses remarked on this, but I felt it was due to status, for even as Senior Registrar he had had to keep a gulley streaming between himself and the nursing staff. I knew this, I was glad of it, it simplified things I felt. And surely, now, as Senior Consultant, the gulley would widen still more, he'd be farther away, even more unapproachable. Of course we were off-duty out here, which made a difference of sorts. Once we entered the hospital precinct, he'd retreat again, I was sure. I'd be Staff Nurse Graine, and have to call him 'sir'.

Conversation, as we walked along, got going very nicely. We were discussing a new type of scanner in X-Ray, when we spotted three figures on horseback, moving at trotting rate towards Warren Rise. I instantly recognised Stephanie Newel astride her chestnut mare. The other two riders were children, both of them on ponies—one on a plump skewbald, who lagged behind. Mrs Newel owned and ran the local Heathside Riding School. She was out with her pupils—this week being half-term. I thought what a fabulous picture she made, her bobbed hair matching the mare's, her back straight in its hacking jacket, her seat well down in the saddle, scarcely rising; she moved like part of the horse. Faintly through the shimmering air we could hear the sound of her voice, hear its cadence, she was urging the children on. I was very keen on riding myself, I hired a mount from the School—a quarter-horse standing fifteen hands, he came from America. Riding was one of the great loves of my life.

Rumour had it that Stephanie Newel was Gareth Bannerman's love, but hospital gossip could rear up high and still not reach the truth. They were friendly, I knew that, for I had seen him at Heathside. He didn't ride, so he must go there for social reasons, I felt. Stephanie was a divorcee, Mr Newel left years ago. They had both been living at Heathside, though, and running the School together, when I first learned to ride, just on eight years ago.

'I've seen you and your black steed pounding the turf,' he said, as we each raised an arm to the vanishing riders; his eye was following Stephanie, the children had dwindled to bouncing dots at her side.

'I wish Orlando were mine,' I said, 'but he's part of the Heathside stock. Mrs Newel lets me have him each time I go, if she can. Now that I don't have a fourteen-mile journey to Seftonbridge each day, I find I have a little more time to ride.'

'I suppose you've ridden from an early age?' He kicked a stone on one side.

'No, not really,' I shook my head, 'I learned when I was fifteen, just after my mother died, she'd have been dead against it. She always was, whenever the subject was raised.'

'Why was that?'

'Because,' I said, 'that was how my father was blinded. He fell from a horse and fractured his skull, wasn't wearing a riding hat. His optic nerves were ruptured. It happened here at Cletford. He always says that Cletford Heath, turning slowly sideways, was the very last thing he ever saw.'

'Really—now you surprise me!' He swatted away a wasp, 'I've always supposed that Mr Graine lost his vision during the War.'

'People often think that, but no, it was the year before the War. He was a medical student here at The Royal, but of course all that had to go. He went to Melton House for training—Braille and handicrafts. He was assessed, rather as nurses are, was advised to train as a Physio. He's been at The Royal now for thirty-eight years.'

'Did he meet your mother after his accident?'

'No, just before. She was a nurse, a probationer nurse, as they used to call them then. She looked after him marvellously well.' (And when she'd died he'd been lost. There had just been Mrs Shoulder and I to carry on in her stead. Not that Father ever complained, and neither did he cling. He was always saying I must have a life of my own.)

'I think someone told me,' G.B. said, as we crossed the road, 'that he was due to retire, fairly soon.'

'He is, next year, when he's sixty-five.'

'How does he feel about that?'

'He doesn't say much, but I have an idea he's dreading it,' I said. 'He's got several hobby things lined up, but they're very unlikely to give him the same satisfaction as physio work.'

We had reached the hospital gates now—*and* the end of the question-time. But probably asking questions was a good way of making small-talk. It was just as I had surmised too—as soon as we stepped on the path, G.B. was streaking across to the sign that said, 'OUTPATIENTS—EYE'.

His mind and concentration were hurtling towards his job—ahead of *him*. He disappeared under the arch.

# CHAPTER TWO

DURING the afternoon Miss Girton, the Senior Nursing Officer, paid a surprise visit to the ward. Gareth Bannerman was with her, it was four o'clock when they came. I should, by rights, have been off duty, but had stopped to talk to a patient, who strongly objected to having her eyelashes cut. Leaving her with Nurse Dane, I went swiftly to the doors:

'Good afternoon, Staff,' Miss Girton turned and led the way into the office. She was a tall, narrow woman in her fifties, who carried herself like a rod. Her dress as befitted her high rank, was a deep Royal purple; it drained her face, but suited her greying hair. She seated herself behind the desk, rested her arms on the blotter, I stared at her wrists, which were almost impossibly small. From the chair at my side, but half behind me, G.B. crossed his legs. I heard the little sound he made, and I saw one half of his shoe—a black slip-on, covered in whitish dust.

It seemed to be a very long time before Miss Girton spoke. A bee zoomed in and out of the window, and two petals dropped from the roses on the sill, before she began: 'No. 2 Side-Ward is vacant at the moment, isn't it, Staff?'

'Both side-wards are free, Miss Girton.' (The

side-wards were single rooms, leading off the main ward corridor.)

'Mr Bannerman wishes to admit a patient tomorrow, for keratoplasty.'

'Oh, I see.' My interest quickened—corneal grafting was special. It literally gave a new eye to a patient with corneal damage. But grafts didn't come available often—I turned and looked at G.B. And he must have read the query curling in my mind, for he nodded and said:

'A graft came in early this afternoon.' He followed this with details of the patient he was admitting: 'She's Miss Anne Malvering, a mistress at the High School. Her left eye was badly scarred in a chemistry experiment. She's been on our waiting list just over six months.'

'She was admitted to Glanelly at the time of her accident,' Miss Girton interposed, 'she was Sir Hugh's patient, but he couldn't do much till a graft was available.'

'Is she working at present?' I asked.

'Yes, but with difficulty,' G.B.'s voice came louder as he leaned forward to me, 'I see her in Outpatients every month, she enquires each time about surgery. It's just bad luck that her uninjured eye has never had good vision. I'd very much like to help her if I can.'

'I've asked my secretary to telephone her,' Miss Girton was getting up, 'It's short notice, but I very much doubt if Miss Malvering will complain.'

'I don't think she will,' G.B. said, rising when Miss Girton did. He didn't, however, as I thought he would, follow her up the corridor; he came back into the office and sat down. 'It won't be easy for you, having a patient out in the side-ward—I mean, of course, with Sister Cheevers away.'

'I shall manage, thank you.' He was doubtful again, his name should have been Thomas. He walked to the window, chin sunk on his chest.

'Well, Miss Malvering's a sensible type of woman, she'll be a good patient, I'm sure.' He looked round as Nurse Bayer came in with a tray of tea. There was only one cup on it, I asked her to bring another. His reaction to that made my brows rise up, 'Not for me, thank you,' he snapped. He hadn't welcomed the interruption, and this I could understand, but I thought he might have refrained from adding, 'I detest the tea-drinking habit,' making poor Nurse Bayer shrink against the wall.

'I welcome tea in the afternoon,' I said, when she'd gone out. 'I find it refreshing, particularly when I'm working overtime.' He reacted not at all to that, and somehow or other, I couldn't drink the tea in front of him. There it sat steaming away, like a kind of flung-down challenge. I couldn't have been more pleased when the telephone rang. I snatched up the receiver, jamming it to my ear. The voice at the other belonged to Miss Girton's secretary, I listened to what she said and jotted it down. 'That was Miss Dacre,' I told G.B., who had one leg out of the door, 'Miss Malvering has agreed to be admitted tomorrow at two. Medical Records are sending her papers up.'

'Splendid! Couldn't be better!' His face cleared

like the sky. 'So providing her cultures show no infection, I can operate on Thursday. Now I'd like to see the room, if I may.' He walked out into the passage, I followed him, and went to Side-Ward 2.

Being a single room it was small, but very adequate. The bed looked hard, he bounced on it, and made a little grimace: 'Better get a sorbo mattress on this, she'll need to be comfortable. The first fifteen post-op days will be very tedious, without having a bed like a concrete block.'

I made a note to send a requisition to Stores for a mattress, I made it on my apron hem, on the hard, starched underside—a habit, or trick, or ploy, from my student days. When I looked up he was watching me, I felt foolish and abashed. Writing on aprons wasn't the kind of think he would expect from a Senior Nurse currently running the ward: 'When do we get Sister Cheevers back?' He lowered and raised the blind, I watched him tighten the cream cord at the side.

'Tomorrow week, the ninth of June.'

'Quite a long time to go. Plenty of time for you to invest in a little red notebook—less expensive than laundry charges, more professional too. I should see to it, Nurse.' He turned and went out of the door.

I returned to the office, I drank my tea in a haze of angry defiance. It wasn't so much the apron incident, as his whole attitude, his constant wishing that Sister Cheevers was back. I suppose, in a way, one couldn't blame him, for Sister was super-efficient, but I wasn't *such* a bad substitute, I was fully competent. One day I very much hoped to have a ward of my own, I had great yearnings, at times, to reach for the stars.

The thing about Gareth Bannerman was that he seemed to be two different men—the one off-duty and the one on, like separate sides to a coin. Both sides disturbed me—in entirely different ways. However I tossed the coin I couldn't win.

I ordered the mattress, signed off duty, decided to call for Father. It was five o'clock, so he might, just might, be ready to leave for home. The Larches was a good mile away, and although he enjoyed the walk, on a warm, close evening like this, he might consent to ride. It was worth a try. I went down to Physio.

As I pushed open the cream doors two of the Physiotherapists were folding equipment, they smiled a greeting to me. The other two were treating patients, and from over the tops of the cubicles I could hear urgent-voiced exhortations—'Raise your right leg higher'—'Good, fine, now look at the ceiling'—'Now let your arm go limp.' There were puffs and groans, a sound like air being forced out of balloons, there was an all-pervading smell of oil and wax. Nell, our guide dog—a golden retriever, mild and brown of eye, came towards me, her harness already clipped on.

'Ready for home then, lovely one?' I bent to stroke her head.

'We both are, but you're late, aren't you, Claire?' Father emerged from the cloakroom, running his thumb over his Braille watch face. One of the younger Physios claimed him, raised a query with him. I sat down on a bench and waited, looking over at the two men—one big, brawny, young, the other (my father) small, with a high, bright colour in his cheeks, with sparse brown hair, brown eyes, just like mine, *his* unsighted, unblemished too—seeming to look at the wall. His navy blue suit hung slackly on him, one could almost see his bones, yet his starved-bird look was deceiving, he had very good health, he enjoyed his work, and didn't look his age. 'What did you say kept you late?' he asked, as we crossed over the car park. He'd agreed to be lazy and have a lift home for once. I opened the hatch door for Nell who, glad to be free of her harness, leapt in and settled down nose on paws.

I explained very briefly about Miss Malvering: 'Lucky woman' he said. Yet he didn't say it enviously, nor with any especial regret. My father, to quote from his medical notes, was adjusted to his blindness. After forty-three years one might expect this, yet I never truly believed it. I couldn't believe, as he'd once had sight, as he knew what sight was like, that he didn't *sometimes* long to see again— 'But, my darling, I see in my dreams and have a whale of a time,' he'd say. His sense of humour was keen and infectious. He was very good company, easy to live with. I loved him very much.

'Is David coming round tonight?' he asked as we stopped at the lights.

'Yes,' I replied, 'at about half-seven, he's coming

in a van. We're going out to Barlow Green to collect Mr Pineham's things. I told you, if you remember, that his wife had recently died, well, after two duff housekeepers—one who pilfered from him—he's agreed to go and live at Melton House as a permanent resident. His son was pleased, he took him in last week. Mr Pineham hated leaving his cottage, he was very upset at the time, but David thinks that once he has his personal belongings around him, he'll feel much better, the awful strangeness will go.'

'It's a thing we most of us dread,' Father said, 'institutional life. However good it might be, and there's none to beat Melton House, we still cleave to our independence and homes. Pity Mr Pineham couldn't have found a Mrs Shoulder.'

I laughed, I changed gear on the hill: 'I don't think,' I said, 'that there are all that many Mrs Shoulders about.'

'True enough,' Father said, 'and it was you who found us ours. You know, Claire, for a lass of fifteen, you showed a lot of sense.'

'Pity I didn't retain it.'

'Oh, you mean that business of Keith. Love makes fools of us all, darling, but you came out of it well. And you're happy enough now, aren't you?' Anxiety tinged his voice.

'Oh, Lord, yes!' I said, but I didn't say anything else. He probably hoped I might do so—confide in him about Dave, but I couldn't do that—at least not yet, so a small silence divided us, then Father bridged it, making me laugh again:

'Is clearing out homes for elderly gentlemen part of David's job?'

'No, it certainly isn't, but you know what David is. Sometimes I think he's incapable of saying "no" to anyone. There are over forty permanent residents up at Melton House now, and he *lackies* for them, they take advantage of him.'

'Well, you won't change him.'

'I don't want to.'

'Wise girl,' he said.

We had reached the new traffic island, which meant we were nearly home, I swung round it, entered Long Acre Road. Our house was the fifth on the left, the one with the overhanging larches, I drove under them, round to the kitchen door. The door was open and from inside the house we could hear Mrs Alice Shoulder singing 'Greensleeves', as she swung the lettuce about.

It was time for her to go home, she met us on the steps—redhaired and tiny, with a Snoopy apron on. She usually stayed until five or half-past, leaving our evening meal ready—either ready to be cooked, or in the fridge, if cold: 'You got the remains of the sirloin,' she told us, filling Nell's water bowl. 'There's a salad, and cheese for afters, duck.'

The 'duck' was for me, she was formal with Father, calling him Mr Graine, or 'that there Mr Graine' when speaking of him to her husband, who did odd jobs in the garden from time to time. Mrs Shoulder lived two miles away, she came and went on her bicycle. She and her husband, Artie, belonged to a cycling club, she didn't come to The Larches at weekends. 'And your young man 'phoned,' she shouted out as I mounted the stairs. 'He thought you'd be home, but I said you weren't, and he asked me to give you a message. He said he was coming round at seven, instead of half-past. If I were you I'd hurry, duck, get a move on like, then you can eat your supper before 'ee arrive.'

I decided on jeans and a workmanlike shirt for the evening's sorting out. I brushed my hair down from its centre parting, and tied it back in my nape. I heard Mrs Shoulder call out goodbye, and looking out of the window, I could see her cycling towards the island, short legs whirling, yellow blouse blowing out like a bag.

David arrived on the dot of seven, at the wheel of a small white van; he sprang down from the cabin, came slowly over the lawn. David never *apparently* hurried, yet he always got things done. He was perfect for people who couldn't hurry, for he'd never fluster them. He was wearing fawn cords and a blue shirt—the cords outlined his leanness, the shirt matched the colour of his eyes.

'Hello there!' he said quietly, standing spidery tall in the doorway. I was washing up, Father was helping, Nell was spread out in the hall, making the most of every possible draught. 'I hope it was okay to come earlier,' he dropped a kiss on my hair.

'Of course,' I said, I turned around and smiled, with my hands still immersed in suds.

'Actually, I was wondering,' he was speaking to

Father, 'if you'd like to come, Mr Graine. There's plenty of room in the van.'

'Thank you, David . . . thank you, but no.' Father dried a dish, felt for the table, slid it carefully on. 'I'm going to be lazy and sit in the garden, I like it this time of day. I like to hear the neighbours working—cutting their lawns and hedges, whilst all I do is breathe in the evening air!'

'I expect you can do with a rest. Physiotherapy's strenuous work.'

'It suits me, I've no complaints,' he went outside with Nell.

'Did I say the wrong thing?' David looked anxious.

'Well, yes, perhaps,' I said, 'it's the thought of retirement that's worrying him, I'd feel the same in his place.'

'I wish he'd change his mind and come with us.'

'He doesn't want to, Dave.'

As I hung up the teatowel he turned me round and kissed me on the mouth: 'How have you been?' He held me loosely, blue eyes searching mine.

'Oh, fine, just fine,' I pulled back a little, then moved in and gave him a hug—a long, thin, bony body—we kissed, broke free, and laughed. I looked at him, I liked what I saw, and I found myself thinking—if only things could stay like this—pleasant, and light, and loving; if only we needn't plan ahead too soon.

A few minutes later we were in the white van, trundling through the town. We passed the hospital, turned left by the heath, took the righthand

fork to Bartlow. The distance was only four miles,
the village soon came into sight—the Pond, the
Green, the Plough Inn, the well with the wishing-
stone, the clunch houses built endways to the road.
Ivy-mantled beech trees darkened the road by the
church, a mill like a spectre with jagged arms stared
out over the beanfields, the clouds were puff-balls,
streaked with pink and gold. Mr Pineham's cottage
was another quarter-mile down the road. It had
white walls and black window-frames, a peeling
green front door: 'The whole place needs a face-
lift,' David said.

It was dusty inside and smelled of mice, a tap
dripped in the kitchen, David turned it off and
produced a list from his jeans. Then together we
began to assemble all the things Mr Pineham
wanted—his Braille machine, a supply of paper, a
typewriter, talking-books, a pack of cassettes, a set
of dominoes, a white stick, a clock, a little bag of
high polished stones. 'They're polished pebbles,'
David said, crossing them off the list. 'He likes to sit
and hold them, run them through his hands. They
probably have the effect of worry beads. Now,
what about his clothes?' He consulted the list again.
We went up to the bedroom and opened cupboards
and drawers. Over the bed, a big one, which took
up most of the space, was a photograph of a young
man in Air Force uniform: 'That must be his son
who was killed in the Battle of Britain.' David
reached up and took it down from the wall.

'Shall we pack it?' I blew off the dust, and wiped
the glass on my shirt.

'Better, I think. We'll put it in with his clothes.'

We found more clothes in the second bedroom, and we filled a cabin trunk, which we dragged out from the cupboard under the stairs. We worked for a solid hour and a half, and I had to confess to tiredness, I was dropping with it, I was glad to climb back in the van. 'I feel so sorry for Mr Pineham,' I said, as we drove to the village. David had suggested that we stopped off at The Plough, for a drink and a sandwich, I felt I could hardly wait.

'I'm sorry for him too,' he said, 'he's lived there all his life.'

'But he couldn't have stayed on his own.'

'No, I honestly don't think he could. If he were simply eighty, and not blind, well then, yes, perhaps. I don't believe in over-persuading people to leave their homes. But I think William would have taken it better if either his son or daughter had offered to have him live with them.'

'And neither did?'

'I'm afraid not,' David sounded regretful, 'the son's wife couldn't cope, the daughter's husband wouldn't. They'll have him for holidays, I dare say, but it's not quite the same.'

'Not the same at all,' I said, and I couldn't help wondering if the Air Force boy in the photograph would have given his father a home. He'd looked so smart in his jaunty cap, so earnest, and so young. The photograph had faded with the years.

The Plough Inn had one or two tables set out on its forecourt. We managed to find a free one, and sat there with our lagers, looking out over the Pond and the Green: 'Getting back to what we were talking about in the van just now,' David said, 'I'd just like to say that if you decide you can take me on . . .'

'Oh David . . .' Not now, I thought, not now, it's not the time.

'Please hear me out, don't get upset,' his hand closed over mine, 'if ever that time comes I'll make sure Mr Graine is all right. There would never be any question at all of him not being wanted by me. If he wanted to live with us he could.'

'That's looking ahead.'

'Hopefully looking,' he released my hand and sat back. 'But subject now closed,' he said, 'you could say I'm resting my case.' I nodded, I was touched by what he had said.

He began to tell me about two new trainees at Melton House—one a man of thirty, the other a youth of eighteen: 'Mark has partial sight in one eye, sees hand movements only. Tom, the boy, had both eyes destroyed lighting a homemade firework.'

'It happens unbelievably often, that sort of thing,' I said. 'How's the boy from Colchester, the one you told me about, the twenty-year-old, who lost an eye during a fight in a pub. I think you said he was coming back in for another holiday soon.'

'Oh, you mean Eric Sindon—yes, he's back with us now. He's having a period of re-training, but he hopes to work for us. There's a job going in the office—assistant to the cashier. He worked for a company in Colchester who've gone into liqui-dation. He's very, very keen to come to us.'

'How is he health-wise?'

'Absolutely fine. He's got a plastic eye. It exactly matches his own eye, you can't tell which is which. He had a rather nasty facial scar, but time does marvellous things—all he's got now is the faintest of faint white lines.'

'Will he get the job at Melton House?'

'I don't see why not. He has all the qualifications, they're bound to give him a try. When you next come up, you must meet him. He rides, by the way. I have an idea he'll be going along to the Heathside Riding Stables to see Mrs Newel, to book himself a mount.'

'Well, good for him! I'm glad to hear it. I know Mrs Newel will say . . .' My voice trailed off, as I saw the two on the steps.

'Someone we know?'

'Yes, it is.' And I still continued to stare, for in the curious way that fate sometimes has of produc-ing people on cue, Stephanie Newel, closely fol-lowed by Gareth Bannerman, was making her way down the stone steps of the Inn.

'Who?' David moved his head.

'Mrs Newel,' I said, 'and our new Consultant—Gareth Bannerman.'

They had seen us, or Stephanie had, I saw her speak to Gareth. They came to our table, David rose to his feet. We had all met before, with the exception of David and Gareth. Stephanie intro-duced them, forestalling me. She looked so different out of riding gear—her skirt was long and full, and multi-coloured; her blouse was a filmy green. Her small face under the polished hair was creamy-hued, dark-eyed. She turned to me, and asked me how I was.

'I think,' Gareth was saying to David, 'that I've seen you at Melton House, but we've not met, have we?' I saw him smile.

'I've heard you sing,' David replied. He was just as tall as Gareth, but much thinner—fair to his dark—a youth against a man. I stopped looking, I hate comparisons.

And as for me, what a mess I looked, in my oldest jeans and a plaid shirt, streaked and grimed with dust. One of the cuffs had a button missing and I'd had to turn it up. I reeked of mothballs, and as for my hair, it festooned me like a tent, the confining band had dropped off hours ago.

Everyone was standing but me, then the men fetched extra chairs. Stephanie and David began to talk about the stock of Heathside. David mentioning the Sindon boy's wish to ride. And somehow or other, I don't know how, we effected a change of partners. David was with Stephanie, I was with Gareth and the talk excluded us; I finished my lager, I saw him looking at me: 'Let's leave them to their horse-talk,' he said, 'take a turn round the pond. I confess to being fascinated by water and Village Greens.'

I was used to taking his orders, I got up at once; not that it *was* an order, for this was the off-duty man—this was the man with whom I had walked, and talked to on the heath—the man whom I thought of not as G.B., but as Gareth Bannerman—or simply Gareth. We slipped away under the lights.

The pond was an oval of black looking-glass. We walked along the bank, waving away little clusters of zinging gnats. Stephanie and he had dined at the Inn, he remarked on the excellent menu: 'But I expect you and David have tried it?' he caught at my arm as I stumbled. I freed myself, answering his question at once.

'Yes, we have, but not this evening. We've been clearing out a house.' I told him about our removal activities, and I kept on talking till we reached the end of the pond where it curved like an egg. We walked round it, saw the Inn in the distance, felt smooth stones under our feet, where the bank rose higher in the way of a miniature wharf.

'I would have thought,' Gareth said at last, tilting his face to the sky, 'that after eight hours on the ward, you'd have had quite enough—enough work for one day, without taking extra on.'

Father had said much the same thing, with much the same effect—I felt they were being critical of Dave. 'The same applied to David,' I said, 'he didn't have to do it. We shared the work, did it together. We even . . . we even enjoyed it.'

'And as a result you're dead on your feet and can hardly walk straight,' he said.

It was true, of course—only too true, but his saying it didn't please me, nor flatter me; I knew I looked a mess. For goodness sake, I behested

myself, don't stumble *again*. I began to walk rather
more carefully, more slowly—we skirted round the
ducks. They slept up here on the stones, we could
see them lying like blobs—brown and headless,
their beaks tucked under the wings. We drew
nearer to the Inn, there was more light, pools of
light spilled out. We could see the diners in the
upstairs' restaurant, glimpse the crowd in the bar:
   'It looks like a stage-set . . . like something from
. . .' I began, but never finished. For suddenly,
without any warning, a duck rose up at my feet. It
squawked and flapped, and streaked for the water,
the others followed suit. And as for me—as for
me—I stepped backwards in alarm, forgetting for
the moment—forgetting—forgetting I was right on
the end of the pond. I felt my heels leave the
edge—I felt myself keeling backwards. I floun-
dered, flailed, fought for balance—the sky and
trees swung round—I fought and fought—then a
jerk, a wrench, a pull on my wrist dragged me
upright. The ground still moved, but was flat again,
and the sky was overhead. There were hands tight
about my waist, they lifted me from the edge, and
Gareth's face was close to mine—touching mine for
a second—warm, hard, rough-smooth, it moved,
and I lay against him—against his shirt—struggling
to get my breath. 'I'm all right now . . . I'm quite all
right.' I made myself move back.
   'That was close . . . a very near thing,' he
gathered up my hair, held it back, stared down into
my face. 'You're not hurt? You're all right?'
   I nodded speechlessly. He released my hair, it

sprang forward again, I pushed at it, trying to laugh: 'It's not my night for walking round ponds!'

'More for falling in!' We began to walk on, keeping well away from the edge. We walked separately, not touching, aware of intense embarrassment, or at least I was, I just couldn't speak, heat prickled my body, Gareth's voice came teasingly out of the dark: 'I doubt if anyone's been in that pond since the old witch-ducking days. You don't qualify as a witch, do you Claire?'

'No, I don't think so,' the embarrassment was going, lifting like a cloud, 'I haven't got the right equipment—no black cat familiar—no broomstick—no cauldron to bubble and stir.'

He laughed and took my arm, and I felt the pressure of his side, as we walked the remaining yards to the tables and chairs. Stephanie and David were still talking. David saw us coming, Gareth suggested to Stephanie that they should go: 'I'm thinking about your 'phone call,' he said.

'Oh Lord, yes, I'd forgotten!' She got up with a swirl of skirt, a toss of her chestnut head. I sat down with David. We were properly paired again. 'I've a 'phone call coming through from the States,' Stephanie explained. 'We'd better go.' Goodnights were said all round.

But she called out again from the kerb, before she got in the car . . . into Gareth's Mercedes, shimmering cream in the dark. 'I saw you two in The Larches garden, jerking up weeds, yesterday. You looked very, very engrossed. What an industrious pair!'

'We take time off occasionally,' David called back. The doors slammed and the big cream car purred off.

'She's going to fix Eric up with a mount,' David told me as we, too, rose.

'Oh good,' I said. Just for a second I couldn't think who Eric was.

'Where did you get to with the tall, dark and handsome Consultant Surgeon?'

'Round the pond, and I nearly fell in,' I laughed but didn't explain. David didn't seem to notice, he kept talking about Gareth:

'Is he Welsh, do you think . . . with the name, and colouring *and* his singing voice. His voice is compelling, rivets you to your seat.'

'I can imagine.' And indeed I could. My imagination was rioting. I sighed deeply as we got into the van.

'I've tired you out. You *look* tired, Claire,' his fingers traced my cheek.

'I *am* tired . . . don't go on about it.'

He looked hurt, and I hated myself. We talked very little after that, but when we got back to The Larches, and I asked him in, he shook his head and refused: 'I'd like to, but I'd better get on,' (he lived-in at Melton House). 'I want to unload all these things, get some of them up to William. He'll be able to handle all his treasures when he wakes up tomorrow.'

'Sounds like Christmas morning.'

'It'll be like that to him. So, goodnight, Claire, sweet dreams and thank you for helping me.' We kissed by simply turning heads, like an old married couple, I thought.

I jumped down from the van, and walked up the garden path.

# CHAPTER THREE

STEVE was assisting Gareth Bannerman in theatre next day. By eleven a.m. three patients were already back in the ward. Mr Mark Steadman (the glaucoma) was the fourth to be returned, I followed the stretcher-trolley through the doors.

The porters placed him on the bed, removed the theatre canvas. I beckoned to Joyce Gale, the Learner Nurse: 'Sit with Mr Steadman, Nurse, until he begins to come round. As soon as he does, speak to him, reassure him quietly. And remember to sit on his left side, on the side of his *good* eye. If you're worried about him, let me know at once.'

'Yes, Staff,' she seated herself, the porters took themselves off, I went along to look at the little boy, Paul. His operation had been over two hours, he'd been conscious and asked for a drink. He was relaxed in a natural sleep, his eye wasn't bandaged, there was no sign of leakage on his cheek.

Mrs Denton, pale hair ruffled in an aureole round her head, called me over, she was sitting out of bed. She was supposed to sit beside her bed, but sometimes she slid her chair forward, she liked to see what was going on in the ward. She was enjoying her stay in hospital, and frequently told me so . . . 'I live on my own, dear. I like company. I get plenty of it here,' and of course she did, for eye patients aren't exactly ill. Their bodies are well, and once the first post-op days are over, they can sit and chat and gossip all they please. 'Mr Blenderman's being kept busy this morning,' she said as the porters came back for Mrs Jean Piltson—a detached retina case.

'His name's Bannerman, Mrs Denton, and yes, he's being kept busy.'

'Keep him out of mischief . . . goodlooking, isn't he?'

I agreed that it would, and that he was, and then I hurried away, because sometimes her comments could go right over the edge. There was no telling what Mrs Denton might say.

As I went out into the corridor, the Admissions Officer was arriving with a new patient, Mr Alec Joiner. After a few minutes' chat in the office, I took him into the ward, introduced him to the patients in nearby beds. He was a languid, intellectual-looking man of twenty-eight. He wore spectacles with grey rims, and the lid of his left eye drooped, giving his face a slightly sinister look. 'This will be your bed, Mr Joiner,' I drew the curtains round it. 'Perhaps you'd like to get undressed, the Nurse will take your clothes. You're just right for a mid-morning drink, you've timed it very well.' His answering smile was slow in coming, but come it eventually did. He was charming, in spite of his drooping lid.

Mr Shone's daughter arrived next. Mr Shone was being discharged. Nurse Islet fetched him, wheeling him in a chair. 'I could walk,' he said to me,

as I met him at the doors, 'you know I can walk,
I've been doing it all the week.' He made to get
up from the chair, but his daughter pressed him
back:

'No, Dad, do as they say.'

'Just ride to the lift,' I said, smiling at him, and
taking charge of the chair. I wheeled him up the
corridor, and out to the line of lifts, the daughter
following, clacking on high heels. The lift arrived,
and in they got, I was left with the vacant chair, I
turned it round, said goodbye to them both:
'You've been a very good patient, Mr Shône.
We're going to miss you a lot.'

'And I'll miss you, dear . . . just cannot thank
you enough.' His eyes were behind dark glasses,
but his mouth with the little moustache was still
smiling as the lift doors rolled across.

I felt a kind of satisfied glow, as I wheeled the
chair back down the corridor. Being in charge of
the ward, even if only pro tempore, had many
rewarding sides to it, it made me feel fulfilled. I like
welcoming patients in, I enjoyed seeing them off. I
liked being relied upon, confided in, and thanked.
And all this probably meant that I was coveting
Sister's job. Had Gareth Bannerman, I wondered,
ever coveted Sir Hugh's? Had he learned of his
resignation with glee? Had he clapped his hands on
the quiet? And if he had, who could blame him—
chances have to be seized—unless one's a cabbage-
plant, of course.

Miss Malvering arrived just after two, during
rest-time on the ward. She was a tall, big-boned

woman, with slightly prominent teeth. She was in
her forties, quietly spoken and calm.

Gareth Bannerman came up to see her as soon as
he'd finished in theatre. He came in a rush, he
looked tense and drawn, his dark face was carved. I
knew he'd been operating since nine o'clock that
morning. The resulting strain must have been in-
supportable. He was terse with me, but I didn't
mind, I even felt relieved. For in no way did I want
to be reminded of last evening. I was trying to erase
it from my mind.

He was kind to Miss Malvering, and his kindness
wasn't all bedside manner; it's easy for nurses to tell
the true from the false: 'She's just the kind of
patient I like,' he said when we came out, 'calm as a
pond.' I jerked a little, and I knew I went very red.
His face was completely straight and impassive,
he even hurried me up: 'When you're quite
ready, Staff, I'd like to see Mr Joiner. I'm due at
Seftonbridge General at five . . . this isn't a social
visit.' I swallowed hard, and dived for the patient's
notes.

I was off duty at four-thirty, and a terrible thing
happened. The car park was full, and somehow or
other, reversing to get out, I scraped against
Gareth Bannerman's Mercedes, and when I got out
to look, I just couldn't believe—couldn't believe—
I had done so much damage. It couldn't be—I
hadn't done it—I closed my eyes, and opened
them, and looked again. My breath came out in a
groan. It was like a wound, a deep jagged scrape,
right across the rear door. It was even slightly

dented. Oh, how could I—how could I have done it! How could I have done it—how could I have done such a thing! I was still standing there, cold in horror, when Bob Carver from Maintenance, passed close by on his way to the porter's lodge.

'STREWTH!' was all he said at first. He bent down and looked at the mark. 'He'll go barmy,' he said, 'he'll go raving bonkers. That car's his pride and joy!'

'Yes, I know.'

He mopped all round the back of his neck with a rag. He had yellow hair and popping blue eyes, he always looked sweaty and hot:

'How did it happen?'

I shook my head. I simply couldn't answer.

He came up to me then, close up, he tapped his nose with his finger, his eyes were artful, he nudged me in the ribs: 'I'd scarper, if I was you. Who's to know who did it? I shan't say a dickey-bird. It could-a been anyone . . . someone who's been and gorn wivvout a word.'

Temptation streaked once, like lightning, then as quickly took itself off: 'Thank you,' I said, 'but I'd sooner own up.'

'More fool yew!' He sloped off, pulling at his crotch.

What to do now? Go in and find Gareth Bannerman, of course. I had simply got to take myself in hand and go and *do it*. I had no idea where he'd be, though. I'd have to get him bleeped. And then I remembered him saying something about Seftonbridge General. He'd got to be at Seftonbridge by five, which meant—he'd be here any minute . . .

I looked up and saw him approaching me.

'Hello, what's up . . . got your car stuck?' His eyes were on my Fiat, which was standing at an awkward angle, its door open wide.

'It's *your* car . . . I've scraped it,' I moved to one side, giving him an uncluttered view of that dreadful—awful mark. I held my breath as a stream of oaths came out.

'Of all the stupid . . . clumsy . . . incompetent . . . for God's sake, girl, CAN'T YOU DRIVE!'

'I misjudged my distance. I can't tell you how sorry . . .'

He had turned back to the car. He actually got right down on his knees and felt carefully over the door. I felt simply dreadful—I felt almost desperate—I didn't know what to say. I babbled something about—sorry again; he looked over his shoulder at me:

'Move your car, will you? Let me pass. I'm going to be late.' His voice was devoid of anger now, it was flat and expressionless.

'Mr Bannerman . . .'

He got in his car. He didn't look at me. I don't think he could bear to. I don't think he could trust himself—couldn't bear the sight of me standing there on the park: 'Will you move your car?' He stared straight ahead over his steering wheel.

'I'll pay for the damage.'

'That's very kind.' He switched his engine on.

'So if you'll take it to your usual garage, and ask

them to send me the bill, I'll settle it straightaway, I won't wait to claim from my company.'

'You can do it any way you please, but you'll *pay for it*,' he said. 'The garage is Martins, I'll leave the car when I get back tonight. Now for the third time, will you move your car, and . . . get out of my way,' I thought I heard him add, as he slammed the door.

With shaking hands, and the certain feeling that the rest of me was stone. I shifted the Fiat enough for him to pass it and drive off. I watched him go . . .

I was very close to tears.

I told Father about it that evening, once I felt less shattered. He knew there was something the matter anyway. He's very intuitive. I told him whilst we were having our evening meal:

'*Oh* dear,' he said reflectively, putting down his fork. 'There are few things that annoy a man more than getting his car bashed in.'

'Do you think it'll be all right when it's mended?'

'Yes, of course it will. Be good as new, I'm sure it will.'

'The car *is* new,' I said, 'he's only had it five or six weeks. He was absolutely livid.'

'He'll get over it, and so will you. It's not the end of the world. Anyone can have an accident, you didn't do it on purpose. Pay his bill and the whole thing will be over and done with. *I'll* pay it, let me pay it, Claire. That's what fathers are for . . . settling bills when their daughters ram Consultant Surgeons' car!'

'No,' I said, 'I'll pay it myself,' but I laughed at

his little joke. He was trying to make me feel better about it, and up to a point he succeeded. But I had a very troubled night, and even when I slept I dreamt of disasters—this time on the ward.

True to his word, Bannerman arrived on the ward at three thirty next day, exactly half an hour before visiting time: 'The child first,' he said with quick peremptoriness, giving me no chance to say a word. Steve made a thumbs down sign, as we followed him into the ward:

'Mood low,' he whispered to me, 'but he'll boost it for the patients. It's we, the minions who suffer 'neath his sting.'

Paul was talking to Mr Freer, who was in the next bed to him. Mr Freer—round, jolly, cheerful, had three little boys of his own. He was telling Paul about their family dog. I drew the curtains round the child's bed, and we all three crowded in. Steve spoke to Paul, but he looked at me, and at G.B. directly behind me. 'Keep looking at Nurse, please, Paul,' his voice was very low, but even so, at such close range, it resounded in my ear. The child stared fixedly, I heard G.B.'s satisfied grunt, and I knew he had noted, as I had, the way the light fell on Paul's eyes—on each cornea, in exactly the same place. This was what he had aimed for, it meant that things had gone well, it meant that the operation was a success. His hand brushed against my shoulder, he eased in front of me, looked at the child at even closer range. 'Well, there you are, Paul, what did I tell you . . . you've got a mended eye.'

'When will Mummie come?' Steve answered his question. G.B. turned to me: 'They can do with swabbing, otherwise fine. We'll get the Orthoptist up. She can put him through some simple tests, and then you never know . . .' he turned back to Paul, 'you may be able to read your Rupert book. You'd like that, wouldn't you?' Paul nodded slowly. As we drew back his curtains, his eyes went straight to the doors.

Mr Steadman was examined next, G.B. reassured him, talked quietly to him, as I re-bandaged his eye: 'It's draining a little slowly, Mr Steadman, but that's all to the good. In a day or two we'll hurry things up with a little gentle massage. We call it "dimpling", we use strange words . . . all to confuse you, of course.'

'Mood rising to jocular,' Steve whispered in my ear. I wished he wouldn't. Gareth's hearing was acute.

He handled Mrs Varsitter, a lens extraction case, with nothing less than genius, I thought. She wasn't, and hadn't been, an especially co-operative patient. She hated having her eyes swabbed—most patients welcomed this. She was quite sure the saline would spoil her skin: 'I feel I should be seeing much better than this with my bad eye,' she said for the umpteenth time, even though she knew the answer, which G.B. gave her again, with his bedside smile:

'Once you get your glasses you'll be absolutely fine. But there *is* an alternative in your case, that you might like to think about. You've got normal vision in your good eye, which is why I've been wondering if, instead of glasses, you'd like a contact lens on your bad one. A contact lens, as you know, fits right up against the eye. This, in your case, would make it easier for both eyes to work together. I'm talking, of course, when everything has healed.'

'No glasses!' she sat bolt upright.

'Not unless you want.'

'Oh, I don't want . . . I don't want at all! I mean, with my looks (she was a curly-haired, elfin-faced blonde in early middle age) they would dwarf me, *ruin* me . . . I've got such small features, you see. My husband calls me Pixie—don't you think that's sweet!'

Steve coughed at my elbow, as I bent to tuck in the sheet.

'I'll see Miss Hendry on my own,' G.B. said as we left the bed. 'You can take your equipage away, Staff,' he meant the dressings trolley, '*and* this,' he touched Steve's truck of notes. So Steve and I left the ward, whilst he crossed to Olive Hendry, left the curtains open, sat down by her bed.

'He's worried about her,' Steve said, 'about her mental state.'

'I know, and I'm not surprised,' I replied, 'she seems to be getting worse.' Once we got to the office I pulled out her notes. I re-read them whilst Steve ate my biscuits again.

Olive Hendry had been in the ward since mid-April, with a badly damaged eye. She had been in a Demonstration March, which had turned into a brawl. Had it not been for Sir Hugh's expertise (he had been at The Royal then), she'd have lost all useful vision in her eye. She had a facial scar running down her right cheek, her eye had a tent-shaped pupil, which in time would settle, and be less noticeable. She was depressed—low—miserable, and I knew that there were times when Gareth Bannerman felt she should be moved to the Psyche Wing. Looking through the viewing window, I could see him sitting beside her, see the fall of her long dark hair, see one side of her face—the undamaged side—she was gypsy-looking, with a great deal of style. It was sad to see her drawing back from life.

In a minute *he* would be coming back, my heart began to thud. Would he say anything about yesterday—would he mention the car? I hoped not and yet I wished he would bring it into the open. I closed Olive Hendry's notes, and as I did so I saw him get up, push his chair back, come striding up the ward.

'Here comes his Imperial Majesty!'

'Oh, shut up, Steve.'

Steve raised his eyebrows at my tone, Gareth's bulk flashed by the window, filled the doorway, he came in and sat down: 'All right, Steve, that's all for now thanks,' his nod was one of dismissal. Steve went out, leaving the door ajar.

And now—and now, I thought to myself, he's bound to mention the car, but he didn't, he tapped the folder of notes on my desk: 'Talking to that young woman's like digging for gold,' he said. He picked up the notes and held them on his knee. 'I saw the mother last night—nervous little woman—means well, but doesn't help very much.'

'I know what you mean.' His hands, for a big man, were almost delicate—the fingers long and tapering, the nail tips very white. Would he mention . . .

'However,' he said, 'she did divulge one thing, one important item of news which she should have told us before. The girl's boyfriend jilted her, three weeks ago—came to see her, just the once, then sent a message in; said he felt they should end things. I can date her depression from them.'

'Yes, it would have been about then.' I remembered the boyfriend coming—or vaguely so, I remembered his bush of red hair.

'She's convinced her attractions are nil,' he went on, 'which is absolute nonsense, of course. She's an attractive young girl, who just at the moment has an eye she has to keep shaded, and a scar on her face that has healed without keloid, and will never need plastic surgery. In a year, with make-up, she'll never know it's there.'

'It's now that counts.'

'I know that. So, what do we do about it? Pack her off to the Psyche Wing—I don't want to take that step. Sir Hugh started her off so well, I'd like to finish the job. She's a kind of . . . legacy-patient, and quite apart from that, I don't like failing . . . I want to get her right!' His chin was sticking out now, at its pugilistic angle. I was beginning to recognise most of the movements he made.

'She needs to be put in touch with someone similarly placed,' I said, greatly daring, for I'd had a sudden idea.

'Who, for instance?'

I was thinking of Eric . . . Eric Sindon at Melton House. Eric's face and eye had been injured in much the same way as Olive's. He, too, had been in a brawl—had been an innocent victim—just like her—and as I thought, the idea seemed to warm. It might be the answer, it might do good, for I remembered David saying what a cheerful, outgoing person Eric was. I explained this to G.B., who didn't grab the idea, but neither did he scoff and turn it down:

'Well . . . I don't know,' he rubbed his chin, 'he may not agree,' he said, 'he may not want to be involved . . . may be short on do-gooding instinct. On the other hand . . .' his eyes met mine, 'I suppose we could give it a try.'

'David could talk to him, sound him out. David's always *more* then willing to help people. He makes a study of it!'

'All right then. Go ahead . . . see what you can do.'

'I'm going to Melton House this evening. I'll try to fix something up.' But I stopped at that point, stopped and listened, I looked towards the door. He did too, for we'd both heard the bubbling and hissing noise coming from the ward kitchen on the opposite side of the passage. It was water boiling—and boiling over; the kettle had been left on, clouds of steam were puffing out of the door: 'It's our new kettle, it doesn't switch off, I'd better rescue it.' I hurried out, crossed the kitchen, switched off at the panel, I mopped up the spillage; no great harm had been done. I opened a window to let out the steam, and through the thinning vapour I saw that G.B. had followed me into the room.

'I don't think I've been in here before,' he stood by the central table, his gaze raking over the stainless steel worktops, the hot-plates, the cooker, the crates of milk, the bread piled up by the bin.

'It's used for breakfasts, mid-morning coffees, teas and bedtime drinks—for preparing them, I mean, of course. It's out-of-bounds to the patients.' I said this walking across to the door, for I thought he wanted to go, to return to the office, or even go back on the ward. But he didn't move, he stood quite still in the middle of the room, then he flexed his knees and sat on the table edge.

'I've not,' he said, looking faintly embarrassed, 'eaten since breakfast-time. I wonder if I might scrounge a coffee, and perhaps a biscuit or two.' He was half-smiling. I stared at him aghast: 'Not eaten since breakfast! But, Mr Bannerman, that's eight hours ago!'

'So my stomach tells me, and my blood sugar's running low!'

'It's nothing at all to joke about,' I heard myself snap, 'and you, of all people, should know better! Oh, I'm sorry, I didn't mean . . . I'll see what I can find in the fridge.' I pulled out ham and tongue. 'I'll make you a sandwich. I think you'd better sit down.'

He said, 'thank you', quite meekly, for him. I heard him sit down at the table, the chair-legs made a squeak on the vinyl floor. I worked with my back to him, trimming the meat, mixing mustard, cutting off crusts, and the silence in the kitchen built up, became the pin-drop sort—apart, that is, from the fridge, which keened and weened at intervals, and apart from the plopping of the clock.

'Claire . . .' When he spoke my name I nearly jumped out of my skin. For I knew with absolutely certainty what was coming next. He was going to mention the business of the car.

'Yes?' I turned round to face him, bearing the plate of sandwiches, sliding it over the table to his hand.

'Thank you. Claire . . . about the car,' my heart began to thud, 'I don't want you paying for it. It won't amount to much. I've seen John Martin, of Martins Garage. I ran the car in last night . . .'

'But Mr Bannerman, we agreed last evening . . .'

'Last evening I was upset . . .'

'But what you said . . . most of it . . . was . . . was absolutely right. I was careless, I wasn't thinking, I felt simply dreadful about it. I still do, as a matter of fact,' . . . our glances met over the table . . . 'and the only way I can put things right is to pay your garage bill.'

'Now, look . . .' he half-rose, then sat down again, as I went on talking fast:

'I've already paid the first half. I went to the garage this morning, early this morning, before I came here. I, too, saw Mr Martin. He'll send me the other half of the bill when he's completed the job. He says this might be Saturday, I told him how urgent it was.'

'But you had no right . . . no right to do that!' He looked incredulous, 'You had no right whatsoever to interfere!'

'I don't look at it that way,' I said, 'I can't see it that way at all. I damaged your car, and you bawled me out, said I'd got to pay. I'm doing so, and I think that evens things up.'

'Of all the childish, silly remarks . . .'

I knew it was, of course. It was rude too, but I simply didn't care. Or at least I didn't care at that moment. I suppose I felt I'd scored. For although he'd been perfectly justified in telling me off yesterday, he had overdone it—grossly so—he had called me clumsy and stupid, had rounded on me, asked me if I could drive. Under no circumstances, after that, would I be in his debt. Paying his bill, especially when he didn't want me to, was paying him out. I was childish, and didn't care.

He didn't say anything after that. He began to eat his sandwiches, quickly and angrily, champing at them, making a sound when he swallowed. When I said I thought I ought to leave him as visiting time had started, he said, 'Yes, please do,' in a muffled tone of voice.

Back on the ward, talking to relatives, keeping an eye on the patients, I didn't feel quite so pleased with my victory. I'd been patronising, I'd been clever-clever, he'd never forgive me for that. Still, there was nothing I could do about it, I would have to leave it now. Later, as I accompanied Miss May, the Orthoptist, down the passage, I looked in the kitchen again, but he'd left some time ago. Nurse Bayer and Nurse Islet were in there, cutting bread and butter. The kettle was boiling, throwing out billows of steam.

That evening at Melton House I talked to David about Olive Hendry. I did so when we'd finished our swim in the big indoor pool that was open to friends of the staff after seven p.m. 'I'm positive Eric will help,' he said, towelling his hair. We were sitting at the end of the pool, watching the other swimmers, before going up to the canteen for a meal.

'Can we go and see him? Can I ask him now?'

'Yes, if you want to,' he said. 'We'll get dressed and go along. I think he's in the Gym. He's got a keep-fit jag on at the moment, and of course I encourage him.' When we got to the Gym he was on the rowing machine.

My first thought was how young he looked, little more than a boy. He was ruddy-faced with a crest of brown hair, his eyes were grey and twinkly. I tried to decide which was the false one. He caught me staring, and laughed:

'It's this one,' he tapped the left one, making a little clink. 'I'm used to it now, don't think about it . . . well, not much, anyway. Now tell me a little more about this girl.'

David and I explained, and he agreed at once to come: 'Sure,' he said, 'course I'll see her. I think I know how she feels. When I first got this . . .' he pointed to his scar, which was hardly visible, 'I felt no girl would fancy me, would ever look at me twice.'

He said this so seriously, so earnestly, that I laughed. So did he, he laughed out loud. He was, as David had told me—an outgoing, cheerful, uncomplicated young boy.

We arranged that he would come to the Unit next day. I would simply tell Olive that he was a friend who did hospital visiting. I warned Eric that she might be difficult.

'Don't worry, Claire. That's all right. I'm not a sensitive plant. I'll weather it. You leave it up to me.'

'He's nice,' I said to David, as we went up to the canteen. 'If he doesn't get through to Olive Hendry, then no Psychiatrist will. I hadn't told either David or Eric about her being jilted. It seemed to me that this had been told to Gareth Bannerman in confidence. No-one likes that kind of thing advertised.

'Not fallen for him, have you?' teased Dave.

'I shouldn't think so,' I said. 'I shouldn't really think so, Dave. I go for older men!'

'Thirty suit you?' (David was thirty.)

'Spot on, of course!'

He looked at me, and his eyes grew serious: 'Well, let me know,' he said, 'when you want to change your name to Cope. It can't be too soon for me.'

Later, driving home in the softly shaded dusk, I

wondered why I couldn't make up my mind to marry Dave. We got on well, we were suited, he wasn't temperamental. And I loved him, surely I loved him, I was happy being with him. Yet somehow or other, ever since Keith, my views on marriage had changed—changed almost without my knowing, changed radically.

Sometimes I wondered if I wanted to be married at all.

# CHAPTER FOUR

MISS MALVERING came back from Theatre at twelve noon next day. I stayed with her until she began to come round. As soon as she stirred I reassured her: 'Try to lie perfectly still. You're back in your room and everything's gone well.'

She looked very vulnerable lying there, her brown hair ruffled, her nose and chin jutting out beneath the double-eye bandage: 'Is it Staff Nurse?'

'Yes, Miss Malvering.' My fingers were round her wrist. Contact helped when both eyes were padded, touch was everything—touch and voices helped patients feel secure.

'I feel thirsty.' She moistened her lips.

'It's the anaesthetic,' I said. 'I'll bring you some tea later on. You can drink it lying down—through a flexostraw—but first I want you to sleep. You're reasonably comfortable, aren't you? You haven't got any pain?'

'No . . . I'm all right.'

'Then I'll leave you to sleep, but your door will be ajar. You'll be able to hear us all moving about, and you know where your bell is, don't you?' I guided her hand to the button near her head.

She had her first dressing done on Saturday. I had told her what to expect. G.B. came up to do it himself, I met him in the corridor as I wheeled the dressings trolley to her room. He had been to the ward the day before and talked to Miss Malvering, also to Mr Joiner who'd had a skin graft applied to his lid. I had schooled myself to forget our argument. I didn't find it difficult. I could work for the surgeon, I couldn't get on with the man.

'How is she?' he asked *sotto voce*, before, we got within earshot.

'Seems fine,' I said, 'she's eating well, makes very few complaints. She's stoic as well as being calm.'

'Well, let's go in then, shall we?' I sensed the excitement in him, intermixed, perhaps, with anxiety.

Her face was turned towards the door, and she smiled when he greeted her. She was nervous, well of course she was. She might be calm as a pond, but she had feelings like everyone else, she could feel apprehension. I hoped and prayed that the graft had been a success. I wheeled the trolley to the bed, turned the bandage up on her forehead, removed the eye pads, asked her to keep her eyes closed: 'Just whilst I wash the lid margins,' I used white lint dipped in saline, then I moved away as Gareth bent over her. I heard him ask her to open her eyes—ask her what she saw—*how* she saw—and I watched him cover her good eye with his hand: 'Now tell me if you can see me clearly—look right up at me—up, up—yes, that's it.'

'A little blurred,' she said, 'but it seems to be getting . . . it seems to be clearing . . .'

'Close and open again.'

She did so and this time she said she could see him better: 'Better, I think, than before . . . before the operation, I mean. Yes, I'm sure I can, but it's just that it seems . . . there seems a clogged effect.'

'That's all right . . . that's normal . . . natural. It's due to the sutures,' he said. 'You won't get perfect vision till after those are out. And remember, too, that the eye has to settle down after surgery. Now, I want to examine it through this loupe, just try to keep perfectly still.' He bent low, his face almost touching hers. When he straightened, she could hardly wait to ask if it was all right.

'Very much all right, Miss Malvering.' I saw him draw in his breath, and expel it gently, I saw him smile down at her. 'All we've got to do now is wait for the eye to heal. And I'd like to pad and bandage *both* your eyes for another three days. This will ensure perfect rest, and then I think, after that, we can leave your good eye uncovered. That'll help a little, won't it?'

'Yes, it will,' she smiled at him. 'And I'm grateful, I'm so grateful!'

His voice was gruff in reply. I could see, though, how pleased he was. It was a heady feeling—special too; Miss Malvering smiled from her bed. It was rather as though, just at that moment, we were all three linked by the feeling that comes when success has been achieved.

Gareth and I went into the office. He put the notes on the desk: 'I hardly dared hope,' he said, 'for such a good result. I'm sorry to double-pad her again, both for her sake and yours, but I don't want her moving too much, not at this early stage.'

'No, of course not. I understand.'

'She's being very well nursed,' he said this looking me straight in the face. I felt my guard slip a little, for he didn't have to say that; he was paying me a compliment. I took it, and grasped it, and held it tight with both hands, whilst I thought—well, perhaps after all, perhaps he's not so bad.

We did Mr Joiner's dressing next. His lid was healing well. A fresh pad and bandage applied. He wasn't, however, immobilised, he could move about fairly freely, even manage to read with his uncovered eye. As we left his bed I saw him reaching over for his book. He seemed to be very fond of reading and, like Father, he went in for crime. I couldn't help wondering if the spoken horrors on Father's talking-books gave one more of a shudder than seeing them in print.

Little Paul Timmins had gone home, an elderly man had his bed. He was Mr Herbert Warren who had come in the day before. He was going to have a naevus removed from the limbus of his left eye. It was encroaching over his eyeball and beginning to look unsightly. The operation was a minor one, he was having it done on Monday, he hoped to be discharged within a week: 'I can remember this hospital full of Military during the War,' he told us. 'My daughter was a VAD, she used to come home with some tales. I was in the Home Guard. They used to laugh at us.' I talked to him for a little while after G.B. had gone. I still couldn't get over the fact that he'd paid me a compliment. I hugged it to me. I practically cherished it.

It was my half-day, I was off at one. I was looking forward to it, even though the skies were pelting rain. Kay Dellar, as usual, was punctual. She came in to be briefed:

'How have things been?' she grinned at me. Kay was dimpled and round, pale-skinned with freckles across her nose.

'Not bad, not bad at all,' I felt like grinning myself. 'Miss Malvering's had her dressing done, the graft has taken well. Mr Steadman's sutures are due out tomorrow, but I'll be here for that. Mr Rosphur and Mr Kelder' (senile cataract patients) 'had their lunch in the Day Room today, they're being discharged tomorrow. Mrs Alston has tenderness of both calves and slight pyrexia, so see she moves her legs at intervals, and help her to the toilet. Mrs Varsitter's allowed her own nightdress now and lies there like Cleopatra. And, well, I think that's about the lot. I'm here tomorrow, Sunday, but off on Monday morning, so I'll see you then . . . one o'clock Monday . . . cheerio, till then.'

'Yes, okay, have a good afternoon. What are you going to do?' She stopped in front of the mirror to pin on her cap.

'Food shopping, being the weekend, although I want to buy a skirt—a glamorous one, something swishy, I seem to live in jeans.'

'We all do, they're practical,' she called as I went

down the passage. I'd change out of my uniform at home.

Saturday afternoon wasn't my favourite shopping time. There was a Saturday market which lined the High Street; Cletford didn't boast a Square. It was still charging down with rain, and the awnings over the stalls flapped in the wind and sent water off in sheets. I did the food shopping in the supermarket, buying lamb, which Father loved. We would have it hot this evening for supper, then tomorrow when I was working, he could finish it up with some of his favourite cheese. I had two loaded plastic bags by the time I got to Harpers—the department store, where I hoped to buy my skirt. The ground floor of the big store was as packed as the street outside. I pushed my way through, trying to get to the UP escalator. I was wearing a scarlet mackintosh, and as I was fairly tall, I suppose, even in such a crowd I was fairly noticeable. All I knew was, I heard my name being called in a voice I recognised—Gareth Bannerman's—I turned, and there he was. And he looked harassed—harassed and hot, even slightly dishevelled:

'Claire, I need your help. Can you come?'

Someone's ill, I thought. Someone's fainted, or had a stroke, or a fit, or a heart attack. All these things spun through my mind. 'What's happened?' I asked. A passer-by jolted me into his arms.

'Whoops! Steady!' He righted me, 'Nothing's happened, exactly,' he said, 'but I'm choosing perfume, I'm very confused, I don't want to make a mistake. I wondered if I could possibly ask you to come and help me choose. The salesgirls are only confusing me more.'

'Perfume!'

'Yes, for a gift.'

It must be for Stephanie Newel. He was looking down at me half-smiling, his raincoat collar was rucked. His hair was damp and trying to curl, my eyes moved over his face—yes, I'd have to help, yes, even for Stephanie Newel.

'Of course I'll help . . . only too glad.'

'Thank goodness for that,' he smiled more broadly, and reached down for my bags.

In Perfumery four doe-eyed assistants were waiting for his return. Rows of tester bottles in racks littered the counter top. The assistants were bent on spraying their wrists and thrusting them under his nose: 'Try this one, sir. I'm sure you'll find' . . . 'Now, this one's very popular' . . . 'I do feel that this one, sir' . . . The din they made was horrendous. No wonder he'd gasped for outside help.

'You'll have to tell me who it's for,' I said, tugging his arm. 'Perfume's a very personal thing, it has to suit the recipient.' It was bound to be for Stephanie Newel . . .

'It's for my Great-Aunt,' he said.

'Your Aunt!'

'Yes, she's eighty-eight, and don't suggest lavender water. If I gave Aunt Maud lavender water she'd empty it over my head. She likes an overpowering perfume, nothing sweet or fresh. She isn't the flowery, ferny type, and her sense of smell is waning, so it's got to be strong, even pungent, as you might say.'

'Well then,' I said, 'I'd get her that one,' and I pointed to a shelf where a small, square flacon stood in on its own. 'It's French, and very alluring, very full-bodied too. And no, I don't want to test it thank you,' I waved an assistant away. 'I know it, you see, I've smelt it before. My maternal grand-mother's French. She spent last Christmas with us, she was wearing the perfume then. She spilt it on my bedroom carpet, so I know it very well, *too* well, and it's certainly very strong.'

'Right, that settles it. I'll have it, thank you.' I saw him reach for his wallet. The assistants sub-sided, the chief one went to the till. As for me, I muttered something about other shopping to do. He didn't detain me, just thanked me, and said goodbye.

As I sailed upstairs on the escalator, I could see him still in Perfumery, waiting for his package to be wrapped. Even from such aerial viewpoint his appearance was arresting. I was just in time to see him thrust the perfume into his pocket before I was borne into Leisure Wear and Skirts.

I couldn't find a skirt I liked. I looked at them all on their rails, pushed them along on their plastic hangers, held one or two up to my front. But it was no good, my heart wasn't in it. Somewhere along the line I'd lost interest—or couldn't concentrate. I'll give up and go home, I thought, I'm simply not in the mood. I'll go home and unpack the shopping, do some of my weekend chores. I bent down to pick

up my bags, found only one of them there. One bag
. . . only one . . . then where on earth was the
other? Where was the one that contained the joint
and all the groceries? I'd left it somewhere. It was
nowhere to be seen. Well, I can't have lost it, it
can't be lost. I did a rapid recap. Gareth had carried
it through to Perfumery, I couldn't have picked it
up. That's where it would be, it'd be there now. I'd
go back quickly and ask. The escalator swooped me
down, and immediately I saw it—plastic and bulky,
dangling from Gareth's hand. 'Oh, you found it!
I'm glad you did. It was good of you to wait. I've
only just missed it, I was just about to dash through
to Perfumery.'

'I daren't come upstairs in case I missed you,' he
reached for the other bag, 'if you've finished your
shopping I'll take these out to your car.' He didn't
say, 'safely out' but his tone of voice implied it, and
I caught the glint of amusement in his eye.

'It's nice of you, but you needn't,' I said, 'I don't
want to hold you up.'

'You won't hold me up. It's on my way. My own
car's on the park. It came back this morning, good
as new.' Another look passed between us. His said:
'Incident closed' . . . mine said: 'Yes, I know, and
the bill's been paid, both separate halves of it.' But
when he turned I followed him, followed his chan-
nelling bulk, to the exit doors that led out on to the
park.

And there we stopped, as did crowds of others,
for outside was raging what could only be described
as a monsoon. The rain was beating down in steel

rods, the sky was indigo; all we could hear was a steady muffled roar. 'Well, we can't brave that,' he said, 'not even in mackintoshes. Let's go upstairs quickly, beat the crowds, have tea in the restaurant.'

My mouth dropped open in sheer surprise, as he handed me one of the bags, took my arm very firmly in his, swept me back to the moving stairs: 'It's the sensible thing to do,' he said, a stair or two below me. 'And we needn't be long, if you're in a hurry to go.'

In the blue and white Wedgewood Restaurant up on the fourth floor, he ordered what Harpers called their Tea of the House. It was sumptuous, to say the least—hot buttered toast and sandwiches, scones and cream and jam, and fancy cakes. I watched it all being put on the table, and I stretched out my hand for the teapot, still in a state not very far from shock: 'I thought you disliked the tea-drinking habit.' I handed him his cup, watching him stir in sugar, take an appreciative sip.

'I don't like tea *breaks* . . . not when I'm working,' he said, 'but tea out, tea as a meal, now that's something else again. When I have a home of my own again, and more leisure to enjoy it, I shall have a sit-down proper tea every day of my life.'

'Oh, I see,' I took the lid off the toast dish, and helped myself to a slice. I knew he lived in The Residency (flatlets for Medical Staff) attached to the hospital building, which must be confining at times. I also knew he was looking around for a place of his own outside. Steve had told me, so presumably he'd told Steve. 'Perhaps, when the new Registrar starts, you won't be quite so rushed,' I said, hoping he might fill me in on that.

'He starts in three weeks' time,' he said, 'name of Mr Spurne . . . Mr Anthony Spurne, he should be all right, I liked him at interview. You won't see quite so much of me then . . . once he starts, I mean. He'll do most of the ward rounds, apart from my weekly one, or bi-weekly, depending on how things go. Oh, and by the way,' he wiped his fingers on the paper napkin, 'you've not told me how your friend from the Blind Home got on with Olive Hendry, when he saw her on Thursday afternoon.'

'No, I haven't yet,' I refilled his cup, 'I suppose I've been putting it off. You see, it didn't go off very well . . . to be honest, it was a flop. I suppose I should have prepared Olive first. I debated whether to do so, then I felt no, better just let him go in, keeping it all very casual, as though he'd dropped in to see several people at once.'

'I'd have opted for that choice myself,' he said, making me feel slightly better.

'She was *so* rude to him . . . rude to Eric. David told me so afterwards. But he says Eric's not given up, he looks on her case as a challenge. He's going to make three more efforts, he says.'

'Stout fellow! I wish him luck.'

I laughed a little then: 'It can't do any harm, can it?'

'Absolutely none. Even her anger is better than apathy, and I'm not so sure, you know, that *some* good hasn't been done; when I went on the ward to see Joiner, she was looking in her mirror, I could see her doing so. Now that, I think, is a very good sign indeed.'

'I'd have liked them to have got on better.'

'In time they still may. But you know, Claire,' I watched his bottom lip curve as he smiled at me, 'we're not playing Cupid; that's a very chancey game!'

'Oh, of course we're not,' My face flamed, I could see it in the teapot, a chrome one with chubby rounded sides.

He asked about David after that. He was being very pleasant—very friendly—this was his nicer side: 'Has he always worked amongst the blind?'

'Yes, always,' I said, 'but at other Melton House Homes, he hasn't been here very long. He's ideal for that kind of work, he enjoys the personal involvement. He never seems to me to want to get away from it. It's his *raison d'être*,' I finished with a laugh.

'Well, we all need one of those, in some form or another.' His comment was cryptic, or I thought it was, and he followed it up very quickly by asking me what I usually did with my Saturday afternoon.

'When I'm not working I'm at home,' I said, 'getting forward for the weekend. We don't have help on Saturdays and Sundays. Father and I fend for ourselves. We don't mind, it's fun for a change, but it needs a little planning.'

'Must do.' I felt his gaze linger, he was practically staring at me. I returned his stare. I felt I passed muster, my cotton dress was new, and although my hair was loose on my shoulders, it was hanging all in one piece, naturally wavy hair stays put in rain.

We began to talk about gardens—and current affairs—and holidays. He told me he had been born in Wales, that his parents lived in Canada, where his elder brother was a mining engineer. 'His company are involved in prospecting for gold and uranium in the Rockies . . . an exciting life, very different from mine.'

'But you wouldn't change with him?'

'Never,' he said, 'although there was a time, not so very long ago, when I considered joining them, entering a hospital out there, but in the end I didn't . . . I decided against it. Now I'm glad I stayed.'

By the time we had finished eating and drinking—and talking—the rain had eased—not ceased, but eased enough for us to leave the restaurant, make our way downstairs, and outside to the park. I couldn't get over how the scene had changed in half an hour. The sun was out, gleaming out, lining the clouds with silver, spangling the puddles like miniature lakes. The rain was falling in a soft, fine mesh, and as we crossed to my car, we saw a rainbow beginning to form, saw it deepen and arch itself up—up and over—a bracelet in the sky.

'Awesome, isn't it?' I heard him say, and I felt his arm round my shoulders. We watched the bow of colours till it died. 'Some people say rainbows bring luck.' He put my bags in the car. I got in and he peered at me under the roof.

'I think that's new moons,' I told him, 'you're supposed to curtsey and wish. The only lucky thing about rainbows is the pot of gold at the end. My mother used to tell me that the pot of gold was happiness. If you found it, it would last you all your life.'

'Elusive things . . . pots of gold!' he smiled and slammed me in. His raincoated form filled the window for a second, then he moved and waved me off. My tyres threw up water as I drove across the park. I could see him crossing over to his car.

And he knows, I thought, as I drove home, how to be entertaining, how to put himself across, when he really wants to do so. But he's temperamental, one never knows how he's going to be. He'd be murder to fall in love with—one would be on a constant switchback—up with his high moods, down again with his low.

Was Stephanie Newel in love with him? Was he in love with her? Were the gossips right? Were they having an affair? Deliberately I stopped the trend of my thoughts at that juncture.

What Gareth did was nothing to do with me.

# CHAPTER FIVE

BUT the trouble on the ward on Monday was *all* to do with me—at least he thought so, and I felt the full weight of his tongue.

I was on lates that day, which meant that my shift ran from one p.m. until eight. I went on duty punctually at one. Kaye gave me the morning report: 'No alarms or excursions,' she said, 'not that we haven't been rushed off our feet,' she unpinned her apron; she was going home, she had finished for the day.

All was quiet on the ward, the rest period had started, I looked in at the side-ward to check on Miss Malvering. As soon as I saw her I knew that something was wrong. There was blood under her nose, not very much, but it was there. When I questioned her she said she'd been out of bed. 'But *why*? Miss Malvering you know that at this stage any movement is hazardous.'

She felt for my hand: 'I had to get out, my bell wasn't working, or if it was, no-one came,' her voice sounded faint. 'I had cramp in my calf, it was agonising, I couldn't straighten it out. I had to get my foot down to try to ease the pain. But somehow or other I tipped forward, and struck my nose on my locker—not hard, not really hard at all, then my eye started to hurt.'

'Your eye!' I tried my hardest to keep my voice level, whilst a dozen alarm bells jangled in my brain. Not her graft—oh please, not her graft, don't let it be that.

'Yes, my bad eye.'

'What kind of pain, and when did this all happen.'

'A sharp pain, and oh, I don't know, perhaps half an hour ago. The lunch trolleys had just gone out, I heard the nurses come back. I was all right then, I'd not fallen then, it was a few minutes afterwards.' Her grip on my hand tightened. 'Nurse have I done any damage . . . nurse, do you think I may have displaced my graft?'

'No,' I said, 'I don't, but we'll need to have a look at it. I don't want to disturb it myself, so we'll get Mr Bannerman up. You're due for another dressing this afternoon in any case, but we'll get him up now. I'll go and give him a ring.'

I asked Nurse Dane to sit with her whilst I went into the office. I shut the door and picked up the 'phone in a hand that was shaking visibly. I dialled Main Switchboard, asked for G.B. to be bleeped.

'He's at lunch,' the voice on switchboard sounded dull, and laconic and bored.

'I can't help that. Please tell him it's urgent.'

'On your own head be it. I'm starting to bleep him now, Staff. Please put your receiver down.' I did so. I hoped he wouldn't be long.

I opened the door, went back to Miss Malvering. Nurse Dane got up looking scared. 'I've checked the bell, Staff, and it's not working, neither is the one next door . . . the one in the other side-ward.'

'Were they checked first thing?'

'I don't know.'

'Nurse Dellar didn't mention it?'

'No, I'm sure she didn't.'

'All right,' I said, 'I'll stay here now. Go to Clean Utility, lay up a dressings tray and bring it straight in here. I'm expecting Mr Bannerman to come up.'

He came almost as soon as the tray, and he didn't look very pleased. I took him into the office whilst I explained.

'FELL . . . she *fell*! You mean out of bed!' I saw the dismay in his eyes.

'She tipped forward, struck her nose on the locker, it seems she had cramp in her legs. Almost at once the pain started up in her eye.'

The dismay changed to shock: 'God Almighty!' he turned on his heel. He was in the side-ward before I could draw a breath.

With Miss Malvering he was calmness itself. To be a superlative actor was an asset at crisis times like this: 'Hello, Miss Malvering . . . spot of pain, I hear . . . been hitting your nose as well?'

'Yes, I knocked it, then the pain started.' She told him what had happened. It worried her that no-one had answered her bell. 'Whenever I've pressed it before, someone's always come at once. I wondered if it was out of order. I tried shouting out, but the extra effort hurt my eye even more.'

'Mm . . . I see. Well, we'll look at it. It may not be very much.'

I turned up the bandage, removed the pads. 'Don't open yet,' he cautioned, 'Nurse'll wipe the lids, dampen them over, the same as she did before.' I did so, and he stepped forward, looked into the grafted eye. I watched his face closely, it was dead pan, I looked at Miss Malvering—I looked at her eye, but from this distance, I could tell very little. 'All right, close up,' I heard him tell her. He nodded to me to rebandage. I heard her ask him if her graft had come away. 'No, no, nothing like that, it's still lying good and flat. What's happened is that your iris has prolapsed, that's what's causing the pain.'

'Is it serious?'

'No, just a nuisance. It means further surgery, a small operation . . . a very simple one.'

Now that she was bandaged again, his face was showing expression—irritation—dark anger—his eyes were nearly slits. He was furious—well, of course he was—this should never, ever have happened. A set-back at this stage of Miss Malvering's recovery *could* be serious.

'Will it mean an anaesthetic and everything all over again?' I felt so sorry for her.

'Yes,' he said, 'it will.'

'When will you do it . . . when will it be?'

'Some time this afternoon. By supper-time you'll be back here, good as new.'

'Why wasn't her bell answered?' he demanded back in the office. He had just rung down to Theatre, booked it for half-two; I would have to start getting Miss Malvering 'prepped.

'Her bell was out of order,' I said.

His head thrust forward at me: 'Out of order! Out of ORDER! You knew that all the time!'

'No, I didn't know. You see . . .'

'Didn't *know*!' his voice vibrated in fury. 'You didn't know . . . but good God, girl, it's your job, your place to know! When did you find out, then? Just now, I suppose . . . just now when it's too late! For crying out loud, Nurse Graine, those bells, every single one of them are supposed to be checked night and morning, twice in twenty-four hours!'

'Yes, but you see, I . . .'

'What's the use of a bell if it doesn't work! It's a lifeline between patient and nurse, it's there to summon help, it's there to prevent an accident, like falling out of bed! And how was it I wasn't told Miss Malvering's subject to cramp?'

'I don't think we knew,' I answered the last stampeding question first. I was getting angrier by the minute, he was giving me no quarter, no proper hearing, no chance to explain, he was beating me into the ground. And in spite of Miss Malvering's terrible plight, the unfairness of his attack was too much to take, I saw him go to the door, and I seemed to burst, I rushed in front of him, slamming the door tight closed: 'Before you go, Mr Bannerman, there's something I want to say. I realise how you must be feeling, and I'm . . . I'm trying to understand. But *I* care too, you know. I care very much indeed. I care what happens to her for herself, not just for her . . . for *your* graft! I mind that she's fallen and damaged her eye, I mind that she's in pain. I mind that she's got to go and be scraped about all over again. *You* mind because of yourself, you mind for all the wrong reasons! You mind because of your reputation, and what Theatre Staff might think! And as for the bells, the life-saving bells, I wasn't even on duty! I wasn't here . . . I didn't come on until one!'

We were standing close, we had closed-in in anger—eye battled with eye—look clashed with look—even our breath crossed swords; it was like fighting physically as we stood there on the carpet. If he dared—I'm quite sure if he dared, he'd have put his hands round my throat—and squeezed hard—and shut me up for good.

I moved to one side, and he found his voice, which came out loaded and thick—thick with rage—fury at me; he got the door open at last: 'Having made your point so succinctly, Nurse, I think we can leave it at that.' His look was black, he looked at me with hate.

'Wire worked loose,' Bob Carver, from Maintenance, told me half an hour later. It would have to be Bob who'd come up to fix the bell: 'Never mind, Nursie, Bob'll fix it, no trouble at all. Same wire served both rooms, which explains the double fault. Not been any trouble, has there? No one's copped it, like?' He loved trouble, when he wasn't in it himself.

'Perhaps,' I said, ignoring his question, 'you'd start in the vacant side-ward, I'll have a word with the patient in No. 2 before you go in.'

'Anything you say, luv. But don't forget me form . . . me proper Requisition Form . . . have to stick to the rules.' He winked and I signed his form at once, and went into to Miss Malvering.

'You'll hear someone scraping about in the wall soon,' I said, 'it'll be the man from Maintenance, coming to mend the bell. I've asked him to be as quiet as he can.'

'I don't mind,' she was biting her lip.

'Is the pain very bad?'

'Let's just say that I know I've got it,' she made an attempt at a smile, 'it's a boring-through, screwdriver kind of pain.'

'You'll be having your 'premed soon, and then you won't feel another thing.'

She went to theatre just before three, she was back again at four. G.B. came up with the porters, still in his theatre greens. Aware of him with every pore, I wished he were covered completely. I wished that as well as his gown and boots, he had a cap as well, and a mask—and goggles hiding his eyes. I knew he was watching every move I made as, with the porters' aid, I positioned the patient, and drew the bedclothes up.

'She'll be all right now,' he said briefly after the porters had gone. We were standing on either side of the bed, looking down at Miss Malvering. She was wearing a different type of bandage—to cover her 'bad' eye only. More of her face was exposed but, in sleep, she still looked vulnerable, her hands and arms were lying outside the quilt.

'I'm so glad she'll be all right,' I said, and I knew

my words sounded stiff. I dragged my gaze from the patient, and made myself look at him. His face didn't 'give' in any detail, it was set in implacable lines. It gave me no help at all in saying what I felt I had to: 'I was rude,' I began, 'earlier on. I was unfair and rude. I'm sorry about it. I'd like to apologise.'

'That's all right. I was hasty myself.' His response was very quick, but he didn't smile as he said the words, nothing about him softened, his eyes were like stones—the hard dark-grey of slate. 'As you'll see,' he looked at Miss Malvering again, 'I've left her good eye uncovered.'

'She's be glad about that.'

'It'll minimise the risk of further mishap, but warn her to keep as still as she can, I don't want her moving about, apart from shifting her legs in bed. That's quite clear, isn't it, Staff?'

As crystal—buzzed in my brain, but . . . 'Yes, of course,' I said. Once again our eyes met in a look of mutual hostility. It was just as well that in her deep sleep Miss Malvering had no knowledge of the animosity spiking over her bed.

He moved to the door and went out without a word to me. I could hear him going up the passage as I sat down by the bed. His feet made quite a different sound in his white theatre boots—a kind of plomping, as though he were very tired.

And considering everything, I was glad to see Sister back from leave next day. She had had a new hair-do, her perm had been cut off—the back was semi-shingled, shaped down into her neck, the

front curved forward attractively under her cap.
She was in her forties, a managing woman, she
enjoyed the position she held. She was good at it
too, and watching her move slimly between the
beds, I wondered how I could ever have thought I
could do her job on my head. I could do the
nursing, I was up to that, but I hadn't got her knack
of seeing that others did their jobs, and did them
properly—the business of the bells had worried me
all night.

'I've been brought up-to-date on most things,'
she said, when she joined me in the office. 'I saw
Miss Girton last night, soon after I got back. I've
seen the Malvering woman too, and I've read
your report of the accident . . . very clear and
concise, I was glad to have it, Staff. I've also seen
Bannerman, he was here when I came on duty,
looking in on Miss Malvering, hindering Night
Sister! And from the roster . . .' she leaned over
and unhooked it from the wall, 'I see Staff Nurse
Deller will be on at one p.m.'

'Yes, she will, Sister, and about Miss Malvering
. . . is she all right this morning? She's not febrile,
or in pain?'

'She's neither, seems quite chirpy, wants an egg
for breakfast.' And she would, I thought, be able
to feed herself with one eye uncovered, Anne
Malvering had hated being fed. I looked at Sister,
for even now I couldn't quite leave alone that
business of her trying to summon help:

'About her fall, I'd just like to say how sorry I am
that it happened. You see . . .' I was stopped in

mid-sentence, by Sister's upraised hand.

'I know exactly what happened, Staff, I don't want to hear it again. No blame attaches to you at all.'

'I could have reminded Kay, I could have made sure that the Ward Procedure was followed item-by-item—left a copy out for her . . .'

'Stop harping back, Staff Nurse, it never does any good. I'll speak to Deller when she comes on duty. Now, get the nurses in and give the report. I'll sit back and listen today.'

In the canteen at lunchtime I sought Kay out. I felt I had to tell her what had happened, warn her of what was afoot. Admittedly there were times when she appeared to be slap-happy, but even so, even counting that, I felt I had to warn her. It didn't seem fair to let her hear of Anne Malvering's accident—for the first time—as soon as she stepped on the ward.

'*I'd* no idea she'd been calling for help,' she said defensively. 'I checked her bell at breakfast-time, at least . . . I think I did.' She stopped chewing, then started again, 'we were very busy, you know . . . I *could* have forgotten.' I knew she had, it was written on her face, but I said nothing. Sister would say it all. 'Good job you went in to see her, wasn't it?' her eyes were on her plate, 'was it awful? Was Banners very upset?'

'Yes, he was. He hit the roof. I told him I wasn't on duty . . . not during the morning, I mean. It . . . just simply came out in the row. I'm sorry, Kay, really I am.'

'Oh, for heaven's sake,' she said, 'I'd have done exactly the same. Of course you had to tell him,' she reached for her pudding and began to spoon it up. 'Anyway, to tell you the truth, I'm not bothered. I'm leaving at the end of the month, giving my notice in. Jim wants me to stop working now he's got this better job. He says we can manage on his money, he doesn't like my hours. He says he doesn't see enough of me, and it's true enough, you know. It's not like a nine to five job, is it, with every weekend free?'

'No, it's not, but I'm sorry, Kay.'

'Oh, they'll soon find someone else. People are queuing up for jobs, even SRNs.' She went on eating, seemingly unperturbed.

Later that afternoon, from the male end of the ward, she caught my eye, and made a shrugging grimace. But over tea she told me that Sister hadn't been all that bad. 'She listened to what I had to say, with that tight little smile of hers. I'm not sure she believed me, but I don't care if she didn't. I can't worry my be-ootiful head about little things like that.'

'No,' I said, 'I suppose you can't,' but I couldn't help wondering if (like her) I was leaving in four weeks time, I could manage to be quite so blithe as that.

As it turned out, the next four weeks were ones of change all round. There was the usual movement of patients—discharges and admissions; the new Registrar, Mr Anthony Spurne arrived. Olive Hendry went home, fetched by her mother and a smiling Eric Sindon; for yes, Eric's persistence had worked, he and Olive were friends; the change in her was almost miraculous. Gareth Bannerman's visits to the ward were less frequent, he was mostly in theatre. Since the fracas over Miss Malvering I had only seen him in passing, and Mr Spurne was easier, far more predictable. One could almost apply to him the adjective, 'calm as a pond'.

Miss Malvering whose recovery G.B. had refused to rush, went home just before one o'clock on Wednesday the eighth of July. I helped her dress, whilst one of the young teachers from the High School sat in the waiting-room, ready to drive her home.

She had lost weight, I noticed, as I fastened the back of her dress. She was leaning forward to the mirror, dragging a comb through her hair. 'I'm sure I see better than ever I did,' she smiled at me in the mirror, 'I feel as though I've been given a brand-new eye.'

'You've clear, unobstructed vision,' I said, 'due to the new cornea. The graft is perfect. Mr Bannerman's very pleased.'

'He's charming, isn't he, so kind too . . . talented and skilled?'

'He's all of those,' I said shortly, packing her comb and brush. *And* he could be short and sharp, *and* he'd got a temper, but the patients never saw that side of him, of course. I hadn't seen very much of him at all during the past four weeks. Anthony Spurne did most of the rounds, and Sister saw to it that she was on duty when G.B. paid us a call. I was glad I'd not had to see him so much, but nothing is all one way, so as well as a feeling of heaving relief, there was also a feeling of loss. I missed our brief chats, I missed our jokes, the occasional badinage, I missed walking with him on to the ward. Now, when I saw him, it was only in passing, and he seemed entirely different. He was Head of the Unit, he was Mr Bannerman doing his weekly round with his own Registrar, his own Houseman, and a gaggle of medical students. He was very grand, he was totally out of reach.

'You'll remember, won't you,' I told Anne Malvering, 'about wearing your dark glasses? Don't go out of doors without them, at least not for a few weeks.'

'Miss Malvering's far too sensible to go against good advice!' came a voice from the doorway— Gareth Bannerman's voice—talk of the devil, I thought. I applied myself to fastening Miss Malvering's case.

He had come up to say goodbye to her. They began to talk together. He reminded her about her drops, and her Outpatients' visits. He took her case to the lifts, and I collected her friend from the waiting-room. And there on the landing, just before the arrival of the lift, Anne Malvering thanked me again, and shook my hand.

'*You* performed the miracle, Mr Bannerman,' her eyes moved to him, then back again to me, before she slipped her glasses on. 'Staff Nurse kept my spirits up, which was no mean task. You worked together for my good. I suppose that's what people mean when they talk of team work inside hospitals. So . . . thank you both.' She coupled us; I wondered if he minded. When the lift had borne her away I glanced at his face.

He was looking at me, smiling too: 'Well, there's praise for you,' he said, 'praise for us both!' Now he was doing it—making us a pair. So he didn't mind, he hadn't minded; I smiled all over my face, I couldn't help it, and I couldn't wipe it off.

The ascending lift disgorged its passengers, Sister was one of them. She looked rather surprised to see G.B. and I footloose on the landing: 'When you're ready to give me the report, Staff, I'll be in the office,' she said. She had just come on duty, and I was off. I explained this to G.B. I moved towards the doors in Sister's wake.

'So you're off for the afternoon, are you?' he seemed in no hurry to go.

'Yes, I am.'

'It's a beautiful day . . . typical midsummer day.'

'Perfect . . . yes.'

'What are you doing? Not wasting it on shopping?'

'Not wasting it in any respect. David and I are riding. We're hiring Orlando and Pegasus . . .' I pushed at the doors with my back—'we're going up to Fenton Wood, and home by the old railway. We've been looking forward to it all the week.'

'Splendid, I'm glad to hear it!' he was full of bonhomie; smiling broadly, he made for the head of the stairs.

# CHAPTER SIX

Mrs Shoulder was always delighted when I went home to lunch. On this particular afternoon she heaped my plate with pie, added creamed potatoes and a mound of garden peas:

'You don't want anything too heavy, duck, not bobbin' about on that horse. There's raspberries for afters, and some nice thick cream, put some roses in your cheeks.' She scurried about the room whilst I ate, flicking dust off shelves, plumping cushions, tweaking curtains, rubbing a smear off the window. She did anything, any small job to keep within talking distance. She probably got lonely on her own. As for me, I worked my way through the lunch she considered light, and I'd got to the raspberries' stage when the telephone rang. She went to answer it, flicking her duster, her voice floated back from the hall: 'Cletford 234 . . . oh yes, yes, just a minute, please,' she turned round, calling out to me: 'It's your young man, duck, sounds upset, I hope there's nothing wrong.'

He's not coming, was my first thought, something's cropped up again. Someone's purloined his afternoon off, or filled it up for him. And he can't say no, he never can, and he's always quite certain that I'll understand and never make a fuss. There were times when I wondered if I ought to do so,

90

ought to urge him to make a stand. I was all for helping people myself, but he let them take advantage. I went out into the hall and picked up the 'phone.

And it was true what Mrs Shoulder had said, he sounded very upset: 'I'm sorry, Claire, truly I am, but I can't get away after all. There's a brass-hat from Headquarters coming. I've been detailed to meet him. It's only just been sprung on me, not ten minutes ago.'

'Dave, it's your afternoon off.'

'I know, but I'll get another in lieu.'

'Well, all right, you can't help it, I suppose,' I sighed and sat down on the chair. He seemed to want to go on talking, and I couldn't be short with him.

'What will you do this afternoon?' He sounded very concerned.

'Go riding, just the same.'

'Yes, I thought you would.' A blankness settled over the line, then his voice came through again: 'You could come here and swim, if you liked, I could join you afterwards. It'd be late, I know, but it might be better than . . .'

'No, Dave,' I said, 'I wouldn't enjoy swimming on my own.'

'You'll be riding on your own.'

'Yes, but that's very different, somehow.'

He agreed that it was, he said 'sorry' again, and he went on to tell me about the Open Day that was planned for Melton House. As I sat there listening, I could see through into the lounge, see the sun on the blue-patterned carpet, see the curtains bulging inwards. It was a gorgeous day, a super day, perfect, just perfect for riding. And how could I be alone, I thought, up on a horse's back, and not just a horse, but darling Orlando—black, and muscled and strong, cantering joyfully, flinging his mane, streaming his tail out behind. I could almost feel him under me, hear the thunder of his hooves, hear his cough too—a clearing of pipes, a horse's mannerism—a kind of HAAaa, before he got into his stride. Orlando and I would depend on each other for company this afternoon. I could talk to him, we could go where we liked—as fast or as slow as we liked. I looked at my watch, said goodbye to David: 'Truly, I'll have to go, or Stephanie will think I've cancelled my ride as well.'

Half an hour later I was driving into the Stable Yard at Heathside, breathing in the unmistakable smell that comes from a horse—grainy and sweet, like apples stored in a loft. Orlando's box was next to the tack-room, and I knew he'd be looking out, but I couldn't see him for another horse and rider were passing by. The horse was Damascus, a roan that I had ridden myself on occasion, and the rider was—I rolled down my window to get a better look—the rider was Eric Sindon from Melton House. He saw me, took his feet from the stirrups, dismounted and came to the car, leading Damascus who didn't look over-pleased.

'It's Miss Graine, isn't it . . . it's Claire?' he bent and peered in at me.

'Yes, it's Claire.'

'You look different every time I see you,' he smiled.

'Well, riding habit's a far cry from nurses' uniform!' I returned his smile, 'it's good to see you, I heard you'd been out a good deal—riding, I mean. It's very good exercise.'

He nodded, 'And I got that job at Melton House, you know.'

'Yes, David told me, *and* that you'd got yourself some lodgings in the town. You don't lose very much time do you?'

'Well, I had some help,' he said. He hesitated, still stood there. There was something else coming, I knew. Damascus got restless, he turned to quieten him, I got out of the car; it was then that he told me the startling news: 'I'm engaged,' he said, 'to Olive. We got engaged last night.'

'ERIC!' Just for a second that was all I could find to say. I stared at him standing there by Damascus, holding the reins bunched tight, trying to keep the big roan stallion still.

'It's a shock, isn't it?' he grinned at me, 'but I fell for her on sight. I fell for her even before she so much as spoke to me, you know. That's why I kept going in to see her. I wasn't doing good works. I wasn't being unselfish, I was simply pleasing myself. Oh, I know she's been in love before, she told me all about it. So I know the score, and I'm not a fool, I know just where I stand. I'm lodging with her and her mother, I'm very comfortable. Olive's going back to work at Harpers as soon as she's properly fit. We're getting married next month, there's no point in hanging around.'

'Oh Eric,' I'd found my voice at last, 'I'm so very pleased for you both. I know David will be too. Many congratulations.'

'I've not seen David to tell him yet,' Eric said, shaking my hand. 'Apart from Mrs Hendry, and my parents whom we 'phoned, no-one else knows— though they will soon enough. I'm applying to Melton House to see if they'll let us marry there— in the chapel—they might agree, as I'm now a member of staff.' Unconsciously he preened himself, and who could possibly blame him? Eric had a whole lot going for him now.

'The chapel's a lovely little building,' I said, 'I've been there often with Father. The chaplain's nice too. I hope it all comes off.'

'Well, wherever we marry, you'll be invited— you and Dave,' he smiled. 'After all, it was you two who brought Olive and I together.'

But was it, I wondered, as I watched him re-mount and walk his horse out of the yard. I'd had the idea in the first place, and mentioned it to Gareth. If he'd said 'no' at that early stage, then the two of them wouldn't have met—unless fate arranged it later on. It was then that the impact of what he'd just told me, really seemed to sink in. They were getting married—*married*—and all arranged in a month. That was all it had taken—a fortnight of sporadic hospital visits, then two weeks living with the Hendrys at their home. Could it possibly work, could it possibly last; I distrusted love at first sight. It could come in a flash and go in a flash. I didn't believe in it—not any more—I had learned my lesson with Keith.

I crossed the yard and made my way over to Orlando, who was whinnying gently, pricking his ear, blowing down his nose.

'He's saddled up and ready, Miss Graine,' Iris, the stable-girl called. She came out of the Tack Room with a bucket in her hand. Behind her was her boyfriend, Tim Hallam, which probably indicated that Mrs Newel was somewhere out of the way.

As I trotted Orlando along the roadside my thoughts continued, at first, to dwell on Eric and Olive's romance, but I soon forgot about them. As soon as I left the town behind there was nothing in my head but the sheer delight of the moment, cantering down Loamer's Lane, watching the toss of my horse's mane, hearing the beat of his hooves, feeling his moving power between my knees. I knew every yard of the way and so, of course, did Orlando. Soon we'd get to the iron pot in the hedge that he always shied at. Yes, here it was, all rusty red, sticking out like a cauldron. Orlando shied and skittered sideways, and then we were safely past, cantering towards the end of the lane that led to the top of the heath—to the long ride that went on, and on, for three miles to Fenton Wood. Here was the end of the lane now, and here was the ride in front . . . long, and hard, green and smooth, like a well-tended race-course. I urged Orlando into a gallop, I let him have his head—and away he went—so fast he went—lowering his back—faster-

and-faster—faster-and-faster—gallop—and gallop—and gallop—My horse a thing of wings—myself a god.

I let him gallop until he stopped, then walked him through Fenton Wood—the thick, damp wood, where the sun never penetrated, where leaves lay carpet-thick on the ground, soggy and odorous. It always seemed to be winter in Fenton Wood.

It was nearly six o'clock when I got back to Heathside. Orlando's box had been mucked out, and spread with clean dry straw. I couldn't find Iris, so I sponged him down, dried and stabled him, gave him a hay-net whilst I cleaned his saddle and tack. I was in the Tack-Room washing the stirrups in a bucket of soapy water, when I heard a car braking outside, then the sound of feet on the cobbles—Stephanie, most likely; my back was to the door, I edged round to face it, still bending to my task, but the large shadow that spread itself over the concrete floor could in no way be feminine. I straightened up and stared—there in the doorway, blocking the sun, and looking in at me, was Gareth. He looked as surprised as I.

'I thought you were Stephanie,' he came further in.

'I thought *you* were,' I said, 'but I think she's out, perhaps you'd like to wait.'

'I'll wait in here with you, if I may.' His eyes roamed round the walls, as though expecting a chair to manifest itself. He took off his jacket and gave it a shake, he looked very hot, poor man:

'I think there's a stool over there,' I nodded towards a trestle, hung about with blankets and stable rugs. He found the stool, a three-legged one, he sat down gingerly; it rocked a little, then steadied, he planted his feet firmly down. And he looked, I thought, more like a well-dressed Vet than a Specialist Surgeon—sitting there in the stone-floored room that smelled of warm leather, and saddle soap, and polish, and horses' sweat. I was aware of him, all the time, but then I always was. I was used to it now, I prepared for the feeling, even steeled myself against it. It was a case of mind over matter, I told myself. But even so—even—so—he could have waited outside, sat in his car, not creaked about on a stool.

I took the stirrups out of the water, and began to rub them up. My hair fell forward and I flung it back, my boot kicked against the bucket, the resulting clang seemed to spin right through my head.

'Shouldn't Iris be doing all that?' he asked as I tipped out the water, swilled it down the drain with a stiff yard brush.

'I like doing it, I'm only too glad to filch the job off her,' I said. 'I like everything to do with horses. It's almost an addiction. Father says there's no cure either, once caught, you're caught for life.'

'Didn't Mr Graine ever want to take up riding again?'

'Yes, but Mother talked him out of it, which was understandable. He still adores horses, though, he comes up here occasionally, and walks round, has a word with each one. Mrs Newel's good, she always welcomes him.'

He nodded, said nothing, and the silence drew itself out; I broke it by telling him Eric Sindon's news: 'Well, what do you *know*!' he exploded, then looked at me and smiled: 'So we did play Cupid, after all, Claire!'

'Yes, we certainly did.' Our smiles seemed to catch and hold us tightly bound for a second—only a second—then I looked away, rubbed down the front of my jodhpurs, 'but it's very quick, isn't it . . . all arranged in a month.'

'That's the way it goes in extreme youth,' he said, 'what does David Cope say about it?'

'He doesn't know, as yet. He wasn't with me this afternoon; he couldn't come after all. But Eric will tell him this evening. He'll be all for it, I'm sure.'

'He believes in the marital state, does he?' His dark head lifted again, once more he looked me in the face.

'He does indeed, he advocates it,' I shook the rubbers out, took my hat from the table, crammed it over my hair: 'Mr Bannerman, I'll have to move you now. It's time for Orlando's feed. I'm supposed to keep this door locked. I get the feed over there.' I nodded towards the Fodder Room.

'All right, I'll come with you.' Up he got, over-turning the stool, righting it, putting it back in place. I wished he wouldn't come with me, for I felt quite sure he was going to ask a great deal more about David and me. I didn't want too probing an interest, and to try to stop it at source, I kept the talk on equine levels, I explained about horses' feeds, told him about the rising price of chaff. I doubt if he were interested, but he made polite noises; he watched me take the feed to Orlando's box.

'But don't come in whatever you do,' I cautioned him over my shoulder. 'He can't bear strangers setting foot in his box.'

'Don't worry, I'm keeping my distance!' he sounded very amused; whereas I probably sounded like the original bossy-boots, very like he did on the ward.

I tipped the feed into Orlando's manger, set the bucket down, came out and closed the lower door. Long before I had got it fastened the sound of his chewing—crunchy-rhythmic—munchy-contented —floated out to us. I stood and watched him over the door, but somehow I scarcely saw him. The man behind me invaded the moment, split the peace of it. I wished he would go, yet wanted him to stay.

'Now if,' I said, and I simply had . . . I had to keep on talking . . . 'if he were mine I could come out here and visit him last thing at night. I expect Mrs Newel does a night round, most caring owners do. The horses seem extra gentle then, endearing, extra loving.' And my words were provocative, I realised that the second they'd left my mouth. I hadn't intended—or had I intended—I heard Gareth make a small sound; I half-turned, became caught in his glance, awareness speared between us—flickered—darted—sharp—live. I knew he was going to kiss me. And I wanted him to, I wanted him to, I wanted him to so much. I swayed towards him, and I saw his face blur, heard his breathing pattern alter, felt his hand at my throat, moving round to my neck—my flesh leaned to his touch. Gareth . . . Gareth . . . I was silent, I knew, but his name thrummed through my body. When he stiffened and held me away from him, it was like being stabbed to the heart . . .

'We have company,' he rasped, and looking up, I followed the drift of his glance. A green Range Rover was turning into the yard. 'It's Stephanie and . . . I think, your father.' The car was pulling up, I saw the glint of Stephanie's hair, the side of Father's face, Nell's pale shape in the seat behind. I made myself move forward with Gareth, and then we were all shouting greetings, Nell plunged out and sat at my feet, I made a great fuss of her. For a few seconds the talk eddied over my head.

'I saw Mr Graine outside the hospital,' Stephanie was saying, 'I thought you'd be back from your ride, Claire,' she was looking down at me, 'And Garry darling, I'm sorry I'm late, but the traffic coming through Seftonbridge has to be seen to be believed.'

'I thought it was something like that,' he said, 'I've been watching Claire feed your horse,' he smiled at Father, went to stand at Stephanie's side.

'What happened to David? He's not here, is he?' Father enquired. He bent to Nell, felt for her handle, she moved and let him grasp it, she remained standing, pink tongue hanging out.

'He couldn't come,' I answered shortly, 'he was wanted at Melton House.'

'He's as bad as Garry,' Stephanie said, 'but things have been slightly better, just slightly, since the coming of Mr Spurne.' Her arm was linked in Gareth's, he had put his jacket back on. The collar was slightly rucked at the back, I saw her put it straight. I averted my eyes, I stared at the cobbled path.

'I think we should be going,' I said, touching Father's arm.

'Oh must you, oh why so soon?' Stephanie's voice rose up. 'Why not do your round of the horses, now you're here, Mr Graine, then why don't you come in for a drink, we're just about to have one. It's not often I have the company of *three* people from The Royal. One could almost say I'm getting hospitalised.'

'I hope not, that means something different,' Gareth said as they turned to the house.

'We'll be five minutes, and many thanks,' Father called after them. With all my heart I wished that he had followed his normal practice of refusing politely when asked to near-strangers' home. We began our tour of the stables, I watched him fondle each horse; only Orlando failed to respond, he was still eating, of course. Annoyed at being inter-rupted, he swung round from his manger, and blew a cloud of bran and oats over his door:

'Good Lord, you might have warned me!' Father choked, as I dusted him down. 'It's like being tarred and feathered! What a diabolical horse!'

'You've met him before.'

'Not during his supper.'

'He's my favourite, you know,' I looked in at him—looked at his flanks, black as ebony, looked at his long neck bent to his manger again.

'I know he's your favourite. You've told me that often enough,' Father said. 'It's because he presents a challenge, a meek horse would bore you stiff.'

'I could love a meek horse too, but yes, you're right, he'd probably bore me. Father, I wish we hadn't got to go in and have that drink. We're intruding, they're only being polite.'

'Rubbish!' he said, Father, at times, could be very, very squashing. 'What absolute rubbish you talk, Claire. We needn't stay five minutes. I want you to tell me what the house looks like inside.'

It was brown, mostly, I noticed, a few minutes later, as we all four sat down in a room the size of a barn, sipping sherry (also brown) and making conversation in forced little rushes with long gaps in between. Father and I, fronted by Nell, were sitting on a Chesterfield. Gareth was in a deep armchair, which made, even him, look smaller. Stephanie was in the opposite one, but mostly she flitted about—a compactly-built, but full-busted figure in cream linen slacks, and a silk shirt with ornamental links. Her skin was creamy, her eyes long-lidded. She was exotic, rather than pretty, and somehow or other the dull room set her off. It was a dull *and* shabby room, more like a gentlemen's club. There were several good pictures, though, most of them horses. I was looking at one above the fireplace, which might have been a Stubbs, when I heard a telephone start to ring, saw Gareth alert.

'Iris'll answer it,' Stephanie said, getting up to open the door. The ringing sounded a long way off, then it stopped and I heard a voice—Iris's voice, just one or two words, then silence, then her steps—the sound of her footsteps, faint at first, then clearer, louder, nearer—till she stood in the doorway, looking in at us:

'It's for the doctor' (she meant Gareth) 'they want to speak to him. It's the hospital,' she added, then turned and went off again. A door slammed somewhere across the hall.

To the accompaniment of Stephanie's sighs, Gareth left the room. He obviously knew where the telephone was, but then he would, I suppose. He was back very quickly, he came straight across to me. And there was something about his bearing and manner that coursed me with alarm—alarm and dread. I pushed myself to my feet: 'There's been an accident at Melton House, involving David, Claire. There's facial damage—damage to an eye; they've taken him into Casualty. They want me there, now, straightaway. It sounds rather serious.'

'I'll come too, I'll come with you!' I saw his nod of assent. Then we ran, raced out to our cars: 'I'll go in my own,' I said. For even at that moment the thought occurred to me that I was going to need my car at the hospital, I might be staying there, staying late . . .

What had happened to Dave . . .

# CHAPTER SEVEN

To see anyone in pain and distress is upsetting and unnerving. Nurses are trained to transcend their own feelings; they are trained—not to be un-caring—but to concentrate all the energies on comforting their patients; they mustn't look shocked, they must never show alarm.

But I didn't feel like a nurse when I saw David in Casualty, lying on a stretcher-trolley, a wad of gauze over one eye. His other eye was firmly closed, his mouth was compressed in pain. He hardly responded when I said it was me, and when I took his hand his fingers stayed limp and lax in mine.

Gareth had already examined him, was admit-ting him at once: 'He's blind, but I'm sure only temporarily,' he had whispered to me outside. Then he'd gone to X-Ray to examine the films, there might be a bony injury; I prayed not. I sat holding David's hand. What had happened, what had caused his injury, was still not very clear. The Casualty Officer said that David had run into some piping—a lorry had backed, and the load and shifted down.

Gareth came back with Casualty Sister, who was wheeling a dressings trolley. I made to get up, but they told me I could stay if I wanted to, so I sat there, I wanted to see David's eye.

'We're going to change your eye pad, old man,' Gareth bent down to him. 'After that we'll get you up to the ward.'

'Okay, thanks,' To hear him speak was a small relief in itself, but the sight of his eye, once the pad was removed, made me catch my breath. The lid was drooping, was markedly bruised, whilst below it the eye bulged out—in a red mass—like the bottom of a plum.

Subconjunctival haemorrhage—registered in my brain. I watched Sister apply a fresh pad, then Gareth motioned me out: 'Are you all right?' He pressed me down on to one of the benches, he sat beside me, holding on to my arm.

'Perfectly all right.'

'You look so white.'

'I'm unlikely to faint!' I snapped, but snapping defensively cleared the way, made the unreal, shocked feeling go, I was able to listen calmly to what he said:

'As you saw, there's considerable haemorrhaging, and that takes time to disperse. What puzzles me most of all is that he can't lift the other lid. It may be due to shock, a kind of hysterical reaction. But whatever it is, it's rendered him sightless, it's the most extraordinary thing.'

'Who brought him in?'

'Dr Shaw—the Melton House Admin. He's in the waiting-room now. Will you go and talk to him, find out exactly what happened. Then afterwards, get him to go home, there's nothing he can do here.

We need one or two more admission details, but you can help with those. Steve's made some notes up for the Kardex,' he passed the papers to me. 'Bring them up to the ward when you come,' he said.

'I can go up and stay with David?' I got up from the bench. It was then I realised I was still in jodhpurs, still in my riding clothes—being astride Orlando seemed weeks ago.

'Of course, why not? You can stay for a time, at least until the shift changes. Stephanie will look after your father. But go and see Shaw now.'

I nodded and went through into the waiting-room. Dr Shaw was by no means old, but he had an old man's demeanour. He was grey-haired and inclined to stoop, his stride was very short; he exclaimed when he saw me, and picked his way over the floor: 'My dear Miss Graine, what a terrible thing! What is the news of him now?' His hand grasped mine, then as quickly dropped it again.

'David's being admitted,' I said, 'we can't tell much at present. Actually, Doctor, we wondered if you could tell us exactly what happened. Sometimes it helps to know how the injury was sustained.' I seemed to have slipped back into my nurse's mien.

'But of course,' he cried, 'I can tell you precisely, it's very clear in my mind. We had the Chairman down for the day, from Headquarters, you understand. We've been having some rebuilding done, he wanted to see the result. I asked David to join us, he gets on well with Mr Sands. Well, we'd just finished taking him round, and were coming back from the workshops, when we saw a lorry just ahead, parked round at the back. It was piled high with scrap metal, mostly lengths of piping. I noticed it wasn't very well loaded . . . didn't look very secure; some of the piping was sticking out a good yard from the back. I remember thinking they ought to tie a piece of white rag on the end . . . for the traffic, you know . . . to warn other motorists. But it was stationary as we approached it, walking up from the rear; we were walking quite slowly and talking together, but then, as we crossed behind it the engine started up . . . quite suddenly, Miss Graine . . . and the load began to shift down. I heard David shout. He was nearest to the tail-board. He tried to jump clear, but a length of piping caught him in the face. I actually saw it hit him, poor lad. He fell down clutching his eye. I brought him here, got him here as soon as I could.'

'Yes, I see.' I felt sick—queasy—I could easily picture the scene. For a second the room shifted round, I gripped the edge of the table, then Dr Shaw's face became clear again, and so did his voice, he was talking about David's next-of-kin:

'His parents, my dear . . . I've rung them, whilst I've been waiting here. It seemed to me best . . . the right thing to do. I'll ring them again, of course, when I get back, and tell them the latest news.'

'Thank you, that's helpful, it saves us a job,' I said, forcing a smile to my face. It stayed there, stretching my muscles, all the time Dr Shaw said goodbye and made his way stoopily out of the doors. I wondered if David would want his parents to be informed so quickly. I knew he didn't get on with them—at least not very well. I hadn't met them as yet, although he kept telling me I must. 'They'll like you, Claire. And for once they may applaud me instead of deride.' When I'd asked him what he meant he said they were over-ambitious for him. I thought they sounded unsympathetic, to put it at its mildest. Would David want them here at this worrying time?

I read his notes, such as they were, up in Sister's office on Glanelly Ward, whilst David was settled in. And as I did so, I still couldn't quite believe it was true. It was David being lifted on to the bed in Side Ward 2—David would be its occupant now—it just simply didn't seem true. I made myself concentrate—I read the notes again:

'Cope, David Alec. Age 30 years. Admitted to Casualty 18.30 hrs. 8th July 81. Collision with load on back of lorry. Loss of vision complete. X-ray reveals no fracture. Light perception nil. Iris, pupil, lens and retina obscured by hyphaemia. Says unable to open right eye. No obvious cause for this. Admitted Ophthalmic Ward for observation and treatment. Query possibly surgery later on.'

'You can go and sit with him now, if you like,' Nurse Rexham (the Staff Nurse who was Kay's successor) put her head round the door. She was a solemn girl, heavily built—a good, caring nurse.

'Thank you, Staff. I *would* like.' Forced smiles were so dreadful. They literally made your facial muscles ache.

'He's out of pain, he's had an injection . . . Pentazocine 50 mg. He should be able to talk to you, at least for a little while. Oh, good, you've got his notes,' she said, 'can I insert a treatment sheet?' I handed them to her, then slipped up the passage to Dave.

His talking posed problems, for he asked me questions I couldn't possibly answer: 'I can't see a thing, Claire, not a thing, and my right eye won't open!'

'I know, Dave, but tomorrow . . .'

'And this one . . .' his hand went up to the bulky gauze pad . . . 'did you see it? What did you think? Did it look very bad?'

'It looked very bruised, there's a degree of bleeding, but once that's dispersed Gareth will be able to see into it. The damage may be slight.'

'That damned lorry. The driver couldn't have looked in his mirror. I was the only one it hit. I felt as though my eyeball had been pushed right into the back of my head.'

His hand moved on the cellular blanket, I grasped it in my own, and this time his fingers curled round, and he seemed to drift into sleep. Afraid of him waking, I sat as still as I could. I sat for an hour—an hour and a half; once I moved, and so did he, he made a small sound, like a long sigh, moved his head on the pillow. I reassured him, said I was there, and once more he slept. Nine o'clock struck, the shifts changed—I could hear it all going on—the sound of footsteps in the passage, the slither of trolley wheels, the murmur of voices, an occasional laugh, crockery sounds in the kitchen. A spoon dropped with a bell-like tinkle, then I smelt boiling milk. The bedtime drinks would be going round.

I ought to go. I had to go, I couldn't stay here all night. I eased my hand out of David's, he muttered, but didn't stir. I got up, but had to be careful, one of my feet was numb. I proceeded with infinite care to the door, all the corridor lights were on. Under one of them, stood Gareth talking to Night Sister Rawle; they both stopped talking and faced me as I approached:

'Have you come to see David? He's still asleep,' I spoke directly to Gareth.

'No, I won't disturb him tonight. I came to winkle you out.' I heard him say goodnight to Sister. She moved off towards the ward doors. I watched her retreating form through a ring of fog. 'I'll run you home,' his hand gripped my arm just above the elbow. It both held me up and helped me along, I couldn't have managed without it. My legs weren't behaving well, they felt like concertinas— one minute all right, the next minute folding up. 'Give me your keys,' he said in the hall. 'We'll use your car, then you'll have it in the right spot for morning-time.'

'But how,' I found the keys in my bag, 'how will you get back?'

'Walk . . . it'll do me good.'

I didn't say no, for I knew that tone—do-as-I-say—it brooked no argument.

He unlocked the car, leaned in, unsnibbed the nearside door, got out, helped me into my seat. It wasn't that I couldn't move unaided, but I kept forgetting to do so, I had to be set in motion like a doll. He looked enormous in my car, his legs wouldn't stretch out properly. He made a joke about them, and I tried to laugh and failed—failed completely—I began to cry instead.

We were roughly half-way home by then, he pulled into the side. He gave me his handkerchief, he didn't say much, neither did he touch me, nor hurry me, nor make me feel a fool. By and by I quietened down, and I thought I felt his hand—just once—cupping the back of my head: 'I know what you're going through,' he said, 'believe me, I know. I know what it's like to see someone you love . . . *the* one you love, lying there, lying injured, lying in hospital. And hospitals at times like that seem alien, scary places, they change from the ordinary habitat of work.'

'Yes, they do, that's exactly it, I hated leaving him. He looked vulnerable . . . helpless . . . childlike. He wanted me to be there.'

'They won't let you nurse him, you know. You realise that, I hope?'

I stared at him in the darkness. I knew what he said was true. It was one of Miss Girton's inflexible

STAFF NURSE ON GLANELLY WARD     113

rules that if a nurse knew a patient—on a personal level—his, or her, care was given to someone else. 'Yes,' I said, 'I *do* know.'

He started up the car: 'You'll be able to see him often, help him with his meals, do small things for him.' The car moved smoothly off. When it stopped next it was in The Larches' drive.

He wouldn't come in, he had to get back, he handed me over to Father, like a brown paper parcel. He waved aside my thanks.

The next few days were difficult ones, terrible ones for David. His pain was relieved, but his spirits were low, there was no change in either eye. And having to be confined to bed gave him ample time for brooding. He became convinced that he'd never see again. On the third day he spilled a beaker of tea all over his sheet. He did it when I was with him, it seemed like the last straw to him. In itself it didn't matter a scrap, we were used to changing sheets, but it upset him—upset him dreadfully, he kept on and on about it: 'Claire, if I'm going to stay like this, I'd sooner be dead,' he said, 'I'm not like your father. I'm not like the others, I tell you, I'd sooner be dead!'

'David!' his words struck a chill, 'David,' I sat on his bed, 'David, please listen . . . it won't happen . . . you won't be blind. Your left eye will open in time, and as for the other one, once the haemorrhage has absorbed, Gareth will assess the damage. It may not be much, all it may need is rest.'

'Are you sure? Do you really think so?' his voice was quieter.

'Yes,' I said, 'I do think so.' I took his hands in mine, I kissed each one, and I hoped and prayed I hadn't overdone it—overdone the optimism, raised his hopes too high. It was difficult to be really encouraging without telling actual lies. And yet it was necessary, vital in fact, to bolster his confidence. Gareth had impressed this upon me, had made a point of it . . . 'Psychological support he *must have*, he's the type of patient who needs it. I can keep his pain within tolerable limits, deal with his medication, but the psychological element is a little more difficult. It doesn't come in dropper bottles, nor in convenient ampoules. I'm going to need your very special help.'

I strove to give it, for David's sake, and on Sunday his good eye opened. It was tested and found to be completely sound. This greatly improved his state of mind, he began to have visitors. Dr Shaw came, other staff and trainees came from Melton House. Father came in before he went home each day.

And as each day passed the swelling of his injured eye went down. It remained very injected (red) but the haemorrhage was absorbing. Antibiotics were discontinued, the covering shade was off, and replaced by dark glasses. David was full of hope. On the ninth day Gareth let him get up and sit by his bed. He could go to the bathrooms in a wheelchair, was allowed to have a wet shave. Mr Spurne, who usually accompanied Gareth when he visited David, told me not to worry . . . 'He's doing just fine, Nurse Graine.'

Yet the eye remained sightless. David kept telling me so: 'I can't see a thing with it . . . nothing at all. It's like, it's as though it's all blocked up.'

'Well, in a way it is,' I said, 'the light can't get through.' But it wasn't really as simple as that, I had read up David's notes. The main haemorrhage had cleared away, but there was blockage in the vitreous, masking any view of the back of the eye.

'Is it ever going to get right?' he asked Gareth on the twelfth day. His drops had just been put in—by me on this occasion; Sister was engaged, and Nurse Rexham was on days off.

'The straight answer to that, David, is that I just don't know,' Gareth said, sitting down on his bed.

'But surely,' he sounded petulant, 'there must be *some* kind of view! You must be able to see something . . . after all this time!'

'Nothing yet.'

'But how much longer?'

'I can't hurry the process. I wish I could. I know waiting around is the worst part of it. To a certain extent nature must take its course.'

David sighed, but said nothing more. I handed him his glasses. He put them on. I wheeled the trolley out.

'He's got very low-spirited again,' Gareth said in the Clinical Room. He had followed me in, I dismantled the trolley, put the bottle of drops in its rack.

'Well, it's not really surprising, is it? David isn't a fool. He knows, or guesses, that after such a long delay as this, there's a good chance he's going to lose his eye. A vitreous haemorrhage isn't good news. He could have retinal damage . . . couldn't he?' I turned round and looked at him.

'It's possible,' was his short reply. His eyes avoided mine, and his face was grim. I made my deductions from that. He went off very quickly too, and no sooner had he gone, then Steve appeared, on his own, without Mr Spurne.

'What's upset "sir"? I've just passed him, brows drawn over his nose. He has a look of a weary Atlas, cracking under the strain.'

'He has his problems.'

'Don't we all,' Steve peered into my face. 'You don't look so good yourself, you know . . . it can't be very easy having your fiancé here . . . on the ward, like this.'

'He's not my fiancé, at least not yet, but you're right, it isn't easy. And added to everything else,' I said, 'his parents are due today. They motored from Berkshire overnight, they're staying at The Crown. They'll be coming into visit . . . this afternoon.'

'But surely that's *good* news?' Steve looked curious.

'Well, I suppose it is,' I replied, 'but oh, I don't know, somehow or other, I smell trouble ahead. I think Dave does too, he's terribly on edge.'

'A mixed blessing, parents,' Steve heard the rattle of cups. 'Any coffee going?' he asked. He didn't wait for my nod, he went across to the kitchen to help himself.

Mr and Mrs Cope arrived at the start of visiting

STAFF NURSE ON GLANELLY WARD , 117

time. I was with David, looking out for them. David was out of bed in a wheelchair, I'd just brought him back from the bathrooms. He'd spent more time than usual, getting himself tidied up.

I knew who it was immediately they entered the corridor—the woman hyper-slim and fair—hair drawn back in a chignon—her cream suit fitting her like a sheath. There was a look of David—he favours his mother—passed quickly through my mind. Mr Cope was shorter, rounded in front; he too was fair—fair going grey—he wore rimless spectacles.

'I'm sure you're Mr and Mrs Cope,' I emerged from the ward, 'David's in here. I'm Claire . . . Claire Graine.'

'Delighted to meet you, Claire.' Mr Cope was genial. Mrs Cope very restrained. She greeted David effusively, though, and I held my breath a little, fearing for his eye, as she pressed her face against his. They asked me to stay for a little while. I could, with Sister on duty. She was seeing them in her office later on.

The talk, at any rate at first, centred on David's accident. Mr Cope said the building company ought to be sued. He (Mr Cope) was a lawyer, and so was his wife. They were partners in a firm called Martley & Watts. David had told me this only recently. They had wanted him to follow them, to study law, but he'd failed to qualify. 'So far as they're concerned, I'm a dead loss,' he'd said. But David had found his métier somewhere else.

'Why a wheelchair, David?' Mr Cope enquired, 'Were your legs damaged as well?'

'Heavens, no,' David said. 'I *can* walk all right, but nothing must jolt my eye, so the going must be smooth—nothing so up and down as feet and legs.'

'But what a long time it's taking, darling!' Mrs Cope exclaimed. She opened her handbag, withdrew cigarettes and a slim silver holder. When a lighter emerged as well, I interfered:

'I'm very sorry, Mrs Cope, but smoking's not allowed. I hate to say it . . . it sounds so rude, but we have to think of the patients.'

'Oh, quite, quite! Forgive my ignorance.' Her handbag closed with a snap. She showed small, even teeth in a brief little smile. She had a cold face, I decided—a cold, bored-looking face. Mr Cope was jollier, but his eyes were analytical; he had eyebrows like neat inverted v's.

As soon as I politely could, I left David alone with them. They would have things to talk about—some of them about me. Mr Cope kept asking when we were getting engaged. So I went to man the ward desk, and was presently joined by Sister:

'Staff,' she said, 'I may be engaged with the Copes, when you go off-duty. They've requested a conference with Mr Bannerman; he wants me in attendance. He'll be up here at four. We'll be in my office, of course.'

'All right, Sister, I'll keep clear,' I said. She went off looking perturbed. Once again, I wondered what was afoot.

I found out next morning when I went into the

side ward. David told me his parents weren't satisfied with the way things were going: 'They want me to have a second opinion, they want a surgeon called Martindale, from The Linzer Clinic in London, to come and see me,' he said.

'*Professor* Martindale!' I stared at him, I could hardly believe my ears: 'David, he's famous . . . an eminent man . . . he'd never agree to come. I mean, why should he, you're in good . . .'

'Dad knows him,' he interrupted, 'or rather, he handled a case for him once. They met on several occasions.'

'But . . .' I sat down with a bump on the chair beside the bed, 'but is this what you want? Do you want him to come? Have you thought about it . . . thought about what it might mean? *If* he sees you, and takes your case, you'd have to go up to London, you'd have to be admitted to The Linzer Clinic. It'd cost the absolute earth, and it's simply not necessary.'

'My parents would pay.'

'Is it what you want?'

He plucked at his sheet: 'I don't know, I can't decide. All I know is, this eternal waiting is driving me slowly mad. What Bannerman says is probably right, but I can't help feeling that something ought to be done to hurry things up.'

'David I assure you . . .'

'And there's also the fact,' he broke in quietly, 'that Martindale's the very best there is.'

'By repute, yes. He's had years and years in which to prove himself.'

'You don't want me to see him, do you?'

I felt goaded, somehow, by that: 'It's what *you* want . . . not what I want. It's up to you entirely. All I know is, if I were you and had got an injured eye, I'd be worried . . . yes, of course I would . . . but I wouldn't change horses midstream . . . not if Gareth were my surgeon, not if I were under his care. I wouldn't change over from him to anyone, not even the mighty Martindale.'

'You think I should stay here?'

'Yes, I do, I think you should stay put. I think you should let Mr Bannerman carry on as he thinks best. It may not be very long now before . . .' I broke off and got to my feet, Sister Cheevers and Gareth were coming into the room. 'Excuse me . . .' I slipped quickly out, I wasn't sorry to go. It didn't occur to me then that my last few words to David had been overheard by Gareth Bannerman.

But they had, and he came to find me before he went off the ward. I was in Clean Utility, sorting dressings packs: 'I'd like a word with you, Staff Nurse,' his face was a thunder-cloud. Even then it didn't dawn that I was the cause of it. I was therefore in no way prepared for his onslaught of words, the accusations he literally flung at my head: 'What right have you to interfere between my patient and myself? I heard you just now, talking to Cope . . . *advising* him to stay put . . . advising him, I've no doubt, against seeing Martindale! How dare you presume to advise him on a delicate matter like this? Don't you think I haven't been into it with him? I spent hours with him last night. He knows exactly what is at stake, what the position is, the advantages of going or staying, I laid it all out for him. The choice is his . . . *his*, Nurse Graine. I don't want him swayed either way. In your dual position as a nurse on this ward and as his personal friend . . . you should have recognised the need for the utmost discretion. You should have held your tongue. You've done irreparable harm!'

'But he asked . . .'

'That has nothing to do with it. He may be your friend . . . a close friend, but primarily he's my patient. As he's told you, the Copes want him moved, they want Martindale to see him. I'm not going to quarrel with that, if that's what he wants. At the moment he's undecided, swinging this way and that. I'd like to see his case right through, naturally I would, but what I don't want, what I won't have, is one of the ward nurses telling him it's best for him to stay put. You don't stop to think, do you nurse, you don't see it from all angles. Supposing, due to your interference, he decided to stay on here, and just supposing that when his eye clears, I'm unable to do much to help him, just supposing in all good faith, I try surgery and it doesn't work! What then, Nurse, what then! What's he going to say . . . how's he going to feel . . . and what's he going to think? He'll remain convinced . . . quite convinced that Martindale could have done better. And how do you think *I* would feel about that.'

'If you'd just let me say . . .'

'I haven't finished. You've got to understand this, if he isn't convinced that I can help him, if he hasn't complete . . . faith, then the worst thing he can do is stay here, both for his sake and mine.'

'He asked me what I thought, and I told him,' I was trembling so violently that I had to lean back against the shelves of sterile dressings packs. The paper rustled and crackled under my weight. 'Any friend, anyone caring about his welfare would have done that.'

'Yes, but you're not just anyone, are you. You're a senior nurse on the ward, and because of that, you have a working knowledge of me as a surgeon. You used that knowledge in your advice to my patient. You had *no right* to do so.'

'You didn't hear all the conversation, you only heard the last part!' For some reason my trembling had stopped, and the hot blind anger that only he, only Gareth Bannerman, could fan to white heat, had hold of me, it put words into my mouth. 'Some of what you say is true, I can see your point of view, but if you'd come in earlier you'd have heard me tell David it was what *he* wanted that counted. It was only when he kept on about it that I felt . . . that I gave an opinion. I didn't intend to use special knowledge, nor to worry him in any way. And I know I'm a nurse on the ward, Mr Bannerman, I'm unlikely to forget it. But I also know that you're rude . . . yes, rude . . . very rude indeed! You can't wait for explanations, you have to be overbearing . . . to override . . . to grind people into the ground! You could have made your point without all that hassle! You've a great deal to learn about how to treat senior nurses on the ward!'

'Persist in this attitude,' he snapped, 'and I'll have you off it . . . damn quick!' He went out and loudly slammed the door.

Somehow I got through the rest of the day, but of course I was very upset. Snatches of what he'd said to me kept coming back into my head. I avoided going in to David's room, I felt that it was best. His parents came during the afternoon.

I was on late-duty on Thursday. I reported on at one, and I wasn't surprised, not in the least, to hear that Professor Martindale had seen David, had examined him in collaboration with Gareth: 'He's being transferred to The Linzer Clinic, by private ambulance, tomorrow a.m.' Sister said, and that was *all* she said. I got other details from David later on.

'Bannerman's been good about it, Claire . . . he was very nice about it . . . said he understood, and all that sort of thing, said it was my right to change, if I wanted to, if I felt it best.'

'Did Martindale tell you what he thought . . . about your eye, I mean?'

'Oh well . . .' David put on his glasses, 'he didn't say very much . . . said there wasn't much to be seen at present, that the fundus was obscured. But he wants me up at the Clinic, to keep a very close watch.'

Which was exactly and precisely what G.B. was doing. But I didn't say so, I didn't say a word, I'd learned my lesson at last.

'What's so marvellous about it all is that there's been no unpleasantness . . . no awkwardness . . .

and the parents are appeased.'

'That's a funny word to use, as though war's been averted,' I smoothed his blanket, tucking it in at the sides.

'If I'd stuck out, there *would* have been war. I've no heart for it at the moment. All I want is my eye put right, I want an end to the waiting. All I want is to get back to Melton House.' And there was something about the look on his face that moved me unbearably. I bent and kissed him, I felt his lips respond. 'I go tomorrow . . . you'll come and see me?'

'Of course,' I kissed him again. And I knew that although I disagreed with every part of the move, there was also, deep within me, a stirring of relief.

I could feel it washing over me as I worked.

# CHAPTER EIGHT

A WEEK later when Father and I were setting off for home, Stephanie hailed us from the entrance to Heathside. I began to brake, 'I'll have to stop, she's coming over,' I said.

'On foot or on hoof?'

'Foot,' I laughed, as Stephanie skimmed the road, reached the car, stooped and looked in at us.

'Hullo, Mr Graine,' she greeted Father, then her gaze swerved to me: 'Claire, I just wanted to ask about David? How is he getting on? It's not a scrap of good asking Gareth, he's as tight as a clam where his patients, or inmates are concerned!'

'David's an inmate no longer,' I said, 'at least not of The Royal. Perhaps Mr Bannerman didn't explain, but he's in the Linzer Clinic. His parents wanted him moved there, so they could visit more easily.' I told the white lie without a blink. She looked a little surprised.

'Lucky David . . . the height of luxury . . . what it is to have parents! I'd rather be in the Linzer Clinic than The Royal any day. But how is he? Has he had an operation? Is there any news?'

'None,' I said, 'no real change, they're waiting for the eye to clear.'

'I hope he goes on all right,' she said, 'I expect

you'll visit him. It's a two-hour journey by train, though, isn't it?'

'Two and a half,' I said, 'including the tube at the London end, but I hope to go next week.' She went off then, dodging the traffic stream.

'Nice girl,' Father said, 'thinks a lot of Bannerman. I wonder if they're likely to make a go of it.'

'If you mean get married,' I swerved to avoid a child on a bicycle, 'probably not. People don't bother these days.'

'Oh, come now, Claire,' he huffed a little, 'some do and some don't, you know. What about Eric and the Hendry girl, they've settled for marriage all right.'

'That's perfectly true, they have, of course.' The wedding was Saturday week, in ten days' time; David would miss it, and I was missing David. I felt bleak and miserable. Nothing was going right.

'Have you got that Saturday off?' asked Father, 'I don't want to go on my own . . . not to a wedding . . . not even at Melton House.'

'The duty rosters are out for next week, and I've got a long weekend. So, yes, we'll go and enjoy ourselves, shall we? We haven't been out for ages, not together, not to a party, not to a celebration.' I chivvied myself into cheerfulness, and Father responded at once.

Later that evening David telephoned, and at last there was news to tell: 'I've a detached retina,' he said, 'which means surgery, of course. But at least I now know what's wrong, and I'm told it's not too bad. The operation won't be for ten days. Some-

thing else has got to absorb, or disperse, or flatten
. . . I'm likely to be here a month. Claire, when are
you getting some time off, when are you coming
up? And tell me about this retina business in plain
layman's language. Martindale talks all the time,
more or less blinds me with science. I'd like to hear
it from you in simple terms.'

So I did my best, and I also told him I hoped to
get up to see him on the Friday before the wedding
at Melton House. I went on to tell him a little about
it, but he didn't seem very interested. He kept
returning to the subject of his eye.

'Well, how is he?' Father enquired, when I went
back into the sittingroom. When I told him, he
remarked that it could have been far worse, which
was very true, for he could have lost the eye.
Father, like me, had thought David's move was
totally unnecessary, and what he said next entirely
reflected my views: 'He might just as well have
stayed here, Claire. All he's done so far is wait.
Bannerman's a dab hand at retinas, everyone says
that. I blame those stuck-up parents of David's,
laying down the law, making trouble, dragging the
boy about.'

I nodded, and agreed with him, forbearing to add
that David was thirty, so scarcely a boy, and there'd
been no question of dragging. All he'd needed to
say was 'no', and refuse pointblank to move. But
'no' isn't very easy to say, at least not for people like
Dave. It's a word that doesn't go very well with
being conciliatory—and polite—and grateful—and
trying to appease.

Since that terrible altercation with Gareth Bannerman a week ago, I'd been able, by stealth, to keep out of his way, for Sister had been on duty each time he came to do his round. But next day, Friday, I could hide away no longer. Sister was on a day off, I had to take her place. It helped a little that Anthony Spurne and Steve came with him. With so many of us the tension was watered down:

'The new admissions first, I think, Nurse,' he said, smiling at me. I let out my breath. I preceded him into the ward.

The first new patient was Mr Burns, an old man of ninety-two, presenting with a glioma on his left eye. This meant that the eye would need to be excised as soon as possible. This had been explained in Outpatients two weeks before. He greeted G.B. with a great deal of pleasure, hitched up to shake his hand. He was a thin old man, with a parchment skin, and straight white hair that stuck out like a skirt from the band of his shade. He allowed G.B. to examine his eye, making no fuss at all. He spoke about his eye as though it were little more than a tooth: 'Be a good job when it's out, sir. I don't mind about it, you know. I can see all right with t'other one, that'll last me, I dare say. When you get to my age you don't go in for a lot of reading, like. So long as I can get about, and watch a bit of telly, I'll not complain. There's folk worse off than me. I've got a very good wife, you know. She's only seventy-five ... quite a youngster. Carrie's my third. I've always had good wives.'

'You're a lucky man,' G.B. smiled, 'and you've nothing to worry about. Your artificial eye will look much better than this one does. It'll match your good one exactly, give a very good appearance. Your wife will be pleased.'

'Oh, that she will, sir! I've told her all about it. Carrie's looking forward to it,' he said.

At the ward desk he wrote up the notes, and gave instructions to me. 'Local anaesthesia in his case . . . guttae cocaine,' he said. 'He'll be first on the list for Monday, so you can start instilling the drops from nine o'clock onwards. Now . . . who have we next . . . Mrs Rumer, I think.' Steve gave him her notes, and off we set again. He saw three patients in the women's section before we returned to the office. Mr Spurne went down to Outpatients, Steve was despatched to X-Ray. I wheeled the trolley into the sluice, having said goodbye to Bannerman, but when I got back, there he was in the office again.

'Can I get you a coffee, or anything, sir?' His presence made me twitchy.

'No, I don't think so, thank you Claire. I'm not waiting around for that.'

I looked at him, a little startled by his use of my christian name—christian name terms, with us both on duty, and he such a martinet, such a rigid observer of protocol! But it eased the atmosphere greatly, because he became the other man—the approachable one—the flip side of the coin.

'I'm trying to apologise,' his words came out in a rush.

'Oh no,' I said, 'don't . . . please don't . . . it's simply not necessary.'

'But we both know it is, don't we?' He put his hand on my shoulder, and any ill-feeling there might have been souring my thoughts of him, vanished on the instant, melted away like snow. He needn't have spoken one single, solitary syllable after that. His touch said it all, the contact was all. I wanted it to go on. 'You were right to call me rude,' he said, 'I was in a foul mood that day. I was piqued by the fact that the Copes plainly thought I wasn't up to my job. I felt professionally slighted, which was very small-minded of me. They simply wanted what they thought was best for their son. I know you spoke up for me, tried to get him to stay, but as I felt then, even that was like a red rag to a bull. I wanted him to stay here willingly, without any persuasions. If he had any doubts I wanted him to go.'

'Yes, I see . . . truly I do, and I shouldn't have called you rude.'

'I deserved it. But I'm glad . . . we've spoken.' He bent forward and kissed my cheek. And the odd thing was, the strange thing was, it wasn't embarrassing. It was perfectly natural—the most natural thing in the world. 'Well, now, having got that settled . . .' he moved back and sat down on the desk, 'tell me how David is. I'm sure you will have heard.'

'I'm sure you will have heard too,' I gave him a straight look. 'I'm quite sure that Professor Martindale . . . out of courtesy . . . will have kept you informed of everything that's gone on.'

He laughed: 'That's true . . . yes, he has.'

'David rang me last night,' I said. 'He told me he'd got a detached retina, and was having a scleral resection in a week or ten days, when the fluid's had time to disperse. He's likely to be in hospital three weeks after that. It's a long and drawn-out business for him. He's longing to get back to work.'

'It's a shame he's going to miss the wedding.'

'I don't think he minds all that much. Are you and . . . Mrs Newel going?'

'*I* am,' he said, 'I'm in the choir, so more or less come with the trappings. Stephanie . . . no, she'll be in Somerset for the greater part of that week.'

'I'm going with Father,' I said quickly, as Steve came bursting in with a set of X-Rays, which he put down on the desk.

Both David and Father had told me that Gareth's voice was compelling. It was that, and much, much more—it vibrated, and soared, and tugged—pulled at the heartstrings, washed in waves, brought starting tears to the eyes. I doubt if there were many dry eyes in Melton House Chapel that Saturday Eric made Olive Hendry his wife.

Olive wasn't a white bride, she wore a silk suit in a raw, natural colour, and a hat with a dipping brim. Her dark, Romany looks were shown to advantage by the suit, the big hat shadowed the injured side of her face. Eric's eyes hardly left her, or so it seemed to me. And in his speech (a very good one) he told the assembled friends he considered himself the luckiest man in the world.

The Reception was a buffet one, so I kept fairly close to Father, fetching his food, and describing the scene to him. Gareth I merely saw across heads during the first half-hour. We met briefly after that, when he said he liked my dress, chatted to Father, then was borne off by Dr Shaw. 'There are far too many people in here,' Father grumbled, as somebody bumped him, and spilled his wine—some of it over me. I scrubbed at it with his handkerchief . . . 'It's not spoiled it, has it?' he asked.

'No, its just the hem, and it doesn't show a scrap.' I wiped the glass bottom, and gave it back to him.

My dress was a pale green voile with a stiffened underskirt, cut tight in the waist, with a heart-shaped neck and puffy shepherdess sleeves. I wore no hat and my hair was drawn back in a coil at the nape of my neck. It was coolest that way, and it made me feel elegant.

At five o'clock when the bride and groom had been driven off to the station, and when Father was yawning, and talking of home, and a decent cup of tea, Dr Shaw, followed by Gareth, came threading through to us. Dr Shaw tapped Father on the arm: 'Richard, I've a little proposition I want to put to you. Perhaps we could go upstairs to my rooms. Gareth will keep Claire company. I'm sure you can spare me a few minutes, can't you?'

Father didn't look pleased: 'I'm not so sure that I can,' he said, 'Claire's waiting to drive me home. She has various things to see to there. We don't want to hang around.'

Gareth caught my eye—he looked amused. Dr

Shaw twittered, and his mouth formed a little round 'o' of surprise:

'Oh, it's all right,' I said quickly, 'I'm not in such a rush. I'll go and sit in the gardens, Father.'

'I'll come with you,' Gareth said. Father went off with Dr Shaw.

'He's not mad about crowded rooms and drinking champagne in the afternoon,' I said to Gareth as we made for the exit doors. 'And he *is* nearly sixty-five. One's apt to overlook that.'

'He doesn't look his age . . . nowhere near it. He's a very remarkable man.'

'He enjoys your singing. He's heard you at concerts. I heard you for the first time . . . today, I mean . . . I enjoyed it too.' I felt, and sounded gauche, but I had to mention it, make some comment, 'it was absolutely beautiful,' I finished, and he caught my hand in his.

'Wedding hymns are beautiful . . . they're not difficult to sing.' He dropped my hand as we skirted the lavender maze.

'Have you had your voice trained?'

'No . . . never. And I rarely sing on my own. I prefer to sing in a crowd, a choir . . . now that I really enjoy. My voice, such as it is, comes from my mother's side of the family. My mother's Welsh, my father's Cornish, which makes me a West-Country man.'

'A West-Country man in East Anglia.'

'Which suits me very well,' he glanced at me, then away at the scene in front.

After the noisy, crowded room, the quiet of the

garden fell about our ears like a muffling shawl.
The air was soft, there was just enough breeze to
move the heads of the roses, to stir the pinks, and
stocks and tobacco plants. The gardens at Melton
House were planted with flowers that gave off
scents, they were bounded by guide-rails of tubular
metal that ran from terrace to terrace, or from level
to level, for the ground rose steeply behind. Right
at the top was a herb garden, set on a southerly
slope, perfect for catching the sun's rays, whose
warmth poured down on the plants, sending the
smell of wild thyme over the earth. The rails went
round in a U-turn here; we sat down on a rustic seat
near a hedge of yew that gave a little shade.

'They make pillows of these things,' Gareth said,
pointing a toe at the herbs. 'They're supposed to
induce sleep or so say the Naturopaths.'

'Yes, I know,' I looked at him, then quickly away
again. In the far distance, down on the road, I could
see a red bus—a double-decker, as small as a
Matchbox toy.

'How did you find David yesterday?'

'Oh, not bad,' I said, 'he's fed up, of course, and
worried about the operation on Monday. His parents were there. They took me out for a meal
afterwards.'

'You must have got home very late.'

'I did, as a matter of fact. I was glad I went,
though.'

'I'm sure David was.'

'He said so . . . yes.' The talk was thinning,
wearing away to nothing, we were wearing it thin,

like pulling out rubber till it got to snapping point. And all the time I knew he was sitting there slewed slightly sideways, looking me over, all over, as he had that afternoon when it rained and we'd had tea in Harpers Restaurant.

'You look like a wood nymph in that dress . . . and almost as elusive.'

I turned and smiled, I laughed a little: 'Last time it was a witch!'

'A beautiful witch . . . so it was . . . when you nearly fell in the pond.' He moved closer to me, much closer, his arm was on the seat, resting along the back of it: 'You're very lovely, Claire.'

I could feel his breath, hear his breathing, I had only to turn my head, just a fraction, just a little, he shifted on the seat. I could get up and walk away from him, I knew he wouldn't persist. The choice was mine—he was giving me that—he wasn't holding me. I turned my head, and was gathered into his arms.

The kiss went on—and on—and on—lips and bodies moved—communicated, soundlessly, giving, receiving messages. I lost all track of the garden, the world, the seat on which we sat. There were my arms and his arms—my hands and his— the swift urgent pulsing of our hearts. When he moved away, pushed me away, got up and stood at the rail—with his back to me—I wanted to call him back.

It passed, of course, that desperateness. Away from him. I trembled, but became myself, not part of him, sense and reason prevailed, and the garden came back, and the breeze cooled my face, and the same was happening to him. He came back and sat down on the seat: 'I didn't intend that.' His eyes were guarded, his mouth a straight line. I was on the outside again.

'No harm done,' I was very flippant.

'Of course not . . . no,' he said. 'Weddings have a lot to answer for.' This time he managed to smile.

'Like Christmas and New Year . . . times for kissing!'

'Claire . . .'

'No, leave it,' I said. He had been about to apologise, and that I wouldn't have. I wanted him, and I knew I did, and I knew he wanted me. It wasn't just weddings—at least not for me—I was falling in love with him. But there was time, still time, plenty of time, to draw back and tell myself 'no'. He could break my heart, exactly as Keith had done.

'Here comes your father and Dr Shaw,' he said, looking over my shoulder. He waited for me to get up, which I did, but he didn't take my arm, as we walked down the path between the rails. He was very slightly in front of me; he looked unperturbed and remote, and arrogant—yes, arrogant; I think I hated him then. Hate and love lie close together. I couldn't, I mustn't love him. I wouldn't love him, I wouldn't let myself.

Dr Shaw was talking to Father. I could hear him hard at it long before the four of us met beside the lavender hedge: 'Ah, you've been to the herb garden, have you . . . a delightful spot,' he said, 'and a great deal of the work, you know, is done by our blind trainees. It never ceases to amaze me what they manage to achieve.'

'I agree, it's astonishing,' Gareth said. I said something in keeping. Father was silent, morosely silent, he was rubbing a piece of lavender between his palms and throwing it down again.

'Your father was telling me you saw David yesterday,' Dr Shaw rattled on.

'Yes, I'm on a long weekend, so was able to travel to Town. He's having an operation on Monday. He'll be glad to get it over.'

'I want to go and see him myself,' he pinched the tip of his nose. 'Our chairman's been several times, but then it's not far for him . . . just a short journey by tube to Green Park. It's rather different for me.'

Back on the car park I steered Father over to the Fiat. Dr Shaw went off with Gareth, we called out our goodbyes. As I fastened my safety belt I caught a glimpse of Gareth's shoulders slanting down to enter his big cream car. He drew off first, I followed, the distance between us lengthened; he pulled away, he was very soon out of sight.

I felt deserted, walked out on, even slighted, which was crazy. For goodness sake don't be so sensitive, I jerked the sun-flap down, I listened to Father going on about Dr Shaw: 'He offered me a job at Melton House when I leave The Royal, Claire . . . a part-time physiotherapy post, they'd provide the equipment, he said. Well, I dare say he meant well, but what does he think I am! They don't need a Physio up there, not even a part-time one. If any of the residents or trainees want treatment, they're brought down to The Royal. He was being charitable, or Headquarters were, and I'm not having that. I want a job, a proper one, I don't want humouring. I'd sooner sit at home and peg a rug.'

'So what did you tell him?' How bright the sun was. My eyes and throat ached.

'No, of course . . . thanked him politely, but gave him a positive no. I've another six months to go at The Royal, something may turn up. But I'm not having something *made* for me, I'll work out my own salvation.'

'And work it out very well, I'm sure. You always do, and have,' I glanced at him, and saw him smile at me:

'Thanks, love,' he said, 'but I'm not so good as I used to be at decisions. I miss your mother, she used to help me. She was very, very supportive. Being married helps.'

'I expect it does.'

'Weddings make me think back.'

'Weddings,' I said, deliberately quoting Gareth Bannerman's words, 'have a very great deal to answer for.'

I saw him next on Tuesday, I expected him to be formal, and he was, but not quite so stiff as usual; he began to talk about David when we'd finished the round, and were in the office again: 'I hear the op was a great success.'

'Yes,' I said, 'it was.' I leaned forward and closed the window against the blowing rain. It was gusty and chilly, our heatwave seemed to have gone. 'To be honest, all they told me was that he was comfortable.'

I knew he wouldn't enlarge on that, due to medical ethics. The Professor, no doubt, would have told him exactly how things had gone. It was enough to know that, so far, everything was all right. David would tell me everything when he was well enough to 'phone, or when I visited him in a week or ten days' time.

'The Professor's delighted with the way things have gone,' he did concede that.

'Thank you for telling me. I've . . . naturally been worried.'

'Yes, of course you have.'

We were facing each other across the desk, which was piled high with papers. I moved and my apron caught a file, which slithered off on to the floor. I bent to retrieve it, so did he, our hands met on the folder. The effect was like an electric shock, he pushed the file at me; I straightened up, just as Steve barged into the room.

'You're wanted down in Casualty, Sir,' he sounded a little breathless, 'a welder from Moffatt Works has been brought in with a flash-burn. His left eye's affected most. I tried to get you before, but I don't think your bleep can be working.'

'I forgot to pick it up,' he slapped his empty pocket, and went striding off.

'I hope I didn't interrupt an intimate tête-à-tête,' Steve said annoyingly, perching himself on the desk.

'You didn't,' I made him get up again. He was sitting on some X-Rays. I rescued them, and put them into their sleeves.

'You'll never guess what I learned last night,' he seemed in no hurry to go on. Surely G.B. would want him down in Cas.

'You're bustling to tell me, so carry on,' I was only half listening. Old Mr Burns was running a temperature. We were very anxious about him. My mind was on him, or it was at first, but Steve's next words made me swing round from the window and stare blank-faced.

'G.B.'s buying Sir Hugh's old house—Park House in East Heath Road.'

'Good Lord . . . *is* he!' I sat down, still staring hard.

'No mistake.'

'But Steve, it's enormous! Are you sure you've got your facts right?'

'Absolutely!' he laughed at me, his news had had maximum impact. 'It's a six-bedroomed, so not enormous, merely a decent size. He most likely got a bargain, you know. It's been on the market three months. He's moving in straightaway, before the purchase is through . . . on a rental basis, a furnished rental. Sir Hugh's furniture's still in situ.'

'But how have you got to know all this? Did he, did Gareth tell you?'

'No, I heard him telling Miss Girton . . . in The Residency, last night. They were sitting fairly near me, in the main lounge downstairs. I couldn't help overhearing, I admit I pricked my ears. Spurne was

with them, he'll be having G.B.'s flat in Residents.
I bet you any money you like G.B.'ll take private
patients. Sir Hugh's old consulting rooms must still
be there intact. All he's got to do is rustle up his list.
I'd say he's made a judicious move.'

'Well, yes, I expect he has,' My mind was digest-
ing facts, 'but I still think it's a very large house for
one man on his own.'

'My guess is he's getting married, or *re*married, I
should say. He's been a widower over three years,
and he's quite a catch, you know. We all know who
he squires around, and even *I* know there's a
sizeable stable-block, and yard, and paddock at
Park House.'

'Oh, I see,' my voice was thick, I cleared my
throat noisily, 'but the stable-block can't have been
used for years.'

'It hasn't. Sir Hugh didn't use it, but he kept it in
good repair. He kept everything in good repair, he
was that sort of man. So you see, perhaps our
Gareth's going to marry the busty Newel, and she'll
move her Riding School to Park House, and they'll
settled down together . . . horses and all . . . I can
see it coming off.'

'That's pure surmise . . . just guesswork,' I
turned to look into the ward, through the viewing
window, which brought my back to Steve.

'Guessing games are always fun,' he said, as the
telephone rang. The call was for him, he was
wanted in Cas. I was glad to see him go.

My mouth was dry, so dry that my lips were
sticking to my teeth. Could he be right? Was he

right? He might be, easily. The room was airless, I opened a window, hardly aware of the rain, which spattered my face and the front of my uniform. Could he be right? I minded so much—I covered my face with my hands, then jerked round as Nurse Islet came into the room:

'Are you all right, Staff?' she stared at me.

'Perfectly,' I said, 'it's just the room, it got a bit stuffy. Yes, Nurse, what did you want?'

'Mrs Knox wants to know if her hair can be washed. I said no, but she's making a fuss.'

'All right, I'll come and see her,' I said. I applied myself to my tasks. I wouldn't think about what Steve had said. It was gossip, pure and simple—apart, that is, from Gareth buying Park House.

# CHAPTER NINE

ON my half-day, ten days later, I went up to Town to see David. I got to The Linzer Clinic just after four. As I walked through the main doors, I was struck, as I had been before (on my first visit) by the hotel-like atmosphere. It was nothing like a hospital, there was no hospital smell, no vast expanse of vinyl floor, no stairs with metal-strip edges, no hospital shop, no clatter of bucket and mop. Instead there was silence, apart from the traffic; there were carpets and new paint, deserted corridors, suites instead of wards.

David's room was on the third floor, with a small bathroom attached; it had long windows that looked out on to Green Park. He was out of bed, in an armchair, looking longer and thinner than ever in a dark silk robe, fastened with a sash: 'I hate the thing,' he confessed to me when I commented on its grandeur. 'It was a gift from my mother. I think she felt it might fit me to my surroundings. It was a parting gift, she and Dad have gone back to Berkshire now.'

'How are you feeling?' I kissed him. I was dying to see his eye. He was wearing dark glasses. All I could see was his smile.

'On top of the world. My eye's fine. Here you are, have a look,' he removed his glasses, stared straight up at me. 'The conjunctival stitches came out this morning . . . the vision in unimpaired . . . its marvellous, Claire . . . the answer to all my prayers!'

'Hold steady, for goodness sake,' I held fast to his chin, I looked at his eye, it seemed perfectly normal, apart from a slight redness, which I knew would go, which would disappear in time. The lid and surrounding skin was still bruised but, again, all this would go. 'Oh, Dave, it's wonderful . . . just marvellous!' I kissed him again.

'I knew you'd be glad.'

'I couldn't be more so.'

'And Melton House,' he said, 'have offered me a month's convalescence with them, just resting up in my flat . . . everything found . . . which is pretty generous of them.'

This was David being grateful again, I felt a stab of impatience. I took off my jacket and sat down next to him: 'Well, the accident you had,' I said, 'happened on their premises. They ought to make *some* sort of recompense, it's hardly a favour, you know. Why, you weren't even supposed to be working . . . not on that afternoon. I know I sound like an awful nagger, but don't be too effacing. You're valuable to them . . . you should recognise your worth.'

'You're good for my ego, and I love your nagging!' he reached for my hand, he held it in his, on the broad arm of his chair. 'Tell me about the wedding,' he said. I did so, feeling guilty— guilty because for me that day had been Gareth and I in the garden. I tried to forget it, I *would* forget it; I described the wedding in detail, I relayed the speeches, I described the people there.

'They came back from honeymoon yesterday,' I finished, 'Eric's working now.'

'They're young to be married, both only twenty. It makes us seem over-cautious . . . doesn't it?' he turned his face to me.

'Yes,' And that was all I could say, all I dared say then. I had known for some time that I couldn't marry David. I had known since that afternoon I had ridden to Fenton Wood, and seen Gareth back at the stables. So I knew I'd got to tell him, but I couldn't tell him now—not here—not in hospital— surely that was wrong. I couldn't tell him, up here in London, divorced as he was from his friends— and his work—and all the things that would take it off.

But his comment, coming so suddenly, made me feel deceitful. I felt I was sailing under false colours, I felt hot and uncomfortable: 'Mind if I look at your view,' I said, crossing to the window. It was half open, diesel fumes wafted in. Down below, in leafy Green Park, couples strolled hand-in-hand, lacquered ladies exercised pugs, tourists thronged to the Palace; the traffic snarled its way to Hyde Park Gate. It was a hot day, it was mid-August— not a day for being in London. I thought of Cletford, already I wished I were home.

'Tea'll be in presently,' I heard David say, and as I turned, someone tapped at the door, a maid came in with a tea-trolley. At a word from David she pushed it towards our chairs:

'It's all right, I'll pour out,' I told her. It gave me something to do. When she'd gone David talked about Eric again.

'It's possible that he may help out with the sports part of my job, leaving me just the mobility side, for a few weeks,' he said. 'Everyone helps each other out at Melton House, you know. It's rather like being one of a family. I feel they're all my friends.'

And they were probably, I thought, a better family than his own. The Copes had been pleasant enough to me, but I hadn't taken to them. They did their duty by their son, but they didn't give him much—not much of the things that really mattered—only those that showed. I could almost hear the sort of comments they'd make to their colleagues in Berkshire . . . 'Of course we had him sent to The Linzer . . . under Martindale, you know; one can't dicker around when it comes to eyes.'

David asked me about the hospital next, and I filled him in with news: 'We've had no-one in the side-ward since you, but the main ward's been full up, of course.'

'Gareth Bannerman's been busy then?'

'Oh very . . . yes, he has. Of course he's got a Registrar now, but you saw him, didn't you?' The bread and butter was very dry. I didn't think I could eat it. I choked a little as the crusts rasped past my throat.

'Off your food?'

'No, not really. It's too hot to eat.' David was hungry, and said so. 'It's a good sign,' I smiled. I poured him out a second cup of tea. 'I think I've slopped it over, Dave. Watch out for your dressing-gown.'

'I don't care a jot for my dressing-gown, I soon won't need it. In another ten days or a fortnight foppish dressing-gowns and hospital beds will be a thing of the past. You know, Claire, during those first few days when I couldn't get either eye open, during that first week at The Royal when I felt I might stay blind, I made a solemn pact with Fate, or whoever decides these things, that if I got my sight back, if both eyes got all right, I'd never ask for another thing, I'd be so eternally grateful . . . and thankful . . . that I'd never grumble again.'

'It's not at all unusual,' I said, 'for patients to feel like that.'

'And I think I've learned a valuable lesson,' he put down his cup, 'what I'm trying to get round to saying is . . . if you've anything to tell me Claire, if you've come to any conclusions about us, and I rather think you have . . . now is the time to deal the mortal blow!'

'Oh David!'

'It's not on, is it? That's what you're going to tell me? Well, that's all right, I understand, I never thought it was . . . not on your side, and when this happened,' he pointed to his eye, 'you didn't feel you could tell me, did you? If it hadn't been for my eye, you'd have given me my congé weeks ago.'

'David, I couldn't make you happy, not in a life-time thing, not in marriage . . .'

'Oh, I think you could . . . very easily. What you mean is, I couldn't make *you* happy. My mother pointed that out.'

I felt angry when he said that—angry on his behalf: 'Your mother hardly knows me,' I said, 'and you *have* made me happy, but it wouldn't work in marriage, David. It's simply not strong enough.'

'I'm glad it's all out in the open, I'm glad we've spoken,' he said. He spoke quietly almost reflectively, there was silence in the room. I couldn't see his expression because his eyes were behind his glasses, he was wiping his mouth on a paper serviette: 'But it needn't all go to waste, surely,' he said so suddenly that just for a moment I couldn't think what he meant: 'What I'm trying to say is, without sounding too much like a grotty old film, we can salvage something, we can at least be friends.'

'Of course we can. I hoped you'd say that.' Relief washed over me. And yet the fact that he *had* said it, pinpointed even more clearly how different we were, how different our thinking was. For if I loved someone, really loved them, friendship, and friendship alone, would be agony—it would never, ever work.

I thought about it on the train going home. I thought of David and I. And I thought of Gareth, I couldn't help it, he was always in my mind. And I knew that once again I was falling in love with a man who cared little for me, apart from the times when mutual attraction flared, when touching became as vital as breathing, when nothing else seemed to matter, and when anything—just then— seemed possible.

And perhaps, after all, I was a witch, perhaps I conjured him up, for when I got off the train at Cletford, and crossed the station yard, I saw him standing in the taxi queue, with a worried look on his face, and a tiny, very old lady on his arm. His aunt, I thought, it must be his aunt—the aunt who likes strong perfume. But why were they in a taxi queue? What had happened to his car? Had they been up to London, or had they boarded the train at Seftonbridge? I hesitated, they'd not seen me, I was crossing to my car. It was still light, only eight o'clock; I looked back as I unlocked the car. Taxis were in heavy demand, and the queue of people was long. Gareth and his companion were more than half-way down it. Ought I to go and rescue them, offer them a lift? Well, of course I ought. It was only human. I couldn't just drive off, and leave them there; the old lady looked fit to drop. Off I went across the yard, approaching the queue from the rear; 'Mr Bannerman . . . Gareth, can I offer you a lift? I've got my car over there?'

'Why Claire, hello,' he relaxed his hold on the old lady's arm; he turned round. 'Did you say . . . a lift?' The noise in the yard was deafening; a bus had drawn up, and was busy disgorging its load.

'Yes, my car's just over there,' I gesticulated wildly.

'It couldn't be more welcome! How very kind of

you! This, by the way, is my aunt, Mrs Williams. Aunt Maud, this is Claire Graine. She helped me choose your perfume. You've got her to thank for that.'

'Did you say you'd got a car, Miss Graine?' a claw-like hand met mine. I found myself looking down into a brown seamed face, into alert eyes set deep under snowflake brows. 'You see, a car is just what we need. A car is what we're short of. Gareth's having trouble with his carburettor, it's at Martins being repaired. We got a taxi coming, but now they seem more scarce.'

'My car's over here, Mrs Williams,' I took her other arm. She was a bony old lady, all angles and points, with elbows like knitting pins. Her hat was a toque, her dress was a foulard silk. She got in the Fiat with surprising agility, drawing her skirts round tight. She settled down, sighing with relief. 'We've been to the theatre, the early performance, at Seftonbridge, you know. It was that thriller play by Emily Sugdale . . . "Murder on a Shoestring" . . . most enjoyable, it gave one food for thought.'

'This is good of you, Claire,' Gareth said, climbing into the back.

'I'm just glad I saw you. I've been up to Town.'

'Oh, of course, you've been to see David. How was he?'

'Fine . . . just fine,' I said. But as I turned out of the station yard, I wondered which way to turn. I hesitated, whilst horns pip-pipped behind: 'Do you want the hospital?'

'Oh sorry, Claire,' Gareth apologised. 'I ought to

have told you, *asked* you . . . can you drop Aunt off first? It's Princes Drive, number eighteen. I know she's very tired.'

'Will do,' I said, I swung the wheel left, and drove down the Avenue. We began to discuss David's eyes, we went into medical details. Mrs Williams sat there, drinking in every word.

'Is the young man your fiancé?' she asked me, when the talk had lapsed again.

'Oh really, Aunt!' Gareth exploded.

'It's all right,' I said. 'No, we're not engaged, Mrs Williams, it's not that kind of relationship.' I added the last bit purposely. What was I trying to do—encourage Gareth, put him in the picture, and why, for heaven's sake—I knew why—I felt ashamed of myself. He belonged to Stephanie, *loved* Stephanie, I was only an also-ran. So be dignified, for goodness' sake, I told myself furiously, just as Mrs Williams spoke up again:

'It seems to me, these days,' she said, 'that relationships abound. There are so many different kinds, it must be very muddling. When I was a girl one was courted, woo'd, then came the engagement period, then the wedding, then the family; it didn't vary at all. There was none of this extraneous stuff, all these shades of grey. I feel very sorry for you young people . . . you can't know where you are.'

'It's a different era, Aunt Maud.' Gareth sounded grim.

Mrs Williams didn't comment on this, she proceeded to her next question: 'Graine,' she said,

'The name, Graine, there's a blind man called Graine . . . a blind masseur at the hospital. Is he a relative?'

'He's my father,' I was glad to find we were on a safer subject, I smiled at her briefly, as we waited to pass a van.

'Is he, my dear . . . is he really! But he's such a wonderful man! He cured my painful neck, you know,' she stretched it for me to see, 'he hung me up on a sort of hook . . . traction, I think he called it. He gave me heat and massage too, I've had no discomfort since. As a matter of fact I was thinking of going to see him about my knees. They creak, you know, at awkward moments. I find it embarrassing. I do think one should try to cure these things.'

'I'm sure my father would try to help, but you'd need a GP's letter.'

'We've just passed Gareth's house!' she exclaimed, speedily changing the subject—so speedily that I very nearly swerved:

'Oh?'

'Yes, Park House, you know . . . used to belong to the Wellesleys. Gareth's buying it, aren't you dear?' She tried to twist round in her seat. 'He wants to get planning permission to divide it into flats. I tell him he shouldn't do it, he ought to get married again, and raise a family, and fill up all the rooms.'

There was no reply at all from Gareth, but he gave a kind of snort. I heard it, but most of all I heard his Aunt's words repeating themselves, echoing in my ears. He was having the house turned into flats, he wasn't getting married . . . not getting married . . . not getting married. So all the gossips were wrong. Steve was wrong. I felt my spirits lift.

Soon after that we reached Princes Drive, and I waited in the car whilst Gareth saw his Aunt safely into the house: 'Will she be all right?' I asked, as he opened my off-side door and got in, drawing his knees up tight.

'She has a companion . . . an ex-nurse,' he said, 'she's very well looked after.'

'She's a dear old lady.'

'Yes, she is. She enjoys life, too, in her way. I'm sorry she regaled you with her views on human relationships. It's her pet subject, and if she could she'd have everyone paired off . . . conventionally paired off into matrimony!'

'It works, for a good many people.'

'For some it does,' he said. 'Claire, I wonder if you'd drop me off here,' . . . we were nearly into the High Street . . . 'it's too late for a meal at the hospital, so I'm taking myself to The Crown. They serve suppers up until ten thirty, so I'm just about right for time.'

'I'll stop at The Crown,' I drove on, pulling up outside the hotel. I expected him to get out at once, we were on a no-parking spot. He opened the door, but still remained in his seat:

'Look, why not join me?' he said, 'I'd enjoy your company. But perhaps Mr Graine will be waiting at home, perhaps you'd rather get on.'

'He won't be waiting, he'll have eaten,' I said, 'at least two hours ago. He never waits in the sense that you mean, he leaves me to please myself.'

'So?' his hand brushed across my knee.

'I'd love to come,' I said. I swung the car on to the hotel park.

We ate mushroom omelettes and chocolate gateau, and biscuits and cheese at the Snack Bar, then took our coffee into the nearby lounge. During the meal we had talked non-stop about the hospital. It provided good, common ground, although its levels were different. We discussed the staff, we made each other laugh. But once in the lounge our conversation became more personal: 'I quite thought you were all set to marry Cope,' Gareth remarked.

'No,' I stirred my coffee, buried my nose in the cup.

'I'm quite sure he asked you.'

I refused to comment on that. I wished he hadn't got back to David. I kept on seeing his face—long and thin, wearing his glasses, informing me in flat tones that his mother had said I'd never marry him. I hoped David would not get in too deep with his parents again. Probably without meaning to they diminished his confidence, they pulled him down, instead of building him up.

'But perhaps,' Gareth reached for the sugar, 'perhaps, like me, you take a jaundiced view of the marriage state?'

'I don't at all,' I told him sharply, surprising even myself, 'with the right partner I can't think of anything more satisfying than being married, and staying that way for life.'

'Well, that's put me in my place!' he laughed, but looked taken aback.

'I didn't mean to sound censorious, I didn't mean to preach. I'm sorry if I . . .'

'Oh, don't apologise. Never apologise for beliefs. I felt the same when I was your age, or not so very much older.'

'But you married, didn't you? I'm sure I've heard . . .' I was getting into deep water. I felt myself crimsoning under his gaze.

'My wife died,' he said quietly. 'I shan't begin again. Her death I regret . . . abhor, if you like . . . my freedom I relish. And now I've shocked you. We've both been honest. Honesty can be shocking. That's one of the many paradoxes of life.'

He was right, of course. He was selfish and callous. How could I possibly love him? Yet I did love him—exactly as he was.

It was dark when we left the hotel. He said he would walk to the hospital: 'It'll do me good to stretch my legs. I'll see you into the car.' He took my keys, unlocked it for me, but before I could stoop to get in, he turned me round to face him, moved forward and drew me close. I looked at him, I was weak with longing, I slid my arms round his neck. It brought us closer, even closer, I leaned against his warmth. I felt his arms hard round my back, and I sank right into him. I heard him say, 'Claire . . .' I raised my face for his kiss. It came softly at first, brushing at first, a drift of his lips on mine—moving away and back again—away and back again—then deep, hard, urgent, demanding—yet tender and loving too. I clamoured to tell him I loved him, but dare not, some reticence remained—some remnants of commonsense prevailed, held me in some sort of check. When he loosed me, when we stood apart, we stared at one another. His hands were cupping my shoulders, I couldn't see his face—not clearly, just the glint of his eyes boring into mine. A car passed us, blaring loudly, and in the quiet aftermath his words fell about me—toneless, expressionless, doggedly making their point:

'Bearing in mind your beliefs and mine, which unhappily don't coincide, I think we had better confine our meetings to hospital ones in future.'

I nodded. I couldn't speak, but when he walked away, it was all I could do not to call him back—not to run after him. If he'd looked back—just once— I'd have gone to him, I knew . . .

But he kept striding on—away from me—out of my life—

# CHAPTER TEN

AT the end of the following week David left The
Linzer Clinic and began his convalescence at
Melton House. Father and I went to see him. He
was glad to be back in his rooms, surrounded
by cards, being visited by friends. One of the
latter was old Mr Pineham who, I was glad to
learn, had settled down well in his new life in the
Home.

I told Father that David and I had settled for
friendship only. To my surprise he said he was glad:
'He wasn't the right one, Claire . . . not for you.
You need someone stronger to keep you in your
place. David would have let you walk right over
him.'

'That's a funny thing to say about your daughter!'
I'd been rather taken aback.

'Not that there's anything wrong with you, darling, you just like your own way,' he said, 'exactly
like your old father! We don't come of pliable
stock.'

And perhaps we didn't, and perhaps Father was
just a little glad—glad and relieved that he wasn't
going to have to make any changes to fit in with
David's and my plans, after all.

Of Gareth I refused to think—except when I
went to bed, and dreamed of him—dreamed of him

ceaselessly. Of course I saw him on Glanelly, but that really hardly counted. It was impossible to believe that the man who came on the ward, who flipped over notes, who gazed in eyes, who chatted at patients' bedsides, was the same man, the passionate man who'd held me in his arms. This one, the new one, was cold, implacable, unfailingly polite. Sometimes I felt I must stir him to anger— anything to rouse him, but I didn't dare, I just carried his orders out. I knew he had moved into Park House, the whole hospital knew that. Anthony Spurne had his rooms in Residents.

There had been a further changeover of patients, but old Mr Burns was still with us. He had never really rallied well after his operation. Then, just when it seemed that the might improve, when his temperature had settled, just as he had begun to take solid food again, his wife had had a form of stroke, and although rushed into hospital, had passed away two days afterwards.

Sister broke the news to Mr Burns, but felt he'd not taken it in: 'I don't think it registered,' she said, 'he just stared at me vacantly.'

I felt that the old man knew all right, I felt he understood, but I also felt he was trying his hardest to push it out of his mind—to disbelieve it—to pretend it hadn't occurred. However, towards the end of the week, when Gareth did his round, Mr Burns detained him by his bed:

'My wife's gone, sir,' he said, 'thought you ought to know. Carrie was my third, you know. I thought the world of her. Now she won't see my new eye, will she, and she won't see me come out. Carrie was looking forward to having me home.'

'I *had* heard, Mr Burns,' Gareth bent to him. I fetched a chair and he sat down, they began to talk together.

'He'll have a hard job to comfort him,' Sister said when she saw them. 'Not that he won't try, mind, but what on earth can you say to an old man of ninety-two who's outlived all his friends, and has no-one close to him in the world.'

'He needs visiting. I can do that,' I said as Anthony Spurne, followed by Gareth, came in at the office door.

'You have enough to do, Staff,' Sister was short.

'I mean in my off-duty time. I can come back evenings . . . it won't be such a big task.'

'You can't bring his wife back, nor stop him dying, and you need your off-duty time.' This was Gareth—for some reason looking annoyed.

'I shall visit him,' I said firmly.

Mr Spurne broke in then: 'It doesn't do to get involved.' He sounded very wise. For a young man he *was* wise, and very predictable. Even after only ten weeks, I knew all his little foibles, and his phrases, and when he'd trot them out.

Mr Burns died at half-past midnight on Saturday the fifth of September. I was with him, for we'd known since lunchtime that the end was very near. I had come back to the hospital just after seven o'clock, and had stayed with him. I was determined that I would. Not that I could help much—none of us could. He died peacefully, almost imperceptibly; he slipped out of the world, asking for no-one, with no-one's name on his lips.

I left the hospital soon afterwards, stiff as a board, and tired, but also feeling glad I'd been there, had stayed with him to the end, for who was to say that he hadn't felt comforted? Mr Spurne would spout cliches, of course, would say: 'What a wonderful age' . . . and 'What a happy thing to go so soon after his wife'. He might even say: 'What a happy release,' I could hear him bringing it out, looking wise and sorrowful, and scratching the back of his neck.

It was chilly for early September. I was wearing jeans and sweater, but I still felt cold as I unlocked the door of the car. The moon was riding high and full, and the heath was bathed in light—silver light, ghostly light. I have never liked moonlight much. It's hard and brassy and unwinking; I have never thought it romantic. Father used to hate it too: 'It was dreaded in the War, Claire . . . bombers' moonlight . . . that's what they called it then.'

As I drew near to Heathside Stables, I slowed down and stared. Iris was there, standing outside, and with her was Tim Hallam. I paid no especial attention at first, just thinking that even for Iris it was rather late to be standing about in the road. Still, there was no accounting for tastes, I raised my hand in a wave, then slowed and stopped, for Iris was shouting my name and running towards me—towards the car—she tried to open the door:

'Oh, Miss Graine . . . Miss Graine . . . can you

help! Something awful's happened!' She was almost in tears—I got out and stood in the road:

'What is it . . . Is it Mrs Newel . . . has something . . . is she ill?'

'It's not her! She's out with her man. She won't be home tonight. It's Orlando. Orlando's run off. We can't find him anywhere!'

'Run off! Run off! But Iris, how could he have? Didn't you fasten his door properly?' I pushed her, and ran across. I ran across the road like lightning and into the stable yard. He must be there, he couldn't have escaped, she couldn't possibly have let him. But she had, he was gone, he wasn't here. I went right into his box. 'He couldn't have got out if you'd fastened him in, he must have been stolen!' I shouted—shouted at Iris who'd followed me into the yard. 'We must ring the police at once . . . lose no time . . . they have means of tracing . . .'

'No! No, you can't do that! No, Miss! He hasn't been stolen.' Iris was looking round at Tim Hallam. I saw him give a nod. 'I got him out of his box, you see . . . got him out when Tim came round. He wanted to ride him, and I got him out, saddled him up and all that. It was only about eleven then, Tim rode him round the yard. It was just for a lark, we didn't mean . . . it was just for a bit of a giggle. But 'Lando shied and threw him . . .'

'Iris! I can't believe . . .'

'He ran off, cantered off. I went to help Tim, up, I thought he was badly hurt, he'd hit his head and his face was bleeding. I had to help him, didn't I . . .'

'And you let the horse go . . . let him *go* . . . let him canter off!'

'I couldn't help . . .'

'Where . . . which way . . . which way did he go? Iris don't you realise . . . it's serious, he could cause an accident, do damage, injure himself . . . kill himself, or someone else! Surely you looked for him?'

'We did, Miss. We looked all over, we went off on the bike. We've looked all over the place. We've been about everywhere!' She was crying in earnest now, in noisy, childish abandon. I couldn't get any sense out of her, I rounded on the boy:

'What happened to that horse, Tim Hallam? What did you do to him? What made him throw you? What made him go off like that?'

He stared at me, his eyes were wary, his cheek bore a graze: 'I didn't do nothing,' his slack mouth quivered, 'I didn't do nothing, Miss. Iris saddled him, I got on his back, and rode him round the yard, and then he chucked me. I didn't do nothing at all.'

In spite of the fact that I loathed the sight of him, loathed them both at that moment, I felt they weren't lying, they were too frightened—too frightened to make up tales, or cover up, or dissemble; I forced myself to be calm. 'You say you've looked for him,' I said, 'tell me exactly where.' Hardly knowing what I was doing I crossed the yard to the Feed Room, collected a hay-net, tucked it under my arm. I boiled with anger as well as fright. What was Stephanie doing, leaving the horses in Iris's care all night? She knew what she was, she knew she was idle and irresponsible. She should be here, looking after her stock. She was with Gareth—where was Orlando? My head hurt as though battered with hammers—Gareth and Orlando—where was the horse? I listened to Iris's words:

'We went all through the town and up on the heath, and round by the hospital, up to Melton House, and back. There was no sign of him, Miss.' Iris was hiccoughing, trying to stem back her sobs.

I thrust the hay-net into the car: 'You ring the police,' I said, 'tell them exactly what has happened, I'm going up to the heath . . . to the top heath by Fenton Wood. He might just . . . *might* just be there. I'll take the car as far as I can, then walk across the grass. He knows the ride, he might be there. He might have bolted there.'

'It's miles!' Even Tim Hallam looked shocked.

'I know that,' I snapped. 'Now, ring the police.' I drove through the town to the heath.

Loamer's Lane wasn't meant for traffic, but a car could get along it, if it was driven slowly and carefully. I rocked along it, looking out all the time for the stocky form of Orlando, black as night, greyed by the moonlight, perhaps. Iris had said he was saddled up—his reins would be hanging loose, the stirrups would be banging against his sides. If I find him, I'll ride him back, I thought. I'll abandon the car. *If* I can find him—*if* I can catch him—but supposing, supposing I can't? And he went off two hours ago, someone else might have caught him—stolen him—I might never see him again. But I *shall* find him—I'm going to find him—think positive—I *will*. I stopped the car at the end of the Lane where it fanned out on to the heath, where it transposed into the racecourse of turf that stretched to Fenton Wood. Of course I'd find him—of course I would. I got out of the car, opened the rear door, pulled out the bundle of hay.

I began to walk down the long ride to the Wood. I scanned the heath for Orlando—no sign of him, just the heath, seemingly limitless, stretching away like a motionless silver sea. There was no wind, there was no sound but the whispering brush of my feet through the tussocky grass. It was eerie, lonely, and the sky had the same kind of silence, the same kind of menace, holding the face of the moon.

I felt I was being watched, I felt eyes stared at me from behind. I quickened my pace, I looked over my shoulder—of course there was no-one there. Look for the horse—look for the horse—that's what you've come here for. I couldn't see him, he wasn't there, he might be in the Wood. He might have trotted right through the Wood and down by the old railway. I'd got to find him, that's what I'd come here for.

The Wood was near, close in front, once again I quickened my pace; my heart banged like a drum in my ears, my feet moved the grass, the hay net bumped weightless on my hip. I had got to find him, walk through the wood, I had got to ride him home. Drop-outs slept up on the heath during the summer months, but they wouldn't steal him, wouldn't harm him, they'd want no truck with a horse. Where was

Orlando—I ought to call, give my special whistle. But somehow I couldn't—I couldn't—just couldn't—I daren't disturb the silence—I couldn't call; I looked over my shoulder again.

Some people said the heath was haunted—oh, for heaven's sake, I thought—don't be fanciful, don't be foolish, it's your own feet rustling the grass. The light was white—bright, so bright— surely brighter than before. I walked on till I reached the fringe of the Wood.

My feet trod twigs that bent and snapped, the Wood was full of noise, little sounds . . . scufflings and rustlings . . . the flick and movement of branches, the squelch of leaves as I ventured further in. The change from light to solid darkness made me go carefully forward, feeling my way, stretching my hands out in front. Once I was sure I heard Orlando, heard a horse's whinny—high-pitched and frightened—heard the crash of hooves. I called, whistled, forgot my fear, I rushed mind-lessly through the wood. Branches clawed at my sweater, something tore at my jeans, my head struck a tree, I stood for a moment half-stunned. It was crazy to go on, I would never make it, I would never get through in the dark; I couldn't do it, I would have to get back to the car. It might not have been Orlando I heard, it might not have been him at all. I tried to convince myself of this, I turned to retrace my steps. As I did so something warm and soft scuttled over my feet. I bit back a scream, I heard my breath hiss; the small sound spurred me on. It spurred me back to the edge of the wood, and out on the heath again—out, once more, on the moonlit stretch, out and down the ride—pelting, rushing back towards the car. I must have run for two miles, I puffed and rasped for breath. My side ached—a stitch pain, I clutched it and ran on. I limped on, drove myself on, the heath danced up and down. The light seemed dazzling, I screwed up my eyes, my ears were full of sounds—there were sounds like hooves, many hooves—pounding, pounding, pounding—the sounds of horses, many horses, the rattle of chariots, the clashing of steel, the shouts of fighting men. It was only the moonlight, moons cause delusions, I knew it was only that, and my own weariness, and those silly ghostie tales. But I kept running, I had to run, I never stopped running once. And the sky was an upturned bowl above, and the sweeps of heath were silver—spinning, and spinning, and spinning away from my feet.

I dived into the car like an animal into its hole. I started the engine, I rocketed down the Lane. And perhaps it was because I was so thankful to be inside, so thankful to be off the heath, so anxious to get home, that I didn't notice the difference at first, didn't notice anything strange—anything untoward about the car.

The smell was the first thing I noticed—a rank body smell, then the breathing—not my own; even then I couldn't be sure—be sure I wasn't imagining things again. I flicked a glance in my mirror, there was nothing there, nothing to be seen. I laughed at myself, that wretched moon had a lot to answer for.

Then it came again—I heard it again, above the hum of the engine—the sound of breathing, the breathing that wasn't my own. There was someone in the car with me—I knew it now for sure—there was someone there—someone there—down on the floor at the back. My scalp moved, and the patch of flesh between my shoulder-blades froze. I had to get out—I had to get out. My foot went down on the brake—it went down hard—the car screeched to a halt, my head jerked forward and back—just as I heard a shifting behind, just as my mirror darkened, just as a hand grasped the back of my seat.

I screamed—I heard it—the sound of my scream; I flung myself out of the car. Behind me came a shout and a crash, but by then I was running hard. A car was coming up the Lane—no, it was standing still, but its headlamps were on—full on—there were three people running in front. They were running towards me, they had come to find me. I tried, and tried to reach them, but my legs were leaden, and my feet were leaden, and they wouldn't—wouldn't move. It was like a nightmare—they wouldn't move—and the world was turning black—the lights were going—

I pitched into nothingness—

The next thing I knew I was in the large brown room at Heathside. I was lying on the slippery Chesterfield. There was an arm under my neck, and a face hanging over mine, a glass was being forced between my teeth. The face was Gareth's, he and Stephanie must have come to find me. The stuff in the glass held brandy, I spluttered as I drank. I heard Stephanie say: 'She's coming round, thank heaven . . . I thought she was dead!' I heard Gareth say: 'Drink it all down . . . do you a power of good,' he sat me up, as though I were a doll.

I wanted to ask questions, but couldn't get one of them out. Just for the moment it was quite enough to sit and drink the brandy, and to feel safe, blessedly safe, I sighed and closed my eyes, then opened them on Stephanie's cry of alarm: 'It's all right,' I muttered, 'I'm all right, nowhere near dying!' She was squatting in front of my knees, she was wearing evening dress—a white one, and her earrings were bracelet hoops. Gareth was sitting beside me; he looked unfamiliar in slacks and a polo-necked sweater—now that was odd, but I couldn't think why it was—coherent thought was eluding me again. There was someone else in the room too—a stockily-built man, slightly bald, middle-aged, with a drooping fair moustache. He was standing on the hearthrug in front of the popping gas-fire; he was wearing a dinner jacket and white frilled shirt. I blinked at him—who was he—he looked familiar—and yet—I couldn't place him; I finished my brandy up. And as Gareth took the glass from me, all that had happened earlier rushed back at me perfectly clearly—horrifyingly clearly; I stared at him:

'Gareth . . . in my car—there was someone in my car!'

'It's all right . . .' he felt for my hand, but the man by the fire explained:

'He was a vagrant, a drunk, I pulled him out. He'll spend the night in the hedge, which was where he most probably came from.'

Stephanie cut him off: 'Claire how could he have *got* in your car, that's what we can't understand?'

'That's easy,' I ground out, my throat felt dreadfully sore, 'I left the car, it was empty for ages. I walked out over the heath to Fenton Wood and back again, I went to look for Orlando. Oh, Stephanie, I never found him, I never even glimpsed him. Once I thought I heard him, but then . . .' my voice broke on a sob.

'Sweetie,' she patted my shoulder, sat on the arm of the Chesterfield, 'Orlando's back, and he's quite all right, we had a good look at him. He came trotting home, happy as Larry . . . at least so Iris said. She and that ghastly boy of hers, closely watched by Gareth, were rubbing him down when Roy and I drove in the yard. It was close on two-thirty then, I couldn't think what had happened. At first I thought that Gareth must have taken up night riding! Then we questioned Iris, or Roy did, he frightened her out of her wits. She told us exactly what had happened, that you'd gone to look for Orlando, *and* where, so we all set off in the car.'

'Your father had rung me,' Gareth said. 'I was in bed, of course. He said you'd been at the hospital, sitting with old Mr Burns, but when it got to two a.m. he'd telephoned the ward, only to learn that you'd left there an hour before. He was talking of ringing the police, but I said to wait for a bit, I'd go to the hospital and make enquiries, look for your car on the park. What I actually did was drive slowly along your home-going route. I thought you might have broken down, or had a . . . had a slight accident. What I didn't expect was to see your horse cantering riderless, and going in the direction of Heathside, I followed it here, I saw Iris. And all the rest you know.'

'My father,' I said, 'how could I have forgotten . . . can I please go and ring him now?' I tried to rise, but didn't succeed, my legs had turned to foam.

'*I* rang him,' Stephanie said, 'as soon as we got back here. I told him you were quite all right, although I doubted it then; you kept fainting off as soon as we got you round.'

'I'm fine, just fine,' I said, but I wondered if this were true. I felt muzzy, but this was the brandy on top of an empty stomach, and on top of fright, and on top of being tired. What a long time ago since I'd been sitting with Mr Burns, since I'd driven home and seen Iris in the road. Would Stephanie keep her on at the stables when she'd been so irresponsible? It was no thanks to her that Orlando was safely home. And who was the man by the fire who had told Iris off? I looked at him, he was smoking a pipe? Surely I ought to know him. Stephanie kept calling him Roy—the name meant nothing to me. Did Gareth mind—I looked at him—he suggested we should go:

'If you feel well enough.'

'Yes, I do.' This time, when I got up, my legs

were all right—well, more or less. Gareth was holding my arm.

'I'll take you home. You can leave your car here.'

'I'll bring it back in the morning . . . deliver it to you,' Stephanie promised me.

It was Sunday tomorrow—it was Sunday *today*—and I wasn't on duty, thank goodness. Gareth and I crossed the room, and I turned and thanked Stephanie, and the man by the fire for their part in the rescue act.

'The thanks are all on our side,' she said, 'you were trying to find Orlando. And as for walking miles on the heath, by yourself, in the dead of night, I couldn't have done it, not even for a horse.'

'But she would have,' I said to Gareth, as we turned out of the yard. 'She'd have done exactly the same as me—gone out to look for him.'

'I doubt it. She has more sense. It was a foolhardy thing to do.' His tone was brusque, I dared not speak again. He was angry, and who could blame him? He'd been up for most of the night, he'd been dragged out because of me, and *because* he'd been dragged out, he'd run into Stephanie and the man. He might not have known she was seeing someone else, he might have found it out for the first time tonight—he was probably furious.

The car was comfortable, roomy, luxurious, but I couldn't relax in my seat. I just wished I could think of something to say to take that look off his face. But he didn't give me any opening, and somehow I couldn't make one. He drove with unbroken speed to The Larches' gate.

Dawn was breaking, we could see the line of it creeping up over the heath, raying out in cracks of light, obliterating the moon: 'Another new day,' he said—not very originally.

'Yes,' I fumbled with my safety belt, my fingers were numb and clumsy-nerveless, I couldn't make them work.

'Here . . . let me,' he unfastened it, I heard the end drop down. I saw his face close to mine—anxious and contrite: 'Sorry I snapped,' his knuckled caressed my cheek.

'It doesn't matter.'

'You gave me a fright, I thought you'd had an accident. When your father rang I could only think you'd had an accident . . . crashed the car, or . . . something like,' he gathered me close to him.

'I'm sorry,' I said, 'I'm very sorry,' I lay against his sweater, it was soft and warm, I could hear the thud of his heart. His finger tilted my face to his, and his kiss was deep, and slow, and meaningful; it drew out the truth, I couldn't hold it back:

'I love you Gareth! I just love you! I love you so *much*!'

'Now, yes . . . perhaps you do.' Little kisses closed my eyes. I felt his cheek against my hair; he said something about 'tomorrow', or 'in the morning'; his voice was thick—thick, and heavy, and blurred. Then another sound cut sharply in, and he moved away from me. Looking round I saw Father coming down the path, Nell at his side, I heard him call again:

'Is that you, Claire? Have you got her, Gareth?'

'Yes, sir . . . safe and sound.'

We met on the verge—Father and I. His hands were icy cold. He was in dressing-gown and slippers: 'I'm quite all right,' I said.

'She needs hours of sleep . . . she's tired, over-wrought,' Gareth said behind me. I heard Father thank him, heard the car start up, heard a last shouted 'goodnight'. Then Father and I were shuffling up the path, Nell leading the way. Vaguely I remember going upstairs, peeling off my clothes, spiralling down into sleep and oblivion . . . down, down, down . . .

Amazingly I didn't even dream.

# CHAPTER ELEVEN

I AWOKE clear-headed at eight a.m. I remembered everything—all that had happened the day and night before. But it wasn't a calm reflection, for the last happening came back first, stood out in blazing letters of fire. I had told Gareth I loved him—told him so quite plainly, told him so without quibble or guile, told him so unasked. How could I have been so foolish—how could I have been so mad—so lacking in pride as to fling it at his head? What had he said to me? Nothing much. Perhaps he hadn't believed me. I hoped he hadn't, for this was the line I was going to have to take. I would have to tell him I'd been out of my mind. I would tell him I'd been drunk. I would tell him that the brandy had produced a temporary euphoria, which had taken over and put words into my mouth.

I thought of Orlando—safe, thank goodness, unharmed and back in his box. I thought of the tramp—only a tramp, who'd been pulled out of my car by the man who'd been with Stephanie last night. I thought of him, I could see him clearly—not very tall, but stocky, with a fair moustache and slightly receding hair. I knew him, well, of course I did, for this morning thought flowed clearly. The man by the fire was Roy Newel, was Stephanie's ex-husband. I wondered that I'd not known him

174

last night, but he'd changed, grown older, heavier, grown a moustache, and added to that, I'd not *expected* to see him. Last night had been dreamlike, confused, unreal apart from the scene with Gareth—when he'd kissed me—and the truth had come out with a rush. It was a truth too, which come what may, I was going to have to deny. Either that, or leave the hospital.

Father was downstairs making tea, I joined him in the kitchen. He was fitting the knitted cosy over the pot: 'I was going to bring you a cup up. How do you feel this morning?' He felt for the back of a chair and pulled it out.

'Sore in the throat, a bit stiff, and incredibly silly,' I said. I also, suddenly (perhaps at the sight of him), felt dreadfully upset. 'I'm sorry I worried you, I didn't think, I just went rushing off. Gareth said it was foolhardy.'

'I thought you'd been attacked . . . mugged, or perhaps had an accident. I felt so helpless, so *useless*. I was just on the point of ringing the police.'

'I'm glad you didn't.'

'In the end I rang Gareth.'

'Yes . . . so he said.'

'He was kindness itself. I got him out of bed.'

'He told me that too, and Father,' I tried to change the subject, 'did you know Roy Newel was back at Heathside? I saw him there last night. He's changed a lot, looks much older, I didn't know him at first. He seemed . . . well, it looked to me as though he were staying there.'

'*Really!* That's interesting!' Father drained his

cup. 'Perhaps they're joining forces again. It's not unknown, you know. Couples divorce, find they miss one another, even miss the rows, miss all the hassle, decide to try again. That may be so in their case, or on the other hand, Newel may be there on business, something to do with the Stables. Heathside may still belong to him.'

'Yes,' I said, 'perhaps on business. Yes, that seems more likely.'

'And talking of business,' he said briskly, 'there's something I want to tell you. I was going to mention it yesterday evening, but you were going back to The Royal, so I thought I'd save it, wait until I'd mulled it over myself. Gareth came here to see me, just before lunch yesterday.'

'Here! *Gareth!*' My voice rose up, my cup went down with a bang.

'We both know who I mean,' Father carried on with his tale. 'As you know, he's in the process of purchasing Park House, is living there on a rental basis, until it all goes through. Well, once it does, once it has, and he's got all the planning permissions, he intends to convert it into flats. He's going to keep the consulting rooms, take one or two private patients, I understand.'

'That's old news. Steve told me that, weeks go,' I said.

'But he's made me a very good offer, which I'm thinking of taking up.'

'Offer . . . what offer!'

'Of three rooms . . . three rooms he's got to spare. He wondered if I might like to set up a

Physio Practice there. He seems to think there's considerable potential, that I might do very well. Of course I'd not take many patients, I'd only be working part-time, and I'd need equipment, a secretary/receptionist; it takes some thinking about. It's a big undertaking for me, even when kept to its lowest, but as you know, Claire, your mother left both of us well-placed. We're not poor, either of us, and the bank would help with a loan. I'd soon repay it, once I got under way.'

'In Gareth Bannerman's house . . . but you can't! You just can't, it wouldn't be right!' I felt and sounded scandalised. 'You can't want to do such a thing!'

'Why on earth not? It's no favour. He's quoted a very high rent. We went into tentative figures. He's the one who'll gain. Gareth Bannerman's no fool, you know, nor a philanthropist. Why be so touchy about renting rooms from him?'

'Father, you don't understand.'

'Now look, here,' his face set in dogged lines. 'I don't want to retire. I want to carry on with my profession. I need to get out and work on a regular day-to-day basis. From a distance and situation viewpoint, Park House is ideal. It's just about the same distance from here as The Royal Hospital is. At first . . . 'er sight, it's exactly what I want.'

'You've decided, haven't you?'

'Yes, I think I have.' His chin came out like Gareth's. They weren't alike not a scrap alike, yet one or two of their movements, their expression changes, were very similar. 'And I thought,' he went on, 'that you might be pleased. I can't see why you're not. If it's Gareth you're objecting to, I shan't see him all that much. I shan't be bringing him home here, if that's what's worrying you. I'd never do anything to embarrass you, Claire . . . surely you realise that.'

'Oh, Father . . . oh, darling Pa!' I went over and gave him a hug. 'If it's what you want, then of course I'm pleased. You just surprised me at first, but now that the whole thing's taking root, I agree it sounds ideal.' I infused the words with enthusiasm—I had to make him happy. But I wished the idea ( and it *was* a good one) hadn't been mooted by Gareth—I wished he'd not be renting part of his house.

'I'm going along there this morning to pace out the rooms,' he said. 'Nell will take me, she knows the way as far as The Avenue. It's the tenth house on the right from there. You've not got your car, have you?'

I told him I hadn't. I went upstairs to dress.

I was making the beds when Stephanie brought the Fiat back. Father and Nell had been gone about an hour. She saw me at the open window, she looked up and waved: 'Well, I've brought it back Claire, all cleaned out.'

'Oh, that's marvellous,' I called, 'but don't go, I'm just coming down. Stay and have some coffee.' I ran down and met her in the hall.

'Okay, will do,' she followed me into the kitchen and sat on the step, with her legs outside; she was wearing her jodhpurs and shirt. 'I wanted to talk to you anyway,' she said, as I measured out coffee grounds. 'I've been meaning to do so for the past six weeks, but keep stalling . . . you know how it is.'

She's going to marry Gareth, I thought. Despite everything she's marrying him. She's overcome all his reluctance to . . .

'It's about Orlando,' she said. I was so surprised I spilled the coffee grounds.

*'Orlando?'* I must have looked stupid, standing there spoon in hand, mouth open, blinking like an owl.

'You won't, I'm afraid, have him much longer. Prepare yourself for a shock. Roy and I are re-marrying . . . marrying each other, I mean. We'll be moving from here, down to Somerset. Roy's got a Stud Farm there. We're selling up here, and taking the horses, combining businesses. A riding School will be added to the Stud Farm.'

'Oh, I see.'

'I'm so sorry, Claire. I know you dote on Orlando, but Roy wants all my stock, you see, and he may want to breed from him.'

'Why of course . . . yes . . . I understand.' Good Lord, what a morning, I thought—first Father and now 'Stephanie, and she was remarrying *Roy*— remarrying Roy and going from here—going miles and miles from here. How did Gareth feel about it, for of course he must know by now. He had prob-ably known for weeks, since before the Sindon wedding. How did he feel? Would he hate it? Was this why he'd turned to me—at least in part, in an on-and-off way, was he trying to fill a gap? Orlando would go, he would go with Stephanie; I concentrated on that:

'So there won't be a Riding School here any more?' I asked, when the coffee was ready. We took it outside and sat on the patio.

'No, there won't, not unless the purchaser of Heathside carries on. And I doubt if he, or she, will, you know. It's not been paying its way. When Roy saw my accounts he nearly fell through the floor—the dry rot floor in my dreadfully shabby old lounge.'

'Oh, I see . . . I didn't realise.'

'Not many people did. Gareth did. I told him. He helped me financially. Twice he stood as Guarantor. He's been a very good friend. I was feckless, and hopeless on my own. Gareth's very business-like, apart from his other . . . accomplishments,' she added this laughingly, looking at me with a shrewish glint in her eye. 'This coffee's superb,' she said quickly, sipping it greedily. 'I hope you're all right this morning, Claire. You don't look it, if I may say so. Last night was the absolute end, and of course it was all my fault. I should never have employed a girl like Iris. I knew she was careless and slack, but as I was nearly always there, I thought it would be all right. Well, she won't get a golden handshake from Roy. She didn't turn up this morning. You should just have heard him, heard what he said; he's been left with all the chores. I'd better not stay here very long, I ought to give him a hand. Oh, by the way,' she emptied her

cup and put it back on the tray, 'I meant to ask you
. . . how's David getting on?'

'Fine now, he's out of hospital, he's got perfect
sight in his eye. He's having a convalescent period
at Melton House at present.'

'Does that mean wedding bells fairly soon?'

'No, it doesn't,' I smiled. I added nothing to this
at all. She tried a little harder.

'Really! Now you surprise me, he seemed so
right for you. You seemed to go so well together. I
quite thought you were engaged.'

'No,' I said, 'we never were.'

'Well, I think that's an awful pity. You're so
obviously the marrying kind. I can see you settled
down with a tribe of children and the sort of husband who'd always give you a hand.'

I said nothing, just kept on smiling. We began to
walk to the gate. When we reached it she turned to
me again: 'Claire, last night, I couldn't help
wondering, thump me if I'm wrong, but it looked to
me as though you'd gone overboard for Gareth.
For your sake I hope you haven't, for he's *not* the
marrying kind. He's a widower, his wife died, that
much I know for sure, but something went very
wrong with his marriage, he never talks about it.
He's got some sort of devil on his shoulder that
stops him trying again. And he can't bear failing,
you know. His pride is paramount. He minds so
very much what people think.'

'We all do, to a certain extent! If we say we don't,
we lie!' I told her in a flash of anger, which I did my
best to hide. 'Thanks for the warning, I don't need

it, but I know you meant well.' I loathed my own hypocrisy, but hers was even worse. She might be marrying and leaving the district, but she still didn't want Gareth to find happiness, permanent or temporary, with any other woman. Perhaps she had wanted to marry him herself.

I opened the gate and let her through. I thanked her for bringing the car. 'And I'm glad about your news,' I told her, 'I hope you'll be very happy. As for Orlando, he'll love it in Somerset . . . all that lovely country.'

'Come and see him soon,' she said, 'We'll be here for another three weeks.' She turned and waved and began to walk down the road. I watched her go, knowing full well I ought to offer to drive her. It was the courteous, obvious thing to do, but I didn't call her back. I didn't want any more questions, and quite apart from that I knew that once I got to Heathside, I'd have to see Orlando. I'd not be able to help myself, and as he was going away, it was best not to see him, best not to ride him again. A lump came into my throat. What a mixed-up morning this was. I started to run as the 'phone rang inside the house.

The caller was Father, he sounded abrupt, he was using his no-nonsense voice: 'Claire, I'm at Park House still. I'd like you to vet the rooms. They seem ideal to me, but I'd like your opinion. Gareth suggests you come down now, there's plenty of time before lunch. Have you got the car back yet?'

'Stephanie brought it just now.'

'Good . . . splendid, then come along, see you in

five minutes.' Before I could say a word the line went dead.

I couldn't go. Well, of course I couldn't. What was he thinking about? I caught sight of myself in the hall mirror—hair still damp from its wash, face peering out, a blue and white dress. And Stephanie was right, I looked peaky and pinched. I reached for the 'phone again. Yet somehow I didn't lift the receiver, for I knew I'd have to go. I couldn't hide away for ever, I'd got to face Gareth some time. Last night's declaration couldn't go unexplained. Once I'd explained, we could both relax, could work together again. He wouldn't have to retreat in alarm, or be so stiff with me, so snubbing that I'd feel he was plunging in knives.

I tidied my hair, I made up my face—blusher made all the difference. I shaded it on. I darkened my lashes and brows. I changed my flatties for high-heeled sandals. I was armouring myself, I could do it, I must. I locked up and went to the car.

When I got to Park House Father and Gareth were sitting in the garden—a walled one, with an orchard at the end. 'Mostly apples,' Gareth said, 'Sir Hugh went in for fruit trees. Goodness knows what he did with all the fruit.' He was talking rather a lot for him, he was formally dressed in a suit, but his jacket was off, and his tie was the blue one with a stripe, the one he'd been wearing that day in June, three and a half months ago, when we'd met on the heath, when he'd stumbled on me eating my lunch in the copse. We had talked about Father's impending retirement then.

The sight of him was having its usual demoralising effect. Even his back view, the breadth of his shoulders, their movement under the shirt, caused a weakness, a surge of love, a rush and push of want. How can I lie and deny it all, I thought, as he pushed a chair in a patch of shade and invited me to sit down.

'Show her the rooms first, Gareth,' Father said comfortably. His chair was a lounger, swing type, 'I'll stay here and have a rest.' He drew his legs up, Nell laid down under the frill.

'Thanks to me we all went to bed at daybreak,' I said, as Gareth and I walked side by side to the house.

'I've not been to bed at all,' he replied, but didn't explain why. We had reached the house, which stood in shadow. It still seemed enormous to me. It was redbrick, with big bow windows, a solid, ornate front door, he pushed this open and we entered a stone-floored hall. 'I'll show you the consulting rooms first,' he said, 'then the rest of the house . . . if you'd like to see it.' He still didn't glance my way.

'Yes, I would. I'd like to see it.' We could have been absolute strangers. His stiffness was rubbing off on me.

'It was built between the Wars, you know, when materials were at their best. It's not new, but not old either, it's been very well maintained. In some ways it's a crime to convert it and spoil its symmetry.' He closed the heavy front door with a little click.

Mention last night now, I thought, get it over

with, then he'll stop avoiding looking at me, and I shan't feel such a fool. So: 'Gareth, about last night,' I began. I saw him turn slowly round. Behind me was a huge oak settle, the backs of my legs were against it. I could feel the smooth cool wood against my calves.

'What about last night?' He was framed in a doorway, his hand was on the jamb. He inclined towards me. For the first time our eyes met and held.

'I said some foolish things in the car. I hope you didn't think . . .'

'Come in here.' He cut me off in the way that only *he* could. I felt nervous, even frightened. I followed him into a room that seemed at first glance to be full of sunlight and warmth. I vaguely registered white and gold, and pale primrose yellow, and green curtains, and a view of the garden beyond. 'Now, what's all this about last night?' He motioned me to a chair, sat down himself, a very long way from me.

'I flung myself at your head, I'm sorry.'

'It put new life into me!' He was laughing, he had to be laughing, yet his face was perfectly straight.

'I'd had a double tot of brandy on top of an empty stomach, I was tired too, and had had a fright.'

'A dangerous mixture,' he said. 'So it was all moonshine, was it? You want to take it back?' His face was still stern, his eyes challenged, his mouth was vulnerable. He was giving me a chance to back down, a chance to save my face. All I had to do was nod, but I found I couldn't do it. I dissembled instead:

'Not *all* moonshine.'

'A qualified answer,' he said.

I was staring at the floor, but I heard him get up, saw him cross to the window: 'Someone's given your car a jolly good polish-up,' he said.

The change of subject shook me, and I felt a sense of affront. Wasn't the other important, then? Wouldn't he pursue it: 'Stephanie brought it back. I think Roy Newel did the cleaning. She told me her news—that she's marrying again, and going to Somerset.'

'Yes, it's been in the offing some time. I think she's very wise. Marrying the same man twice too—a case of the devil you know.'

'She said you'd been good to her.'

'Did she now?' he turned round, one of his eyebrows rose: 'It worked both ways, as it happened. Stephanie helped me too. I was, *am* grateful to her,' his long mouth quirked. 'You've been having a girlish gossip, have you? Steph's been painting the scene, our past relationship, a little too vividly.'

'She hasn't, she didn't. She was very . . . discreet. She didn't say much at all . . . only mentioned that you'd never be likely to follow her example, she said that you'd never marry again.'

'I think perhaps she said more than that.' He came closer and looked down at me.

'Only that your wife had . . . had died. And we didn't . . . weren't gossiping.'

'You couldn't have gossiped, not about my wife, no-one knows about her, except Aunt Maud who followed me here from Wales. Eve was killed in a road accident, whilst running away with her lover. The man in question was a friend and colleague. That's it, in a nutshell, Claire.' He put out a hand, I put mine in it. He drew me up out of the chair. 'Come over here. I've been nerving myself to tell you this for weeks. It'll help you to understand why I've behaved as I have with you.' We sat on a kind of low chaise-longue—a piece of the Wellesley's furniture. He held both my hands very tightly, as he told the rest of the story. In a way we held on to each other, I think. 'What was so shocking,' he said, 'was that I'd never suspected a thing. I loved Eve, I thought she was happy. There were differences, things weren't perfect, but I felt our marriage worked.'

'Did the man live?'

'No, he died . . . Alec was killed on impact. Eve was brought to the hospital at Llandroft where I was Registrar. She lived long enough, just long enough to tell me she was sorry. What she said had no significance till I got home and found her note . . . her goodbye note. It was all done by the book.'

'Oh Gareth . . . what can I say!'

'I came here soon afterwards . . . grieving for Eve, grieving for Alec, trying not to couple them. I found it painful to face up to, and the bitter taste of failure was in my mouth for a long time. It made me marriage-shy.'

'Oh God, I'm not surprised,' I cried.

'But I didn't enjoy my freedom. I lied in my teeth about that. I've felt half a person these last three years . . . terribly incomplete. Then I met you and I fell in love. I fought like a tiger against it. You were twelve years younger, you loved Cope, or I thought you did. And even when I learned the truth, I was still afraid to speak. I'd failed in my marriage, it had been a sham, or the last two years of it had. So I wouldn't risk it, I opted for safety, which was shot to pieces last night when your Father rang me, frightening me to death. An accident . . . was my first thought; I went off searching the roads. Then I saw Orlando bolting home, then I heard where you'd taken the car. I was still quite sure that something terrible had happened. When I saw you running, heard you scream . . . I could only feel relief . . . *relief*, Claire. At least you were alive!'

'I'm so sorry!' It was natural then to move into his arms.

'You told me you loved me last night, I didn't dare to believe you. I thought it might be what you said . . . reaction to events. I had to give you every chance to take it back, if you wished. I want you, and I love you, Claire, but it has to be two-way. So what are you going to say to me now?' He cupped my face in his palms, raising it enough to kiss my lips, drawing back again, waiting for my answer which must have shone from my eyes:

'I love you so much . . . so much,' I said, 'so much that it hurts. I've loved you since that afternoon we looked at the rainbow together.'

'To marry?' His face came nearer.

'To marry,' I said, 'to marry and be together all our lives.'

When he kissed me this time, when I kissed him, it was different from before—different and even more wonderful, with doubts and fears assuaged. He was mine, I was his—he loved me, I loved him—I felt safe and secure and happy—so happy, that one day I felt quite sure Gareth and I would find the pot of gold that's supposed to lie at the end of every rainbow . . .

Perhaps we already held it within our grasp . . .

We were married at Cletford Parish Church on the seventeenth of October. We had a reception afterwards at The Crown. Gareth's parents and brother came from Canada, my Grandmother came from France, Aunt Maud came from Princes Drive. Crowds came from the hospital, several from Melton House, including David, which pleased me very much.

Father gave me away, of course, he was thrilled about it all: 'The proudest day of my life since I married your mother,' he said. Gareth said I looked too lovely to be true.

We've been married fifteen weeks now, and Father has sold The Larches. He lives at Park House, where he has his own separate flat. Gareth persuaded him to do this, and he acquiesced very readily. Mrs Shoulder housekeeps for us all.

Gareth sees patients at the house three afternoons a week. I act as his nurse/secretary, for I decided to leave The Royal; it seemed the best course, and Gareth wanted me to. When Father starts his Physio Practice in six weeks' time, I shall be his receptionist too, so I'll have plenty to do. The house needs to be run efficiently, for apart from Father's small flat, we didn't convert it after all; we left it as it was. We both want children—a large family, so need all the rooms. When we told Aunt Maud she started knitting at once.

Oh and there's someone in the yard, too, who needs a good deal of attention. He's Gareth's wedding present to me, he was purchased from the Newels. He's black and muscular, with a hogged mane, and, yes, his name is Orlando. He's got one of the old loose boxes, and a paddock all his own. One day we may buy another horse, for he ought to have a companion. Gareth says we'll most likely end up with a full-scale riding school. I don't think it would worry him if we did.

I always visit Orlando at night—late at night, as one should. Horses are extra gentle then, endearing, extra loving, but I must confess I don't stay very long, I hurry back into the house where Gareth will be waiting for me . . . my dearest, dearest Gareth . . .

Safe in his arms I want for nothing more . . .

# Doctor Nurse Romances

Amongst the intense emotional pressures of modern medical life, doctors and nurses often find romance. Read about their lives and loves in the other three Doctor Nurse titles available this month.

### MATCHMAKER NURSE
#### *by Betty Beaty*

Mr James Jarvis, orthopaedic consultant at the Frantfield and General, is reputed to leave a trail of cast-off crutches, mended bones and broken hearts behind him. But, Nurse Hester Stanton vows, he will not get away with ruining her sister's life for a second time ...

### DR PILGRIM'S PROGRESS
#### *by Anne Vinton*

In her first job as a fully-qualified doctor Jane Pilgrim is relieved to think that her new boss will be the kindly old Dr Potts. But Dr Potts dies before she arrives at Northingham Hospital, and Dr Richard Graves, his successor, proves to be a very different – and dangerously attractive – proposition.

### A NAVAL ENGAGEMENT
#### *by Elspeth O'Brien*

Surgeon Commander Alexander Carlton Roscoe RN does absolutely nothing for her pulse or her blood pressure, Sister Kitty Martin insists. Yet why does the very thought of the dynamic surgeon, who is also a wounded war hero, make her heart beat faster?

## Mills & Boon
### the rose of romance

# 4 BOOKS FREE
## Enjoy a Wonderful World of Romance...

Passionate and intriguing, sensual and exciting. A top quality selection of four Mills & Boon titles written by leading authors of Romantic fiction can be delivered direct to your door absolutely FREE!

Try these Four Free books as your introduction to Mills & Boon Reader Service. You can be among the thousands of women who enjoy six brand new Romances every month PLUS a whole range of special benefits.

- Personal membership card.
- Free monthly newsletter packed with recipes, competitions, exclusive book offers and a monthly guide to the stars.
- Plus extra bargain offers and big cash savings.

There is no commitment whatsoever, no hidden extra charges and your first parcel of four books is absolutely FREE!

Why not send for more details now? Simply complete and send the coupon to MILLS & BOON READER SERVICE, P.O. BOX 236, THORNTON ROAD, CROYDON, SURREY, CR9 3RU, ENGLAND. OR why not telephone us on 01-684 2141 and we will send you details about the Mills & Boon Reader Service Subscription Scheme — you'll soon be able to join us in a wonderful world of Romance.

Please note:– READERS IN SOUTH AFRICA write to Mills & Boon Ltd., Postbag X3010, Randburg 2125, S. Africa.

- - - - - - - - - - - - - - - - - - - - - -

Please send me details of the Mills & Boon Reader Service Subscription Scheme.

NAME (Mrs/Miss) _____ EP6

ADDRESS _____

_____

COUNTY/COUNTRY _____

POSTCODE _____

BLOCK LETTERS PLEASE

SISTE

When Sister Bridie Stewart accepts a post as company nurse at the London Head Office of Pan-
European Oil her career enters a challenging new
phase. But is her new boss, Dr Gregory Brandon,
just a little *too* high-powered for Bridie?

*Books you will enjoy
in our Doctor–Nurse series*

# SISTER STEWART'S DILEMMA

BY

MEG WISGATE

MILLS & BOON LIMITED
London · Sydney · Toronto

First published in Great Britain 1982
by Mills & Boon Limited, 15-16 Brook's Mews,
London W1A 1DR

Australian copyright 1982
Philippine copyright 1982

ISBN 0 263 74023 4

Set in 10 on 12 pt Linotron Times
03/0982/

Photoset by Rowland Phototypesetting Ltd
Bury St Edmunds, Suffolk
Made and printed in Great Britain by
Richard Clay (The Chaucer Press) Ltd
Bungay, Suffolk

# CHAPTER ONE

'A LOVELY evening for a walk, Bridie. I would have liked to come with you,' said Mrs Stewart. 'Where did you go? Up to the loch? It always has been a favourite haunt of yours.'

Bridie sat in the friendly family kitchen, watching her mother's nimble hands preparing supper.

'Yes,' she replied. 'I find it's a good place to go when I've some serious thinking to do. At this time of year, with all the autumn colours, it's really lovely. And the dogs certainly enjoy it.'

'It gives them an appetite right enough,' agreed her mother, nodding towards the two waving tails and sounds of delight where two large plates of canine supper were being consumed. 'Serious thinking, Bridie? What's a young head like yours doing full of serious thoughts? Especially on an off-duty visit home.'

'Oh, I don't know, mother. I feel I've got into a bit of a rut with the surgery and everything. It's rather a dead end, you know. And, well, Neil and I . . .' she trailed off.

'First rush of passion died away a bit?' She looked up to see her mother twinkling at her. 'I'm sure I don't have to tell you, Bridie. The first passion does die away a little, but it gets replaced by a sort of permanence, a growing kind of deep affection. At least, that's how it's been with your father and me.'

Bridie's parents had married fairly young. Her mother

5

had continued nursing at an Edinburgh teaching hospital, while her father had been based in a joint practice in the city suburbs. But with the arrival of Bridie's elder brother James, her father had taken the sole practice out in Glenairton, with its comfortable grey stone house, and here they had lived in great happiness for nearly thirty years. They were, she reflected, one of the happiest married couples she knew. An almost perfect match. Her mother was thoroughly content, providing support for her husband as almost a medical secretary and at the same time following her interests in the village social life. Her father must be one of the last really traditional family doctors, managing his far-flung practice on a sole basis still, despite periods of intense pressure. It was a good life and not one to belittle.

'Of course, you're right,' said Bridie, 'but well, sometimes I feel a bit unadventurous. After all, Jamie's making a career for himself in the Merchant Navy and sister Lizzie is doing well at university in Edinburgh.'

'Aye, well, the problems of youth! I expect the truth is you've been hearing from your little tomboy friend Mary, filling your mind with ideas about London and fresh fields down South.'

Bridie remained silent, for her mother was certainly perceptive enough. The warmth and security of her parents' home and the easy, undemanding welcome they always gave her were important parts of her life—a far cry from the unreal atmosphere of oil-boom Aberdeen and the busy shore-based surgery she ran there for Pan European Oil. And yet she knew that even the excitement and driving force she felt in Aberdeen were beginning to pall.

'That'll be your father's last patient now,' said her

mother at the sound of the front door closing. She had an uncanny way of knowing when the surgery waiting-room was empty. 'I expect he'll be ready for his dram.'

Dr Stewart liked a drop of whisky after completing evening surgery and Bridie enjoyed bringing it to him when she was home.

'Supper's nearly ready,' she said, following her father into the drawing-room.

'Hello, pet,' he said, putting an arm round her shoulders. 'Had a nice couple of days? It's back to the oil town tomorrow, eh? Never mind, that nice young man of yours will be glad to see you back, I've no doubt. It's about time you brought him to see us again, isn't it?'

'Yes, daddy,' she smiled and kissed her father on the cheek, keeping quiet counsel. She chatted on with him about friends and activities locally and then spent a pleasant evening before retiring early to be ready for the journey back to Aberdeen in the morning.

As she was drifting off to sleep she recalled the application she had made for the senior sister vacancy at Head Office. It had been addressed to the Personnel Director at Pan European's Mayfair address, just off Park Lane. There was bound to be strong competition for the job and the company circular had stated that it was also being advertised in the nursing journals. She wondered what Neil's reaction would be, if she were called to London for an interview.

Neil, although he had not actually proposed, implicitly made it clear that he intended her as the dutiful wife of the Highland GP that he would become—once he had the opportunity at the right practice. He had, of course, been an influence on her taking the post at Aberdeen, where he was also based as Scottish Regional Medical Officer for the company.

It was not that she disliked the idea of marriage and settling down—and Neil was a lovable man whom it would be hard to better. Their relationship had been going for four years and she felt safe and warm within it. It was just that she also felt stifled. She was good at her job and she thrived on responsibility. But she felt she had not yet finished testing herself against what the world might throw at her. Also, there was quite a lot of that same world which she wanted to see. For instance, she had only visited London half a dozen times. The last occasion had been an Easter trip to stay with her old nursing-college friend, Mary. She had enjoyed taking the place of Mary's absent flat-mate during the Bank Holiday break and she had found the short sight-seeing jaunts exciting—to say nothing of the concerts, discos and restaurants of every ethnic culture which London had to offer. Even the rhetorical antics at Speaker's Corner had fascinated her. London had the same vibrancy as Aberdeen, but was less coarse, more polished. Most of all however was the feeling of opportunity. Room to develop one's skills, expand, meet different people, forge out a really worthwhile career. Perhaps that was why she had applied for the job at Head Office.

Thirty-six hours later saw her bustling into the Aberdeen surgery, trim and well organised in her crisply laundered uniform. It was only a short step to work from her little bed-sitting room and she felt refreshed after her few days' leave.

'Good heavens, Jean, you've had a tidy up,' she said to the surgery receptionist as she breezed in. 'Magazines in a neat pile. Telephone directories in the right order. Not a coffee cup in sight. What's brought this on?'

'Well, Sister Stewart, there's a message from Dr Fillingham to expect a visit from a Head-Office VIP some time today. We don't know exactly when.'

'And where is Dr Fillingham?' asked Bridie.

'He's gone out to Forties Field *Endeavour*. They've some problems in the rig's sick bay. He couldn't postpone the trip.'

'Ah, yes. Thank you, Jean. Well if you say there's a bigwig coming I'd better make sure the surgery's neat and tidy.'

She entered her private domain, hanging up her coat and checking herself in the cloakroom mirror. Neat and efficient-looking, she mused. Her startlingly blue eyes stared back from the reflection. They were particularly striking because of the contrast with her jet black hair. It was an unusual combination. She tucked a stray curl into place and positioned her nurse's cap on her short, trim hair style. She was not a great one for make-up, content to rely on mascara to emphasise her long lashes, with a hint of blusher on her cheeks and just a touch of lipstick. Her complexion was fresh and clear, slightly inclined to paleness which was especially attractive against the dark hair and brows. It served also to deepen the vivid colour of her eyes. She was not a stunning beauty, she thought, but attractive enough in an easy, natural way. Looking critically at the image that stared back at her from the glass she felt the effect was good. Fortunately she had never had problems with her figure. She was naturally slender and ate sensibly. She smoothed the bodice of her uniform and tweaked the waistband straight. Certainly smart enough to receive a VIP.

She wondered who it could be as she went into her office and consulted the diary for the morning's activities. It was fairly quiet; general surgery for minor ills until eleven-thirty and then a couple of medical screenings before noon. She would need to spend the afternoon updating the medical supplies inventory and processing any top-up requirements for helicopter shipment out to the sick bays on the rigs. Not a terribly demanding day, she sighed. Perhaps their visitor would liven things up.

She bustled around the various examination rooms and cubicles, checking with Jenny, her senior nurse, that all was neat and tidy.

'It's all right for some,' laughed Jenny, referring to Neil's visit out to *Endeavour*. 'Gadding around the North Sea in a helicopter, leaving us to cope with the big chiefs from Head Office!'

Jenny was a bright youngster from Liverpool with an infectious sense of humour. She was a good nurse and Bridie tolerated her slightly irreverent manner, knowing that she could revert instantly to a cool ordered efficientcy when the occasion demanded.

'I don't know why he doesn't take you with him now and again. It would be good to see some of our colleagues in their working environment, instead of just a signature on the bottom of a pharmacy requisition. I know, strictly speaking, women aren't allowed on rigs, but the rules are easing all the time. On the Norwegian rigs, they even have nurses doing the medics' jobs full-time. Anyway, you'd only be visiting. Go on, tell him you want a tour of Forties Field. I would.'

Bridie had made no secret of her relationship with Neil Fillingham and was quite sure that Jenny imagined her engagement to him would be only a matter of time.

'Quite so, Jenny,' she said lightly. 'Maybe I will at that. But Dr Fillingham likes to think he can entrust the shore operation to us. So let's get on, shall we?'

She had been tempted to say that it was Neil's view that a woman's place was very much in the home. That maybe he saw the shore-based surgery as the equivalent of home in his professional life. But she was certainly not prepared to discuss Neil's idiosyncrasies with a junior, no matter how good their working relationship.

'I'll be wheeling them in, then, shall I?' enquired Jenny. 'It looks as though it's all dressing changes and physio this morning. Bags I the nice pipe-line engineer who's come in again for heat treatment on his back. It's a very nice back. Perhaps he'll let me rub it for him.'

'Jenny . . .' said Bridie reprovingly, trying very hard to keep a stern face.

'Sorry, Sister Stewart,' said Jenny, immediately contrite. She sped out to the waiting room, colouring slightly.

The morning surgery passed smoothly enough. She felt it necessary to refer only one case for further treatment—a drilling foreman with a rather nasty eye infection. She suspected a piece of embedded grit was the cause. She dressed it and arranged a pool car to take him down to Aberdeen General for examination by a specialist. She was confident this would have been Neil's decision had he been here.

The medical screenings also went well, with Jenny assisting ably. Towards noon, she was organising the last few tests, taking a blood sample from a mountain of a man, who so dominated the examination couch with his bulk that she feared for its ability to support him. Paradoxically, considering his size, he went positively ashen as she took the sample. She was obliged to disguise her activities with light conversation about the weather, his work, anything . . .

'I'll leave you with Nurse,' she smiled down at him. 'She just has to take an electrocardiogram check and a quick chest X-ray. Then you get a nice cup of tea and a biscuit. Come back in three days for a physical examination with Doctor, when he'll go over your results. OK? Make an appointment with Jean in reception.'

'Yes. Thank you, Sister,' he said with some relief. 'I don't suppose you could make it a packet of biscuits could you? This fasting for twelve hours before my medical hasn't agreed with me at all.' He smiled ruefully.

'Well, we'll try and do better than the regulation digestive biscuit. We might even manage a couple of custard creams,' she said in tones of mock sympathy. 'However, I'm told there's a good fish and chip shop just round the corner.'

'Thanks, Sister,' he said, his mind completely distracted from the blood test.

Just like little boys, they are, she thought to herself.

She left Jenny to it and made her way out through surgery reception and up the stairs to Neil's office. She needed to check through the pharmacy requisitions and see if there was anything urgent in his midday mail.

Yes, she was good at her job, she thought with a sense of satisfaction. She felt she knew instinctively how to handle patients, to put them at their ease, provide sympathy but not involvement, to keep a proper sense of perspective. More responsibility would be so fulfilling, but she could not see Neil letting her develop it. She would talk over her future—their future—with him when he returned from Forties Field later that day. They were bound to go out somewhere this evening.

She hastened in to his office and stopped short. A complete stranger was sitting at Neil's desk. He was absorbed in some papers, an elegant tan leather document case open beside him.

'Oh!' she said, coming up short. 'I er . . .'

Her first instinct was to apologise for bursting in. But then she remembered that this *was* Neil's office and curiosity stayed her. At which point the stranger looked up. She felt the most extraordinary jolt as his eyes seized hers. They were the most penetrating eyes she had ever seen. Surely the intensity of his gaze could not be sustained. He seemed to look right into her. She felt a sense of relief as his glance dropped, followed by a sense of resentment as his eyes ran down her crisp uniform, her legs, her trim ankles and then back up again. It was not a look so basic as to give offence, but rather caused her a feeling of unease, as though he was well aware of what lay beneath her professional attire. She felt colour rising to her cheeks.

'Dr Gregory Brandon,' he announced himself. 'And you are . . . ?' The voice which accompanied the steely grey eyes was in marked contrast—almost a drawl. It issued from a lean, virile frame, with broad shoulders and a deep chest. His face was equally lean, with a firm strong jaw and finely chiselled features beneath immaculately groomed dark hair. The hands, now interlinked before him on the desk, were slender and long-fingered, but with a definite suggestion of latent strength in their loose clasp.

She recovered her poise, took a breath and walked forward.

'I'm Sister Stewart,' she said. 'And I should like to know what you are doing at Dr Fillingham's desk, looking through his papers.'

'I am in fact looking through *my* papers,' he replied levelly. 'In addition, since I am Chief Company Medical Adviser to Pan European Oil, I feel quite entitled to sit at one of our employee's desks.' He paused coolly. The expression in his eyes had somehow changed into something approaching boredom.

Bridle felt confusion overwhelm her. Normally very self-controlled, she was dismayed to find she was practically stuttering. 'Oh, I'm sorry, Dr Brandon. You must be from Head Office. We were expecting a visitor. I had no idea you had arrived.' The words came pouring out in a rush.

'I'm not surprised you were unaware of my arrival. There was nobody manning reception as I came in. Is that normal?' he enquired sarcastically.

Bridie over-reacted. 'It certainly is not,' she flared. 'I expect Jean had just popped out for a moment.'

'I see.' There was a silence which she felt compelled to break.

'Well, anyway, she would only have been away from her desk for a minute or two. And it's been fairly quiet this morning. If you had just given us a little more notice of your visit . . .'

'That's something I never do,' he interrupted. 'I like to see things as near as possible to how they usually are.'

'Catch people out, you mean,' she retorted, instantly regretting it. Good heavens, she was behaving like a petulant student nurse.

For the first time, humour appeared in his eyes, transforming them totally. 'Possibly,' he rejoined.

He really could look quite attractive, she thought and began to relax a little.

'How long will you be here, Doctor?' she asked. 'I expect you'll want to make a thorough inspection of the surgery facilities downstairs this afternoon, and meet the staff. I'm afraid Dr Fillingham's out in the field today, but he'll be back later this afternoon. I'm sure he'd spend some time with you this evening.'

'That won't be possible,' he said airily. 'I have a luncheon appointment with the Chairman and will be engaged all afternoon. And I fly back tonight.' His mood had changed again, reverting to his former laconic detachment.

'But Sir Rupert's not here as well, surely,' said Bridie. The Chairman of Pan European was something of a national figure, often reported in the Press. She remembered suddenly what she had read in the paper that morning.

'Of course,' she went on. 'The company's sponsoring a Pro-Am Golf Tournament at the Royal and Scottish today and he's attending, isn't he?'

'Precisely,' came the reply.

He rose to his feet, uncoiling to about six feet, and walked round the desk to the window. Looking out, with his back towards her, he continued, 'I'm leaving at twelve-forty-five. I'd like a verbal report from you, taking fifteen minutes, and a tour downstairs, taking thirty,' he said, consulting an extremely elegant wristwatch. In fact, everything about him was elegant, she pondered. The shoes looked as good as any you would find in Princes Street, Edinburgh, and the suit was beautifully cut, the jacket hanging from broad shoulders to narrow hips supporting perfectly creased trousers.

'Well?' He turned to face her.

She blinked.

'Er, well, Dr Brandon, I hardly think three-quarters of an hour is sufficient for a thorough look round. You say you are engaged this afternoon?'

'Correct. I am playing in the Chairman's Invitation Match.'

'I see.' She compressed her lips. He was obviously not interested in the Aberdeen Medical Centre at all. It was simply an excuse to bring him in the company jet for a pleasant day's golf on one of Scotland's finest links. What a thoroughly unlikeable man—and he called himself a doctor!

'You appear to be wasting what little time we do have, Sister Stewart. Please make your report.' He indicated her to a chair before the desk.

She bristled, her annoyance at his peremptory manner almost gaining the upper hand. She sat down in the chair while he remained standing, leaning casually on the corner of the desk and looking down at her with the most patronising air possible.

She retreated into her professional shell and delivered a terse, efficient and economically-worded precis of the Aberdeen operation. She put in many of her own comments on systems and staffing patterns, not all of which Neil would have supported. He listened in a distant manner. She felt at times that he was not listening at all. Probably anxious to join the gin-and-tonic brigade at the Royal and Scottish, she thought. She finished her report.

'Not in agreement with all the company's medical systems, then, Sister Stewart?' he enquired sardonically.

'I wouldn't say that,' replied Bridie coolly. 'It's just that there is always room for improvement.'

'With only two year's service with the company, you are remarkably sure of yourself,' he said swiftly. 'What makes you think you are qualified to comment on things above your head?'

She felt anger mounting within her. How dare this superficial, so-called Medical Adviser be so arrogant? She adopted tones of icy calm.

'I certainly would not presume anything, Dr Brandon,' she said with tight self-control. 'I believe I run an efficient surgery here and I would be failing in my job were I not to note and suggest possible improvements.'

'Good,' he said, abruptly closing the conversation.

He walked to the door in another sudden about-turn of mood.

'And now, a swift look round, Sister. We have . . . er . . . twenty minutes.' He strode off down the corridor towards the stairs. She followed—rather lamely, she thought crossly. For all the world he could have been some Eastern prince—with her as a dutiful female following two steps behind.

The tour was lightning swift. She was hardly surprised when Jenny's irrepressible personality seemed to catch his fancy. She felt a mild annoyance and interrupted Jenny in mid-sentence. 'Dr Brandon, you might care to take a look at our new glaucoma screening apparatus. It's next door . . .'

'I am quite familiar with the latest tonometry equipment, thank you, Sister.'

Colour suffused her face.

'I need to make a telephone call,' he said abruptly. 'I'll use the 'phone in reception. While I'm doing that, perhaps you would fetch my document case from Dr Fillingham's office.' He glanced at his watch. 'I'm running behind schedule.' Without waiting for a reply, he turned and left the room.

Bridie found herself shaking with anger as she made her way upstairs. The sheer arrogance of the man! Running behind schedule indeed. It was only a golfing schedule after all. Rarely had a person irritated her so much in such a short time. And now he was treating her like a fetch-and-carry messenger. She entered Neil's office and went over to the desk. He had even forgotten to close up the case. Her eyes strayed across the uppermost document in the case, as she reached across to shut the lid. With a feeling of shock, she realised she was looking at her own handwriting.

SURNAME:  Stewart
CHRISTIAN NAMES:  Bridie Jane
POST APPLIED FOR:  Senior Sister, Head Office
Medical Department.

It was her application for the Head Office job. And of course . . . she sank down in the chair in horror. This patronising, superficial man was the final recipient of her application. No wonder he had known her length of service. What an impression she must have made! A real chance of bettering herself and she had almost certainly ruined it by taking such obvious exception to his lofty manner. What an idiot she had been. She had better try to make amends. Picking up the case, she sped down to reception. He was just replacing the telephone receiver. Summoning a smile, she handed him the case.

'There you are, Doctor. A pity it's been such a flying

visit, in every sense. Perhaps you'll be able to come and see us again. Dr Fillingham will be sorry to have missed you.'

The flash of friendliness she had seen earlier briefly warmed the steel-grey eyes.

'Thank you, Sister,' he said curtly. 'It's been most pleasant. Now I must go.'

He turned and, seemingly in one movement, was through the door and into the back seat of a long, sleek Jaguar, which had just drawn up outside. It felt as if a rather powerful force had just left. Jenny, standing next to Bridie, must also have felt it.

'What a dishy doctor,' she said. 'I'd love to work in *his* surgery.'

'Don't be childish, Nurse,' said Bridie and, turning on her heel, stalked off. She did not hear Jenny's gasp of surprise at this un-Bridie-like show of temperament, nor see the glance she exchanged with Jean, the receptionist.

The afternoon passed quickly enough. After a light lunch in the site canteen, where she regained her composure, she busied herself with the myriad details of surgery administration. She was quite surprised when, at around five o'clock, she became aware of the smell of pipe smoke in the office and a familiar figure standing behind her.

'Hallo,' said Neil, giving her a perfunctory peck on the cheek. 'What a day! I hate riding in helicopters. I've got a tendency to air-sickness and the pilot's been chucking us up and down like an express lift.'

'Poor darling,' she smiled. 'Well, everything's tidy here. You don't need to hang around. I've just got to pop these few things in the post and then I'm finished too. We've had quite a day—or morning rather, with our VIP paying us a flying visit.'

'Tell me about it this evening,' said Neil wearily. 'I must get back to the flat and freshen up. I feel wrung out.' He paused. 'I take it you do fancy doing something this evening? I thought perhaps we might go for a drive out to the Inverkirrie Castle for a steak and a bottle of wine.'

'That would be fine, Neil. I'd like to go out this evening. I've had better days, especially first days back after leave.'

'Right then, I'll pick you up at seven-thirty.'

It was not a very successful evening. Neil did nothing to assuage Bridie's worries that she had spoiled her new job hopes, but seemed more concerned that she had given a good impression of the Aberdeen surgery to their visitor. In fact, she gave up talking about her own hopes and aspirations when Neil made it plain that he felt she was far too inexperienced to tackle a more demanding post.

'Your place is up here in Aberdeen with me. I don't know where you get all these ambitious ideas from, Bridie.' He ran a hand through his curly fair hair and emitted a cloud of pipe smoke. 'You need to be a dedicated career girl to go for that kind of job— and you're a home-bird, aren't you?' he said complacently.

'Am I, Neil?' It seemed the easiest thing to say.

'Of course. You wouldn't have got the job anyway. Well, shall we go now. I'm tired.'

Normally, she would have accepted Neil's offer of a cup of coffee at his flat. But somehow a feeling of resentment had crept up on her. She pleaded a headache and was relieved when Neil agreed to drop her straight back at her bedsitter.

On her own in bed later that night, she felt a pang of bleakness. She felt strangely unsettled by her brush with the languid Dr Brandon. How stupid she had been not to connect him with her job application. She had almost certainly ruined what little chance she had stood. He probably saw her as Neil did—a provincial nobody who would never measure up to the demands of a more responsible position at Head Office.

She hugged her arms round her knees and tried to forget the day's events. It seemed that sleep was a long time coming.

# CHAPTER TWO

THE next morning heralded one of those dreary Aberdeen days when a dank, south-east wind brought an endless stream of low, scudding rainclouds in off the North Sea. The town's citizens greeted this with traditional dour acceptance and went about their business with a kind of glum tolerance, shoulders hunched and collars turned up against the elements. Only the oil men, immediately recognisable by their tartan reefer jackets, heavy boots and all-weather working gear, seemed impervious to the conditions.

Normally outgoing and optimistic in the mornings—even on grey days such as this—Bridie found it unusually difficult to get going. She had not slept very well. But then she realised it was Neil who had upset her with his dismissive attitude to her ambitions—although ambitions was almost too strong a word. She did not look upon herself as a single-minded career girl. All she wanted was to expand her horizons a little—and what Neil seemed to imply was that further responsibilities were beyond her.

She realised she was frowning at herself in the hall mirror as she slipped on her topcoat. That certainly would not do. Start showing your disappointments and little frustrations on your face and, pretty soon, permanent lines would begin to appear. She took a deep breath and purposefully picked up her umbrella.

'Don't forget your letter.' The cheerful face of Mrs

McGregor, her landlady, appeared through the kitchen door. 'It's on the hall-stand in front of you, dear.'

'Thanks, Mrs M,' she said. It was London postmarked and addressed in her friend Mary's handwriting. She tucked it into her bag. It would make good reading in the coffee break.

Mrs McGregor stepped into the hall and regarded her quizzically. 'My, you're looking a wee bit downcast, this morning,' she said. 'Trouble with your love life, would it be? You take my advice, Bridie Stewart, and make up your own mind about things. Men, they're all the same—they like to think they're the stronger ones, but I have a feeling it's us womenfolk who decide all the really important things.'

'Yes, Mrs M.' She smiled in warm affection. She did not have time to become involved in one of her landlady's homespun philosophy conversations, but appreciated her concern. Mrs M was very like Bridie's mother in many ways. 'Well, time to be off. I'm a bit behind, this morning.'

'Mind you're well wrapped up. There's a touch of winter in the air, I'm thinking,' said Mrs McGregor, opening the front door.

'Don't worry, I put on lots of warm layers today, Mrs M. I've even dug out my winter boots. See you this evening.' She hurried out and along the glistening, grey streets.

The first part of the morning passed interestingly enough. There was a meeting with a representative from a drug company, who wanted to present some of his company's latest research into hypothermia and its effect on the body's ability to absorb medication. She found the subject fascinating and had no difficulty in keeping up with the conversation, even though Neil did most of the talking.

It was not until coffee time that she remembered Mary's letter. Shutting the door to her office, she settled down to read it. It was, of course, full of Mary's slightly scatty personality, flitting from one topic to another with amazing agility, treating everything with the same degree of enthusiasm. In fact, it was difficult to reconcile this style with Mary's responsibilities as a theatre sister at St Clements. It seemed that her romance with one of the registrars there was blossoming.

'He's asked me down to Sussex this weekend to meet his parents. Dear Bri, this *has* to be good news, doesn't it? I've spoken to his mother on the 'phone and she sounds really nice. I hope we get on OK. Don't know what to wear. I think I'll go late-night shopping in Bond Street on Thursday. Fenwick's is so reasonable, you'd be surprised. But then you know, don't you? We had tea there on Easter Saturday and you bought that unusual silver evening bag. What did Neil think of it? Don't tell me he didn't even notice it. You never did say.'

She smiled to herself at her friend's headlong approach to life. They had been almost inseparable as student nurses and she really missed Mary's company. Fancy her remembering the little shell-shaped evening bag. She could not answer Mary's question about Neil's reaction, because, truth to tell, they had not been anywhere she felt was sufficiently grand for her to take it. It was still wrapped in tissue in its box in her room.

She read on, through Mary's bubbling stream of gossip. It seemed she was about to have to deal with a mild domestic crisis. Mary's flatmate, also a nurse at St Clements, wanted to specialise in obstetrics and had decided to move to Bristol, where there was a hospital which provided good opportunities for midwifery. This meant Mary was in need of a replacement for the flat—and fairly quickly.

'It's so important to get the right person,' she had written. 'It's no earthly use advertising. You get all sorts of odd types. Even a surprising number of fellows, despite specifying a girl. Mind you, you get quite a few indeterminate chaps these days, who aren't sure *what* sex they are. Actually, I do believe that type's supposed to be very neat and tidy . . .' Bridie laughed aloud. Was this the quiet, rather diffident girl she had first known as an eighteen-year-old student? She read on.

'Wouldn't it be great if you could come to London. We'd have such a good time. I know you'd love it. I suppose it's Neil really. That's why you won't. It's so silly. There's enough opportunity for both your careers.'

Suddenly the feeling of restlessness was back. She felt an unaccountable sense of frustration. She skimmed through the last paragraphs of Mary's letter, refolded it and slipped it into her bag. Perhaps her mother was right. Maybe Mary did have an unsettling effect. Certainly she was not behaving very well towards Neil recently. She resolved to try harder.

Somehow, however, as the days went past, she found herself making more and more excuses for not seeing him outside work. It was not difficult to find feminine reasons for wanting early nights and, after the evening which followed Dr Brandon's visit, the excuses had become more frequent and easier to make.

Even Jean, their receptionist, noticed something amiss and commented on it one morning as she handed over the mail.

'You've been looking a bit down lately, Sister Stewart,' she said. 'You ought to let Dr Fillingham prescribe you a tonic.'

'I'm OK, thank you Jean,' smiled Bridie. 'It's probably the thought of winter approaching.'

People were kind. It was nice of Jean to be concerned. She *must* shake off this strange feeling of depression. It would be nice if Neil had noticed she was looking a bit low and offered a diversion or two away from the rather narrow little world they shared. But he seemed completely preoccupied with his own concerns. Her feelings of disloyalty towards Neil were becoming increasingly frequent these days and she realised too that she hardly ever suffered from an accompanying feeling of guilt. Daydreaming again, she chided herself and went into her office, dropping the bundle of unopened mail on the desk. She called to Jenny.

'I think we'll break the rules this morning, Nurse. We have twenty minutes before surgery. Let's see if Jean can produce an early cup of coffee.'

'Yes, Sister,' came the eager reply.

She dispensed with her coat, checked her uniform and began opening letters. There was the usual pile of publicity material from the drug companies, a batch of internal memoranda, most of which seemed to emanate from Neil—and a letter addressed to her, marked *Private and Confidential*. She turned it over. Pan European Oil, it said on the reverse, Park Lane, London, W.1. She slit it open and started to read. Her heart began to beat wildly. It was from the Personnel Director.

'Further to your recent interview with Dr Gregory Brandon, the Company is pleased to offer you the post of Senior Sister, Head Office Medical Department . . .'

An overwhelming surge of elation rose within her. They were offering her the job! It could hardly be called an interview that she had with Dr Brandon, but he had decided after all that she merited the job. How wonderful!

'Coffee,' trilled a voice.

She started.

'Oh, thank you . . . er . . . Jenny. Close the door behind you, would you please.' She completely failed to notice the look of puzzlement on the young nurse's face.

The letter went on to specify the details. The salary was confirmed, considerably more than she was earning now, plus a substantial London weighting. It seemed they were anxious for her to start from the beginning of next month. Good heavens, that was Monday week. A copy of the letter had been sent to Dr Neil Fillingham, to whom it was suggested that her replacement should be Jenny as Senior Nurse. The internal telephone interrupted her racing thoughts.

'Would you come up please, Bridie.' Neil's voice sounded unusually abrupt.

'I've surgery in five minutes, Neil—'

'Five minutes is all we'll need.'

He was sitting behind his desk, a strange expression on his face.

'Neil, isn't it marvellous? There was me thinking I didn't stand a chance, but I've got it! Aren't you pleased for me?'

'You're not accepting the job of course.' It was a statement, not a question.

Her next rush of excited words died in her throat. 'What do you mean, Neil?' she stuttered.

'I said, you're not accepting the job are you? It was a

nice little daydream and it's actually ended in an offer. But you know London and Head Office aren't really for you. You'd be a little out of your depth there, wouldn't you? In any case, I need you up here with me.'

She experienced a feeling of gloomy inevitability. Neil was not at all pleased for her. Somehow this realisation was not tinged with any sadness. She made one last attempt.

'But Neil, can't you see it's important for both of us? You might even want to come down to London yourself. And it's not for ever. It's something I want to do. Maybe just for a year. The experience will always stand me in good stead, whatever the future holds for us . . .'

'You've just got ideas above yourself,' he said angrily. 'And look at the state you'd leave me in. He held out his copy of the letter and slapped it with the other hand. 'They're suggesting that young empty-headed girl, Jenny, should take over running the surgery. A frivolous type like that. Ridiculous.'

'She's perfectly capable, Neil,' said Bridie wearily.

'She's still wet behind the ears,' he said scathingly.

'Neil, I don't really have time to discuss it. I have surgery now. We'll talk about it later.'

She made her way downstairs with a strange feeling of indifference. She realised she had almost expected Neil to react as he had. Surprisingly, his outburst appeared not to have affected her at all. Any feeling of disappointment she might have had was secondary to a much greater feeling of suppressed excitement.

She remembered this was the second letter she had received from London in the same week. The first had been Mary's. With news, amongst other things, of a spare room in her flat. Everything seemed to fit together so well. A red-letter week indeed. She resolved to give herself twenty-four hours to make up her mind. Her father had always said one should sleep on a big decision. She would ring him tonight. He always gave her good advice.

She passed the rest of the day in something of a daze. Fortunately, her duties did not bring her into contact with Neil, nor would she see him the following day, since he was attending a regional conference in Edinburgh. She went home and, having enjoyed some supper with Mrs M, who was always glad to provide her with an evening meal when given enough notice, put through a call to her parents after her father's evening surgery.

Dr Stewart was a man who delighted in his children's achievements, not out of any feelings of self-gratification, but rather for the sake of their own happiness. The result was that all three children had developed their abilities to the utmost, free from any parental possessiveness. At the same time, the family bonds were, and always would be, outstandingly strong. His reaction was almost predictable. He asked several highly practical questions about the job, her view of whether the economics would work with London's cost of living and what plans she had for accommodation. Having satisfied himself on these various points, he said, 'Well, Bridie. It seems a good opportunity for you. I can't see any reason why you shouldn't take it.'

She had made no mention of Neil and, following her lead, neither had her father.

They discussed other practical considerations, like the advisability of her parents' garaging her little red Mini; how much of her accumulated possessions at Mrs M's

should now be stored at Glenairton, pending their possible removal to London; the fact that he would convey all
the news to her mother, who was out visiting a neigh-
bour; and they rang off.

She was glad not to have spoken to her mother, who
would certainly have asked about Neil. She did not trust
herself to discuss the subject and, sitting alone in her
room later, sipping a mug of cocoa, she found herself
quietly crying. She felt a great sense of disappointment
in Neil. It was remarkable that you could think you knew
someone intimately, for quite a long period of time and
then discover, in reality, that you hardly knew them at
all.

Well, perhaps their relationship needed a bit of a jolt.
Being apart might well make them appreciate each other
more. They could visit each other regularly. She knew
Mary had a folding settee-bed in her lounge and he
would enjoy some weekends in London. She would
show him the sights once she felt sufficiently qualified as
a guide. It would be fun. She decided to convey these
thoughts to him at the earliest opportunity and immediately felt better.

She woke the next morning refreshed and completely
clear in her intentions. What a marvellous thing sleep
was. It gave your mind a well-earned rest and let your
sub-conscious make its own decisions while you slept.
Things always seemed to have dropped into place by the
morning. The day passed in a flurry of activity. She
decided that in view of their urgent requirement of an
immediate decision, she should telephone her verbal
acceptance of their offer and follow it up with a written
confirmation. She paused momentarily to consider
whom she should telephone and was very glad to find a

valid reason why it should not be Dr Brandon. She felt
somewhat wary of him after their last meeting and
wanted to renew their acquaintanceship on a face-to-
face basis. The telephone was less than perfect as a
means of communication.

She decided to ring the initiator of the letter, the
personnel director. A pleasant, mature voice boomed
down the long distance link, expressing delight at both
her acceptance and her forethought in prefacing a letter
with a telephoned acceptance.

'Dr Brandon's been very anxious to get the post
filled—he has many concerns and this will absolve him of
one of them,' he said. 'I shall look forward to welcoming
you to Pan European House on November 1st, Sister.
Ask for me personally when you arrive. Do you want us
to book you into a hotel? I believe the letter explained
that the company would pay accommodation for up to
three weeks until you get yourself fixed up.'

She explained that she was hoping to resolve that
question herself, thanked him and rang off.

Next on her list was a call to Mary, whom she tracked
down in St Clement's staff rest room. Mary's whoop of
'How fantastic, Bridie' could hardly have earned her any
marks for decorum amongst the junior nurses. They
discussed ways and means, Mary reassuring her that of
course the room was still free, and that she couldn't wish
for a better flat mate. Bridie planned to travel down on
the inter-city train on Saturday week. Mary would meet
her at King's Cross, time to be confirmed.

By the end of these two conversations, she was buzzing with excitement. It was an excitement that she was
obliged to contain, since everything would have to remain confidential at Aberdeen until Neil could read his

copy of her formal letter of acceptance. She certainly must afford him that courtesy.

That evening she regretfully told Mrs M that she would be leaving in a week. Her landlady was obviously sorry to lose a tenant she had become fond of, but wished her well and, true to form, dispensed a fair amount of philosophical advice.

Bridie neatly parried any questions about Neil and retired to her room to start sorting out her possessions. She should really telephone Neil to tell him she had finally decided to take the job, but it seemed easier to put the confrontation off until the following Monday.

Saturday morning found her on the road early, heading for Glenairton with her Mini crammed full of cardboard boxes and assorted luggage. Her parents greeted this influx of paraphernalia with their usual calm and pretty soon she was perched on a stool in the kitchen, discussing her news with her mother and enjoying a welcome cup of coffee.

'And what has Neil to say to all this, then?' said her mother with an enquiring look.

'I shall explain to him,' said Bridie firmly, 'that this is something I need to do and that he must accept that we may see less of each other for a while. If we have something worthwhile between us, then it can surely stand our being apart for a short spell. Anyway, I think it will do us both good. We'll have regular visits to each other. I think we've just fallen into a rut.'

Mrs Stewart nodded, seemingly reassured—and changed the subject to lighter matters.

Thus also did Bridie convey her feelings to Neil over an after-work drink the following Monday. He adopted a hangdog expression and she felt pangs of guilt, but stood her ground.

'I can see you've made up your mind,' he said sulkily, 'and nothing I say will change it.'

'No, Neil, it won't,' she said gently. 'But don't let's be glum. Let's plan a weekend for you to visit me.'

The rest of the evening passed half-heartedly and she made another excuse for an early night. She returned the warmth of his goodnight kiss as they sat in his car outside her front door, but she could not help feeling that something was missing from their relationship.

Any remaining misgivings evaporated during the rest of the week, as preparations for her departure took over. Events merged into a blur, culminating in the farewell drinks she bought for everyone on her last evening. There had been a collection for her and she was presented with a digital clock radio and positively showered with good wishes, hugs and kisses from the many people in the Aberdeen complex. Neil put in a brief appearance but faded away early on. She felt a sense of disappointment but it was soon dissipated by her friends and colleagues, including by now a boisterous and very amusing group of construction engineers, who insisted on making an evening of it.

The following grey and rather misty morning found her speeding southwards in an inter-city express, feeling as excited as a schoolgirl.

She enjoyed the driving power of the train. It really was exhilarating, hurtling South, she thought, as she made her way along the length of the swaying coaches to a leisurely lunch. It was fun too, eating her meal next to the ever-changing scenery rushing past the window. She was fortunate enough to have a table to herself and was content to sit alone with her thoughts and tingling feelings of anticipation. She decided to indulge herself with a half bottle of wine and passed most of the afternoon in a gentle doze.

Mary greeted her at King's Cross rather in the fashion of a whirlwind and Bridie found herself and her luggage scooped up, whisked across the concourse and into a friendly London taxi at the speed of light.

She asked how Mary's visit to Sussex had gone the previous weekend.

'Well,' said Mary. 'This is it, you know Bridie—the real thing.' She paused and then suddenly pulled off her left-hand glove.

Bridie stared at the sparkling engagement ring.

'Oh, Mary. How wonderful! Congratulations!' She hugged her friend and kissed her on the cheek. 'I'm so happy for you,' she said. Although, if she were honest with herself, she would have also acknowledged a quickly dismissed pang of envy as she remembered her ailing relationship with Neil. 'When did it happen?'

'He proposed last night. I can't wait for you to meet him. I know you'll like him. His parents are absolutely fantastic too. Actually, if you're not too tired, we thought we'd take you out for a little welcome-to-London celebration. There's a bistro just round the corner from the flat.' Mary's eyes were shining.

'But you and Barnaby would want to be on your own, it must be difficult to get the same off-duty times.'

'Nonsense,' said Mary. 'That's fixed then. Never mind the unpacking. The whole of London awaits you.' She laughed gaily.

And so it was for the rest of the afternoon. Mary's

infectious personality bore Bridie up and into a flurry of details about London, the flat, ways of travelling to and from her new job and countless other topics. She felt as though she had passed through a timelock into a new, exciting world. She gave a squeak of delight at the room that was to be hers, with its neat divan and bright furnishings.

'Looks rather bare now Fran's gone,' said Mary. 'A few posters on the wall will put that right. There's a friendly travel agent round the corner. Rather a nice young man in there too. He'll soon fix you up.' She winked and giggled.

'It's lovely,' said Bridie simply. 'I've got a few bits and pieces of my own to put around. It'll be so nice to have the use of the kitchen. And a separate living-room. Mrs McGregor's was always very nice, but this is so much better. Honestly, Mary, I can't believe how quickly everything has happened. I'm so lucky.'

'You deserve it. Now, Barnaby's coming at seven, so have a bath and put on something exciting and we'll go out.'

Barnaby turned out to be a really nice young man and very much in love with Mary. They appeared to have a cosy, relaxed awareness of each other, both physically and emotionally. Barnaby was a charming conversationalist, but she noticed his eyes kept drifting back to his fiancée and she suspected their hands were firmly interlocked beneath the table. Mary seemed to expand in her happiness, as though the security of Barnaby's love had enabled her to blossom too.

Bridie sighed. She and Neil had never been like this. But perhaps, after a break . . . She looked idly over Mary's shoulder at a tall man ushering a very glamorous blonde in through the door. There was something familiar about him. Suddenly a current seemed to leap across the room as his eyes met hers and she experienced the same jolt as when she had opened that office door in Aberdeen.

Dr Gregory Brandon inclined his head in a curt nod of recognition. Again, she felt the intentness of his gaze sear through her. She gave a clumsy sort of half smile in return, but he had turned and was asking for a table, to which he motioned his companion. The girl beside him was dressed in the very latest fashion. She was wearing a pale pink zippered jump suit which, whilst doing justice to her figure, appeared to be at least one size too small. It stretched tightly over her body, emphasising the full roundness of her breasts and Bridie noticed that the zip appeared to be undone strategically low. So this was the sort of woman Dr Brandon found attractive, she mused. She became aware that Mary was looking at her expectantly.

'Sorry, Mary,' she said.

'I said, who's your attractive friend?'

She felt herself blushing absurdly and stammered that he was in fact her new boss.

'Wow,' giggled Mary. 'No wonder you've come rushing down to London at one week's notice. I shall have to keep an eye on you.'

Bridie found herself protesting and frantically sought a fresh topic of conversation. She was relieved when the first course came—a delicious paté—and she was able to turn her attention to eating. It was an excellent meal, amply washed down with the bottle of Beaujolais which Barnaby had ordered.

As they ate, she found her eyes kept straying back

across the room. He was sitting with his back to her and his sleek, dark head moved and nodded in talk with his companion. In fact, their heads were extremely close together and they were deeply engaged in an obviously absorbing discussion. Certainly, he appeared to be far more talkative than when she had met him in Aberdeen, where he had been uncommunicative to the point of rudeness. As their meal progressed, the girl occasionally put her head back and laughed—a gushing sort of sound which Bridie immediately labelled as affected.

Returning from the powder room after coffee, she collided with a man pursuing the opposite course. She found a strong, steady hand gripping her elbow and looked up into those remarkable steely grey eyes.

'Welcome to London, Sister Stewart.' He stepped back and regarded her, his eyes taking in her simple blue blouse and dark skirt. She was aware of the same cool appraisal she remembered from their first meeting and again felt a sense of discomfort.

'Thank you, Dr Brandon. What a surprise! I wasn't expecting to meet you again until Monday.' She was determined to get their relationship off on the right footing.

'The country mouse comes to the big city,' he smiled patronisingly. She kept her cool and returned the smile lightly.

'Yes, having a very nice first evening with some friends—actually one of them's my flatmate. I was very lucky to find somewhere to stay so easily. I know it's terribly difficult to find accommodation in London these days. Do you live in this area yourself?'

'No,' he replied and ventured no further information.

'Well, I mustn't keep you from your friends.'

'Nor I from yours,' she said pointedly and made to move past him, but he remained blocking her route back to the dining area.

'Well, see you Monday then,' she said awkwardly, waiting for him to move aside.

He continued to regard her intently and then said abruptly, 'Yes—Monday.'

He stepped sideways and she was able to brush past, very aware of his presence.

Mary and Barnaby had not observed this meeting and were very much involved with each other. Bridie was glad. That meant she was not obliged to comment again on the rather disturbing Dr Brandon. Back at the table, she found herself smothering a yawn and apologised.

'Yes, it must have been a long day for you,' said Barnaby, smiling. 'I'll get the bill and then I think you'd better get some sleep, Bridie.' She smiled gratefully.

As they left the restaurant, she noticed Dr Brandon was again deep in conversation with his blonde companion. He did not look up, although she was almost certain he was aware of their departure.

# CHAPTER THREE

MONDAY morning found her making her way through Mayfair, clutching the pocket street directory that she had found was an essential purchase for London living. Her destination was in the next street and, turning the corner, she came upon the building which housed Pan European's head office. It rose imposingly from street level and conveyed an impression of airiness and light, with lots of glass in evidence. She felt a tremor of excitement as she pushed through the swing doors into a tastefully furnished and luxurious reception area.

The immediate impression after the rush of the West End streets was of quiet. This was due partly to the acoustic tiling on the ceiling and partly to the beautiful carpeting, which stretched in an unbroken run from wall to wall. Soft lighting and attractive groupings of indoor plants abounded and two impeccably groomed girls sat behind the impressive reception desk. One of them looked up and smiled.

'May I help you?'

'Yes. I'm starting work here today,' announced Bridie, with more self-assurance than she felt. 'My name is Bridie Stewart and I'm to ask for the personnel director, Mr Andrews.'

'Ah, yes.' The girl checked a sheet on her desk. 'Sister Stewart, transferred from Scottish Region. Welcome to Head Office.'

'Thank you,' said Bridie, warmed by this show of friendliness and efficiency.

'Mr Andrews normally arrives at quarter to nine, so I think you're a little early, even for him. Why don't you take a seat? He won't be long.'

'Oh, am I that early? Yes. Thank you.' She turned, casting a swift look at her wrist watch. It said eight-thirty. She had been so concerned about being punctual on her first morning—and finding her way on the Tube—that she had completely over-estimated the journey time. She subsided into a deep leather armchair and picked up a newspaper from the coffee table, more to hide her confusion than to read, for her attention was fixed on the comings and goings in reception. The day started early for Pan European, with telephones tinkling at the desk and an increasing flow of staff through the entrance and into the busy lifts. She was aware of a quickening in her pulse as she sensed the power and efficiency of this nationally-important company. She was determined she was going to make a success of this job. She might be a little naive, arriving too early on her first morning, but she was a good nurse and she would soon establish herself.

She noticed the reception girl pointing her out to a grey-haired, authoritative looking man, whom her gaze had singled out from the busy traffic of people through the foyer.

He made his way over, an easy smile on his face.

'Good morning, Sister Stewart, and a warm welcome to Pan European House. My name's Andrews, Personnel Director. Nice to match the face to the voice,' he said, referring to the previous week's telephone conversation.

'Thank you, sir,' she said, rising to her feet.

'No need for the "sir", my dear. Board directors don't expect to be called that by our heads of departments. Post boys and juniors, perhaps, but certainly not our new senior sister. Come along up to my office first of all and we'll sort out a few details.' He led her over to the lifts.

'You're very prompt, I see,' he said, pressing a call button. 'That's excellent. I think one can achieve more in the first couple of hours before coffee than all the rest of the day put together. Mm?' She smiled her agreement. Thank goodness she had been over-early. She was off to a good start.

The lift arrived and they entered, along with several other people. Two secretaries followed them in and stood chattering in the corner while the car filled. 'Which floors?' enquired one, a scarlet-painted fingernail poised above the row of buttons. Bridie was aware of a heady perfume pervading the enclosed air of the lift car.

'Good weekend?' the girl asked her companion, nonchalantly pressing the correct floor numbers as everyone made their requests.

'Unutterably boring,' came the blasé reply. 'How about yours?'

'Pretty average,' replied the first girl. 'Went out to dinner on Saturday. Nothing spectacular.'

'We'll just have to find ourselves a couple of millionaires, Britt.' The girl called Britt laughed affectedly and Bridie realised with a start that it was Dr Brandon's blonde companion of the other evening. She examined her with renewed interest.

The girl was dressed for her business environment

today. A fashionable coat hung open to reveal an expensive looking silk shirt of which Bridie thought too many buttons had been left undone. A smart black skirt tightly hugged her hips. Very high heels and matching bag completed the ensemble. Bridie felt more than a little mousey by comparison. Dr Brandon would probably have said 'country mousey,' she reflected gloomily. Some shopping for clothes would be a priority next Saturday. Mary would have to give her some help, she decided.

To match her sophisticated outfit, this worldly London creature was wearing what Bridie considered to be an excessive amount of make-up. It could not be good for her skin, she thought critically, to cover it up with all those artificial layers. Well, if this was typical of London stylishness, she was not going to follow suit! She was proud of her own clear, fresh complexion and looked after it carefully. Nothing was going to make her hide it under expensive cosmetics and probably ruin it in the process, she told herself defiantly.

'This is our floor, Sister Stewart.' Mr Andrews' voice interrupted her thoughts.

They all disembarked, the two secretaries moving on down the corridor. 'This is the Executive Directors' floor. The chairman's office is there, Board Room there—and this is my office.' He opened a door off the corridor and ushered her through an outer office—his secretary's—and into an inner room. 'Make yourself comfortable, Sister. I'll just dig out your file.'

'It's very nice of you to welcome me personally, Mr Andrews.'

'Not at all. I make it a policy with all our key people and anyway, I have a note here from Dr Brandon asking

me to ensure you're looked after on your first morning.'
He bent to unlock the desk drawers.

'He's not here just yet, then?' she asked.

'No. Dr Brandon doesn't arrive until about eleven-
thirty most mornings. Ah there you are, Jill. Jill is my
secretary, Sister Stewart. She'll show you round, introduce you to people and take you down to your new
surgery. I expect you're anxious to see it.'

'Well, yes, I am,' she said.

'A few formalities first, though,' he said, opening her
file. The formalities were swiftly dispensed with and she
was soon embarking on a brisk tour of the building. She
was told that Dr Brandon's office was also on the
Executive floor.

'He doesn't have a secretary of his own,' explained
Jill. 'The chairman's secretary, Britt, does any confidential work for him.' She smiled. 'He's not really the type
to do lots of memos and reports. Any correspondence
which you yourself may require will be done by a
secretary in the Personnel general office.'

'I imagine most of my work will continue to be hand-
written,' smiled Bridie, 'but thanks anyway.'

'—and talking of Britt, here she is. Let me introduce
you.'

She found herself shaking hands with Dr Brandon's
companion. Britt gave no sign of having recognised her
from the bistro or the lift that morning, but eyed her up
and down condescendingly and Bridie found her dislike
of the girl growing. Suddenly she wanted to get down to
her territory and don the uniform of her vocation. She
was not going to compete with these sophisticated
secretary girls until she was good and ready. Jill cheer-
fully agreed to take her downstairs—Bridie felt she was

relieved to be able to get back to her own work.

Her surmise that her sister's uniform would give her a sense of purpose proved correct and she was soon examining her new surroundings in greater detail, feeling more at home with each passing minute. There was a pleasantly furnished small office, within a suite which also comprised examination booths, screening rooms and a small personal wash-room, all separated from the main corridor by an outer door. A brief glance at the filing arrangements and Kardex system showed that her predecessor had been a person of high efficiency. As to the medical facilities, she found they were quite unexpectedly superior. One room housed the very latest type of electrocardiogram machine and the visual acuity, hearing test and lung function monitoring equipment was the best obtainable. She found herself wondering if all this was not a little too extravagant for a building housing five or six hundred people. Even the equipment in Aberdeen was not up to these standards.

She unlocked the drugs cupboard to discover an inventory which a fully established pharmacy would find hard to surpass.

She returned to her office and opened the appointments diary. This morning had been left thoughtfully blank, she observed, but there was a pre-tropical medical check and some booster shots for a Mr McCabe that afternoon. She sat back and considered her surroundings. The idea of a cup of coffee suddenly suggested itself and she realised that it had been some considerable time since breakfast. As in most large offices, coffee came from a vending machine, which was situated by the lift, just outside her department's door.

As she made to grasp the handle, the door suddenly

opened inwards and she was staring up at Dr Brandon.

'We're always bumping into each other, Sister,' he said. For a brief moment, humour danced in the grey eyes as he looked down at her and then it was gone.

'I was just getting some coffee. Would you like one?' she offered.

'No thank you, I really can't abide that machine stuff. I'll have a proper cup when I get upstairs. You carry on, though.' He moved past her, sat down at her desk and opened the appointments diary.

She felt a flicker of irritation, but maintained her intention and fetched herself a coffee. It was only instant, but quite a reputable brand, she noticed. His dismissal of it, with the implied suggestion that her taste was less than discerning, was a little unwarranted. The medical department did not sport a coffee percolator, even if the Executive Floor did. She supposed that his girl-friend, Britt, would be only too pleased to prepare him a cup.

She controlled these thoughts with a firm resolve and remembered her intentions of establishing a sensible working rapport with him. She re-entered her office. Of course, she had no right to resent it, having worked in the department for only a few hours, but she found his taking-over of her desk and chair somewhat annoying. It suggested a possessiveness she was not prepared for. He looked up as she came in.

'Well now, Sister. What do you think?' He cupped his lean chin in one hand and waved the other in an all-embracing gesture at their surroundings.

'Well,' she said, 'it's absolutely first-rate. The quality of equipment is really excellent and I'm sure I'll be able to provide a really good medical service.'

'Good,' he said—rather smugly she thought. 'I've had carte blanche from the chairman on the specifications and I've gone for the best. Let me know if you're unsure of any of the procedures.'

'That won't be necessary, thank you,' she said coolly. 'My predecessor has carefully filed all the operating manuals and it won't take me long to brush up.' She paused and then continued, 'Yes, it's an excellent establishment, far better than Aberdeen—or in fact anywhere I've worked, in a straightforward surgery.'

'Do I detect a note of criticism, Sister?' He raised a finely arched eyebrow. 'I should tell you that although there are only six hundred people in this head office, they include some of the most vital people in Pan European. In addition, there is a constant traffic of key personnel to and from our vital international interests. This Mr McCabe you're seeing this afternoon, for example,' he tapped the appointments book, 'he's our Chief Underwater Operations Engineer. He's flying out to the Gulf tomorrow to supervise some important marine terminal constructions. And I need hardly remind you how dependent our ailing economy is upon oil.'

She had certainly not been prepared for this mini-lecture, but kept a still tongue and lowered her eyes.

'Of course,' she said.

'Fine. Now I think we should take a quick look round.' He stood up abruptly.

She was whisked around the surgery in a manner which at first she would have described as perfunctory. However, when she asked a question about aligning the visi-tester, he went to great lengths to explain, sitting before it himself and showing her how the patient's chin and forehead were to be positioned to check each eye. She found herself responding to his patience.

To clinch her understanding, he insisted she sat before the machine herself. She felt his hands on the side of her head, gently but firmly aligning her chin and forehead. She was surprised at the casual strength and coolness of his fingers and was aware of his lean frame pressed aginst her back as he checked her position. He was wearing a very attractive after-shave, she noticed.

'Well?'

He was asking her sight-testing questions and she hurriedly gave some answers.

'So you're not colour-blind, Sister,' he joked, 'and you've a fast understanding of technical points. Let's go back to your office and I'll just run through the stock and order medical supplies system with you.'

Back in her office, he glanced at his watch. 'I haven't got long. I'm scheduled to see Sir Rupert at twelve-thirty.'

They launched into the details of administration, all of them simple procedures which she readily understood. The telephone rang and he picked it up.

'Brandon,' he said tersely. 'Yes, she is here. Who's calling . . . ?'

His expression hardened. 'Oh, I see.' This last phrase was uttered in tones of heavy sarcasm. He passed her the receiver.

'A personal call,' he murmured, with studied boredom, and leaned back in the chair.

Who on earth could it be? She had not given her new telephone number to anyone yet, even Mary.

'Sister Stewart speaking.'

'Bridie, it's Neil. I've had a hell of a time tracking you down. Why didn't you tell your switchboard you'd arrived.'

She gave a sigh of exasperation. 'Neil. Look, I'm sorry, it's impossible to talk now. Can I call you this evening?' Dr Brandon was eying her disdainfully and she felt a spot of colour in her cheeks.

'Never mind that,' crackled Neil's voice. 'Look, you've made a terrible mistake moving down there. I must talk to you about it.'

'I just can't discuss it now, Neil.' Her cheeks felt ablaze and, even though she was pressing the receiver against her ear with all her might, for fear Neil's words could be overheard, she had the distinct impression that Dr Brandon's penetrating gaze was reading her every expression with consummate ease.

'Then I'm going to fly down on Saturday. There's a flight at eleven a.m. I'll get to Mary's flat at about lunchtime.'

'Yes, yes, Neil,' she said, wanting to end this conversation at any cost. She felt as though she were under a microscope, her every emotion on display. Somehow it seemed vitally important for Dr Brandon not to be party to any details of her personal life.

'See you Saturday, then,' said Neil.

'Yes. Goodbye.' She practically threw the receiver into its rest, her emotions at fine pitch. She stammered out apologies and made hopeless attempts to recapture the details of their interrupted conversation, but an air of aloof detachment had settled on him.

'The problems of your love life seemed to have disrupted your train of thought, Sister. They say absence makes the heart grow fonder, but I've rarely seen such a display of fondness after so brief an absence.' He had risen to his feet and appeared to be addressing his remarks to the ceiling.

'It's not like that at all,' she said tautly.

He proceeded to add insult to injury with his next words. 'A lot of girls find it unsettling when they first arrive in London from the provinces. Many go completely off the rails—and the majority don't stick it very long. London can be very lonely.' He was treating her like a child, patronising her, mocking her. She felt a prickle of tears behind her eyes.

'I shall be perfectly all right, thank you,' she said, barely able to conceal the shake in her voice.

'Fine.' He opened the door. 'Well. I think we'll leave all this humdrum administration for now. Anyway, I have to meet Sir Rupert.' This last was said with his back to her.

'Enjoy your lunch,' she flared. The words came out unbidden, her tone of voice instantly regretted.

He paused, as if to turn, but moved on instead, throwing a curt 'thank you' over his shoulder. She heard the outer door close. Very near to tears, she sat down. How could Neil have been so thoughtless? To have a telephone conversation like that forced upon her in front of the condescending Dr Brandon. She suddenly felt rather small and very lonely.

Gradually, however, her natural resilience gained the upper hand and, after a few sniffs, she made her way to the surgery's wash-room, splashed some cool water on her face and repaired her make-up.

By this time, it was almost her own lunch-time and, picking up her on-site bleeper, she locked the surgery door and went in search of the company dining room and the excellent subsidised lunch which Mr Andrews had described to her earlier.

She found his secretary, Jill, in the queue and joined her, taking a tray. This led to introductions to other members of the staff and she found herself rapidly welcomed into a pleasant and sociable meal. The conversation at table ranged over many subjects and she found the events of the late morning soon faded into the back of her mind.

Surprisingly quickly, it was time to return to the surgery and she busied herself checking that all was in readiness for Mr McCabe's check-up and inoculations.

Mr McCabe immediately wanted her to call him Jock. He turned out to be a big bluff Scotsman with a mop of red curls and a genial manner.

'I'm sure the first tropical medicine shots I had made me feel worse than the real thing,' he grinned. 'I hope you're going easy on that jungle juice, Sister.'

'You'll only have a mild reaction,' she reassured him, as she deftly swabbed and inoculated. 'These are just boosters. When do you fly out to the Gulf?'

'I've a few days leave to take first and then there are a few important events due over the next few days. I guess it'll be after that.'

Jock kept up a stream of anecdotes and she found she was warming to his quirky sense of humour. She was grateful for his chatter, for it concealed any slight unfamiliarity she felt with some of the screening apparatus.

She explained to him the workings of the spirometer, handing him the tube and asking for a big breath.

'Goodness, that's excellent,' she exclaimed, as the automatic pen traced out the curve of his exhalation on the graph paper. She removed the sheet. 'You're almost off the paper, Mr McCabe.'

'Aye, well, you need a good pair of bellows if you're to be a diver,' he replied.

'I can see that,' she smiled.

'Actually, it's really due to the fact that I played the bagpipes as a child.' The dry manner in which he delivered this quip caught her sense of humour and she laughed.

'Seriously now, have you never played the bagpipes, Sister?' She shook her head.

'Well, your education's been sadly neglected. I could arrange to give you lessons for a small fee. You never know when a skill like that might come in useful.' They laughed together.

'I take it Mr McCabe's not quite ready for his physical examination.' A voice heavy with irony penetrated their shared amusement.

She turned to find Dr Brandon standing in the doorway. He was looking at her with raised eyebrows, his finger holding back a cuff pointedly, to expose his wrist-watch.

'Er no, Doctor, sorry. We just have to take weight and height measurements. We're a little behind.'

'Quite,' he replied.

Assessing the situation, Jock interjected, 'I was a wee bit late myself, Doctor, so it's my fault.'

'I see. Well perhaps Sister would bring you along to the examination room when you're ready.'

She completed the remainder of the tests in a subdued manner. A pall had been cast over the earlier, relaxed atmosphere. Jock, being a man of tact, preserved a sympathetic silence.

In due course, his examination complete, Jock's head reappeared round Bridie's office door, his fingers tightening his tie and buttoning his collar.

'That's me then, Sister. I'll be away—and thank you.'

'Goodbye Mr McCabe. Have a good trip out to the Gulf.'

'May see you before I leave,' he said cheerily.

She made her way back to the examination booth, where Dr Brandon was making some last notes on Jock's sheet.

'An extremely healthy man, I would say,' she ventured.

He looked up. 'Do you usually flirt with your patients, Sister?'

She felt a flash of anger. 'I certainly do not,' she retorted hotly.

'In that case, you certainly have a frivolous manner. I had hoped you were a more mature person. This may not be a ward in a teaching hospital, but I do feel we should maintain *some* professional standards.'

Inwardly, she blazed. How could she respond to this without saying something irrevocable? She fought with herself, with her sense of outrage at this imperious man. How dare he talk about her professional standards? He was more dilettante than doctor, with his long lunches, his part-time hours and his golfing diversions. Knowing that he would take her silence as a form of sullenness, she nevertheless was obliged to maintain it for fear of losing her self-control. She fixed her gaze on the papers he was holding, anything rather than meet his eyes. She could feel the hotness in her cheeks. He passed her the file and stood up, regarding her.

'Well, I shall wish you good afternoon.' He paused and she thought he was about to add something. But he turned and left the room. She heard the outer door close.

This time there was no holding back the tears. She sat down on the edge of the examination table and wept. What a thoroughly horrid first day. She could not understand why he was treating her so unfairly. Doubts crowded in. Perhaps she had taken on more than she could cope with? Perhaps she really did stand out like some callow country cousin? Perhaps one had to have a tough and aloof veneer in order to survive in the high-powered London head office of a multi-national oil company?

Confused and downcast, she filled the rest of the afternoon with minor adminstration and made her way home in a mood of complete contrast to the excitement and anticipation of her morning journey.

Fortunately, Mary had been on early duty and was already home. Seeing Bridie's face, she immediately sat her down at the kitchen table and produced a pot of tea. It did not take much of her gentle probing before Bridie was recounting her day's experiences.

'Well, Bri, it's not for me to say really, but I take a pretty dim view of Neil 'phoning you like that.'

'I suppose that's just Neil,' said Bridie resignedly. 'I could have died though, with Dr Brandon witnessing that call. Oh I do so want to make a go of it. I can, can't I, Mary?'

'Of course you can, silly. He wouldn't have offered you the job if he didn't think you could do it. I mean he's a man of some experience. How old, do you think?'

'Mid-thirties I suppose. But he looks younger.'

'Well, there you are, then. He's probably worked with dozens of people and is a very good judge of ability. You've just got to give it a little time. It's all been quite a change for you, you know. And talking of change, why don't you? I'll rustle up some supper.'

Immensely cheered by Mary's combination of jollying along and good, solid, common-sense, she relaxed into a pair of familiar and well-loved jeans, an extremely floppy sweater and a pair of loafers. The two girls enjoyed a quiet domestic evening collapsed in front of the television.

She drifted off to sleep, full of determination to prove herself to Dr Brandon and not to let his attitude throw her. He certainly was a man with charisma, she thought ruefully.

The rest of the week passed in an increasingly relaxed manner. She found herself becoming more and more used to her surroundings and was introduced to department heads and the other members of the Board. Sir Rupert Gallimore turned out to be every inch a Company Chairman. She was immediately aware of his presence and sheer force of personality, but this was tempered by an innate kindliness, just discernible beneath his serious exterior.

Her commuting to and from the flat had developed almost into a routine by the end of the week and she found herself approaching the Tube journey with the air of a seasoned Londoner. In fact, it was not until Friday that she really directed her thoughts to Neil's weekend visit. Although the passage of time had mollified her anger at his thoughtless telephone call, she felt distinctly cool about his impending arrival.

Mary insisted on dragging her out on a clothes-buying

expedition on Saturday morning. She enjoyed the infor-
mal attitude of the little boutiques and shops to which
Mary took her. She made mild protests about self-
indulgence, but Mary would have none of it. By midday,
she had bought several items which, by their very
interchangeability, would provide her with several
outfits ranging from very formal to smartly casual. She
laughingly remarked to Mary that downright casual was
the least priority, since the majority of her wardrobe fell
into that category already. One slight indulgence, purchased very much with Mary's encouragement, was a
closely-cut, smooth-fitting straight dress in black silk, its
simplicity enhanced by a single scarlet rose at the shoulder. Bridie expressed some concern at the boldness of
style at the neck-line, but Mary assured that it looked
absolutely right. She made this last purchase with her
credit card, again at Mary's instigation. She insisted that
the dress was an 'investment' and laughed mischiev-
ously.

They returned to the flat at noon, indulging themselves by spending a pound each on sharing a taxi. In
high spirits, she was almost looking forward to Neil's
arrival . . .

Until she saw him sitting on the doorstep under an
almost palpable cloud of gloom. He glared at the two
girls.

'But Neil, you said you were catching an eleven
o'clock flight.'

'I caught an earlier one.'

'But why didn't you ring?'

'How was I to know you'd be gadding around London
on a spending spree.' He stared balefully at the assorted
parcels they were carrying.

Any pleasurable feelings of anticipation at the thought of seeing him evaporated. She felt an acute sense of embarrassment at Neil's peevishness and she almost had to force him to acknowledge Mary, which he did with obvious ill-humour. Mary, displaying her intelligence and diplomacy, announced the necessity to do a little food shopping and immediately went out again.

Afterwards, Bridie felt that the scene which followed was one she observed as if detached, rather than one in which she participated.

It became abundantly clear to her that Neil's motives for wanting her back with him in Aberdeen were far more to do with selfishness than with love. Strangely, she accepted this almost with relief, as though a period of intolerable waiting was over. Any display of emotion by Neil was centred solely on anger and bitterness, with no hint of sorrow.

'You must realise you've made a mistake by now. I know that head office quite well, you know. It's all high-flying whizz-kids and air conditioning. Not your scene at all.'

She had by this time resorted to silence as the only viable defence.

'Look Bridie, if you persist with this, it's the end of our relationship, you realise that?'

She looked up sadly. 'What relationship, Neil?'

He stared at her, then turned and strode from the room. The front door slammed behind him and she sat numbly at the kitchen table until she heard Mary's key.

A look from Mary's concerned eyes was all it took to release a flood of tears while her friend gently comforted her. This too passed, however, and when it was over, she experienced a feeling almost of absolution, of release. An episode in her life had drawn to a close.

# CHAPTER FOUR

THAT evening was spent reflectively at home. It had been necessary for Bridie to reassure Mary that she did not mind being left on her own. Barnaby was cooking dinner at his flat and Mary wanted Bridie to come as well, but she would have none of it, insisting that her friends made the most of a rare Saturday evening together.

In fact, she half expected that Mary would spend the night with Barnaby and this proved to be the case. She affected no surprise when her flat-mate returned mid-Sunday morning. Any comment would have been totally inappropriate, since for Mary and Barnaby to share each other completely was simply a natural extension of their love. A serenity and fulfilment seemed to emanate from Mary—and Bridie felt a quickly banished pang of envy for her friend in her happiness.

During the early part of the following week, she became aware of a sort of expectancy and suspense within Pan European House. The discreet, subdued conversations between senior executives in corridors seemed more prevalent than usual. Even Sir Rupert, with whom she travelled up in the lift one morning, exuded an air of suppressed excitement. Catching her looking at him, he smiled.

'Big week, m'dear, big week. Much afoot,' he said.

She wanted to enquire further, but they had arrived at her floor.

She would have liked to ask Dr Brandon, but felt she

should concentrate on proving her abilities in the surgery before showing interest in Company business outside her own particular role.

She wanted to make several improvements to the surgery operation and, discussing them with him, thought she detected a glint of approval in his eyes. He certainly listened to her attentively and she found herself gaining in confidence.

'Sister Stewart,' he said. 'You will find that I am only too ready to give people full responsibility where they show ability to carry it. If you feel you can improve our standards here, then please implement your ideas.' He smiled. 'You will not find me slow in criticising you if standards slip.'

She responded to his lightness of mood. 'Of that I'm sure, Doctor.'

For the first time, she held his gaze without wavering. His eyes had softened. Small lines crinkled at the corners. and the steel grey seemed to grow less cold. She still felt, however, that they were eyes which looked into her rather than upon her.

By mid-week, the air of excitement in the company had reached fever pitch, manifested in an invitation to department heads and senior executives to a cocktail reception in the large Board Room the following evening. 'During the course of the evening the chairman will make an important announcement' ran the memorandum.

Bridie, flattered by her inclusion in the function, immediately began considering what to wear. The black dress she had bought would be perfect, but she made some discreet enquiries as to how formal such occasions were. She learned from Jill that the chairman usually liked people to make an effort. This was easy for the men, who could get away with their business suits, but the ladies usually changed into something a little special.

Mary joined into the spirit of the occasion with her customary verve. 'I told you that dress was a good investment,' she bubbled. 'What about accessories?'

'I thought my black bag and . . .'

'But you've got your silver shell bag,' said Mary. 'That would be stunning with the black dress. I tell you what. You can borrow my silver sling-backs to match. We're the same shoe size. Come on. Let's have a dry run.'

There was no appeasing Mary until Bridie had put on the full outfit. She surveyed the result in the bedroom mirror. It was really quite good. She looked trim and elegant. The simplicity of the black dress suited her neat figure. The neck-line was a little daring, but certainly not vulgar.

Mary was far more enthusiastic and kept giving pronounced nods of satisfaction and approval. 'You'll knock them cold, Bridie. It's sensational.'

It was only after she had rung to book a taxi to take herself and her outfit to work in the morning that she was allowed to relax.

As the day progressed, she found herself looking forward to the evening with increasing interest. The lunch-time conversation in the company dining room was full of conjecture about the coming announcement. Two surprisingly solemn young men from Accounts dolefully predicted a take-over and a lively argument developed with the Buying Department, who were convinced it was to be a merger. She felt herself caught up in the general excitement and the afternoon seemed to drag past.

Eventually, she heard the buzz of voices and sounds of movement outside her department, which signified the departure of the administrative staff at five-thirty. She had an hour to get ready.

She had hung her dress up behind the office door. There was little enough space in the tiny washroom adjoining her room, so she left the dress hanging up while she washed and attended to her make-up. One advantage of her self-contained surgery was the privacy it afforded on occasions such as this.

Of course, a real luxury would have been a shower, she thought, as she slipped out of her uniform in front of the wash-room mirror. Filling the bowl with water, however, she enjoyed a simple wash and was soon ready to apply her make-up. She looked at the low-cut black bra into which she had changed. Yes, the dress would be a little daring, but she could carry it off. She giggled too at the sheer black tights and silky bikini briefs she was wearing. The latter were flimsy to say the least, not something she would normally wear, but a very necessary adjunct to the close fit of the dress.

She began to apply the suggestion of make-up which she preferred, taking a little more trouble than usual with her eyes. Satisfied at last, she checked her watch. Twenty minutes left. Plenty of time to step into her dress and attend to the finishing touches.

As she slipped out of the washroom, a figure emerged from her office. She realised with horror that she had forgotten to lock the outer door to her department. She stopped dead in her tracks as their eyes met. He was totally aware of her embarrassment but did not avert his gaze.

'Oh, Dr Brandon. I was just changing.' The absurd

statement came out in a rush and died. Her mouth went dry as his eyes dropped to her gently swelling breasts and plunging bra. Her arms flew across her body in a classic gesture of modesty. She felt her heart thudding as his eyes slowly travelled back to meet hers. Her whole being seemed to blush.

His eyes gleamed and a seemingly interminable silence ensued. She stood there trembling and helpless, wishing and wishing she had something to cover herself with. She certainly was not going to turn her back and flee into the washroom. How stupid to have left the outer door unlocked.

And then, suddenly, he broke the long silence. 'What is the meaning of this?' His eyes blazed with anger.

She returned his ire. 'I told you. I'm changing for the party,' she retorted. And then, rather lamely, 'There's nowhere else.'

'I see. And running round the surgery half-naked is called changing, is it?'

'You have no right . . . Please . . . I just forgot to lock the—At least have the decency to . . .' She was near to tears of humiliation now.

Her earlier sense of mischief at her risqué underwear was dissipated in the stark reality of the situation. She remembered just how wispy was the material and her cheeks flamed scarlet.

His jaw was working and he seemed about to say something. Why was he just standing there? A red mist settled over her vision. The pig, she ranted silently. As anger reasserted itself, she stepped forward, resorting finally to outright challenge. Her hands dropped to her side, fists clenched. By this time, she was uncaring, unaware even, of the revealing nature of her scanty attire, the gentle curves of her body and the whiteness of her skin.

'Will you please get out of my way.' She raged out the words, one at a time, eyebrows raised and nostrils flaring.

His transfixed expression suddenly changed and he stepped aside. She darted past, backed into her office and furiously slammed the door. She found she was trembling uncontrollably, her knees weak and quivering. She sat down on a chair, its surface a cold shock against the backs of her bare legs.

She heard the outer door to the main corridor close and she rushed out to turn the key. Leaning back against the door, she closed her eyes with relief. It was impossible to dismiss the memory of his eyes travelling intimately down over her body. As she slowly calmed, she sought to maintain her indignation at his seeing her in this way, at his frank appraisal of her femininity—but it was surprisingly difficult. But why had he been so angry? She had not committed a gross misdemeanour and most men would surely have followed their male interest with either amusement or even a fine display of gallantry—perhaps even open admiration. But he had just been angry. She shrugged these thoughts off and refocused her thoughts on dressing. At least their next meeting would be in the crowded atmosphere of the cocktail party and any awkwardness at the memory of their encounter would be easy to dilute in the social hubbub.

She smoothed on her tights and stepped into the dress. A quick trip back to the mirror to check hair and make-up and she was ready. A touch of her very special perfume on wrists and throat, then she surveyed the finished effect in the mirror and nodded a silent signal of approval at herself, firmly thrusting down the memory of her recent embarrassment.

Upstairs, the gathering was still at the polite, inhibited stage. Feeling confident that she looked her best, she moved into the throng and joined Mr Andrews, who was chatting with Jock McCabe.

'Well, Sister Stewart,' said Jock appreciatively, 'a touch of glamour is just what I need. You'd have no trouble filling your appointments book if you dressed like that on duty.'

She smiled her pleasure at his honest compliment and lack of guile.

'Seriously, you should pity the poor oil man— banished to a derrick off a desert shore, with only men and camels for company. It should be a Personnel policy to supply drill-crew comforts like Miss Stewart here. Don't you agree Mr Andrews?'

The conversation continued in this light, bantering vein and required no great effort from her, other than laughing rejoinders to Jock's endless and highly entertaining stories. She covertly examined the other people in the room.

She had judged her attire well, she observed with a sense of relief. The women were all dressed to the same degree as herself and she relaxed in the knowledge that not only did she conform to the spirit of the occasion, but also looked smart and fashionable. She was aware of several admiring glances and found she was beginning to enjoy herself. There was no sign of Dr Brandon. This surely would be an occasion he would attend. After all, his life seemed to revolve around social functions and good living. Indeed, her own life had undergone quite a change, she pondered, as she sipped what was undoubtedly a champagne cocktail of some description.

'Is this champagne mixed with orange juice?' she whispered to Jock.

'Chairman's favourite,' he replied. 'It's called Buck's Fizz. Very powerful aphrodisiac. Have another one.'

Bridie felt a good-natured desire to smack Jock's wrists and laughingly made the gesture. She changed the subject.

'What's this evening all about, Jock? Do you know? I bet you do.'

'Well, I maybe have an inkling,' he grinned boyishly. 'But the only people who really know are the Executive Board. Talking of whom . . .'

The door from the chairman's suite at the far end of the boardroom opened and several of the senior directors came in, following Sir Rupert. Bridie noticed Dr Brandon bringing up the rear. He certainly moved in high-powered circles.

Sir Rupert made his way to the head of the long, beautiful rosewood table and waited. Such was his presence in the room that conversation stilled in an instant. Even those with their backs to him became aware that something was impending. She was equally aware of Dr Brandon's tall figure, as he stood amongst, but a little aloof from, the other directors. Her heart turned over in an upwelling of embarrassment as she recalled their encounter of an hour ago. She forced her mind back to the present.

'Ladies and Gentlemen, I have just returned from a press conference at the Park Lane Hilton, where I was delighted to make the following announcement to the national and international press, television and radio news services.' Sir Rupert raised a single sheet of paper.

'Pan European is pleased to announce a major new discovery of North Sea oil. The undersea well has been "brought in" by PX 7, the company's latest and most advanced rig, operating on the furthest fringes of the Vikings Field . . .'

A cheer arose from Sir Rupert's audience. He raised his hand for silence and went on to give details of the new find's capacity and expected operational dates. He made reference to the delight expressed in government circles and by the Prime Minister, with whom he had been in touch earlier in the week.

An excited buzz of conversation ran round the room.

'That'll help the old balance of payments no end,' said Jock, still at her side, 'to say nothing of the company's prosperity.'

'You did know about the new discovery, didn't you?' said Bridie.

'Yes, I was on PX 7 when the well came in,' he said. 'The excitement was quite something, I can tell you. We were expecting a strike, but we'd been told very firmly to keep it quiet.'

'Why such a secret?'

'Something to do with the Common Market Energy Conference tomorrow—and foreign-exchange rates. All a bit above me, I'm afraid,' he grinned. 'You'd have to ask Sir Rupert about that. I'm just an engineer.'

Bridie savoured the excitement in the room. There were several poppings of champagne corks as Sir Rupert charged the glasses of his colleagues. She caught a glimpse of Dr Brandon raising his glass in congratulation, engaged in easy, relaxed conversation. She was glad of the press of people which separated her from him.

It was a good atmosphere to feel part of, she thought happily. The excitement was very much a shared one, with voices all around raised in animated conversation. She found herself drawn into a fair amount of repartee with various young men in the company. At the same time, she felt there was a lot of genuine interest in her as a person. There were many enquiries as to her background, her reasons for coming to London, how she was finding the transition, and so forth. She enjoyed this immensely, responding with equal interest in other people and was glad to find her social acceptability so easily achieved.

The passage of time appeared to accelerate and she was amazed to see a television monitor being wheeled in so that everyone could see Pan-European's announcement become public on the news. Further cheers greeted the announcer's words.

It appeared that a group of the more extrovert individuals were all for going on somewhere and extending the evening with a little supper and dancing. Largely with Jock's encouragement, she found herself being carried along with this suggestion.

'All we need is a small armada of taxis,' he said. 'I'll organise that with some of the chaps. You fetch your coat. We're off to have some fun at the Maverick. See you in reception.'

'Where's the Maverick,' she cried, but he had gone.

She hesitated. A night out in mid-week was not something she was used to. But it was a night out in London and she had caught the party mood. It would be nice to dance to a little good music and she felt confident in her dress, well able to go somewhere sophisticated. Why not? She needed to ring Mary, though. They had got into the habit of making a casserole to share on some week-day evenings and she should tell her flat-mate she was eating out.

She decided to call from one of the secretaries' offices and, entering the first, picked up a receiver. As she did so, Sir Rupert appeared in the doorway.

'That's not a direct line, my dear. You can use the personal one on my desk if you like.'

'Oh thank you, sir. I wanted to ring my flat-mate. Some of us are going dancing . . .' She followed him into his inner office.

'Are you now?' he twinkled. 'Might almost join you myself, but I have to take it easy these days, or so your medical colleagues tell me.'

He picked up his brief-case from the large desk and made towards the door. She stared blankly at the array of telephones and communicating devices on the desk.

'Use the ivory-coloured one, Sister. Have fun.' He was gone, leaving the door ajar.

She dialled the number and looked round the office. It was decorated and furnished in perfect taste. It was also perfectly enormous. She giggled and plonked herself down in the large upholstered executive chair behind Sir Rupert's desk.

Mary, perceptive as ever, detected her high spirits immediately. Bridie had to answer several questions about the party as well as explain that she might be late and would be having supper out.

'Buck's Fizz, eh?' laughed Mary. 'Just you watch it, my girl. All this fast living will be your downfall, mark my words. It'll be black coffee in the morning. Be good.' She rang off.

Bridie replaced the receiver and, on an impulse, spun herself in the enormous chair.

'Outside your normal territory, aren't you, Sister?'

The gyrating chair brought her round to see Dr Brandon framed in the doorway. His eyes had that softer quality of humour she had noticed before. He really was quite a different person when he smiled. He moved into the office.

'Sir Rupert offered the use of his direct line. I had to ring Mary.' She realised she was being defensive again. She rose to her feet and moved round the desk to retrieve her handbag.

'What an unusual bag,' he said, picking up the little shell and lightly touching the silver scallop and the silver tassle on the clasp. Perhaps he was laughing at what he considered to be an item of frippery. She felt unsure of herself.

He handed her the bag and their eyes met. He was regarding her intently.

'Sister Stewart, I feel I should apologise for my rather unnecessary display of anger earlier this evening. It must have been most embarrassing for you to be surprised in such a compromising manner.'

A fusion of awareness passed between them. She knew he was remembering how she had last appeared to him. They were both remembering. She felt her heart thudding again. It was extremely hard to maintain her composure and return his surveillance.

Suddenly he stepped forward and, reaching an arm round her waist, crushed her to him. A gasp escaped her parted lips as her head tipped back and she found her cheek pressed against his. His head was lowered into the sensitive softness of her neck. She felt his lips brush her skin and sensed again the elusive, musky fragrance of an expensive eau de toilette. Her next intake of breath was almost stifled as his mouth came down on hers. She was rigid, her arms still held away from her in shock, but slowly, against her conscious will, she felt herself melting, aware of everything about him—his cool lips, the surprisingly fine tracery of his eyelashes closed on tanned cheeks, the fierce pressure of his arms and the innate strength of his body. She closed her eyes and found her arms weakening and coming to rest on the hard strength of his.

In an instant, he had stepped back again. She stood limply, one hand reaching out for the edge of the desk, trying to catch her breath. Her mind span, like a dizzy ferris wheel.

Again, the force of his gaze assailed her. She tried to return it.

'You've dropped your bag,' he said thickly, stooping to reach to the floor. He held it open with one hand and dropped back some items which had tumbled out.

'Surprising what a silver shell can hold,' he murmured, with a return of his indolent manner. He snapped the bag shut, turned and left her.

She stood staring at the door through which he had vanished. An overwhelming sense of unreality pervaded her. It was a feeling compounded by the muffling opulence of her surroundings—the low ceiling, the deep pile carpet, the luxurious furniture and subtle lighting.

Seeking the reality of the outside world, she moved to the windows forming one corner of the room and looked out. The office was on the top floor and she felt suspended above the scene below. It was as if she was observing another world, the streams of light and the traffic below separated from her by both distance and silence, with the double layers of glass.

What an extraordinary man he was. The memory of his lips on hers was sharply defined. She was disturbed at the way her emotions had reeled. Perhaps it was the champagne? After all, that was something to which she was by no means used. She nodded to herself, remembering the validity of Mary's advice, and began to relax. She was more than a match for Dr Brandon and his cavalier ways. Maybe she was not as brittle and sophisticated as his London playmates, thank goodness, but she certainly was not to be trifled with. She smiled wryly. This would teach her to keep her defences up. You needed to develop a kind of protective outer shell in order to survive. It seemed to be one of the most important aspects of London life.

She realised she was staring at herself, her reflection in the dark glass superimposed on the London skyline. Yes, she would cope quite adequately with this new life-style. One hand went up absently to her hair. She remembered the dancing expedition and sped down to collect her coat from the surgery.

Jock was jumping up and down in reception.

'There you are! Come on. We managed to get hold of the last taxi in London.' She was bustled into a cab already containing a highly entertaining marketing manager from the party. He was escorting one of the market research girls with one of the grandest displays of old-world chivalry Bridie had ever witnessed. In fact, so outrageous was his waggishness, that she firmly refused to get out of the cab when they arrived at the Thames Embankment and he airily announced that the final stage of their journey was to be waterborne. She looked at Jock helplessly.

'Come on, Sister Stewart, it's true,' he grinned reassuringly. 'That's the Maverick, over there.' He pointed to what looked like a paddle steamer, dressed fore and aft with coloured lights, moored some considerable distance off in the waterway.

'But how . . . ?' she said uncertainly, stepping on to the pavement.

'Quite civilised, my girl—and *quite* safe. Fully approved by the Greater London Council.'

With Jock's firm hand under her elbow, she soon found herself aboard a glass-roofed launch full of chattering young revellers. A brief surge across the tideway, with an exciting glimpse of brilliantly-lit buildings reflecting back in the dark waters, and she was stepping into a world of infectious rhythms, pulsing strobe lights and chattering voices.

'Come on, let's find the others,' said Jock, leading the way into the crowd.

She had always enjoyed dancing. As a little girl she had excelled in the traditional reels and was always on her feet to the last at Hogmanay. With growing up had come the pleasure of dancing with a partner, whether in a more formal ballroom sense or, as now, less inhibitedly, to disco music.

An endless stream of partners demanded her attention. She was grateful for Jock's insistence that she should fuel her physical reserves with something called a Maverick Half-Pounder—which turned out to be truly delicious American style hamburger with the most delectable garnishings. She declined more offers of wine, never being a girl who took anything more than the odd drink or two. Anyway, she preferred the natural stimulation of the music and the company.

Dancing a slow number with the raffish marketing manager who had so ably entertained them in the taxi, she noticed the tall figure of Dr Brandon on the opposite side of the floor. He was dancing with Britt.

'Our Dr Brandon's really getting stuck into Britt,' grinned her partner rather vulgarly, catching her glance. 'Quite a lad, our Gregory.'

'So I see,' she mouthed coldly, for there was no doubt as to the truth of his observation, even if crudely put.

The girl's arms were twined round his neck and, as they moved to the dreamy beat, she could see that his head was bent down, his face hidden in the flowing blonde hair. He must have said something, for her head went back and Bridie remembered the gushing laugh.

'He likes the dolce vita, I take it,' enquired Bridie in icy tones.

'Bit of a dark horse, really,' said her partner. 'Don't see much of him around the company. Deals with the directors mostly—but then I'm a healthy type, don't often need doctors. Mind you, I think I'm developing a need for intensive medical attention. Perhaps you could give me a thorough examination later on, Sister?'

His insistence on harmless flirting occupied all her attention. In fact he started off quite an evening's entertainment and she smilingly found herself fending off exhortations to cool fevered brows, monitor rapid pulse rates, cure irregular heartbeats and so forth, from the assorted company of grinning jesters and laughing girls. At last, someone made a reference to the rest of the working week and the party began to break up.

Yawning, she found herself on the launch, speeding

shorewards. Her coat hung round her shoulders, held there by a friendly arm from Jock.

'Quite an evening, Bridie,' he smiled down at her.

'Mm—really great,' she replied and patted her shoulder.

He insisted that they share a cab. Her flat was on the way to his hotel.

'My last night in the old country. It'll be all sand and camels from tomorrow.'

'Poor Jock,' she said, in mock sympathy.

Pausing at the first set of Embankment traffic lights, their cab was overtaken by a low-slung, white car. As it drew up alongside, she recognised Britt's profile in the passenger seat and, looking down past the girl's short hemline, observed a familiar, elegantly clothed sleeve, a Rolex Oyster watch and a slim hand resting nonchalantly on the stub gear lever. The car powered away from them as the lights changed, a sleek, potent thing, effortlessly surging forward along its unchallenged track.

'Nice set of wheels, that,' said Jock. 'Porsche 924 Carrera. About £20,000 worth of machinery.' He was unaware of the driver's identity.

She smiled to herself and leant companionably into Jock's encircling arm. 'A playboy's car, would you say?' she enquired innocently.

'Very much so.' A pause. 'Mind you, a playboy with very good taste,' he added.

At her flat, she turned as Jock leaned across to give her a goodnight kiss on the cheek and squeezed his hand.

'Have a good trip, Jock. And watch out for those dusky maidens. I'll buy you a pint when you get back.'

'You're on, Bridie,' he laughed and was gone in a rattle of cab engine.

Slipping thankfully into bed, she quickly reached that plane of delicious dreaminess that just prefaces oblivion. It was a dreaminess invaded only by a memory of cool, firm hands pressing her forward to masterful, expert lips which were confidently claiming hers.

# CHAPTER FIVE

MARY's theatrical antics in the morning caused Bridie much amusement. She opened proceedings by gently tapping on the bedroom door and entering on tip-toe with a cup of coffee in one hand and a tube of Alka-Seltzer in the other. These were raised enquiringly. Bridie shook her head laughingly.

'Perhaps an ice pack?' whispered Mary in sepulchral tones.

Bridie picked up a pillow and made as if to throw it.

'OK, OK, so Cinders escaped from the ball un-scathed. Any Prince Charmings?'

Bridie outlined the events of the evening. Somehow, those involving Dr Brandon were left out and she con-centrated more on the cocktail party and the night out at the Maverick.

'The Maverick, eh? Very trendy. Honestly, Bri, you've only been in London a couple of weeks and you're hitting the highest spots already. Who brought you home then?'

She described Jock. It was easier talking about the friendly Scotsman than Dr Brandon, who she had de-cided was nothing more than a superficial philanderer. The memory of her encounters with him was still unset-tling however, and she did not want to describe them to Mary. She even found herself telling white lies about how she had prepared for the cocktail party and the events that had taken place while she was getting changed. Omitting an embarrassing confrontation with Greg Brandon was like leaving a gaping chasm in the story—noticeable by its very absence—but she could find no reason for this reticence. It remained a story she withheld. For the time being, anyway.

She was aware of a strange quality about those events. As if some half-remembered dream had continued the story during the night. She recalled waking up once or twice with an image of him in her mind—an image which she had angrily thrust away. She became aware that Mary was looking at her quizzically.

'I said, I saw the television news about Pan European. Was that what the party was all about?'

'Oh, yes. Yes. Good news isn't it?'

Mary studied her intently. 'I'm sure you're not telling me all, my girl.' This was said in tones of exaggerated seriousness. 'There is a new man in your life. Admit it. And it's not Jock,' she added.

'Oh, Mary, don't be silly.' Bridie swung her legs out of bed.

'Withholding vital information, eh? I am your guide and mentor in wicked London. Spurn me at your peril. It'll end in tears, mark my words.'

Bridie shooed her irrepressible flat-mate out of the room and began to prepare for the day ahead. She banished all thoughts of the previous evening from her mind.

Rattling to work on the Tube, she felt surprisingly lively, considering she had had only six hours' sleep. This was not the case with all her colleagues. One of the attractive girls in reception, whom she had noticed dancing energetically at the Maverick, looked decidedly wan. Through the morning, she found herself dispensing a fair number of analgesics and quantities of sympathy to several sore heads. Of Dr Brandon there was no sign.

She was sitting in her office around noon, inserting extra data into the Kardex system, when the internal phone shrilled insistently.

'Sister Stewart, can you come up, immediately? It's Sir Rupert. He's complaining of feeling unwell.' Britt's normally honeyed tones had an unusual ring of urgency.

Bridie hurried to the lift and pressed the button for the Executive Floor. Britt was on the telephone in the outer office.

'Yes, yes, Greg, two blocks away. Understood.' She paused. 'Yes, Sister Stewart is here. Right.' She replaced the receiver. 'I managed to contact Dr Brandon on his car phone. He's just turning in off Park Lane. He'll be here in a minute. He'll know what to do.'

Bridie ignored this slight on her resourcefulness and hurried in to the Chairman's office. Sir Rupert was sitting back in one of his easy chairs. His eyes were closed and he looked pale. She took his wrist in one hand and felt his brow with the other. 'How are you feeling, sir,' she questioned.

'A little peaky m'dear, a little peaky.'

Britt interrupted. 'Sir Rupert has this lunch arranged with the Secretary of State for Energy and it's been on his mind.'

'I think we could do with a blanket from surgery. I wonder, could you fetch one? A red one—from one of the examination rooms.' For a moment, it seemed as though there would be a battle of wills between the two girls. But Britt nodded and went.

Bridie turned back to Sir Rupert. She slipped a thermometer into his mouth and checked his pulse. The
results of these two investigations indicated nothing
untoward and she was puzzled.

'Can you tell me how you felt, sir?'

'Bit dizzy, really. Room started to go round. Thump-
ing headache, I'm afraid.'

'Well, let's make you comfortable for a start.' She
deftly undid his collar, pulled a coffee table over, placed
a cushion on it and lifted up his feet.

'Thank you, m'dear.'

The door flew open. Dr Brandon gave her a curt nod
and moved over to the chairman, pulling a stethoscope
from the medical bag he was carrying.

'Temperature's normal, doctor—and pulse—'

A raised hand imperiously interrupted her. He gave
no sign of having just made a headlong dash from his car,
and looked as immaculate as ever.

'Would you help Sir Rupert off with his jacket, Sister.
And loosen his shirt.'

She complied and waited as he applied the stethoscope and listened intently, his lips set in a purposeful
line.

She could not help noticing that Sir Rupert's colour
was improving. In fact, he really looked quite normal
now. Dr Brandon's expression remained set, however,
and he proceeded with a swiftly efficient examination.
She somehow sensed that she was inhibiting him by her
presence. A doctor would normally be asking questions
of his patient, but he was curiously taciturn. He walked
across to Sir Rupert's desk and, taking a slim gold pen
from his inside pocket, scribbled something on a memo-

slip. He folded the paper and handed it to her.

'Sister, would you be so good as to collect this medication from your surgery?' She made to open the slip and read it.

'As quickly as you can, please.'

'Oh yes, of course, Doctor.'

She hurriedly left the office, almost bumping into Britt, returning with the blanket. The door closed behind her. Alone in the outer office, she opened the slip of paper and glanced down. To her utter amazement, she realised she was looking at a request for a simple analgesic, of the type she had been handing out to hangover cases all morning. All that ailed the Chairman was merely the result of too much champagne the night before. And as for that charlatan of a doctor, he was simply pandering to the whims of a hypochondriac! She turned back to the door in a white-hot fury. How dare he treat her as a simple messenger!

She made to re-enter the office, but the closed door was a silent barrier. How cosy! The three of them in there, all indulging in a tableau of mutual admiration. Well, if these were her duties for some of the time, then so be it. She turned, tight-lipped, and embarked on her errand.

Returning a few minutes later with the tablets, she found she was still seething. Greg Brandon was merely a lover of fast living, fast cars and fast women. In fact, he was an insult to their profession. Bridie had always had some reservations about private medicine and, of course, she had been deeply influenced by the unstinting vocational devotion of her father. This so-called Company Medical Adviser was nothing more than a confidence man, earning an opulent living from the vapourish

imaginings of an over-privileged captain of industry.
Why, he was not even a full-time medical adviser. She
had never once seen him in the office early or late—
and the middle of the day seemed largely given over to
lunch.

She checked this silent railing with an effort. She did
not feel it was in her character and she had always taken
pride in her self-control. The worthwhile side of her post
far outweighed these wet-nurse aspects. Only that morning a memorandum had come from the purchasing
director, co-opting her on to a committee to assess the
performance of a new type of thermal clothing for use on
the rigs. She would be required to set out a matrix of
physical monitoring checks and generally supervise and
interpret the inflow of data from out in the field. This was
a project which she would enjoy and to which she could
contribute. This was the sort of responsibility and challenge which she wanted.

She felt compelled to knock before re-entering the
office. There was a feeling that she had interrupted a
deep discussion, for all three were regarding her silently.
Dr Brandon turned away and she saw him replacing an
opthalmoscope in his bag. She smothered a desire to
enquire why an opthalmoscope was necessary to diag-
nose simple symptoms of over-indulgence. It seemed
that the doctor threw himself into his role with great
enthusiasm, right down to his demeanour of heavy
concern. But then it was a small price to pay for the
life-style he enjoyed. She made a great effort to conceal
her dislike and handed him the anodyne he had requested.

'The medication you required, Doctor,' she said
coldly.

'Sir Rupert should take them now.' He busied himself with packing his medical bag.

She poured the Chairman a glass of water from his desk carafe.

'Britt, you'll get on to the Ministry as we've agreed—and cancel the table at my club.'

'Yes, Sir Rupert.' Britt withdrew into the outer office.

'And have a light lunch sent up from the company dining room, Mr Chairman,' said Dr Brandon. 'I think you can allow yourself an hour or two's rest. You're not receiving that trade delegation until three o'clock, I think you said. I'll tell Britt to block all calls until then.'

'Thanks, my boy,' Sir Rupert sighed and, catching Bridie's eyes upon him, smiled wearily. 'He keeps telling me I'm overdoing things. Now and again I fear he's right.'

Bridie nodded. She had come across many hypochondriacs in her nursing career. In her experience, proffering sympathy was rarely a wise treatment, since they seemed to absorb it like insatiable sponges. However, her professional approach was inevitably compromised by the doctor's presence. And indeed, Sir Rupert did look rather lost and vulnerable. She patted his hand and, remembering the blanket, tucked it round his legs and made him comfortable.

'Now, do as Dr Brandon says, Sir Rupert. A short snooze will see you right. If you need anything, I shall be down in my surgery.'

'Thank you, my dear.' Bridie saw a flicker of genuine appreciation in the Chairman's eyes. Ah well, nurses in need were always nurses indeed, no matter how serious or trivial their patients' ills, she thought, remembering the ethics of her profession.

She was aware of another pair of eyes upon her. He held the door open. As they moved into the corridor, he paused. 'A word with you, Sister. In here will do.' He opened the door to the empty Board Room and, depositing his bag, sat down on the edge of the table, one leg dangling languidly.

She was acutely aware that they were alone together. Even in the spaciousness of the Board Room, there seemed an absurd air of charged intimacy. It was not surprising that he enjoyed such success with women. She found reassurance in the thought that she was not to become one of his prizes. And yet, he was a man of such abrupt changes of mood. On occasion, he displayed all the qualities of a competent, responsible medical man. If the circumstances of Sir Rupert's case had not been so ludicrous, she could at least have afforded him her professional respect.

'About Sir Rupert.' His eyes were serious. Indeed, there was no trace of artificiality about him at all. But surely he was not going to persist with this travesty of the chairman's malaise? They were not talking in front of the children now. Was he going to further insult her intelligence by continuing the charade with a member of his own profession? She waited unbelievingly.

'I want you at all times to be contactable by Sir Rupert's secretary. If you leave the building for any reason, you must let Britt know and give her a contact telephone number. It is important always to be near a telephone during normal working hours; that is, nine until five-thirty. Other arrangements exist outside those times.' His tones were clipped and precise.

She stared at him. She could hardly believe her ears. This was fawning upon the chairman to the point of servility.

'You are to carry your bleeper at all times. And no switching it off in the lunch break.'

'I assure you, Dr Brandon . . .'

'For example, where is it now?'

She realised angrily that she had left it on her desk. When she was sitting down, it dug uncomfortably into her ribs if she wore it in its proper place on her waist-band.

'Your predecessor clipped it here.' Amazingly, he had read her thoughts. 'You'll find the clip will hold quite securely.' He reached out and caught the edge of her apron top between finger and thumb. She felt his fingers brush lightly against her.

'Right, then?' He looked at her, as if inviting questions, his mouth curved in a sardonic smile, one eyebrow raised. For a moment she wanted to provoke him into admitting his obsequious approach to the chairman, but the moment passed and she nodded vaguely.

'May see you later, then, Sister.' He was gone in a lean, flowing movement of immaculate tailoring. The door clicked itself smoothly shut.

What an infuriating mixture of moods he was. Here was a man who waxed hot then cold, domineering then friendly, hypocritical then sincere. She clenched her fists in frustration. The effect of his mercurial nature on her was quite alarming. In fact, she had been all set to vent her opinions upon him in no uncertain manner and he had de-fused her completely by picking on her silly bleeper.

There was something about Dr Gregory Brandon that made her over-sensitive and insecure, something which pushed her constantly back onto the defensive. It was an effect she had not experienced from any man before and it was extremely disquieting. Every instinct in her young body warned her that she must keep a safe distance between them. Arms' length at least.

The days passed and she threw herself into her responsibilities whole-heartedly. She was delighted to find that her opinions and training were needed for many things outside the day-to-day running of the surgery. She found herself drawn into a number of projects, ranging from industrial safety to the design of drilling-platform sickbays. Although she found many of the discussions ranged beyond her scope, there were occasions where she had a real role to play and found herself able to make her points confidently and forcibly.

To her immense surprise she realised that she was even being lobbied by the sales director of a protective clothing company. He apparently valued her influence within Pan European and invited her to lunch at a particularly attractive French restaurant in Covent Garden. Although she found his praises of his company's products a little less than fascinating, she found herself enjoying the meal. She had felt it necessary to shop for a smart business suit and a pair of classic court shoes which she could wear on occasions such as this. She kept her spare wardrobe in the surgery suite but, since that first occasion of changing from her uniform, always made sure the outer door was firmly locked.

Catching a glimpse of herself in a mirror-tiled wall, she was conscious that she looked smart and fashionable in the pleasant surroundings of the restaurant. Her companion had said the place was designed by a particularly well-known man, who also influenced a famous chain of contemporary furniture shops. Apparently his work was often featured in the glossy, monthly magazines. She had discovered that she was beginning to be a little more adventurous with menus and had chosen an excellent avocado vinaigrette, followed by a delicious sea-food dish. Waiters too held no terrors for her now. One simply had to be courteous and clear in one's requests.

She could not say this for her companion, however, for with his rapid imbiding of wine came an unnecessary amount of officiousness at the quality of the service. He then almost spoilt the meal by making remarks to her about the lack of understanding he received from his wife. Bridie sensed that his next move would be an invitation to a cosy little dinner *à deux*. She adroitly turned the conversation to the need for her return to the surgery and a convenient cab eventually saved the situation. These business lunches needed care if you were a single girl, she smiled wryly. This was one story she certainly *would* relate to Mary.

Sitting in the back of the cab, she felt a happy sense of self-assurance. The busy life in the capital's streets excited her and she felt she was becoming a part of it. She enjoyed the challenge of her job and reflected that the widening of horizons she had hoped for was beginning to happen. Not that she had aspirations of becoming a tough career woman, but it was satisfying to set new goals and begin to achieve them.

Pausing in her office to check the afternoon diary before donning her uniform, she heard the outer door crash open. She rushed out of her office to see a white-faced young man leaning weakly against the open door, his face twisted with pain.

'Sorry Sister, but I've got this terrible stomach ache. I wonder if you could give me something.'

With a huge effort, he stood away from the door and, for a moment, looked as if he was going to faint. She ran forward and caught his arm.

'Come along. Let's have a look at you.'

He moved forward and, with a groan, pressed his other hand to his abdomen. She led him gently into an examination cubicle and motioned him to lie down. He did so, stretching his legs out straight at first, but then drew them up in obvious pain.

'Right, let's have a look now. It's Robert from Buying isn't it?' She remembered him as a management trainee member of one of the committees. She popped a thermometer into his mouth and loosened his collar. His pulse was high and temperature above normal. It could be a case of food-poisoning.

'What did you have for lunch?'

'Nothing since breakfast, Sister. Couldn't face anything.'

'Let's have a look at your tum.' She unbuttoned his clothing and ran light fingers down over his lower abdomen.

'No, just relax. I won't hurt,' she reassured as she felt him tense. Everything was stretched taut, like a drum. 'Tell me if you feel anything.' She applied the gentlest of pressures and he yelped with pain.

'Sorry, Robert. Bit tender there, eh?' She stepped back and pursed her lips. 'Have you had these pains before?'

'Well, yes, Sister, but never this bad. It's been getting worse all morning. I didn't think I was going to make it up the stairs to see you.'

'Don't worry, Robert. We'll soon sort you out. Now you just stay quiet for a minute. Yes, lie like that if it's easier.' He had turned on his side with his knees drawn up. She pulled a blanket up over him and hurried back to her office. She picked up a telephone and dialled Britt's number.

'Do you know Dr Brandon's whereabouts?' she asked quickly.

'Who's calling?' came the faintly bored reply.

'It's Sister Stewart and I want the doctor urgently.'

'Oh, I think he's still at lunch . . .'

'What? At three o'clock?' Bridie erupted.

'I can find out if you like—'

'Yes, please do. And when you do, tell him I've a case of acute appendicitis down here. It'll probably be peritonitis by the time he gets back from lunch.' She crashed the receiver down.

She returned to Robert. He could not have heard the conversation, but he looked distinctly worse. Small droplets of perspiration clung to his brow and his face was completely devoid of colour. She made a decision.

Returning to her office, she made several telephone calls. The first summoned an ambulance. With the second, she was able to contact Mary at St Clements—which happened to be Pan European's nearest hospital—and asked her to warn their casualty department of the nature of her emergency. Finally she called down to reception, telling them to send the ambulance men directly up in the lift—and have the chauffeurs clear any Company cars which were blocking the drive-in to the front entrance.

The ambulance seemed an age. She sat with her young

patient, gently holding his hand. He squeezed it with such pressure, as the paroxysms of pain gripped him, that it felt as if her bones would crack. She had taken in a small bowl of water and a pad of lint which she used to cool his forehead.

Her intuition led her to distract his thoughts by references to little, inconsequential matters, always a good policy with people in stress states.

At last the ambulance men arrived. They had the good sense to bring their stretcher up with them and, with practised and easy skill, they soon had Robert installed upon it.

'You're coming too, Sister?' He looked up.

She hesitated briefly. 'Of course, Robert,' she replied, catching an affirmatory nod from the ambulance man.

They sped to one of the lifts. Thank goodness for Pan European luxury, for it was large enough to take the stretcher flat. Robert looked helpless, down there on the low-slung trolley. She crouched down to still the look of apprehension in his eyes.

They swept out through reception. She remembered to ask one of the receptionists to inform Britt of her whereabouts. She was determined not to give the absent Dr Brandon any cause to criticise *her* professional standards, even though she would have plenty to say about *his* lack of availability in a real emergency. Not that she really needed him.

A chauffeur cleared a gap in the passing traffic and, in an instant, they were on their way, lights flashing and siren blaring. She had witnessed the skill of ambulance drivers in Edinburgh and Aberdeen, but it was nothing, compared with the density of London conditions. A disorientating blur of passing vehicles assailed her as she looked into the cab through the partition window— buses, cabs, cars, lorries flew past as the driver tore through the traffic, with a controlled disregard for the rules of the road.

In moments, they were wheeling into Casualty at St Clements. A team were ready for her and she was relieved to see Robert smoothly absorbed into the efficiency of the hospital. Sipping a cup of coffee in the waiting-room later, she looked up in surprise to see Barnaby and Mary coming towards her.

'Pretty good diagnosis of yours, Bridie. A real flare-up. You don't often see an appendix take off like that, but when they do . . .' He grinned.

'You're operating, then?'

'Yes, as soon as we can. We've given him sedation now. He's much more comfortable. Oh—he's worried about informing his parents. I said you'd probably take care of that.'

'I think he's a bit smitten,' added Mary. 'You've obviously made quite an impression as a ministering angel.'

Bridie smiled and said she should be getting back and would get in touch with Robert's parents.

Quite a day, she thought, climbing into the second cab of the afternoon. She glanced at her watch. As with many emergencies, the sequence of happenings had compressed into a very short space of time, for it was four o'clock. All in all, she felt she had coped with the situation very well. Especially with the lack of support from her so-called superior. She paid off the cab and went in through the swing doors.

'Is Robert all right, Sister?' One of the reception girls

looked concerned. 'What was it? We've all been very worried. He looked dreadful as you took him out to the ambulance.'

'An erupting appendix,' smiled Bridie reassuringly. 'He'll be as right as rain in a few days.'

The girl looked relieved. 'Is there anything I can do?'

'Well yes, I need his parents' telephone number. I suppose I can get it from Personnel. Or perhaps . . .' There was a faint pink tinge to the girl's cheeks. Bridie smiled at her own intuition again. She had been sure she had noticed Robert in the girl's company the previous evening at the Maverick.

'Well, I think I might have it here.' The girl dipped into her hand-bag below desk level and jotted a number down on her pad.

'Thank you. That's certainly saved me a search.' Bridie started towards the lift. 'Oh, he won't be in much condition for visitors for a while. I would think tomorrow evening would be the earliest. Shall I let you know his progress?'

The girl's pink cheeks burgeoned into a bright red. 'Oh yes, thank you, Sister,' she blurted.

Bridie concealed a smile. It was true, she thought. The whole world did love a lover.

As the lift arrived, there was a minor commotion outside, a protesting squeal of tyres. A tall figure appeared in the swing doors and strode across the reception area to where she held her finger on the 'door open' button. The doors slid closed behind them.

'I understand there's been an emergency. My message-handling service had trouble contacting me . . .'

She regarded him disdainfully. The difficulty had

probably been in tracking him down to some expensive restaurant or other.

'. . . although, judging by your casual attire, the emergency can't have been too severe,' he added sarcastically.

She realised that she was of course still wearing the smartly tailored suit she had changed into for lunch. Unbelievably, he was going to take her to task for being out of uniform. Her jaw gaped in total amazement. 'You have the nerve, the cheek, the unmitigated gall to suggest I should have delayed calling an ambulance— wasted time putting on a uniform—it was an acute case of appendicitis—*and* I was right—*and* where were you I might ask?' Her sense of outrage obliterated everything. She was unaware that he had stepped back in shock at this tirade.

'It may not have been such a crucial emergency as Sir Rupert's,' this said with heavy irony. 'But the lad was in great pain and I could have done with some professional guidance about pain-killers.'

'Sister Stewart . . .'

'It seems to me,' she rushed on headlong, 'that our way of working together is perfect. I'll worry about the little things, like a case of impending burst appendix and you concern yourself with the big things—like Sir Rupert's dyspepsia.'

The lift doors opened and she realised it was her floor.

To those awaiting the lift, the effect must have been akin to the curtains opening on a highly dramatic scene in a play, for they were both stock still, regarding each other fixedly. His expression had remained one of shock and hers one of angry frustration, her head thrown back, eyes flashing.

As she left him in the lift and stalked down the corridor, she felt his eyes burning into her back—even after the lift doors had closed.

# CHAPTER SIX

IN THE calm of the evening, she began to feel some remorse for her outburst. Mary was working a late duty, so she had the flat to herself. She would have welcomed the benefit of Mary's counsel. 'Well, you've really done it this time, my girl,' she said to herself. There was nothing worth watching on television and she had resorted to a sort of mindless flicking through magazines whilst nibbling at some cheese and crispbread.

She could not understand her lack of self-control with him. It was undeniably true that he should be contactable in any emergency and right had certainly been on her side. But it was no excuse for losing her temper like that and she felt very annoyed with herself. Heavens, he may even have been totally ignorant of what had happened with Robert. That willowy, decorative female, Britt, had very little sense of reality and could quite easily have bungled the messages.

And so she went on, alternately dwelling on his shortcomings and then finding excuses for them. He really was the most infuriating person she had ever worked with. She kept remembering the expression on his face when she had let fly—almost one of hurt.

Walking into her surgery the next morning, she found, to her amazement, six red roses neatly arranged in her office vase. A note was clipped to the open page of her diary.

'My sincere apologies for my unthinking remark yesterday. I see you are free at coffee time. Perhaps I might join you—there is a project I wish to discuss.

                                            G.B.'

She leaned over her desk to smell the flowers. They were absolutely beautiful—as fresh as could be. Their fragrance filled the room, the vibrant colour contrasting dramatically with their clinical surroundings. She sat down in her chair and stared at them. They must have been put there very early. What a man of surprises he was. And now of course she really regretted the scene in the lift. She would certainly need to make amends for that; in fact, more than that, she *wanted* to make amends. She felt a sense of anticipation, unusually intense.

At least she would give him no cause to disapprove of her appearance this morning. She took particular care, checking herself in the cloakroom mirror. She had not put on any lipstick today but, on an impulse, fished in her bag and applied some. In the same impulse she took out her precious bottle of Cabriole perfume and dabbed the minutest hint on the inside of her wrists.

A tour of the surgery and examination rooms satisfied her that everything was in order on that front and she settled down at her desk to study some field data on the protective clothing tests. She did not hear the outer door open and gave a start when his tall figure entered her office.

'Oh, Dr Brandon, good morning.'

'Good morning, Sister Stewart. May I?' He indicated a chair in front of her desk.

'Er, yes. Please.' This display of courtesy was a little

unnerving. The situation was exacerbated by the vase of flowers which stood between them on the desk. Neither of them actually looked at it, but each was aware of its presence. She even thought she detected a faintly amused gleam in his eye as they regarded each other. She took a deep breath and plunged ahead.

'It was very nice of you. They're beautiful. Thank you,' she said, struggling to control the faint pink in her cheeks. 'You really shouldn't have. The apology should have come from me. I should not have spoken to you as I did.'

'Nor I to you,' he said. 'I heard the full story later. You acted impeccably and deserve every commendation. I take it the young man's OK?'

'Yes.' She was thankful to get on to a safer topic of conversation. 'There have been no complications. He's rather dopey this morning, after surgery of course, but absolutely fine. I have some friends at St Clements who are keeping a special eye on him.' She explained about Mary and Barnaby.

'Excellent—and his parents?'

'Spoke to them yesterday. They're visiting him this afternoon.'

'Well, you seem to have covered everything. And as for our little altercation, let's put it down to a lack of communication. I really wasn't aware of what had happened, Bridie, and I apologise.' He leaned forward and touched her hand.

She found the combination of his genuine smile, his use of her Christian name and the lightness of his hand on hers somewhat heady. His eyes held hers and again she felt them looking into her, but this time she was looking into his as well. It was almost as if some inner understanding passed between them. She dismissed this ludicrous notion vehemently.

He cleared his throat noisily. 'Right then, how about some coffee?'

'It's only from the machine I'm afraid.' Good heavens, she was almost twinkling at him, remembering their last exchange about coffee.

'That'll be fine,' he said airily.

Glad of the diversion, she took a couple of coins from her desk drawer and made for the door. She was very self-conscious as she rose, with his eyes upon her, but she remembered the care she had taken with her appearance and was sure her uniform was absolutely perfect. Why, she had even clipped her personal bleeper to her apron front as he had asked.

Returning a minute or two later, she found his mood had changed to one of brisk practicality. He was poring over an architect's plan which he had unrolled on her desk. The vase of flowers had been used unceremoniously to hold down one end of the roll. She was very aware of the square set of his shoulders and the tilt of his head as he scrutinised the plan. He took the proffered coffee and sipped it. She waited patiently.

'Well, Sister Stewart, this is a plan for a medical wing in a new shore complex the company is planning to build at Skavanger in Norway.'

'Skavanger?'

'Yes, the new discoveries made by PX 7 in Vikings Field are just the beginning. We're really on the brink of another huge breakthrough. But all of this is very confidential. You see, Sir Rupert must keep this sort of information restricted. It's all tied up with corporation taxes and Government subsidies. I certainly don't pretend to understand all the implications.' He smiled ruefully, 'What it does mean, though, is that the company needs another shore installation like Aberdeen, but on the Norwegian side of the North Sea. And it's the medical services wing of the installation which concerns us.'

'Us?' said Bridie.

'Yes, Sister. I need your help. Because of the confidential nature of this project, we cannot involve any but a small group of people at Head Office. Such a group needs very special selection. I was very interested in the comments you made in Aberdeen when I interviewed you, regarding service improvements to the centre there. I believe we can implement many of your ideas at the Skavanger complex.'

He turned his attention back to the plan, a lean, sensitive hand gently tugging at an earlobe as he scanned the scales and elevations on the blue-print. He was totally unconscious of the effect his words were having upon her.

Her heart bounded. This was what she had come to London for! She knew she had a contribution to make to projects such as these—vital projects, important to the nation's future. She felt an elation almost out of proportion to the situation. And yet, to have such confidence shown in her by this strange, mercurial man was hauntingly exciting. She gave herself a mental shake and forced her attention back to earth. She studied the plan, leaning forward, very conscious of his face a few inches from hers. An immaculately manicured finger pointed out features on the plan.

'Medical facilities are ground floor of course. Access to the main building here—and here. Ambulance and transport bay here. Oh, and ramps duplicating every ground level kerb and step.' His enthusiasm was disarming.

She pursed her lips, a little frown appearing on her intelligent, pretty face. 'It looks very good. The trouble is, I don't really follow these blue-print plans very well. It's a bit difficult to tell . . .'

He straightened abruptly. 'I quite agree, Sister Stewart. The shell of the building already exists and certain of the internal load-bearing partitions are in position. However, the final touches of lay-out can only be solved by personal attention. How's your diary over the next few days? I think we should fly out to inspect the site.'

In something of a daze she checked—and found the next two or three days were relatively light, certainly well within the capabilities of a temporary agency nurse. She gave a sort of mumbled assent.

'Excellent. I'll have Britt arrange us a flight. I take it you've a passport? Would you be able to leave tomorrow? Afternoon 'plane to Oslo, stop over, then local flight to Skavanger, overnight stay, then back on Friday. OK?'

She nodded dumbly. He rolled up the plan and tucked it under his arm.

'Britt can also give you the number of a nursing agency we've used before so that you can book a temp. I'll arrange a stand-in for me in case of emergencies.'

And in an instant, he was gone, leaving her with that sense of breathlessness to which she was fast becoming accustomed.

It was practically impossible to force her attention back to her work and her mind kept jumping ahead to the coming trip.

Britt telephoned through during the afternoon with the flight details. 'It's SAS Flight 262, 15.40 from Heathrow, check-in one hour before. Dr Brandon will meet you here at two p.m. precisely. He'll take his car out to the airport.' Bridie was certain she could hear a note of envy in the girl's voice.

'Oh, Dr Brandon suggests you take adequate warm clothing. It's rather cold in Norway at this time of year,' she added unnecessarily. 'There is a company field clothing allowance, so I daresay you'll be able to buy something suitable. Personnel will give you all the details.' She rang off without waiting for a reply.

Bridie tightened her lips in irritation. Britt had made it sound as if she were a completely untravelled novice. She had not been abroad much, it was true, other than a package holiday or two and a school trip. But she was no stranger to a rigorous climate. She felt like ringing back this soft Londoner and telling her that Scotland and Norway had a great deal in common, not least of which were similar cold winters.

She had brought her fleece-lined three-quarter length sheepskin coat down from Glenairton, and also her walking boots and warm trousers. She dug these out of her travelling trunk that evening, to the accompaniment of excited questions from Mary.

'Gosh, you lucky thing. You're fast becoming an international executive—and you'll have that attractive boss of yours as company for a whole forty-eight hours.'

'Oh Mary, don't be silly. Now what have I done with my passport?'

Early the next morning found her at Lillywhites in Piccadilly, hurriedly adding a few vital items to her wardrobe. With the Company allowance, she purchased a beautiful oiled wool Icelandic sweater, which the assistant said would keep anyone warm, even at minus fifty, and a quilted blue husky. These two, combined with her sheepskin coat, should be quite adequate. She added a knitted wool hat, which, in dire conditions, could be pulled down round her ears. Finally—and stilling any possible joking comments with an aloof stare at the young assistant—she selected a pair of thick knitted woollen tights. They may not be glamorous, she reflected, but she was certainly not going to look silly by shivering with cold. And nobody would see them.

On an impulse, she also purchased an attractive new hold-all, with a matching flight bag. She felt her faithful old suitcase, which had accompanied her since student days, could at last be pensioned off. It would mean repacking everything during her lunch-time, but worth it, for she felt smart and confident with her new luggage.

Thus equipped, she stood in reception at two o'clock, attempting to look nonchalant, but with her heart thudding with suppressed excitememt. There was a glance of open envy from the receptionist as she handed Bridie her air ticket and itinerary.

'Right Sister. Let's go.' He swept past her.

Standing beside him, as he loaded their bags into the open tail of the white Porsche, she sensed him making an appraisal of her attire. 'We're a bit over-dressed for the beginning of our journey,' he said, shrugging off a high-collared chunky anorak and depositing it in with the luggage, 'but we'll need all our warm layers when we get off the 'plane in Oslo.'

'Yes, that's what I thought,' she said. 'I've got a couple of extra layers packed ready in my flight bag.'

'Good girl.' He smiled at her, slamming shut the boot.

In an instant, they were purring down Park Lane, into the Cromwell Road and up on to the M4 flyover. She felt a vigorous thrust in the small of her back as he nosed the powerful car into the outside lane of the motorway. She looked across at the speedometer and saw the needle steady on the speed limit. There was no sensation of frantic dash, for he drove without ostentation, seeing opportunities in the press of traffic and taking them easily and lightly. There was a distinct feeling that he enjoyed the aesthetics of the beautiful white machine, but held its high-powered performance in great respect and control.

'You take the window seat, Sister,' he said, as they made their way down the narrow aisle of the aircraft cabin. 'There won't be a lot to see. It'll get dark quickly as we fly North, but the take-off's interesting.' He paused. 'I take it flying doesn't bother you at all?'

She shook her head smilingly and felt a ridiculous sense of pleasure as he nodded approvingly.

It transpired that they were travelling first-class and she stretched her legs out in luxury. It was so different in comparison to the cramped conditions of flying tourist class on package holidays. Here she felt as if she were sitting in a superbly upholstered armchair.

The smiling Norwegian stewardess fussed round them. She thought the girl was paying particular attention to her companion, answering his questions about the weather ahead with obvious pleasure. Bridie cast a glance at his profile, as he asked about head-winds and so forth. He really was an extremely attractive man, but appeared unaware of the effect he was having on the stewardess. He turned his head and Bridie quickly averted her gaze.

'We have a jet-steam with us,' he said. 'It should take ten minutes off our flying time.'

She nodded, not really understanding.

He opened his brief-case and took out a sheaf of papers. 'I really must check through this typescript. I hope you'll excuse me. It's an article for the *European Heart Journal* and the copy date's this Friday. I've promised the editor he shall have it the minute I return from Norway.'

'Of course,' she replied. 'What's the article about?'

He looked at her, obviously pleased by her interest. 'Well, actually it's about ways of obtaining early warning of cardiac conditions amongst people working in the extremes of heat and cold, both of which are fairly common in the oil industry. Cardiac complications have always been an area of special interest for me . . .'

She noticed that his eyes were alight with involvement with his subject. This was an aspect of him she had not seen before. He gave an example or two to illustrate his points and she found herself readily understanding the direction of his thesis. As he talked, she found his enthusiasm infectious. He gestured with his hands as he talked—something else which she had not noticed before.

They were interrupted by the stewardess checking their seat belts and she realised they were stationary at the end of the runway, waiting for take-off. She had not flown often enough for the excitement to have been dulled and she felt a thrill as she heard the shriek of the jet engines rising in a rapid crescendo.

There was a sensation of driving power as the brakes were released and they hurtled down the runway, the ground flashing past the window, and then the giddy feeling as they left the ground in a stomach-plummeting climb.

She looked across at him. He was deep in his article, as though the take-off had not happened. He must have flown many times, she realised. Well, perhaps it was a little unsophisticated to be excited at the flight, but she had not shown it too much—and anyway she was enjoying herself. He finished checking the last few pages of the typescript while they ate a light meal served by the stewardess.

'May I read it?' she enquired, gesturing at the manuscript.

'Of course.' He passed it across.

She found it of immense interest. As she read, it became apparent that he must somewhere be doing a considerable amount of research and correspondence. She wondered where this could be, since there was certainly no sign of it in the office or surgery. She turned her head to ask, but he had fallen asleep. His face was softer in repose, the angle of his jaw less pronounced. She noticed the fine filigree of eyelashes and a memory assailed her of an arm tight around her and hungry lips seeking hers. A hand reached down and retrieved the open flight magazine which was about to slip out of his fingers and she saw the stewardess smiling down at her. It was a conspiratorial, indulgent sort of smile, as if she assumed he belonged to Bridie. She realised with a start that this would indeed be a natural assumption, for they were both dressed casually.

It was also an assumption she found absurdly attractive and she shook herself mentally, withdrawing her eyes from him. His sleeping face was turned towards hers against the crisp linen head-cloth on the seat-back. Greg Brandon could really be quite a nice man, she mused. The little crisis over Robert's appendectomy had cleared the air no end and he had stopped patronising her professionally.

She realised she was enjoying very much being in his company. He was entertaining and witty—and, yes, he really could be rather kind, if you could penetrate that strange exterior. She had to remind herself sharply of his philandering tendencies. It was only a few days ago that he had arrogantly made a pass at her! The memory of that kiss and the press of his muscular body against hers lingered in her thoughts.

She looked back across at him, sleeping so innocently. It was a pleasant thought which the stewardess had unwittingly raised—of the two of them as a couple—but she must remember the gulf which lay between them. He lived in a different world from hers, separated from her socially and professionally—to say nothing of emotionally. And then of course there was the Britt girl . . .

She felt a slight sensation in the pit of her stomach as the jet began its descent to Oslo. She must have been day-dreaming for quite some time. Perhaps she had dozed a little, too. She felt pleasantly relaxed. The seat-belt sign flickered on, accompanied by the cabin staff announcing their imminent landing.

She was regarding him as he awoke. His eyes opened, looking directly into hers. As sleep faded, recognition followed and she found they were smiling warmly at each other. It was a moment of intimacy, but quickly gone, for she handed back his article and he busied himself replacing it in his brief-case

'Rather a dull travelling companion, I'm afraid,' he smiled ruefully. 'I was trying to get this article finished last night, burning a little midnight oil.'

'And now we're arriving in the land of the midnight sun,' she smiled.

'Well, not quite,' he said, but laughed. It was a pleasant, relaxed sound.

Very soon, they were in the arrivals hall and queueing for passport control. The easy-going relationship established in the plane seemed to sustain itself. A grin appeared on his face.

'Show you my passport photo if you'll show me yours,' he teased.

She realised she had been holding the document down against her body. Heavens, she had only been seventeen when the picture was taken! It would be intriguing to see his, though. Laughingly, they exchanged passports.

A younger version of him stared up at her. Of course, the frozen effect in any passport photograph was there, but so was the strength of personality in the lean features. His hair was shorter now, with today's fashion, but he had changed hardly at all, for she noticed it was an almost expired ten-year passport. It was full of entry stamps in many languages. She looked back at him to compare photographic and real images. He was regarding her seriously.

'A very attractive young lady,' he said abruptly. She felt a silly sense of embarrassment. Then they were through the customs formalities and he was waving a cab out of the rank.

She had first noticed the coldness of the air as they disembarked from the aircraft and, standing outside the airport building, she began to take greater stock of her surroundings.

The cold was most intense on the exposed parts of her body—her ears, for example, and the tips of her fingers as she removed a glove to button her coat. There was a drying sensation in her nostrils. But the air was crisp and the cold did not seem to penetrate, probably because it carried far less humidity than in England. It was strangely exhilarating. There had been plenty of snow but the streets and pavements were efficiently clear. There were none of the dirty ruts of packed ice or slush which only too often followed snow-falls in England.

The cab into which they climbed was pleasantly warm and amply equipped for the climate. She commented on the Norwegians' efficient approach to their winter.

'Yes, they're well organised. Every car carries chains for the wheels as well. They even have heaters which can be timed to be switched on while the car's parked, so they're always warmed up to climb into. Central heating's a way of life, as you'll find at the hotel.' He leaned forward. 'The Grand,' he said to the driver and she felt a thrill of excitement.

'Is there really a hotel called The Grand in Oslo?' she said laughingly.

'There certainly is. One hundred and fifty bedrooms and four-star. Very comfortable.'

Which indeed it was. She could hardly wait for the porter to deposit her luggage and leave, so that she could explore her room. She found she had a private bathroom, colour television and a breathtaking view over Oslo. The lights of the city seemed crystalline in the clear air. She left the curtains open at the double-glazed windows. She felt a delicious sense of gaiety and found she was looking forward to dinner immensely. They had arranged to meet in the bar for an aperitif in half-an-hour.

Quickly, she ran the water for a bath and added some of the special oil she had bought in the Heathrow duty-free shop, swirling it round to make luxuriant piles of bubbles. She slipped out of the clothes she had travelled in. The bathroom was very Scandinavian, with pine louvres and lost of glass. Her reflection stared back as she appraised herself critically. Quite well-proportioned really—and she was determined to keep it so, she thought, regarding the gentle swell of her breasts and the trim curve into neat waist and flat stomach. Hips not too pronounced and moulding smoothly into slender thighs. Her legs were really her strong point, long for her height and a slim, elegant shape.

She luxuriated in the bath, enjoying the penetrating warmth of the water. How strange to be in a country where you could enjoy the sensuous pleasure of a steamy, fragrant-smelling bath immediately after coming in from the icy cold of outdoors. She lifted a leg indolently and idly traced patterns with her toe on the condensation which misted the tiles.

Half an hour later, she was making her way through the lounge to the plushly-decorated cocktail bar. A gentle chink of glasses and a subdued hum of conversation formed the background.

She found him sitting languidly on a bar stool, from which he stood to greet her. 'Would you prefer to sit at a table?'

'No, here's fine. There's more to see,' she smiled. She almost regretted this as she perched on an adjoining stool but, apart from his eye dropping to a brief glimpse of thigh as she settled herself, she managed the manoeuvre perfectly.

She had dressed with care, selecting a knitted jersey wool dress in the same blue as her eyes. She had known it would travel well in her luggage and she felt it flattered her figure. A thin silver cord caught it in at the waist and an antique silver brooch, which had belonged to her grandmother, adorned the close-fitting material above her breast.

'What would you like? There's a very light Finnish vodka. Clean-tasting, like the air outside.'

'You sound like an advert.' He stared at her sharply and then, seeing the merriment on her face, relaxed, laugh lines appearing at the corner of his eyes.

'It sounds lovely. With tonic and lots of ice, please.' She noticed that he was drinking the same.

'I've got a menu here. Take a look.'

She scrutinised the choice with interest. 'Ooh, there's a smorgasbord,' she exclaimed.

'Yes, lots of exciting fish dishes. Very good for hors d'oeuvres. You can pick a main course from the à la carte over the page.'

The smorgasbord *was* exciting and they lingered over it enjoyably, plates in hand, trying to make up their minds. Finally, she selected a mixture of little items, including some smoked salmon which literally melted in her mouth.

They had been shown to a quiet table in the corner of the restaurant. She sipped at the Moselle wine which he had ordered and looked around her, enjoying the atmosphere. Attentive waiters moved softly about the room, discreetly serving the diners. Each table had a candle-lit centrepiece and the gentle light reflected back from the sparkling glassware, giving a subtle luminescence to the wine. It lit his features, softening them, and now and again caught his grey eyes. She found herself hoping she looked equally attractive.

'What happens tomorrow?' she asked.

'Well, it's an early start. We take a company plane to Skavanger and then spend the day at the complex.'

'The company keeps a 'plane and pilot in Norway?'

'Well, a 'plane yes. A small, light aircraft—a Cessna actually—and, as a matter of fact, I shall be the pilot on this occasion.'

'You fly?' she asked in astonishment.

'It's a hobby. I enjoy the freedom and detachment of flying. I learned in the University flying club. Flying the company's aircraft is a good way of keeping up the hours necessary to maintain my licence.'

She must have looked extremely surprised, for he paused, smiling at her. 'Don't worry, Bridie. I'm perfectly safe.'

She thought she detected an amused gleam in his eye and had an uncanny feeling that he was about to reach out and take her hand. They stared at each other. His eyes bored into hers and she felt a giddy thrill of anticipation and excitement.

'I'm sure you're safe.' She finally managed to break the silence and was glad of the diversion caused by the waiter bringing their main course. Greg Brandon might be safe as a pilot, but she was by no means sure he was safe in other ways. She steered the conversation on to other subjects. He expanded on his love of flying and of fast cars. He claimed they were his only two indulgences. He asked about her childhood and upbringing in Scotland and she described her parents and family.

The meal passed surprisingly quickly and they moved to the lounge to take coffee. He sat back in the deeply-upholstered armchair, long legs stretched before him, fingertips together, steepling his hands. She smiled at him. It had been a wonderful dinner.

'You're right,' she said suddenly. 'Real coffee is heaps better than the instant vending-machine type.'

He laughed gently and shrugged.

'Do we have to get up really early?' she asked.

'Well, our first meeting's at eleven o'clock. It's about three hundred kilometres—about an hour's flying, including take-off clearance and so forth. And there are pre-flight formalities at the airport. We should leave here at seven-thirty local time. I'd set your bedside alarm for six.'

'But I don't have one.'

He stared at her, then smiled. 'Yes you do. It's in the bedhead, next to light switches and television controls.'

She remembered the confusing array of knobs.

'I'm not sure I . . .'

'I'll set it for you. It's quite easy—'

Was he laughing at her naivety again? She kept silent, smiling her thanks.

'—and I suppose we really ought to hit the hay if we're to be up early.' He rose to his feet and she followed suit.

Clicking open her bedroom door, she was glad she had tidied her other clothes away. He went over to the bedside and adjusted the settings with quick, light fingers. 'There we are. Look, it's just two switches really.'

'Yes, I see. I'll know next time.' She smiled her

thanks, trying to keep her voice light, for his presence close to her, in her room, was highly disturbing. He straightened and looked at her.

'Right, Bridie. See you downstairs for breakfast at seven. Sweet dreams.' His eyes seared into hers. Suddenly he stepped forward and she was in his arms. Elbows together, she futilely pushed against his chest, but his lips were brushing her cheek, seeking her mouth. Her mind was a dizzy blur.

He tightened his arm round her waist and she tried to step back, forgetting the bed behind her. They fell together on the quilt. Somehow her gesture of non-compliance had become an invitation and she felt him pressing down on her. She tried to turn her head away, but his lips found hers, open in protestation. His tongue entered and explored her mouth and, against every voice of reason, she found herself responding. Her arms slid down and around him. She felt the muscular strength of his shoulders. His mouth left hers and moved sweetly down the line of her jaw, into the soft, sensitive parts of her neck. She arched her head back, her mind racing in a confusion of thoughts and emotions.

A delicious, plunging abandon pervaded her. She exulted in it and then, in the next instant, recoiled from such dangerous recklessness. And yet, the delicious play of his touch on the nape of her neck filled her with a deep need which began to obliterate her feelings of doubt and self-control.

She felt his hands expertly find the zip at the back of her dress and sensed it slide down, cool fingers caressing the curve of her bare spine. Nimbly, he unhooked her bra and slid the dress off her shoulders. His mouth returned to hers as his hand moved gently over her, cupping her swelling breasts, his fingers teasing her nipples.

'Bridie,' he murmured hoarsely in her ear. She felt the hard strength of him pressing against her.

A voice, completely unrecognisable as her own, penetrated her tumbling thoughts. 'No. We mustn't, Greg. Please.'

His eyes opened, staring at her. There was a long silence and it was as if time stood still.

'You don't really want me to stop, do you?' he breathed, his fingers tracing a tingling pattern across her skin. Her brain was a rushing maelstrom.

'No. I mean—I don't know.' Suddenly he was kissing her again and her heart was pounding. She did not want him to stop, it was true, for never in her life had she felt so—

Then she felt his arms relax their pressure. She fell back from him, her breath coming in uneven gasps. His eyes were dark with passion, the pupils enormous. She could feel his legs weighing down on hers.

'You're right. This is utterly impossible.' There was anger in his voice. Suddenly, he rolled aside and sat on the edge of the bed, the lean curve of his back towards her. She felt cold and deserted, very conscious of her nakedness. The jersey dress was in disarray. He stood up and turned to look down on her, staring at her exposed body. Her arm instinctively rose to cover herself and her other hand sought her hem, tugging the dress down to its proper place.

He seemed about to say something, but then turned on his heel and stormed from the room, leaving her trembling, a deep aching longing within the depths of her being.

She lay there for a long time, trying to rein in her racing thoughts. She knew that, in truth, she had not wanted him to stop, that she had wanted him to go on and on, to take—and give—fulfilment and delight. She knew, with absolute and inescapable certainty, that she had fallen in love with him.

# CHAPTER SEVEN

GRADUALLY, the whirling vortex of her thoughts slowed and calmed, but still she did not move. The memory of his touch burned within her and she savoured the excruciating tenderness of the recollection. Never before had she felt so aroused. Fires smouldered within her that she had not known existed. Certainly, no other man had reached the very centre of her being as had Greg Brandon. She felt a deep yearning for him.

But it was a yearning tinged with great sadness. He had been angry with her. Perhaps he thought she was just a silly child from the provinces—or worse still, a teaser. He was, after all, a man of the world, who had probably had many love affairs. Her eyes swam with tears as she remembered his obvious liaison with Britt. How could she compete with sophisticated, easy girls like that? Could that sort of creature be the type he really wanted? She realised that, by comparison, her very inexperience might make her a dull lover. But yet she knew this would not be true, for the passion she had felt was capable of an even fiercer intensity. Given full scope, it would completely engulf her in a tidal wave of sensuous giving. It had only been a small part of her that had asked him to stop. The rest of her had wanted to unfold for him, and wrap him in her love.

A horrifying thought struck her and she sat up, shivering. Perhaps he had asked her on this trip just to go to bed with her. He might have thought the excitement would go to her head, make her easy prey. She slipped out of her clothes and into her nightie and dressing-gown. Yes, that could be it, she brooded, angrily brushing her teeth and removing her make-up. It was probably the expected thing for girls to sleep with their bosses in the upper echelons of Pan European. He should have added that requirement to her job description if it was indeed the case, she thought savagely. It would not be easy to face him at breakfast. Well, she had never been a sleep-around girl and she was not going to start now, no matter how much it was expected of her. With this resolve, she slid into bed, the billowy Norwegian duvet settling around her, providing a cocoon of relaxing warmth. She was chilled, her hands cold, and she hugged them round herself. She fell into a fitful sleep, half-aware of recurring glimpses of a dark head in the curve of her shoulder and aroused grey eyes looking into the very depths of her soul.

She dressed in her full cold-weather clothes the next morning, filled with a firm resolve to hold her own during the coming day.

She was purposely a few minutes early for breakfast so that he would have to seek her, rather than vice versa, but he had preceded her and was sitting in the dining-room, a clip-board propped up against the coffee pot before him. She took a deep breath and, with studied nonchalance, approached the table. Even so, two spots of colour were burning fiercely in her cheeks. She addressed a point above his head.

'Good morning, Doctor,' she said.

'Morning, Sister, just checking our flight plan, these kippers are delicious, really fresh, you should try them.'

This was all said in virtually one breath. He did not look up.

She had not been prepared for this. Meaningful glances, perhaps. Even anger. But not bluff good humour. Perhaps this was the way company affairs were conducted. Except they were not having an affair, she reminded herself sternly. The waiter pulled back her chair and she sat down, feeling awkward and clumsy.

'Did you sleep well?' He looked up and her heart turned over. She nodded dumbly and frantically sought the menu. She indicated orange juice, muesli and coffee.

'I've rung the airport. Weather's good. Should be a pleasant flight, but they're not too sure how long it's going to stay settled.' He was completely buried in his reading matter again.

What had happened in her bedroom was obviously of little importance to him. He was probably like a lot of men. They felt obliged to try it on, to bestow the largesse of their love-making on a girl, whether she desired it or not.

No, to credit him with the guile of planning this trip just so as to persuade her into a night of love was unfair. He was simply a rather superficial, philandering playboy who would take his opportunities as they came up. But she knew she could not ignore this surge of excitement at being in his company. Her emotions would have to be kept firmly in check, for another episode like last night's could well be her downfall and she could not bear the pain of just a casual affair with him.

He had arranged for their baggage to be brought down and they were soon speeding out to the airport in a cab.

Once there, he left her in the departure lounge while he went off to collect the latest weather report and to file their flight plan, whatever that meant. She had never flown in a light aircraft before and felt a thrill of excitement, tinged with some trepidation. He would be a good pilot though, she reflected. The assured manner with which he handled his Porsche suggested that—and everything about him exuded confidence.

Her surmise proved correct for, seated in the aircraft, he flicked through the pre-flight checks with practised ease, sensitive fingers lightly touching switches, eyes noting readings on the dials, an absorbed expression on his face. Her seat was next to his in the cockpit and she was looking straight out ahead where she would see the runway unfold before them. It was quite unlike the sensation of sitting inside an ordinary passenger airliner.

The array of switches and dials bemused her and she made no attempt to understand them, being very happy to sit and watch the activity of Oslo airport. All the runways and tarmacs were clear of snow, but the floodlights reflected a white mantle covering the buildings. It was snug and warm here in the cockpit, for the engine had been turning over for some time. She heard him asking for take-off clearance and he turned to her with a boyish grin.

'Here we go then!' he said, and moved some levers forward.

The runway lights streamed towards them like an arrow-straight motorway. The Norwegian dawn had not yet broken, although there was greyness in the sky to the East. Then they were climbing, his strong hands easing back on the controls, a tiny frown of concentration on his face, alert eyes surveying his instruments.

She looked down as the airport lights and buildings dropped away and they soared into a dark abyss. She gasped involuntarily as he swung the aircraft confidently into a steep bank and it seemed for all the world as though the ground below them was moving up alongside. She realised that, in reality, she was looking at the ground over her shoulder. It was rather like being on one of those chairplane rides at a funfair.

He was gesticulating at her. 'Earphones,' he shouted over the engine's noise and pointed at a headset on her seat back. She slipped it on and his voice crackled in her ears. 'Bit different to Scandinavian Airways, eh?' He was chuckling, for all the world like a little boy with a toy. And yet this aircraft was no toy and obviously required skill and mastery in its handling.

'We're heading West and climbing. We'll be up through the cloud cover soon.' He returned to the business of flying, making adjustments here and there, pulling levers. She heard him talking authoritatively on the radio, using some obscure jargon, but in English, surprisingly. He was completely absorbed. All thoughts of last night were probably long gone from his mind, she thought sadly. She was no more important to him than a brief diversion—not as exciting, even, as flying this aircraft.

The sky was growing lighter but she noticed wisps of cloud scudding past the window. The cloud intensified and suddenly they were plunged into a grey limbo. She looked across at him, her eyes widening in apprehension.

'Don't worry, we're only climbing up through the cloud base. We'll be out of it in a short while.'

She sat back, reassured. Gradually the greyness lightened and then they suddenly burst through into a world of such beauty that she gasped with delight. The cloud through which they had climbed had become an unbroken expanse of white cotton wool, stretching below them from horizon to horizon. It was tinged with pink for, behind to the East, the sun was rising, reaching out fingers of light in front of them. The sky was an azure blue, the deepest she had ever seen. It was a cerulean canopy stretched above them.

'Quite a sight isn't it?' He was smiling at her, wanting to share the pleasure of the moment. She nodded and averted her face, for her eyes were misting at the warmth in his expression. She gripped the armrests of her seat and fought to control the trembling of her mouth. He was still talking, peering upwards.

'I hope it lasts. That's cirrus cloud up there, coming in from the South-West. Often heralds bad weather.' He was indicating thin wispy mare's tails of cloud, but she hardly noticed, glad of the respite to find a tissue and blow her nose.

They fell silent, the aircraft droning steadily on. She noticed that here and there beneath them the clouds had taken on darker shadows and some appeared to be more angular than others, the pleasant cottonwool effect was lost. She attracted his attention and pointed. He indicated a switch on her headset so that she could talk to him.

'Bad weather?' she asked.

He was laughing at her. 'No. Guess what they are.'

She looked down again and shook her head.

'They're mountains,' he said. 'That's Telemark you can see and the surrounding ranges.'

She realised that she was looking down on the tops of

mountains pushing aggressively up through the white, billowy softness of the clouds. What a trip this was turning out to be! She was experiencing things she had never dreamed of before.

Her thoughts turned to the day ahead and she went over in her mind the ideas she felt she could contribute to the new Skavanger centre. All too soon, she heard him talking over the radio again, asking for landing clearance. The cloud below had been thinning for some time and was clearing as they approached the coast. Up above them the mare's tails had joined together into a sort of haze and there was a halo round the sun. She looked down and caught glimpses of soaring mountain tops and sudden plunges into narrow fingers of water reaching in from the sea.

'Fjords,' he said.

'Yes, they remind me of the sea lochs in Scotland,' she replied. They were beginning their descent and ahead of them she could see what must be the landing strip at Skavanger. It reached out between two peaks, almost into the deep still waters of a fjord. He touched the aircraft down with consummate skill, his hands moving over the controls with gentle assurance. There was the lightest of bumps and a rumble of wheels as they taxied to a halt.

Soon they were clambering out, to be met by a charming Norwegian, named Carl, who turned out to be the general manager of the site.

'Ah, Dr Brandon, you have brought us poor Norwegian boys some glamour, ja?' A pair of bright eyes twinkled at her. 'Come. We go in and have coffee. Your first visit to Norway?'

She smiled and nodded, following the two men across

the tarmac, glad of the grip of her walking boots on the frozen ground. The air was a distillation of icy purity. She drew it into her lungs like a cleansing force.

Their morning meeting swung into effect and she found herself ably contributing ideas and suggestions. He had completely re-assumed the mantle of their working relationship. It was as if they had never shared any intimacy at all. She found this a relief in many ways, because she could pretend it had not happened. Without this self-created illusion, she could hardly have got through the meeting, let alone participate. She was surprised at the extent of her ability to join in the discussions, but found it no great strain. In fact it was very enjoyable and both Greg and the Norwegians listened carefully whenever she had a point to make. Her opinion on various matters was frequently sought and she answered unselfconsciously and fluently.

By lunchtime, they had completed a tour of the medical wing and were sitting in the Site Manager's office, drinking steaming mugs of coffee and eating large door-step sandwiches. She found these something of a struggle and smiled wryly to herself. Despite being treated as 'one of the boys', she was somewhat out of place in this man's world. Everybody seemed so bulky and larger than life, wrapped up in their anoraks and sheepskin coats, all wearing heavy boots. Why, they had even unceremoniously issued her with a bright yellow hard-hat when they had toured the site. She had caught him grinning at her sardonically, but she had ignored the mockery in his eyes and strapped it on with a haughty shake of her head, making no comment. He had brought an extremely expensive-looking Pentax camera and had busied himself shooting various aspects and features of the site. From time to time he spoke verbal notes into a pocket dictating machine.

'We have made good progress this morning, I think,' a Norwegian engineer was saying when the 'phone shrilled.

Carl, the general manager, picked it up. His expression changed from relaxed good humour to steely seriousness. He rapped out several questions in Norwegian and tugged at his chin with one hand. Then he looked up and addressed Greg Brandon.

'Doctor, there has been a bad accident on one of the drilling platforms. There is no danger but there are injuries and the sick bay medic on the rig cannot judge their seriousness. He has asked for assistance. We should fly any bad cases off in the chopper, but the weather is deteriorating. Can you fly out and assess the situation before it really clamps down? Our duty doctor is already storm-bound on a rig out in Forties Field.'

'How soon could we leave?'

'Immediately. We have a chopper and pilot standing by, ready to go.'

'I would like to take Sister. We may be able to treat the injuries actually on the rig.'

'Of course.'

Bridie interrupted. 'But surely, women aren't allowed on the rigs—'

'Rubbish,' snapped Greg. 'This is an emergency and I need your help.'

'Things are less rigid on the Norwegian-operated rigs, Sister,' said Carl in a gentler tone. 'On some of them, the medic is actually a woman.'

She was swept along on a surge of activity. For the

second time that day she found herself aboard an aircraft—a helicopter this time, with a capable-looking Norwegian at the controls. In comparison with the Cessna, the accommodation here was spartan.

Climbing up into the body of the machine, the revolving blades cutting the air with a peculiarly insistent whistling rhythm above her head, she had glanced up at the sky. The earlier weather had now been replaced by an ominous pattern of cloud, streaming in off the sea. She caught a look of concern in Greg's eyes as he held out a firm hand to help her aboard.

'Doesn't look too good. The forecast is a deep depression moving in off the North Sea. Storm-force winds in the next six hours. We've just enough time,' he shouted.

Soon they were lifting up and away, across the unfriendly sea. She looked down and shivered. It looked desolate and brooding, coloured a flat, slate-grey. They seemed to be flying very low.

'How far?' she mouthed at him and he raised his watch, lifting his fingers three times. Fifteen minutes. Gradually, she discerned an outline of derricks and steel towers climbing up from the horizon. As they drew near, the full size of the platform was borne upon her. She had heard that the large rigs supported two hundred men on a steel 'jacket', whose legs actually stood on the seafloor. It was like a man-made village sitting out here in the forbidding ocean.

The rig towered up against a background of dark, menacing clouds. Four great steel legs rose from the restless, surging waves. She could see a flat area, with a circle and the letter 'H' painted within it. Surely they were not going to land there?—it was minute! She closed her eyes, glad he could not see her face. But with her eyes shut, it was worse. She could feel them descending in a series of swoops. The wind seemed awfully strong, buffeting them sideways. She opened her eyes, and the 'H' circle was closer, but refusing to stay in one place, moving in and out of her field of vision. Gradually, however, it steadied and they were down. The outer door was swung open and she could see a crew running out restraining lines. She caught a look of admiration in Greg's eyes as he and the pilot exchanged thumbs-up signs.

She clambered down onto the steel deck. The wind caught at her, a hard spatter of hail stinging her cheek. She was glad of the warm tights and husky which she was wearing under her outer coat. There was a look of surprise on the face of the oil-man who had taken her arm. The rig had obviously not been signalled that a nursing sister was accompanying the doctor.

'I'm Sister Stewart. This is Dr Brandon. Where are the injured?' she shouted. This was no time for polite introductions. Responding to her tone, he nodded.

'Follow me, both of you,' he yelled, voice straining against the rising wind.

They negotiated a series of narrow walkways and stairs, their boots clanging against the steel structure. Their guide led them through a doorway and banged the door shut behind them. He was a craggy-jawed Texan, all stubble and weather-worn features.

'What happened?' asked Greg.

'One of the diving-stage cables parted. We were just hoisting the guys inboard, two of them, and the line went, the son of a—' He stopped, looking at Bridie. 'Sorry, ma'am.'

'And?' pressed Greg.

'One of them got caught by the flying cable end and the other was pitched out on to the deck. He fell awkwardly and he's still unconscious. The medic's done his best in the sick bay but we just don't know if we should move them. I'm sure one of them needs stitches.'

'Let's have a look, shall we?'

They entered the sick bay and Greg made a rapid assessment. One man was conscious but obviously in shock.

'Nasty wound, there, Sister, but it's clear of anything vital. Shot of morphine's needed, I think, and a temporary dressing. Perhaps you could attend to that while I take a look at the other man.'

She set about her ministrations and was rewarded by a look of relief in the man's eyes. He would need hospital attention right enough, but she made him comfortable and smiled down at him. She felt Greg tug her sleeve.

'I'm a bit concerned about the lad who's unconscious. He could have internal injuries. We should really get them both back to hospital at Skavanger as quickly as possible. It might be a rough ride with the weather closing in. That's a very nasty front coming up from the south-west.'

'We'd better get going then. What does the helicopter pilot think?'

'He says if you're going to go back, then you'd better go pretty quick,' interposed the medic.

As the two stretchers were loaded into the helicopter, she felt the force of the wind tearing at her, like unseen hands snatching at her clothing. Both men were firmly strapped in and the stretchers were securely anchored to special fixing points. The one to whom she had given a shot had drifted off into an anaesthetised state. The other was still unconscious. She tucked blankets around them both and made sure they could not be thrown about.

The scudding cloud was very low and she gave a shiver of apprehension. She caught a glimpse of the sea—there were far more whitecaps now and streaks of foam on the surface. The waves were much larger and had built up very quickly. They could have only been down in the sick bay for half-an-hour at the most.

'Come on.' The Norwegian pilot was shouting down at the deck crew. 'We go.' Greg pulled the hatch shut and secured the clips. She saw men struggling to pull chocks away from the wheels and, with a roar of the engine, they lifted away. The wind caught them like a feather and tossed them aside. She heard a stifled curse from the pilot and she was thrown heavily against Greg in the adjoining jump seat. She caught a horrifying sight of steel superstructure as they seemed to slip down below the very platform itself. A monstrous pillar of steel—one of the rig's legs—confronted them through the window. It was so close that she could see the rivets and joints, streaked with rust, as it stood like some sort of massive breakwater, leaning into the crashing seas which furiously hurled themselves against its base, raising clouds of spray high in the air. It was an alien, terrifying sight and with a cry she turned and buried her face in Greg's chest. She was sure their headlong plunge would end in disaster, that the wind would hurl them into the boiling sea like a piece of flotsam.

His arms tightened strongly around her and she

clutched at him, her eyes squeezed shut. For what seemed an eternity, they were tossed hither and thither and then, gradually, the pilot regained control.

'It's OK now. We'll make it all right.' Greg's voice was in her ear. She was still holding on to him like grim death.

Their eyes met and she knew he was going to kiss her. Knew that she wanted to kiss him. Their mouths met and her lips parted. They probed each other with fierce passion. She was straining up at him with all her senses. She could feel the rough coldness of his skin against hers and tasted the salt which the sea spray had left. Their mouths parted and she looked up into his eyes.

'I was frightened,' she said. 'I'm sorry.'

He smiled gently and shook his head. 'So was I,' he said. 'But we've got a good pilot.'

She suddenly remembered their flying companions. The pilot, up forward, was concentrating on his controls. Her two patients were completely secure. The restraining straps and stretcher design had performed well.

'We'll be stable now. Wind's behind us. The return trip will be in double quick time.'

A matter-of-fact tone had returned to his voice. He unclipped his seat belt and moved up forward to peer out, exchanging a glance with the pilot, who raised his eyes heavenwards, pursing his lips in a silent whistle. He turned and motioned her to join them.

Feeling more secure now, she unhooked herself and moved up to the cockpit. He pointed downwards.

The sea was a dramatic sight. Curling combers moved before them, marching inexorably on to the coast. Here and there, long streaks of white marked the surface. Now that the trauma of their headlong departure from

the rig was over, she was almost enjoying herself,
exulting in the driving, overpowering forces of
nature.

'Some blow, ja?' the pilot shouted. 'This part of the
world we sometimes call a weather engine. Often very
bad storms. The hundred-year storms are the worst.' He
caught the expression on their faces and went on. 'Every
hundred years they say, there is very bad storm. The
winds—maybe one hundred knots—and the seas—they
would reach almost to the top of a drilling platform's
legs.'

He corrected their course as a side gust caught them.

'Myself I have not flown in one. Yet! OK?' They saw
the humour in his eyes and he threw back his head in
a great shout of laughter. It was infectious and they
joined in. It was a release from the tension they had all
felt.

The landing at Skavanger was relatively easy, compared with their earlier experiences. They had moved
slightly ahead of the advancing front and the mountains
provided some protection against the North Sea gale.
Greg had radioed ahead for an ambulance to be waiting
and they soon had the two injured men established in the
local hospital. Satisfied that everything possible was
being done for their patients, they began to relax. Carl,
the site manager, found them sitting in the hospital
waiting room in something of a daze.

'You were not expecting such an eventful trip, I
think?'

'That's true enough,' said Greg and they both smiled
ruefully at Carl.

'It is a bad storm. Blowing up even more now. You
could not have delayed your return from the rig much

longer. But now we all relax. Tonight you will have dinner with my wife and me—and stay in our house.'

'But we're booked into a hotel. You mustn't go to any trouble,' said Greg.

'Now you are unbooked without going to any trouble.' He smiled. 'And I have your luggage in the back of my car. Come.'

He would hear no further argument and they allowed themselves to be shepherded out to a large Volvo estate car. The wind was fierce, carrying snow flurries with it. They drove steadily out of town and Bridie could hear the steady thump of the car's snow chains on the packed icy surface.

Carl's wife was a friendly, buxom lady, who fussed around them like a mother hen. She was called Marga.

'We have plenty of room. It is so much nicer than the hotel. And I enjoy visitors.'

'It is the least we can do,' added her husband.

'Well, you're very kind,' said Bridie gratefully.

'Good. Now you would like to wash. A nice hot shower perhaps?'

She smiled. 'That would be lovely.'

'And the doctor also? But ladies first, yes?'

'Of course,' he asserted curtly. It was impossible to guess what he was thinking. The gulf between them had returned and it was as if he had never taken her in his arms in the helicopter.

Marga smilingly showed her to a guest room, pointing out the shower on the way. The doctor was taking the room belonging to their absent student son, on the other side of the landing.

She peeled off her layers of clothing with relief and,

slipping on her dressing-gown, made for the shower. The stinging jets of water made her gasp and she stood there, enjoying the tiny needles of luxuriously hot water play on her body. Gradually the tensions of the afternoon faded and she stretched her arms above her head, the spray pounding on the shower hat Marga had thoughtfully provided. She seized the soap and smothered herself with fragrant lather. As the water sluiced it away, playing over her body, she felt herself growing calm, more able to control the memory of that desperate, searing embrace in the helicopter. They had been eager for each other in the stress of the flight. She had read somewhere that people who had survived plane crashes or similar disasters had an immediate and overwhelming desire to make love to each other. Even perfect strangers. That anything like that had passed between them out there over the storm-ridden North Sea was impossible to imagine here in this comfortable, secure house. It had just been the stress of the moment, she told herself, a human reaction entirely. But in her heart, she knew it was more than that, that it was part of the way she felt about him. Towelling herself briskly until she glowed, she shook on some talc from her toilet bag and, wrapped in her dressing-gown, flew back to her room, innocently unaware of the trail of fragrance she left behind her on the landing.

She dressed simply for supper, in a creamy-coloured silk blouse and pleated skirt. Thank goodness she had packed another outfit and was not obliged to put on the same jersey dress she had worn at the hotel. It held too many memories. The same beige suede sling-backs went just as well with this ensemble and she enjoyed smoothing on the sheer tights she wore with them. They were such a relief from the woolly ones which had swathed her legs all day.

Supper was a delightful occasion. Marga had prepared a delicious casserole and she spooned out steaming platefuls for them. She and Carl were very fluent in English and the meal was sprinkled with much humour. Like many Norwegians, they had a close affinity with the Scots—and indeed the British generally. Carl recounted many stories of his father's exploits during the last war. He had been a radio operator for the Resistance and still kept in touch with many of his old comrades, both Norwegian and British.

What an adventurous race they were, Bridie reflected. It was as if they had the sea in their blood and the rigours of their climate were nothing to them. Here they were, sitting snug and warm in this friendly house, whilst outside, the full force of a North Sea storm hurled itself at the windows. She wondered if Greg also felt the romance of Carl's stories, but he gave no sign, smiling politely as the conversation ebbed and flowed.

As they were drinking their coffee, she heard a telephone ring and Carl went to answer it. He returned a moment later.

'Your patients are both well. The man that was concerning you, Doctor, has nothing more serious than severe internal bruising and concussion. He will be recovered soon, with careful attention. And the other,' his eyes danced, 'will talk about nothing but a blue-eyed, raven-haired beauty who flew him from the sea's dangers in a silver bird. I wonder who he can mean, Sister?'

She felt Greg's eyes on her and the colour rising in her cheeks. She mumbled something about anaesthetics producing odd effects and sipped her coffee.

'That reminds me,' Greg's voice was gruff. 'I'd like to telephone London. May I please book a call? It's a Company charge.'

'Of course, but I will book it for you,' said Carl. 'It will take only a minute.'

She felt the food and wine beginning to make her sleepy. She waited for Carl to return and then made her apologies.

'I am not surprised you are feeling tired, my dear,' said Marga. 'It has been a long day—and an eventful one, ja?'

She made her way up to bed, a delicious languor in her limbs. There was a longing too, but she tried to dismiss this. He had not paid her much attention at supper and this was how it should be, she reminded herself sharply. This was what she wanted. He was merely an exceptionally pleasant travelling companion.

Brushing her teeth in the bathroom, she heard the tinkle of the 'phone downstairs. The wind was still howling round the eaves and she looked forward to her inviting bed. She would sleep well, whatever blizzards were blowing outside.

Returning to her room, she heard a low murmur from downstairs and recognised his voice.

'. . . yes, it's possible, an early flight. Yes. Yes, in time for lunch. The usual place. You'll book it, good. Well goodnight, Britt . . . and sweet dreams.' The receiver clicked down.

She stood stock-still, a feeling of cold rejection sweeping over her. The warm pleasure of the evening had vanished. In its place was an overwhelming loneliness.

She rushed to her room and, tearing off her dressing-gown, hurled herself beneath the covers. Had she noticed, she would have been glad that the shrieking wind drowned the sounds of her sobbing. For her heart was breaking for love of this impossible, unattainable man.

# CHAPTER EIGHT

THE loud, ringing sound of steel striking something solid penetrated her consciousness. Daylight was streaming into the room and there was a sound of voices from outside. She realised that the noise she could hear was of snow being shovelled from a driveway. Her heart lifted at the recollection of where she was—and then suddenly plummetted as full recall of the previous evening came back to her.

She knelt up on the bed and peered out of the window. The fury of the storm had been spent and the scene was tranquil. The glare of light reflecting from the white vista was dazzling and she screwed up her eyes. Carl was shovelling snow from the slope in front of the house with easy, swinging movements, while Marga sprinkled a white powder, presumably salt, where he had cleared a path.

Bridie's breath misted on the window. Then, remembering the snug warmth of the duvet, she slipped back under it and lay idly on her back. She felt heavy-limbed, her mind numb. She had not slept well, and did not feel refreshed, as she normally did in the morning. Her thoughts retraced the events of the previous day. The storm had been fierce, but it must have died away quite suddenly, for it was still clear in her memory, along with the tumbling stream of emotions which had also possessed her. Despite all her instincts of self-protection, she knew Greg Brandon had become a central force in her life. She concentrated on trying to recall his face but, strangely, the detail of his features escaped her. All she could recollect was a powerful image of his presence. How could it have happened— that she had fallen so desperately in love with this elusive, restless man? She stared up at the pine-clad ceiling. The gulf between them was enormous, socially as well as emotionally. She had always felt that when she really fell in love, it would be total and absolute. Her innermost values were for constancy and for deep lasting bonds—but for all that she had fallen for a man who preferred women who would give him none of those qualities. And yet, she yearned for his touch, for his strong arms around her and his gently caressing fingers . . .

A tap at the door sharply invaded her thoughts. The homely, cheerful face of Marga appeared, her cheeks rosy with the effort of snow-clearing.

'You are waking. Good. I will make some breakfast. Hot Scottish breakfast for a cold Norwegian morning. Porridge with eggs to follow. In twenty minutes, yes? Carl will be finished then.'

Bridie nodded a smiling assent and Marga's face disappeared.

Down in the kitchen, she leaned against the table edge, while Marga busied herself with preparations for the meal.

'Some storm, wasn't it?' said Bridie. 'But there doesn't seem to have been a lot of snow.'

'No. It was a big wind, mostly, from the West, not bringing much snow. A little hail, yes. It was a wind to make drifts, to blow across and block the drive. Carl, he makes much complaining. But some breakfast will cheer him I think.'

Bridie smiled. 'Can I do anything, set another place at the table? You've only laid three.'

'Ja. Three.'

'No, I mean, there's you, Carl, the Doctor and me. We'll need another.' She opened the cutlery drawer.

'The Doctor has gone. He did not tell you?'

'Gone?' A collection of cutlery dropped with a clatter from her startled fingers.

'We thought he had explained. He wished an early arrival back. He flew himself to Oslo very early this morning, once he was sure the storm had blown out. He wanted to catch the morning flight to London. Carl drove him to his aircraft at six o'clock.'

She had resolved to put him from her mind once they were back in London, but she had hoped they would enjoy their last day together. Now even this slight pleasure was denied her. She felt a prickle of tears and was glad Marga was preoccupied with cooking. She had been looking forward to being in his company on the return trip, despite her knowledge that their relationship could never go any further.

'He said he would call at your room on his way to bed to explain the change in plan. You must have been asleep.'

She blinked back tears. 'Oh yes. I expect so. Shall I call Carl?' She wanted a reason for a minute or two on her own.

Finding a tissue, she paused in the hall-way and regained her composure. It was just as well, she thought. She would not now see him again until Monday—a weekend in which to get things in perspective and put back together her shattered emotions.

Carl stomped in through the door at her call, beaming a smile. 'And how is our raven-haired blue eyes this morning? You sleep good, I hope? Now we eat, ja? I have big appetite.'

Over breakfast, they tried to persuade her to stay for the weekend. There was a ski-ing club apparently, with lots of young people, and she would be made very welcome. But somehow the magic had gone from the trip. She felt she wanted to get back to the familiar things of her life, needed the security of her own environment.

'I think perhaps, Marga, that our guest has a young man in London she is anxious to see.'

She lowered her eyes sadly but Carl mistook this for confirmation of his theory. 'Ja, that is so. Next time, you bring him to visit us too. We will make you both very welcome.'

She nodded dumbly, feeling a lump in her throat. They could not know it, but she had already visited them in the company of the only man she would ever want.

'So. It is to be the other possibility Dr Brandon suggested. If you did not wish a weekend stay, then you can catch the afternoon flight from Oslo to London. It always calls here on Fridays and Sundays. It is for the oil men to make their weekends at home. Soon I am to drop Marga off shopping. Perhaps you would like to come? Or stay here and I will collect you later.'

She smiled her thanks. 'No, I will come with Marga. I might even buy a present or two to take home.'

'Good,' said Marga. 'We will have lunch together in Skavanger. Carl can join us—if we can drag him from his work.'

'Did Dr Brandon say why he went early? I would not

have minded getting up as well and going with him.'
There was a falter in her voice.

'Oh, he wished you to have a good sleep and see
something of Skavanger. He thought also the ski-ing
might keep you for the weekend. He is a nice man, ja?'
Carl laughed. 'But he could not have known about your
young man.'

She averted her face and concealed her feelings by
helping Marga clear the table. The truth was, she
thought sadly, that he did not wish to be diverted from
his rush back to be with that Britt creature.

An hour later found her in Marga's company, explor-
ing the shops in Skavanger. It was exciting, examining
unfamiliar goods and hearing business being conducted
in a foreign language. Knowing that Mary and Barnaby's
wedding date was to be fixed soon, she took the opportunity of buying a set of beautiful Scandinavian wine
glasses as a first step towards their wedding present. She
also could not resist buying two very sensible items of
Norwegian clothing—pairs of warm, soft moccasin-type
slippers with long woolly socks, in brightly coloured
stripes, already attached. They would keep her and
Mary warm in the cold of London's winter, she explained to Marga. She found she was able to purchase all
of these items with her credit card. She had not known
that it could be used internationally. She had brought
some travellers' cheques but the credit card method was
so much easier.

Skavanger was a pleasant little community and she
enjoyed the friendly welcome of the Norwegians. Marga
was well-known and popular and, by lunchtime, Bridie's
head was awhirl with the stream of faces to whom she
had been introduced.

The sadness of the early morning was still with her, but gradually she was able to force it to the back of her mind. Carl joined them for a pleasant lunch and, all too soon, she was repacking her flight bag with her presents so that Carl could carry her luggage into the little airport building.

Her Norwegian friends made a great fuss of her as she prepared to go through Passport Control—a huge bear-hug from Carl and a kiss on both cheeks from Marga. For a moment, she almost changed her mind about staying for the weekend but then, clinging to her earlier decision, she turned and, giving a last wave, made her way through to the embarkation gate. The flight was full—apparently Greg had managed to get her booked in to one of the last remaining seats when he passed through that morning—and there would have been no shortage of stand-by takers had she decided to stay on and cancelled the reservation.

She did not have the luxury of a first-class seat, because the whole flight was economy-booked, nor did she have a window seat. Compared with the excitement and thrill of the flight out, she felt decidedly gloomy. They had been airborne for only a short time when she felt a slow languor creeping over her, to which she surrendered, and passed most of the journey in a fitful doze.

At Heathrow, she made her way to baggage control and waited for a glimpse of her holdall coming up on the endless belt carousel. She had kept her flight bag with her as cabin baggage so as more easily to protect the glassware she had bought. The bustle of the airport failed to excite her and she felt extremely jaded. Nevertheless, she decided against the luxury of a taxi. Even though she could charge the cost up to Pan European as a travelling expense, she felt it was rather extravagant. Anyway, the new extension of the Piccadilly Line Tube out to the airport would serve her needs quite adequately—and the flat was only a brief step from South Kensington station.

Mary was out when she arrived home and she unpacked slowly, with an odd sense of unreality. She was quite hungry and decided to take the easy solution, wandering round the corner to collect a take-away Chinese meal. She had hoped Mary would be home, but as she gnawed at the spare ribs she had bought, staring blankly at a silly television programme, she remembered that Barnaby had some tickets for the ballet and they had planned a night out.

Feeling rather bleak and just a little alone, she turned off the television and decided on an early night. She had bought a novel at the corner shop earlier and, curled up in bed, she eventually lost herself in the book. The events of the last few days must have taken their toll because, within a remarkably short space of time, she found the book dropping from her hand to land with a flutter on the floor. Summoning her last ounce of energy, she reached for the bedside light switch and fell into a dreamless sleep.

She was amazed to find she had more than slept the clock round, for the time on her digital radio alarm read ten-thirty when she woke up the following morning. The flat was quiet. Perhaps Mary had stayed with Barnaby.

She felt refreshed. The sleep had done her good. She still felt a pressing weight of sadness, but things seemed to be achieving a better perspective. She stretched luxuriously under the covers and raised her arms, yawning.

The whole trip seemed like a dream, she reflected, staring round the familiar room, full of her personal bric-a-brac. Had she really seen clouds pierced from beneath by harsh Norwegian mountains? been carried through a North Sea storm to a village on iron legs straddling the sea-bed, been made love to by—

She stopped this passing procession of images firmly. Over this coming weekend, she would get a firm grip on her feelings. It was not to be, between Greg Brandon and her, and the sooner she stopped lingering over such bitter-sweet memories, the better.

She swung her slim legs out of bed and slipped along to the bathroom. She noticed Mary's door was shut and, passing it on the way back, heard a sleepy voice call out, 'Yoo-hoo, globe-trotter.'

She stuck her head round Mary's door. 'Yoo-hoo yourself,' she said to the tousled mop of hair on the pillow. 'Tea? Coffee? Orange juice?'

'Mmm, a cup of tea would be heaven, Bri.'

'Coming up.' She pulled the door shut.

The giggles with which Mary greeted her Norwegian slippers present gladdened Bridie's heart.

'Fabulous. But you don't think I'm getting cold feet about marrying Barnaby, do you?' she joked. 'Although I do literally get cold feet. Could be a problem in our marriage. I might well be advised to wear these on our wedding night. Could kill a bit of passion, though.' She held up the slippers and scrutinised them with such seriousness that Bridie burst into laughter.

'I'm sure the best cure of all for cold feet is having someone to warm them up for you. But those are for use when Barnaby isn't available,' she cried.

'They're lovely, Bri. Thank you!' Mary's company

was an antidote for Bridie's gloom. She was lucky to
have such a good friend, she thought.

An inevitable stream of questions about her trip
followed and Mary sat gaping as Bridie described her
adventures. She lightly passed over much mention of her
travelling companion. Fortunately, this was easily
achieved by dwelling on the sheer drama of her other
experiences.

The two girls passed an enjoyable day together, catching up on what Mary described as their 'to do' list. Bridie
was a little apprehensive about another evening on her
own and, when Mary suggested they should make up a
threesome with Barnaby, she was glad.

'You're sure I won't be playing gooseberry,' she said
uncertainly.

'Nonsense.'

'Where shall we go?'

'Well, Barnaby's been telling me about this pub in
Fulham which some of his friends have been to. They
have some good folk-singing groups there.'

'That would be lovely, if you're sure . . .'

'Now don't start all that again,' said Mary good-
naturedly. 'I'll ring him and tell him his evening's organised. He'll be delighted.'

The recommendation of Barnaby's friends proved
excellent. The music was in a special room at the back of
a traditional London pub. It was filled with an enor-
mously appreciative and enthusiastic audience. The
atmosphere was infectious. Bridie had wondered if it
would be full of serious-faced individuals demanding
absolutely authentic folk music, but this was not the case
at all. Many popular tunes were played and nobody
minded if you joined in the choruses. One particular girl

singer stole the evening. She was stunningly attractive, with long hair and a loose, flowing dress. She sang beautiful and haunting songs to her own accompaniment on a guitar and, quite frequently, the silence in the room as she sang was absolute.

One love ballad was of Scotland and the Highlands and the effect on Bridie was devastating. She was overwhelmed with such feelings of sadness and homesickness that tears flowed down her cheeks and she felt a great heaviness in her heart.

'Bridie. What on earth's the matter?' Mary's concerned eyes held hers.

'Oh I'm sorry, Mary. I'm just being silly. You must excuse me.' She fumbled and made her way awkwardly to the wash-room.

'Now then, Bridie. Come along,' she said to herself in the mirror. 'You're just indulging yourself.' She splashed cold water on her face and felt thoroughly ashamed. It was just the combination of a beautiful Scottish love song which she had learnt as a child, being surrounded by so many people enjoying themselves and—yes, she must be honest—the sight of Mary leaning back against Barnaby, loving the music, his chin on the top of her head and arms tight round her waist. Envy was an emotion she despised and she thoroughly rebuked herself.

The door opened and Mary appeared. 'Are you all right, Bridie?' she asked, her voice anxious.

'Yes. Of course.' She squeezed a smile. 'I just got homesick. I'm a bit tired after all my gadding about I expect.'

Mary was relieved. 'Nothing wrong with feeling homesick. It happened to me too—sort of creeps up on you. Gradually goes away, though. Come on, let's have another glass of wine. Barnaby's really worried.'

She found that the tears had been something of a release and she was able to join in the rest of the evening with something approaching her normal spirit. When Barnaby suggested some supper at the little bistro they had visited on her first night in London, she readily agreed. However, she found that her appetite was blunted and she settled for a light meal of melon, followed by scampi.

Mary and Barnaby were driving down to Sussex for Sunday lunch with his parents, so Bridie found herself alone again the next day. She busied herself with domestic tasks, relieved by composing a letter to her parents which told of her visit to Norway. Although it was a cold November day, it was quite bright and she resolved to take herself out during the afternoon. She had always wanted to visit the Victoria and Albert Museum and knew it was within easy walking distance so, donning her sheepskin coat over jeans and sweater, she set off towards the Brompton Road.

London on a Sunday afternoon was pleasant, compared with the pandemonium of a week-day, but even so the museum was quite crowded. She spent a pleasant couple of hours browsing amongst the beautiful prints and fabrics, although the thought kept recurring that it would have been so much nicer to have had a companion to share it with. She steadfastly refused to let herself dwell upon the possible identity of such a companion.

By Monday morning, she was confident that she had tamed her unruly emotions, even to the extent of being able to deal with him at work without betraying her feelings. She would indeed be called upon to do this, she remembered, since there was to be a meeting that morning with the architects who were consulting on the Skavanger site, at which they would both be present. She was half-expecting him to call into her surgery before the meeting so that they could discuss the conclusions from their trip, but he did not. Thus, she passed the first part of the morning in a state of studied composure which, far from relaxing her feelings, actually seemed to wind them tighter. She spent far too long making the decision as to whether she should go to the meeting in her uniform or change into her smart suit. In the end, she opted to stay in uniform. It was more appropriate, she told herself, angrily thrusting away the thought that his opinion might have influenced her decision.

She stepped into the lift and pressed the button for the basement theatre, where the meeting was to be held. She was checking herself in the lift's mirror when it stopped at the ground floor. The doors slid open to reveal Greg waiting there, as immaculate as ever. Their eyes met and her heart rocked, all the laboriously built intentions of the weekend vanishing in one lurching split second.

There was a silence and then, 'Good morning,' they both uttered in unison. She realised the lift doors were going to shut, leaving him still standing there and she reached for the 'Doors open' button to prevent such a ridiculous situation. The doors began to close but were stopped with an awkward, irritated sort of clatter.

'The meeting's in the basement theatre,' she said unnecessarily as he slipped in past the doors. They descended and she was acutely aware of being in close proximity to him in the confines of the lift. Wherever her eyes focused, she found she was looking at him, for there were mirrors everywhere. In the end, she gazed with an expression of idiotic expectation at the floor indicator panel, waiting for the B for Basement light to illuminate. She realised he was doing the same.

'I wonder if the architects are here yet. We're due to start at eleven, I believe.' He glanced at his watch. 'I imagine we'll have coffee first.'

The lift doors opened and he stood aside to let her out. As she passed him, he remarked, 'I'd have thought this was an ideal occasion for that smart little business outfit you were wearing the other day.'

'Oh—I thought that . . .' She caught sight of the mocking gleam in his eye and realised he was laughing at her. She swept past with her head held high.

The architects had indeed arrived and turned out to comprise a group of earnest young men, all elegant pin-stripe suits and pocket calculators, long blueprints rolled up under their arms and briefcases with numbered combination locks. She felt more than a match for them and was glad to have worn her uniform. It gave her an easily recognisable role within the group. She was introduced to several of them over coffee. She found this a little difficult, since when she was asked whether her views on the Skavanger plans were to be discussed in the meeting, she could not reply with any certainty, for there had been no opportunity to compare notes with Greg. She caught his attention.

'I really think we should have discussed our thoughts on Skavanger before this meeting. I'm feeling a little foolish,' she said in an angry undertone.

'Oh, I wouldn't worry about that. I'll cover it for both of us. Did you have a good weekend's ski-ing?'

Bridie positively gaped, utterly lost for words. Her

contribution had been dismissed in one patronising sentence. This was it! Final confirmation that he had asked her on the trip for one reason alone, to become one more notch on his belt. And when he had been thwarted in this intention, he had left her behind to play, just like a little girl, whilst he rushed back to the easier charms of his secretary creature.

'I returned to London on Friday, actually,' she said tightly, in tones of icy calm.

There was a look of puzzlement on his face and then the Company Project Manager was announcing that they really ought to get started. They took their places at the table.

'Shall I kick off?' Greg looked round the meeting. There was a murmur of agreement.

'Gentlemen, as you know, Sister Stewart and I made a personal inspection of the Skavanger site last week and I'd like to de-brief you on our conclusions. I have some slides.' He rose to his feet and, nodding towards a small projection window at the rear of the room, moved forward to stand alongside a silver screen. The lights dimmed.

What followed was one of the most concise pieces of reporting and recommendation she had ever heard. He held everybody's absolute attention and spoke rapidly and articulately without once referring to notes. Not only that, but she gradually realised that every single comment she had made during their visit had been heard, assimilated and developed as part of a grander plan, all within the dazzling quicksilver of his mind. Slide followed slide, illustrating this point and that. She had not realised he had taken so many shots—and to have had them processed so quickly. Although it was he who was presenting the report, she felt it was very much a joint effort from both of them. She felt her heart swimming in a kaleidoscope of emotions. She almost felt proud of him and smothered an absurd impulse to applaud as he finished. The lights came up to an impressed silence.

'Well, thank you, Greg. You and Sister Stewart seem to have done most of our work for us.' The Project Manager smiled and a murmur of agreement ran round the table.

She suddenly felt brimful of confidence. The rest of the meeting passed in a rapid interchange of views and decisions, to which she frequently contributed. Now and again, she caught his eyes upon her, gently approving. It was uncanny. With some of the questions, she felt she knew his answer before he uttered it and quite often they found themselves nodding in unspoken agreement across the table. It was almost as if they were a natural team.

'Well, thank you, gentlemen—and Sister Stewart. A very productive session. I think we'll have a progress meeting in one month; same venue and time. Does that suit everybody?' The Project Manager brought the meeting to a close and chairs slid back, briefcases appeared and papers were collected.

As she was gathering up her notes, she felt a light touch on her elbow and turned to find his grey eyes smiling down at her.

'Well done us, wouldn't you say? It will be quite a medical centre at Skavanger, I think. I'm most grateful for your help.'

'Oh, no, really. It has all been most interesting,' she stammered. 'I've enjoyed it.'

'Good. Well, I must leave, I'm afraid. I may see you later. Perhaps you would like to—'

'Dr Brandon. You are OK for the next meeting?' He was diverted and the moment between them was lost, for he was reaching for a pocket diary, reviewing dates and appointments.

'I'll have to check with my secretary. Can she let you know?' In an instant he was gone, an arm raised in farewell.

She felt that increasingly familiar sense of isolation. He was probably going off to lunch with his girl-friend. She knew she should not let it hurt, but the truth was that it did hurt, with a sweet tender pain she could hardly bear.

Some of the earnest young pin-stripes wanted to buy her lunch at a nearby Italian restaurant, but she politely declined and took her leave, to the accompaniment of appreciative glances and much 'Nice to have met you. See you again. Thank you Sister' etcetera. She found she could not even face the social clamour of the company dining-room and retired to the haven of her surgery with some cottage cheese and fruit from the sandwich bar next door.

As she sat at her desk, absently dipping into the tub of cheese, her thoughts turned back over the last few weeks. She had certainly realised her ambitions. London had been everything she had expected, for she felt a different person to the girl who had worked in Aberdeen. She knew she was coping well with all these new challenges and there was much satisfaction to be derived from her new career. But the lack of fulfilment in her work had been replaced by a much more acute lack of fulfilment in her heart. She knew too that what she felt

was not just an infatuation brought on by the heady pace
of London life. She might be young and inexperienced,
but she had a great deal of common sense, more even
than her extrovert friend Mary. Bridie knew that she had
inherited a legacy of level-headedness from her parents
which would stand her in good stead whatever life
brought her.

What she felt for Greg Brandon had never been
matched before in her life and most certainly would
never be matched again. He now seemed to occupy her
every thought, his image clouded with the knowledge
that they would never come together. She was not the
sort of girl to whom he was attracted, nor could her
sensitive spirit stand up to the casualness of his approach
to life in general and women in particular.

With an effort she pulled her mind back from this
reverie. She must find an outlet in work. She rose and set
about filing some of the paper-work which had been
generated whilst she was away. The agency nurse had
been efficient and had left a comprehensive note of
various actions taken and items requiring her attention.

The telephone rang whilst she was absorbed in this
and she lifted the receiver.

'Surgery. Sister Stewart speaking.'

There was a silence.

'Hallo. Sister Stewart,' she repeated.

A sound of stertorous breathing. Was this some sort of
crude hoaxer? She felt anger rising.

'Who is this?' she snapped.

Her eyes widened as she heard a voice like a gra-
mophone record running at too slow a speed. 'Sister . . .
It's Rupert Gallimore . . . please come quickly.'

'Sir Rupert. Where are you?'

A silence.

'Sir Rupert?'

'. . . office . . .' There was a clatter, as of the receiver falling on to a hard surface. She flew from the room, pausing only to collect her panic-bag. Experience had taught her to always have an emergency medical kit available for instant call. How useful it would be on this occasion she could not tell.

The building was quiet, still in the lull of the lunch break. She pressed all three lift call-buttons on her floor and paced up and down. 'Come on. Come on,' she muttered, and breathed a sigh of relief as a car arrived with a ping of its bell. She pressed the Executive Floor button and prayed no-one would stop her ascent. She knew with certainty that, whatever ailed Sir Rupert this time was no mere attack of dyspepsia. She had heard a man sound like that before, in an intensive care unit. She cleared her mind of conjecture and tore down the Executive corridor as the doors opened.

Sir Rupert's outer office was deserted and she dashed through, flinging open the door to his inner sanctum.

Her eyes took in the scene at a glance. The remains of a working lunch were on the coffee table. Beneath it, a widening stain was spreading on the deep pile carpet where a glass of orange juice had been spilt, its contents running across the glass surface of the table, soaking documents and dripping over the edge.

Sir Rupert himself was standing by the corner of his desk, from which a telephone receiver hung incongruously by its cord. He was swaying, staring at her speechlessly. His face was drained of colour, his lips bluish. He had one hand clasped to his chest, the other fumbling in his waistcoat pocket, then holding out a bottle of pills. Even as he paused, his knees buckled and he slid to the floor, brushing telephones and intercom from the desk with a clatter.

She rushed forward and knelt beside him, taking the capsules from his grasp. She glanced at the label. Glyceryl trinitrate.

'Sir Rupert—you suffer from angina, don't you?'

He looked up, his eyes clouded with pain. He nodded once, almost imperceptibly and then his eyelids fluttered and closed. His head fell back.

# CHAPTER NINE

FOR a moment, time stood still. Then her professional training took over. First contain the situation. Then treatment. With one hand she undid Sir Rupert's collar and, with the other, groped for one of the telephone receivers from which a metallic voice was emitting. It was a company operator, obviously confused by the scatter of signals on the switchboard downstairs.

'This is Sister Stewart. I have an emergency with the chairman. Please try to contact Dr Brandon and inform him. I believe he has some sort of car telephone. If you can't raise him within three minutes, call me back on this extension.' Her instructions were crisp and precise. Then she went to work. Sir Rupert's capsules were of no use, even if she could administer them, since they were for prevention, not treatment. They were completely incorrect if he had indeed entered some form of cardiac arrest. She swiftly felt for a pulse and tensed as she found none. She struggled to straighten his heavy bulk and loosen his clothing. The telephone shrilled and she grabbed it.

'Bridie. It's Greg. I'm in the car. What has happened?' His voice was surprisingly clear.

'Sir Rupert's in cardiac arrest. Angina pectoris. I am applying compression and mouth-to-mouth. I need oxygen quickly.'

'I will be with you in five minutes and an ambulance in ten. Can you manage?'

'I'm trying.'

'Good girl.'

There was a click and she hurled down the instrument. Grabbing a cushion from the settee, she slipped it under the chairman's neck. She checked the airway was clear and began compression on his chest. The only cases of arrest she had experienced before had been in a hospital environment where all the benefits of electric shock equipment were available. Now she had none of these facilities and her panic bag contained nothing of use in this situation. She worked frantically, aware that her slim frame was tiring with the effort. She applied herself alternately to cardiac compression and mouth-to-mouth resuscitation. Beads of perspiration ran down her face and she tore at the neck buttons of her uniform, gasping for air.

'Slowly, more slowly,' she urged herself. 'It is the oxygen from your lungs that he needs. Panting and puffing will do nobody any good.' An eternity passed and she felt her muscles growing weaker with the exertion.

'Greg, Greg, please hurry,' she breathed.

She fell forward, her ear to the chairman's chest, fingers feeling for the vital carotid pulse in his neck. Suddenly she felt a flicker, like a trapped bird fluttering in a cage. Desperately she breathed into his mouth, pausing to watch his chest fall in exhalation, waiting for signs of life in his own involuntary muscles.

Yes. A barely perceivable movement, but unmistakably his own. He was breathing. She had contained the situation. She fell sideways against the desk, her breast heaving as she sobbed for breath. Through half-closed eyes, she saw the bluish tint slowly fading from the

Chairman's lips. The door crashed open and Greg was kneeling beside her. Skilful fingers and stethoscope affirmed her own conclusion. He grasped Sir Rupert's shirt sleeve and, with a rending of stitches, tore it asunder in one stroke from wrist to shoulder. A hypodermic appeared from his bag like magic, with a phial, and in seconds he had administered an injection. He turned to her.

'Ambulance will be here any minute. Are you all right?'

'Oh Greg, I'm so glad you're here. I thought I was going to lose him.' Her voice choked.

'Of course you weren't. A capable girl like you.' He paused. Suddenly, his hand was cradling her neck. He pulled her to him fiercely. Their lips met in a searing kiss and she pressed against him. In that instant of passion, frightening in its intensity, she knew that she wanted him, needed him, would do anything for the love of him. She wanted to tell him how much she loved him, to give herself freely to him, no matter how he felt about her.

They broke apart, breathless, each aware of the surging force of the embrace, each suddenly red-faced with the knowledge that these feelings were improper in their present situation, an affront to their professional standards.

A trio appeared in the doorway—two smart ambulance men, in a uniform she did not recognise, with Britt bringing up the rear.

'Straight downstairs gentlemen. The back lift please. Yes, you can move him. Yes, oxygen if he needs it.' One of the men was carrying a portable unit. 'Now then, Britt. A phone call to the receptionists if you please—'

He turned to the ambulance men. 'Who else observed your arrival?'

'No-one, sir. Just the girls in reception. The lift was empty.'

'Right then, Britt. You know what to do.'

Bridie watched incredulously as he and Britt exchanged a nod of complicit understanding. They seemed to have a perfect rapport. And yet, seconds before, he had taken her, Bridie, in his arms and kissed her with a passion she had known from no man before.

Britt disappeared through the outer office.

The men were gently and efficiently sliding Sir Rupert on to their stretcher. Britt re-appeared. 'OK,' she nodded to Greg and again Bridie caught a glimpse of some shared secret knowledge. She felt an outsider, almost an intruder.

'Come along,' Greg snapped and the entourage sped down the corridor. Britt was holding open the door of a lift at the back of the building, which Bridie recognised as the one in which goods were delivered. Fortunately, it was spacious and able to accommodate all of them, but it seemed that Britt and one of the ambulance men were not coming, for the doors closed, leaving them on the Executive floor.

They lurched downstairs, painfully slowly in comparison with the express lifts at the front of the building. Sir Rupert's eyes flickered and focused momentarily upon her. She leaned down and patted his hand.

'Just you relax, sir. Everything's under control. We're taking you somewhere we can properly look after you. Don't worry.'

Greg was standing next to her, a preoccupied, set expression on his face. The lift hummed to a halt and the doors opened to reveal the goods entrance at the rear of the building. 'Right. Gently does it.' Greg stepped out. 'I'll lead the way.' He began kicking aside cardboard boxes which threatened to block the way of the wheeled stretcher.

'OK Sister, I'll do the work if you could just steer.' The ambulance man applied his not inconsiderable weight to the rear of the trolley and she found herself at the front, manoeuvring a path at Greg's instruction, out to the mews exit.

As they emerged, she saw an ambulance being reversed down the cobblestones. She recognised the driver as the man they had left upstairs. He must have taken a front lift and driven round from the other side of the building. It was not a normal Ambulance Service vehicle, but a specially converted large Citroen estate car. It had the words Transmedic International sign-written along its sides. The rear entrance seemed an awfully inefficient method of getting Sir Rupert out of the building, but presumably the traffic was unusually heavy at the front. She had often seen cars and taxis jammed solid in Mayfair. She made to question Greg about this, but his expression forbade any conversation other than that necessary to load the stretcher into the ambulance. She stood aside to let the men effect this. One of them climbed into a jump seat alongside Sir Rupert's stretcher and the driver took his place behind the wheel. Greg opened the front passenger door, turned and beckoned to her.

'Sister Stewart.' He hesitated for a moment. 'It is imperative that knowledge of these events is limited to yourself, myself and the Chairman's secretary. Is that perfectly clear?' She was totally unprepared for this authoritative and formal tone and responded automatically.

'Er, yes. Of course, Doctor.' She paused, not really understanding. 'But the receptionists and the switchboard girl know there has been some sort of emergency. Won't they naturally . . . ?'

'Yes. Britt is taking care of that. I'm sorry, we can't delay. I'll explain when there's more time.'

With a lithe, fluid movement, he slid into the passenger seat and the Citroen purred away. The flashing blue light on its roof was at variance with the lack of a siren's wail. It was dream-like, as if she were watching a silent film. It turned at the bottom of the mews and was gone, leaving her with an even heightened feeling of unreality as she looked along the empty cobblestones.

She retraced her steps to the goods lift and returned to the surgery floor, her mind in a whirl. The speed with which things had happened in the last half-hour had left her dizzy. She realised she was passing staff in the corridor who were only just returning from lunch. She checked her watch and was amazed to see that it was only two-fifteen.

Her office had an odd, deserted air about it. Her tub of cottage cheese still reposed on the desk, a spoon flung down next to it. The coffee she had bought to accompany her lunch was still tepid. She sat in her chair and absently spooned at her snack. She could not understand the need for such secrecy. Why, they had virtually smuggled the Chairman out of the building.

A ghastly thought struck her and she felt as if a cold hand had touched her. Supposing Greg was guilty of some negligence in his professional duty. Perhaps he had mis-prescribed some medication or other. Perhaps it was all a huge cover-up. And that girl friend was in it with him. She had an inherent distrust of Britt. She shook her imagination free of these stampeding thoughts with an effort. This was ridiculous. But her mind rampaged on. If it were true, what should she do? Her love for him made her want to support him, but her ethical standards were paramount. She could not be a party to any form of malpractice. She simply must get to the bottom of this. She would go and confront Britt now.

Britt was on the telephone when Bridie walked purposefully into the office, her entrance acknowledged with a barely lifted eyebrow.

'No, I'm afraid the chairman's been called to an important meeting in Geneva. No, not for several days . . . and then he's scheduled for some leave. The managing director's handling all his affairs. Can I have him call you? Thank you.' She replaced the receiver and fixed Bridie with a supercilious stare.

'Why all this secrecy?' blurted Bridie. 'I don't understand.'

'I'm afraid you'll have to ask Dr Brandon that.'

'Don't you dare patronise me. I have a right to know,' spat out Bridie. 'Sir Rupert is as much my patient as Dr Brandon's and I demand to know his condition.'

Britt's expression of indolence actually seemed to intensify. 'I'm afraid you'll just have to wait to speak to Greg. Oh, is this yours?' She reached down behind her desk and picked up Bridie's emergency bag. She held it out between finger and thumb as though it might contaminate her.

Bridie snatched it. 'I demand to know which hospital Sir Rupert has been taken to,' she raged.

'Well, it's the Welbeck Square Clinic . . .'

'Thank you.'

'. . . but it's no earthly use ringing them. They will only talk to a restricted list of callers.' The telephone rang. 'You'll have to excuse me.' She lifted the receiver. 'No, I'm afraid the chairman's been suddenly called to an important meeting in Geneva. Not for several days . . .'

Bridie found herself out in the corridor, shaking with rage. Although it was out of her character, she had derived a certain pleasure in slamming the door on Britt's honeyed tones. She made her way back to the surgery, worried and preoccupied.

She remained worried for the next week or so. She tried to discuss it with Mary but found it difficult to frame her concern in words. It was impossible actually to suggest that Greg was involved in anything unethical. Mary's reaction was to tell her not to worry, Dr Brandon knew what he was doing, it was not her concern and so forth. Also, she had the distinct feeling that Mary was unusually wrapped up in her own affairs. Bridie had come home one evening to find her and Barnaby in the living-room, surrounded by holiday brochures, diaries, maps and estate agents' circulars. They would not commit themselves, but it was obvious that a fair number of wedding plans were being laid. Bridie was feeling particularly tired that evening, and had retired to her room with a steaming bowl of soup, leaving her friends to their happy deliberations. Her room seemed rather lonely.

At Pan-European, it seemed as if a curtain had descended on the chairman's activities. She felt a grudging respect for Britt's ability to smooth things over and account for the absence of such an important figure in the company's affairs. Even the arrival of the private ambulance had been explained away as simply a demonstration of the Citroen model to the company medical adviser. To all enquirers, Sir Rupert was incommunicado.

And so it remained until the following Thursday morning, when a telephone's shrill tone interrupted some eye tests she was giving.

'Good morning, Sister Stewart. This is the Welbeck Square Clinic. Sir Rupert Gallimore has asked me to telephone you.'

Bridie recoiled in surprise. 'Yes. Thank you. I see,' she said in a rush. 'How is Sir Rupert?'

'He's doing extremely well and seeing far too many visitors. He would be most grateful if you could spare him half-an-hour today. Is that possible?'

'Well, yes, of course.'

'Good. Now he knows you are an extremely busy person and wonders what time would be convenient to you.'

'Oh, yes. W-would you hold on please.' Still rather stunned, she flicked open her diary. 'I've several appointments during today, but nothing later on this afternoon. Would five o'clock be all right? I could come on my way home. Where are you exactly?'

'Five o'clock is fine. You'll be able to have tea with Sir Rupert. Have you got a pencil and I'll give you the address. We're not far from you.' She jotted it down. It was almost with walking distance, quite close to Bond Street Tube.

'See you at five o'clock, then.' She hung up.

She was delighted to hear that the Chairman was on the way to recovery. Why on earth would he want to see her?

She could hardly contain her curiosity during the rest of the day and five o'clock found her tripping along a street just north of Oxford Street, peering up at the numbers through the November gloom. A discreet brass plate indicated that she had navigated herself correctly. She pushed open the large mahogany door and found herself in a beautifully-proportioned hall. A room to her right was marked 'Visitors'. She entered and was met by a friendly smile on the face of a charming Indian girl in a flowing sari, sitting at an antique table.

'You must be Sister Stewart. Sir Rupert's been looking forward to your visit all day. I'll just buzz for someone to take you up.' She reached across to a compact and very modern switchboard sitting on a side desk.

A few minutes later, she was being led upstairs and along passageways by a smiling nurse. The Clinic was quite spacious and had been skilfully converted from the second and third floors of an elegant Regency terrace. Sir Rupert was ensconced in a comfortable, modern room, all pastel colours, subdued lighting and sleek furniture. He was propped up in bed and was positively beaming at her as the nurse ushered her in.

'Hallo m'dear. Welcome. Welcome. Sit down.' He waved at a chair.

'How are you feeling, Sir Rupert?' she enquired, sitting forward and regarding him with some concern.

'Not bad at all, m'dear. Not bad at all. Thanks to you, mind. I'd have been a goner if it wasn't for you—'

'Oh, I'm not sure about that,' she protested.

'No. It's a fact and you know it.'

'You're feeling better. That's the main thing.'

'Yes. They're even letting me up and around now.

Got to take things easy, so they tell me. But you know more about these things than I do.'

'Well, yes. You must take more care. No strain or pressures. It's the worst thing.'

He was regarding her benignly. He really was a very nice man. Nothing like the hypochondriac she had once suspected.

'I expect there are a few questions buzzing around in that pretty head of yours?'

'Actually, to be frank, Sir Rupert, there have been some things I haven't understood. It *has* been awfully cloak and dagger you know. I was told to keep everything to myself and I've done that—but I did wonder why . . .'

'Well, that's why I've asked you here, Bridie. Yes. Apart from wanting to thank you of course,' he added hastily. There was a pause and she waited expectantly, slightly surprised that he knew her first name. 'Do you know anything about stocks and shares, business generally?'

'Not really. My father has some money invested in unit trusts and he's always looking in the *Scotsman* to see how they're going. But I don't really know anything more than that companies are made up of shares and they're all bought and sold on the Stock Exchange.'

'Quite right, Bridie. And have you heard of something called a take-over bid, when one company buys enough of another company's shares to control it?'

'Yes, I have.'

'Good. Well, you see, there is this company—it's not a company really, more like a bunch of international money men.' His tone was scathing. 'They want to gain control of Pan European. But they haven't got the interests of our company at heart. They haven't got the interests of the country at heart either. If they took control of Pan European, they would milk all the profits out of our North Sea operations and not invest for the future. And we do have to invest for the future. Not just more North Sea exploration, but there's the Irish Sea as well. And we must research other forms of energy, because one day the oil will run out.' He paused and she feared he was tiring himself.

'Please don't become exhausted, Sir Rupert. It's not worth it.'

'It's all right, Bridie. I'm fine. And it is worth it. The Company owes you an explanation. Are you with me so far?'

She nodded. 'I can see it's important to stop these men gaining control of Pan European. But how?'

He was looking at her expectantly.

'You mean, if Pan European shares were to drop in value, then these financiers could buy them and take over the Company . . .'

He nodded vehemently '. . . and?'

Suddenly, everything dropped into place '. . . And if news got out that you were ill, weren't completely in command, then people would think the Company wasn't being properly run and the value of the shares really would drop.'

'Yes. Exactly. So?'

'So it's very important for your heart condi—I mean, illness, to be concealed.'

'Yes. You're a bright girl, Bridie. You needn't mince words either, m'dear. A heart condition *is* what I've got. But it's the best kept secret in the company. You see, I can't even trust some of the members of the Board. I won't go into details, but people can make a lot of money out of take-over deals, to say nothing of the scramble for jobs under a new regime. It would destroy the company as we know it.'

'But Sir Rupert, you can't run the entire company single-handed. You must—what's the word—delegate to other people.'

'Indeed I must, Bridie. But I need a successor. I've been grooming our Managing Director for the job. He's a brilliant man, but he needs six months—and he must have the vote of the Board.' He leaned his head back. 'Yes, Bridie. Six months and I shall take a back seat.'

'Well, Sir Rupert. You must take care of yourself in the meantime.' His eyes were closed and she feared he really had exhausted himself. She sat quietly.

Now she understood the need for all the secrecy. Sir Rupert was the key figure in Pan-European, always appearing in television programmes, often quoted in the press. She would not have thought it possible to conceal news of his illness from the public in such a fashion. But if news had leaked out, it would have seemed as though the company really was leaderless. No wonder Greg had been so firm. If only he had taken her into his confidence. Another thought struck her and she looked up. Sir Rupert was regarding her steadily.

'How long have you been aware of your angina condition?'

'Two years.'

'And how long has Dr Brandon been with the company?'

'Two years.'

'Did he—?'

'It was Dr Brandon who first diagnosed the condition

at his consultancy in Harley Street. He is one of the best heart men in England. He has a dazzling career before him. I asked him to act as Company Medical Adviser— he was well aware of all the implications you and I have just been discussing. He agreed to the post, but only if he could continue with his work in Harley Street and also have access to company resources to help him with his researches. I really don't know how he manages to pack everything in. He is one of the most dedicated and hard-working men I have ever known, I wish we had a few more like him in our senior management.'

She must have been gazing at him raptly.

'Mind you, he plays hard as well. He's an extremely good-looking young man.' Sir Rupert's eyes were twinkling at her. She felt her cheeks burning. She was glad of the diversion caused by the door opening and tea being brought in. She stood up and poured for them both. She could not resist plumping his pillows and straightening his bed clothes before handing him a cup.

'Always the nurse, eh?' He gave a chuckle. 'Tell me about yourself—or at least add to what young Greg has told me.'

They passed a pleasant ten minutes or so, gently chatting. She told him about her family, about her brother in the Merchant Navy and sister at university. He had children of his own but much older.

'It's all weddings and christenings m'dear,' he complained. 'Costs me a fortune in presents.'

She laughed, eyes shining to see him so lively and fast-witted. It was moments like this which made all her training worthwhile. It was true. She really had saved his life, or at least prevented something worse. A starvation of oxygenated blood to the brain, no matter how slight, would have diminished his mental faculties, even turned him into some sort of vegetable. She had seen this frequently in her career and suppressed a shudder at the thought of a vital man like Sir Rupert suffering such a fate.

'Well, Sir Rupert, I really think that's enough excitement for today.' The smart young nurse was standing at Bridie's elbow.

Sir Rupert raised his eyes heavenwards. 'You see how they boss me around.'

'I agree with them, Sir Rupert,' she smiled, 'and we all want to see you fully recovered—as soon as possible.'

'Thank you, my dear. I do hope you'll visit me again. I'm told I can take a restricted interest in the company's affairs from next Monday, but I have to remain here under all these eagle eyes.' His face became serious. 'Well, Bridie, it has been a delight to see you. I do hope I may be able to be of real help to you one day. If there is ever anything I can do, you must promise to let me know.'

'I was really just doing my duty, you know, but I promise to tell you if I should ever need your help.' She took his hand and shook it. It was ridiculous. She almost felt like giving him a hug.

Outside it had been raining and the lights of the traffic reflected up from the wet streets. She joined the throng of homeward-bound commuters. Mary had been working an early duty and popped a warming casserole into the oven. The two girls took trays into the living-room and curled up in easy chairs in front of the gas fire. Mary was obviously very excited.

'We've fixed the date, Bri,' she burst out. 'Isn't it wonderful. I'm actually feeling a bit frightened now we've got to this stage. It's going to be a May wedding.'

'Oh Mary, I'm so happy for you. Will you be getting married in Scotland?'

'We thought about it, but most of Barnaby's family live down South and practically all our friends. There are some lovely churches in this borough and, after all, I am a resident. And my family's so small—it's only Mummy and Daddy, really. It would be far easier for them to come down here, rather than everybody go up there. Barnaby and I are going up on the night sleeper this Friday to discuss it all with them.'

'Where will you live?'

'We're thinking of buying a house out in west London. I'll continue nursing for a while, but we both want children. I expect we'll have to wait a little while though. You can take over the lease of this flat, Bri, and we'll soon find you a flat-mate. There are always notices on the board at the hospital.'

The conversation carried on in this vein for most of the evening. Bridie felt unsettled by all this talk of weddings, but she was overjoyed for her friend and did not begrudge her a moment of her happiness. It was difficult to ignore her feelings of emptiness, however, in the solitude of her own room. Her thoughts returned to what Sir Rupert had revealed that afternoon. In so many ways had she misjudged Greg Brandon. She had thought him a superficial person with shallow motivations and lifestyle. But he was in reality a gifted man of drive and determination, she could see that now. She also knew that there would never be a man like him again in her life. She had fallen in love with him when she could only see his faults. Now that she understood the difficult role he played within the company and had glimpsed the dedicated professional man he really was, it made everything a hundred times more difficult.

She had come to London hoping that a more worthwhile career would fill the gap in her life. True, her new job had more than measured up to her hopes, but she had now found herself with an even more unattainable dream. Mary's news had brought everything into sharp focus. Bridie knew that she would throw away her career and her new exciting way of life in one instant, could she but realise this warm, passionate love she felt for Greg Brandon.

The next morning, she was more able to concentrate on her work, now that her mind was clear of concern about Sir Rupert. She could not, however, bring herself to acknowledge Britt with anything more than a formal nod when she passed her in the corridor.

Most of the morning was occupied with an assessment meeting on the new thermal clothing tests and it served well to distract her thoughts from Greg. When she returned to her office, however, and answered the 'phone to hear a female voice announce it was Dr Brandon calling, her heart jumped. There was a click and his voice came on the line.

'Hallo, Bridie. How are you? I hear you've paid Sir Rupert a visit.'

She was practically stammering at the sound of his voice. 'Yes,' she blurted. 'It was such a relief to see him bright and perky, almost his usual self.' She hesitated. 'I wish you'd told me, Greg,' she added reproachfully. 'You could have trusted me. I've been thinking all sorts of things . . .'

'Yes, Bridie, I'm sorry. I should have put you in the picture. But I needed his authority to do that and I obviously couldn't trouble him until he was better.' He paused. 'I really would like you to try and understand.'

'I do really, Greg. I'm sorry.'

There was an awkward silence.

He cleared his throat. 'I've actually rung to ask you a favour, but I don't think I've got the nerve to ask it now.'

'Yes, you have,' she laughed. 'You've got enough nerve for both of us. What is it?'

'It's silly really. I've only just got back here from Pan European House and I've left the Skavanger file on Britt's desk. I'm very tied up this afternoon and I wanted to work on some equipment specifications at the weekend. I don't suppose you could . . .'

'Bring it round? Of course I can. I was going out to get some shopping anyway this lunchtime. I'll bring it now. Where are you?'

'I'm at my consulting rooms in Harley Street.' He gave her the number. 'You're sure it's no trouble?'

'Of course not. See you in about twenty minutes.' She replaced the receiver, her heart beating wildly at the thought of seeing him. He might even ask her out to lunch. If he did, she would offer her help at the weekend on the Skavanger project. He might welcome it—and the flat would seem lonely with Mary and Barnaby in Scotland. She controlled these thoughts and reached for her top coat. She stopped, realising he would hardly ask her out to lunch in her uniform. She looked at her watch. She had said twenty minutes, but she could take a cab and save ten. She slipped out of her office and, with a rueful smile, locked the outer door to the surgery. She did not want any more embarrassing situations— although Greg was at a safe distance.

In five minutes she had made the transition into her

suit, checked her hair and make-up, collected the file from Britt's empty office and was hailing a taxi, spirits high and the blood singing in her veins.

The cabbie knew his job and she was soon making her way up some steps in Harley Street and ringing a ground floor bell marked Gregory D. Brandon. The door was opened by a pleasant, middle-aged receptionist.

'Sister Stewart? Would you like to go straight in? The doctor is expecting you.' She indicated a room off to one side.

She tapped at the door and, without waiting for a reply, entered the room. She stopped dead in the doorway, her cheeriness vanishing like sun behind clouds. Britt was standing in the room, her hand in Greg's. He was obviously about to kiss her.

Britt turned. 'Hallo Sister. Have you come to see Greg? We're just off to lunch.'

'I see.' Bridie swallowed.

'It's a special celebration, you see. Look!' She held out a hand and Bridie found herself staring at the brilliant sparkle of an engagement ring. The scintillating reflections burned into her eyes, mocking her, taunting at her dreams.

'Aren't congratulations in order, then?' Britt's mouth was twisted in a sardonic smile.

'Oh, er, yes, of course. Congratulations.' She stared at the floor. 'I've brought your file, Doctor.' She dropped it onto a nearby chair without looking up. 'You must excuse me, I have some shopping to do.' Her words trailed off into a barely disguised falter and she turned and fled from the room.

'Bridie?' She heard a voice behind her, but she was gone, through the front door out into the street, bumping into passers-by in her flight and scarcely noticing. All she knew was the sick feeling that clutched at the pit of her stomach. Everything else was blankness and oblivion.

# CHAPTER TEN

LOOKING back on that Friday afternoon she found she could remember very little of it. Unsure of her self-control, she did not even want to answer the telephone in case it should be him on the other end.

She was hurt and bitter, and angry at her own delusions. She had told herself often enough that she was not Greg Brandon's sort of girl and it had taken his engagement to Britt to finally convince her of this truth. Seeing that her diary for the afternoon was empty, she decided to leave early and made her way home on the clattering tube train. London seemed an alien, ugly place, full of brittle unfriendly people rushing hither and thither.

Mary was also early and found her sitting in the kitchen, still wearing her top coat and staring dismally into space.

'Hello Bri. You're early. Is anything the matter?'

'No. I'm OK, thanks. At least . . .' She could feel the hot prickle of tears behind her eyes. She held them back. Even though Mary was her closest friend, she couldn't bring herself to tell her that she had been stupid enough to fall in love with her boss. She fished for a tissue and blew her nose loudly. She was certainly not going to carry on like some love-sick teenager.

'I think I'm just a bit overwrought. I haven't been sleeping too well. I'm not sure if I'm cut out for this Head Office life. It's all a bit too high-powered.'

Mary was concerned. 'Well, you're certainly not the

Bridie we're used to. I don't like the idea of your being on your own here this weekend. London can be an awfully lonely place.' Her expression suddenly brightened. 'Why don't you take a trip home? You could come up on the sleeper with Barnaby and me. You'd be home by midday easily. We could all travel back together on Sunday night too.'

Bridie looked doubtful.

'Go on,' said Mary, 'it would do you good and your parents would love to see you.'

'I don't know . . .'

'Oh, come on. Listen, it's only five o'clock. We can dash round the corner to our friendly travel agent and book you a sleeper. We've even got our coats on still.' Bridie found herself caught up in her friend's enthusiasm and, in a quarter of an hour, was back in the kitchen staring dazedly at her rail ticket and sleeper reservation. Mary put the kettle on.

'Good heavens, I'd better ring mother and tell them I'm coming. I hope she can meet the train. It's practically a two-hour drive from Glenairton to Aberdeen.'

Her mother was delighted at the prospect of a visit from her elder daughter. 'I don't know what time the train gets in—about ten o'clock, I expect,' Bridie speculated.

'Don't you worry dear. I'll ring the station at this end. I'll meet you at the ticket barrier. Your father will be really pleased. See you tomorrow!'

Barnaby soon arrived and, while Mary cooked them all a simple supper, Bridie threw a few clothes in her flight bag. She did not need to take much, apart from her toilet things, nightie and a change of underwear, since she had left a fair quantity of casual clothes at Glenairton. She decided to travel in jeans and a sweater, with her sheepskin coat as insulation against the colder temperatures she expected further north.

'Catching sleepers is an odd thing,' mused Barnaby, sipping a mug of coffee. 'You sit around at home until you're thoroughly tired and ready for bed and then you go out into the night to catch a train. Silly, really.'

'Well, it certainly saves a lot of daytime travelling, darling,' insisted Mary.

'What time do we need to be at King's Cross?' asked Bridie. 'I've never travelled on a night train before.'

'About elevenish,' replied Barnaby. 'It's worth being early so that I can nobble the sleeping car attendant and offer financial inducements to put you both in the same compartment.'

'Can you do that?'

'With my charm, anything is possible.' Barnaby was smiling broadly.

He was true to his word, for at midnight, she and Mary were established in a compact, swaying compartment as the Inter-City night express pulled out of London on its long journey North.

Mary was a seasoned traveller. 'It's impossible for us both to get ready for bed at the same time. It's all clashing elbows and bottoms,' she giggled. 'You go first and grab the top bunk. I'll lay on the bottom one and read my book until you're finished.'

Bridie was impressed by the cleverly designed fittings for hanging things and so forth and, after taking off her make-up, brushing her teeth and slipping on her nightie, she clambered up into bed. She was aware of her friend going through similar motions and then Mary's face appeared on a level with her own.

'Right then. Hope you sleep OK. Actually, the motion of the train soon sends you off. Quite nice really. Like being rocked in a cradle. 'Night.' Her head disappeared—and then popped back up. 'Oh—and no losing any sleep over Dr Gregory Brandon.' Bridie's eyes widened in amazement. 'Well, it wasn't that difficult to see, you know,' said Mary, with a wry smile. 'It was written all over your face that first night in London, when you saw him in the bistro. And ever since you've been back from the Norwegian trip, you've gone from bad to worse.'

Bridie's eyes misted at her friend's kindness and perception.

'It won't do, you know,' went on Mary. 'Now listen, you're off to Scotland for a nice weekend. Time will soon sort things out.'

'Yes, you're right,' said Bridie, smiling through tears.

'OK,' said Mary and, nodding firmly, disappeared again. 'See you in Scotland.'

'Goodnight, Mary—and thanks,' Bridie called back.

She reached for the light switch and snuggled down in the crisp, white sheets. They had pulled the window drape, but there was a chink through which an endless flicker of light showed. Gradually, this too diminished as the express left the metropolis and hurtled into the darkened countryside. She was left alone with her thoughts. This train was speeding her away from the only man in her life whom she had ever really loved. She could not wipe her mind clear of the memory of him and Britt standing there, the engagement ring glittering on the girl's finger. Eventually, the soporific effect of the swaying train dulled even this image and she slept.

Next morning, the trio met for breakfast in the dining-car as the train covered the last stage of the jouney and, very soon, they were trooping down the platform at Aberdeen to be met by Mrs Stewart.

After the greetings were completed, Bridie asked if Mary and Barnaby wanted a lift, but they insisted a taxi was the best solution, as Mary's parents lived on the opposite side of town to Bridie's route homewards.

'Good old Min,' said Bridie, affectionately patting the roof of her little red car.

'Yes, I thought I'd give her an airing. Your father said it would charge up the battery,' said Mrs Stewart.

Bridie insisted on driving and they were soon on the road to Glenairton. Mrs Stewart plied her with questions about her life in London.

'You're not looking your normal bright-eyed self, dear,' she said after a while. 'I hope you haven't been overdoing things.'

'Oh, don't fuss, mother,' said Bridie good-naturedly. 'I expect it was the journey. You don't get a really good sleep on the overnight train.'

'Well, you can catch up tonight.' They settled into a companionable silence as Bridie drove along, loving every minute as the beautiful, well-loved scenery unfolded before them. Although it was barely December, there was quite a covering of snow, particularly on the high ground.

She spent a pleasant afternoon with her parents, loving the warmth and security which the family home seemed to exude. As the evening approached, however, she felt more and more tired and had little appetite for supper. Sitting in front of a blazing fire later on, she even found herself shivering, a dismal ache in her limbs.

'I think I'll turn in,' she said at last. 'It's been a long day—and night, for that matter.'

'I hope you're not sickening for anything, Bridie,' said her mother, regarding her with concern. 'You don't look at all well.'

'Oh, I'm all right. I just need a good night's sleep.' She made her way upstairs, glad to tumble into bed.

Her mother's fears proved correct, however, and she spent a restless night, tossing and turning. When Mrs Stewart knocked on her door with a cup of tea in the morning, she took one look at Bridie's face, with her hair clinging damply to her forehead, and went to the bathroom medicine cabinet for a thermometer.

'It's there you stay, my girl,' she said, examining the reading. 'It's a slight fever you have. All these London 'flu germs, I'll be bound. Let's hope it's only the twenty-four hour variety.'

Bridie acknowledged that she felt most unwell. The ache in her limbs was worse and her surroundings seemed unreal. 'But I'm booked on the night train back, with Mary and Barnaby—'

'I'll ring them.'

'—and there's the surgery tomorrow. There's nobody to cover.'

'You must have an agency you can call on?'

'There's the Grosvenor. They run a twenty-four hour, seven days a week, service.'

'I'll ring them as well.'

'The number's in my address book. In my handbag.' She waved vaguely at the dressing table.

After that mild initial protest, she allowed things to take their course. Her father confirmed the 'flu diagnosis and she spent an uncomfortable day and night in bed.

She woke up—it must have been midnight—to find the sheets damp and a raging thirst in her throat. She might have called out his name for, in her feverish imaginings, she had been sure Greg was in the room, standing over her. With remarkable clarity, she had watched him sit on the bed, the pupils in his grey eyes large and smouldering, and lean down towards her. She felt his lips on hers, gently at first and then with more urgency. She was responding hungrily, her arms round his broad shoulders, pulling him down. His hands were caressing her body, moving inside her nightie, arousing burning desire within her. 'Yes. Yes, Greg, my darling,' she whispered.

The harshness of reality dawned on her as her muddled thoughts suddenly focused on the empty room. She reached for her glass of water, trying to slake the fire in her body and mind. Then, overlapping with these emotions, came the reaction. Tears soaked into the pillow and she slipped into an exhausted sleep.

The next morning, she woke up feeling clear-headed. She was somewhat unsteady on her feet, as she discovered, on making her way to the bathroom. Bowing to her mother's advice, she spent the day in bed. She had the distinct impression her mother was enjoying fussing over her and she let herself be coddled. It was really rather pleasant for a change.

As she lay in bed that day, gradually regaining her strength, she thought how painful life was going to be, working with Greg, coming into daily contact with him. She did not think it was something she could bear. Always she would be wanting to reach out and touch him, wondering how it would feel to run her fingers through his crinkly dark hair, caress his lean, strong jaw. Britt would be there too, looking on mockingly—almost as if she knew the depth of Bridie's feelings. It would be impossible. She simply could not carry on working there. It would make her life a misery. In fact, life in London had very little to offer her now. Even Mary would be drifting away as her marriage to Barnaby drew near. It was only a few months away. Sadly she came to the conclusion that she would resign from her job. She was too proud to carry a secret torch for Greg, her unfulfilled love for him torturing her every working day. The best solution was to change her life completely and try to forget him. She made her way rather shakily downstairs to find some writing paper and ask her mother if she would post a letter on her village shopping trip that afternoon.

Propping the writing-pad on a book against her drawn-up knees, she leaned back on the pillows and composed a letter to Sir Rupert. She was going to ask for an immediate release from her contract—she knew she really could not bear another day in Pan European. It was an unusual request and one which would normally be refused, but the chairman had offered his help if ever she needed it and she was going to take up his offer. She struggled over her reasons for resigning—she felt compelled to give some. She stressed that she had enjoyed working for the company and eventually, and rather lamely, referred to 'personal reasons' for wishing to leave. It was a difficult letter and took some time to complete, but she eventually sealed and addressed it to Sir Rupert at the Welbeck Square Clinic, marking it PERSONAL. She had no fear it would concern him while he was still recovering, for he had begun resuming an interest in the company's affairs and anyway she was a very small cog in the Pan European machine.

She gave it to her mother to post, who made no comment other than to register satisfaction that Bridie was well enough to write letters. She did not feel able to tell her mother of her decision, for that would have meant lengthy explanations and she was not ready for that.

She lay back in bed, feeling rather empty. Her thoughts kept returning to Greg but, every time she felt a wave of bitter-sweet tenderness for him, she remembered Britt and the glitter of that arrogantly shown-off engagement ring.

By the next day she was up and about. She told her parents that she had contacted the office and arranged some leave. Although this was something of a white lie, it was also the truth. She was rather withdrawn and quiet around the house, but no remarks were passed about this, her parents assuming it was the after-effects of the 'flu.

Wednesday morning dawned bright and clear, with a crisp winter sun, and Mrs Stewart encouraged Bridie to take a walk up to Loch Glenairdrie. 'It will give you an appetite for lunch, dear. Put some colour in your cheeks,' she urged.

Bridie hesitated for a moment, but Angus and Sophie, the two labradors, had heard the magic word 'walk' and were circling around her, tails waving with interest, an anticipatory look in their soft, brown eyes. Faced with such appealing expressions, she could not refuse. Donning her old walking anorak, scarf, gloves and a pair of wellingtons, she loaded her two canine companions into the back of her mother's estate car and set off up the road to the loch.

She parked and opened the tail-gate to let out the

scrambling dogs. 'No jumping in the loch,' she called after them. 'You'll get a nasty cold shock.' She smiled as they raced off, barking joyously and snuffling frantically at the snow. Angus even took a mouthful and shook his head at the frozen taste of it. The layer of snow was fairly light and several days old, for there was a clearly defined track round the loch where other walkers had trodden.

The outlook was breath-taking, as always, the snow adding an extra dimension of beauty. She drank in the scene, assailed by the thought that it would have been so much nicer to have had someone to share it with, a feeling which had become more and more frequent since she had known Greg. She thrust the notion away bitterly and made her way along the track, head down and pensive. It was difficult to recapture the mood of the last occasion she had walked the dogs here, back in October. She had felt very unsettled then, she remembered, eager for change—and very disillusioned about Neil, she now realised. How fatuous to have imagined that she and Neil could ever have had a future. Looking back, it seemed as though it had been another girl taking that walk. So much had happened since to completely change her outlook. She had absorbed new experiences, taken on and won new challenges. But now it seemed as though all her resolve and ambitions of such a short time ago he turned sour.

Down by the road, a Range Rover had pulled up, a figure emerging from the cab. Someone else coming up to enjoy a walk through this winter landscape, she mused, her feet crunching on the snow. She really did not know if she would take another job in London or stay up here in Scotland. She might even go abroad. There was always a demand for good nurses in the developing countries and it would be worthwhile work. Perhaps she would write to the Ministry of Overseas Development and discuss it with her father.

She had reached the head of the little loch now and began making her way back along the opposite bank. The figure from the Range Rover was approaching on her side. It was a solitary figure, probably a gillie. There was something familiar about the set of the shoulders. She realised with surprise that he was running towards her, waving. Suddenly, she heard her name being called, the sound drifting down on the crisp, clear air. She stopped and stood stock-still in utter amazement. One of the dogs, noticing her stare, also froze, one paw raised, muzzle pointing towards the approaching man.

With a slithering, sliding run, Greg Brandon stood before her, his chest heaving with exertion, breath hanging clouded in the cold air. His eyes were dancing, alight with the pleasure of seeing her. She stood speechless, her heart bounding, questions rising on her tongue, overlapping one upon the other in her spinning mind.

'Greg, what on earth are you doing here?'

'I've come to ask you something,' he said, trying to regain his breath.

'But how did you find me?'

'Your parents. I called at the house. Your mother gave me directions. She said this was your favourite haunt.' He looked round at the loch, the pines with their white mantle of snow and the soaring Cairngorms in the distance. 'I can see why.'

He was looking at her and she ached to hold him, feel his strong arms encircle and enclose her.

'But I don't understand. Is there some emergency?' A

sudden thought gripped her. 'It's not Sir Rupert?' she cried in alarm.

'Sir Rupert's fine, almost his old self. In fact, it is mostly he who's responsible for my being here. Said I needed my head examining to let you go. He'd received your letter, you see, and—'

'Oh Greg, please don't make it difficult for me. I've made up my mind to leave Pan European and—'

'It's not your job at Pan European that I've come to ask you about.' He was very close to her now and had taken both her hands in his. Suddenly she was in his arms, crushed fiercely to him. Muffled in winter clothes, she could feel only his face, the skin cold against her and the warmth of his mouth. She felt herself melting into his kiss, her eyes closed in a sweeping wave of delicious abandonment. Then she was pushing him away.

'But Bridie, what's the matter?'

She struggled to control herself. 'Greg, please. Can't you see? You're just playing with me and I can't bear it.' She turned away and he caught her arm, gently and insistently.

'But, Bridie, don't you understand? I've come to ask you to marry me.'

It seemed that there was a very long silence. She felt a tremor of exultation deep within her. He was looking at her, an expression of agonised suspense on his face.

'But Greg, you're engaged to Britt and—'

'Whatever gave you that idea?' His jaw gaped in surprise.

'The ring. Last Friday. You were both going out to celebrate—'

'We were going out to celebrate *her* engagement. She's going to marry that young Marketing Manager. It was a whirlwind romance, apparently. I was going to ask you to come for lunch as well, but you rushed off.'

'But I thought she was your girl-friend. You were always going around together, meeting out of hours. I thought you and she were—'

'That was just part of the job. I needed to keep tabs on Sir Rupert, judge what sort of pressures he was undergoing, assess how the politics of the company were affecting him. I had to do that unobtrusively. I thought Sir Rupert explained all that.'

'But not about Britt—'

'Britt was just a go-between. Nothing more. Oh Bridie, how crazy that you should think—' He was smiling broadly at her. 'Britt's not my sort of girl at all. Far too flighty.'

The tremor of exultation was a river now.

'I've known *you* are my kind of girl ever since Norway. But I wouldn't allow myself to fall in love with you. I wanted you very badly that night in Oslo—but I couldn't take advantage of you. When I heard you sobbing your heart out in your room that night we stayed at Carl and Marga's house, I knew it was to do with me. I couldn't bear to see you upset, so I rushed back to London on my own. I had hoped you would stay and have a nice weekend in Norway and get me out of your thoughts. The complications of a love affair in professional life can be very difficult and I couldn't subject you to that. You're far too nice a person.'

'And I thought you were angry with me, annoyed at having such an innocent little companion on a business trip.'

'Never, my darling.'

'And now, Greg?'

'And now, Bridie, I just love you,' he said simply. 'But you haven't answered my question.'

The river of exultation rose and flooded her being. She reached up and flung her arms round his neck.

'Yes, oh yes, Greg, my love.'

He spun her round and round, until they collapsed uncaring on the crisp white snow, the dogs jumping and weaving, barking frenziedly.

She lay looking up into the clear, azure sky, joy and laughter dancing within her. It was the same sky of a short while ago, but then it had seemed a setting for the end of something.

Now she had only the feeling of a beginning . . .

# Doctor Nurse Romances

# Romance in the wide world of medicine

Amongst the intense emotional pressures of modern medical life, doctors and nurses often find romance. Read about their lives and loves in the other two Doctor Nurse titles available this month.

### NURSE ON TRIAL
*by Clare Lavenham*

Paula Garland is shattered after she fails her SRN because of a traumatic experience in her final year, so when she is given a second chance to sit her exams she resolves to put the past behind her. Then she meets Dr Justin Stewart and it seems as if history will repeat itself . . .

### THE UNCERTAIN HEART
*by Sheila Douglas*

Nurse Linda Mannering is regarded as a sensible, down-to-earth and conscientious nurse by her superiors, so she seems the ideal choice to look after the charming and difficult patient Paul Nicholson. But even sensible nurses have hearts . . .

## Mills & Boon
the rose of romance